AMERICA LOVES
JOHANNA LINDSEY

ALL I NEED IS YOU

Johanna Lindsey

All I Need Is You

AVON BOOKS  NEW YORK

AVON BOOKS, INC.
1350 Avenue of the Americas
New York, New York 10019

Copyright © 1997 by Johanna Lindsey
Excerpt from *Captive Bride* copyright © 1977 by Johanna Lindsey
Excerpt from *A Gentle Feuding* copyright © 1984 by Johanna Lindsey
Excerpt from *Love Only Once* copyright © 1985 by Johanna Lindsey
Excerpt from *Hearts Aflame* copyright © 1987 by Johanna Lindsey
Excerpt from *Once a Princess* copyright © 1991 by Johanna Lindsey
Excerpt from *Angel* copyright © 1992 by Johanna Lindsey
Front cover art by Fredericka Ribes
Inside front cover art by Elaine Duillo
Inside cover author photo by John Russell
Visit our website at **http://www.AvonBooks.com**
Library of Congress Catalog Card Number: 97-27864
ISBN: 0-380-76260-9

First Avon Books Paperback Printing: December 1998
First Avon Books Hardcover Printing: December 1997

AVON TRADEMARK REG. U.S. PAT. OFF. AND IN OTHER COUNTRIES, MARCA REGISTRADA, HECHO EN U.S.A.

Printed in the U.S.A.

WCD 10 9 8 7 6 5 4 3 2 1

For A.J.
His father's pride, his mother's joy,
and his grandparents' delight.
Welcome to the family, kiddo.

Chapter 1

Texas, 1892

"*I* don't give a damn if you are part owner of that ranch, you're not going to run it!"

"That's not fair and you know it! You'd let Tyler run it if he was here."

"Tyler's a full-grown man now. You're just seventeen, Casey."

"I don't believe you said that. He's full-grown at one year older'n me, when women my age have husbands and three kids already? But that's not grown up enough for you? Or is it just because I'm a woman? And if you say it is, I swear I'll never speak to you again."

"A welcoming thought at the moment."

Neither of them meant it, but you couldn't tell that by looking at them. Courtney Straton watched her husband and only daughter glaring at each other and sighed long and loud, hoping to get their attention. It didn't work. The argument had escalated from heated words to shouting, and when Chandos and Casey argued,

1

subtlety didn't work. She doubted they even recalled that she was there.

This was an old argument. However, it had never been this heated before. Ever since Fletcher Straton had died last year, the ultimate fate of the Bar M Ranch was in question. The ranch would have belonged to Chandos, but Fletcher, knowing his son, had put a provision in his will that if Chandos refused the inheritance, the ranch would then go in equal shares to his three grandchildren. Which was exactly what had happened.

Chandos didn't need the ranch. He had done well for himself. The incentive had been there, to prove to his father that he could match him, and he'd done that well enough. He might not own quite as many acres, but he had just as many head of cattle, and his house was nearly twice as large as Fletcher's, which made it almost a mansion.

Combined, the Bar M and K.C. ranches formed one of the biggest spreads in Texas. Because they were owned by father and son, most folks had always considered them combined. It was only the father and the son who didn't, and now only Chandos who still insisted on keeping them separate.

But separate didn't mean allowing his daughter to run the ranch. He was quick to temper, and Casey wasn't helping matters by turning stubborn on this particular subject no matter how serious she was about it.

They were much alike, these two. Unlike her two fair-haired brothers, Tyler at eighteen and Dillon, who was only fourteen, Casey took after

Chandos in temperament and in looks. She got her hair from him, black as pitch. She got her height from him, making her, at five feet nine inches, about the tallest girl in the county.

The only thing Casey had inherited from Courtney was her remarkable eyes. On Casey, they were like softly glowing amber jewels. And for all that she professed to be a woman and *was* one by the standards of the West, where young women married at such young ages, she was late in filling out. Tall, lean, and lanky like her father, though without his muscles.

Yet she was a very pretty girl, if she would be still long enough for one to notice. Trouble was, Casey was never still. Standing, sitting, she was always in motion of one sort or another, pacing, or talking with her hands, or walking with long, masculine strides.

But if you caught her in a quiet moment, you'd notice how large her eyes were, how flawlessly smooth her skin was under her tan, how her nose was shaped rather pertly. Her brows were a bit too thick, her chin a bit too stubborn—like her father's—but added to her finely chiseled cheekbones, these features weren't so noticeable. What was disconcerting, though, was that she had the same uncanny ability as Chandos to hide her emotions when she chose to, completely, so that you had no idea whatsoever what she was thinking or feeling.

This wasn't one of those times. But Casey had another of Chandos's traits—strategizing. When one tactic didn't work, she usually resorted to another.

Shouting hadn't worked, so she switched to a

calmer tone. "But the Bar M needs someone in command."

"Sawtooth is doing well enough."

"Sawtooth is sixty-seven years old. He was retired and living peacefully on his little spread when Grandpa died. He agreed to take over the reins only until you could find someone else. But you haven't found anyone willing to take on those responsibilities without demanding half the profits, and you refuse to manage the place yourself."

"I have enough headaches here. I don't have time to divide myself—"

"But I do, and I *can* do it. You know I can. The Bar M is one-third mine. I have every right—"

"You're not even eighteen yet, Casey—"

"What's eighteen got to do with anything, I'd like to know? And besides, I will be in a few months—"

"Which is when you should be thinking about getting married and starting your own family. You can't do that if you're saddled with running the Bar M."

"Marriage!" the girl snorted. "I'm only talking about a couple years, Daddy, just until Tyler finishes college. There isn't anything I don't know about running a ranch. You saw to that. You taught me all I know about ranching, all I know about surviving on the trail—"

"Biggest mistake I ever made," Chandos mumbled.

"No, it wasn't." Courtney spoke up finally. "You wanted her to be able to handle any situation if we weren't around to handle it for her."

"Exactly," Chandos said. "*If* we weren't around."

"I want to do this, and you haven't given one good reason why I shouldn't."

"Then you haven't been listening, little girl," Chandos said, frowning. "You're too young, you're a female that the forty-some wranglers on the Bar M are *not* going to want to take orders from, and you've reached the time in your life when you should be looking for a husband. You won't be finding one with your nose buried in ranch accounts and coming in off the range each day sweat-soaked and filthy."

Casey was red-faced by then, most likely from anger, though it was hard to tell. "Marriage again!" she all but sneered. "There hasn't been a man around these parts in the last two years worth my taking notice of. Or do you want me to marry just anyone? If that's the case, I can think of a dozen men who are eligible. I'll go rope me one tomorrow, if that's what it'll take to—"

"Don't be impertinent."

"I'm being absolutely serious," Casey insisted. "You'd let a husband of mine run the Bar M, wouldn't you? You'd find that perfectly acceptable. Well, I'll have a candidate for you no later than—"

"You'll do no such thing. You will *not* marry just to get your hands on those account ledgers—"

"I've had my hands on those account books for months now, Daddy. Sawtooth is half blind, if you didn't realize it. Trying to tally the ledgers gives him a powerful headache that actually makes him physically ill."

It was Chandos who was red-faced now, and there was no doubt in his case that it was from anger. "Why wasn't I told about this?"

"Maybe because every time Sawtooth rides over here to see you, you're out on the range somewhere. And maybe because you won't step foot on the Bar M to find out why he came over in the first place. And maybe because you don't really care about the Bar M. You'd just as soon see it fall to ruin now that Grandpa's gone, just to spite his memory."

"Casey!" This from Courtney in an appalled tone.

But Casey had already blanched. She'd gone too far and knew it. And before her father could blast her for doing so, she ran from the room.

Courtney started to assure Chandos that Casey had just let her emotions run away with her, that she hadn't really meant what she'd said; but, tight-lipped, he marched out of the room right behind Casey. Only not to follow her. He headed off toward the back of the house, a more direct route to the stable, while she'd run toward the front.

Which was entirely too bad. Chandos shouldn't have let the argument end like that, with Casey riddled with guilt now, but still determined to change her father's mind. He should have been more explicit with his reasons. He should have pointed out that he didn't want to see Casey get hurt when she failed, which she was bound to do.

The cowboys on the Bar M might accept her

for a while, because they knew her as Fletcher's granddaughter, but inevitably there would be new men, and those who didn't know her and hadn't known Fletcher would start dissension soon enough. It might be different if she were an older woman, a widow or the like, but she wasn't. Most men simply wouldn't take orders from a woman, much less one they considered a young girl.

But Chandos hadn't mentioned any of that, at least not clearly enough. Courtney would have to talk to her herself, though she would give her a day or two to calm down first. Casey was unpredictable when her emotions were riled.

Chapter 2

When Casey stormed from the room, she
didn't head upstairs. The front porch was closer,
and at this time of the morning it was usually
empty and peaceful. Today was no different.

It was a big porch, only ten feet wide but
some eighty feet long, fronting the entire length
of the house. It was filled with small white tables and chairs, a couple of two-seater swings
that her father had built, and a profusion of
plants that her mother babied and that hid the
numerous spittoons the ranch hands made use
of.

She moved to the railing, gripping it until her
knuckles turned white. As far as the eye could
see was Straton land, either her father's or her
grandfather's, vast plains dotted with the occasional hill or a lonely stand of trees around a
watering hole, and the usual cactuses and fauna
of Texas. There was a forest on the northern border, but you couldn't see it from the house. A
creek bed divided the two properties. Farther
south, they shared a freshwater lake teeming

with bass. It was stark land, it was beautiful land. Yet on that fine spring morning Casey noticed nothing.

She never should have said what she did to her father, but then, he'd been *so* unreasonable. And choking on both guilt and anger wasn't an easy thing to deal with. Anger she was used to, growing up with two brothers who delighted in teasing her. But guilt was another matter, and for something that might be true . . .

What else was she to think? Her father had always given the impression that he really didn't care about the Bar M. He didn't want anything to do with anything that had ever belonged to Fletcher Straton. Everyone knew that. Yet Casey had loved her grandfather. She had never understood why he and Chandos couldn't bury the hatchet, so to speak, and get along after all these years. Fletcher had made every effort. But Chandos was unyielding.

She knew the history, of course—how Meara, Fletcher's wife, had left him, apparently because of his unfaithfulness. She had taken their son with her, and although Fletcher had searched far and wide for them, intent on bringing them home, they had completely disappeared.

He didn't find out how they had managed to elude him so thoroughly until years later, when Chandos showed up at the Bar M. He had been lucky he hadn't been shot on sight riding in on his pinto, wearing buckskins, his long black braids, and little else. He'd looked like a fullfledged Indian, all except for his deep blue eyes, Meara's eyes, and the only way his father was able to recognize him.

To hear Fletcher tell it, Meara had left him in a fit of temper without taking the precautions she should have before running off. She and her child had been captured by Kiowas and sold to a Comanche. They had been fortunate, though. The young brave had taken Meara to wife and adopted Chandos. A few years later, another child was born of that union, Chandos's half-sister, White Wing, whom he had adored.

He had been a child himself at the time of the capture, and it wasn't until ten years later, when he was eighteen and ready to take his place in the tribe as an adult, that Meara had sent him home to his father. She had wanted him to experience living in the white man's world before he chose the Comanche way of life.

That had been a mistake. Chandos had gone, because he would have done anything his mother asked of him, but his decision had already been made. He had been raised by the Comanches. As far as he was concerned, he was a Comanche.

But he wasn't averse to learning all he could from the whites, as he had thought of them at the time. *Know thine enemy* wasn't only a white man's creed. The trouble was, Fletcher, thrilled to have his son back, thought Chandos was there to stay, so he couldn't understand his son's hostility. And Fletcher, stubborn, belligerent, and autocratic in those days, had managed to increase that hostility, not lessen it.

They argued constantly, with Fletcher trying to mold Chandos into the son he wanted him to be. But Chandos was no child at that age.

The breaking point came when Fletcher ordered his men to corral Chandos and cut off his braids. It was quite a fight, to hear Fletcher tell it, with Chandos wounding three of the men, and that was when he took off, three years after he'd shown up. Fletcher had thought to never see him again.

Later, the old man discovered that Chandos had returned to his tribe to find most of them dead, massacred by a group of whites, his mother and sister both raped and killed, and this had happened the very day he'd gone home to them. For four years he and the few remaining men of that small band of Comanches had tracked down the killers to exact their revenge, and brutal it was, as brutal as the massacre of all the women and children of the band had been. It was during that time that Chandos had met Courtney Harte, Casey's mother.

They had fallen in love. Chandos had eventually made the decision to settle on the property that belonged to Courtney's family and adjoined his father's; he wanted to compete with Fletcher and prove that he could be just as successful at ranching without his help. He'd had a fortune in the bank in Waco that Fletcher had given him long ago, but he never touched that money, likely never would. What Chandos created, he did on his own.

Chandos and Fletcher, father and son, never made peace, at least not that anyone was aware of. And even though Fletcher was dead, Chandos hadn't buried their differences with him. Yet one day the two ranches would be combined through Chandos's children, and that probably didn't sit well with him at all, which was why he'd as soon see the Bar M go under than get the proper management it needed.

But Casey never should have said so aloud. She could believe it all she liked, but to actually say it was an insult of the worst sort, and she had never insulted her father before.

She didn't hear any footsteps come up behind her, yet she was asked, "You gonna cry now, missy?"

Without turning around, she knew who had joined her and must have been near enough to overhear the fight she'd just had with her father. She'd gotten pretty close to Sawtooth after Fletcher's death, close enough for him to easily question her and expect answers.

"What good will tears do?" she replied in a tight voice.

"Never served no purpose in my opinion, 'cept to make a man squirm. What are you gonna do, then?"

"I'm going to prove to Daddy that I don't need a husband to get by, that I can work in a man's world just fine without having one tied to my apron strings."

"Not that you'll ever wear aprons." He chuckled at the idea of it. "But just how you gonna do that?"

"By getting a job that isn't suited for a woman," Casey answered.

"Ain't many jobs that are suited for a woman, let alone those that ain't."

"I mean *really* unsuitable, dangerous maybe, or something so strenuous a woman would never consider it. Wasn't that Oakley girl a bull-whacker for a time, and a scout, too?"

"From what I heard tell, that Oakley girl looked more like a man than some men do, dressed like it, too. But what's your point? You ain't thinking of doing something stupid like that, are you?"

" 'Stupid' is a matter of opinion. The point is, I need to do something. Daddy isn't going to just miraculously change his mind. He's as hard-headed as they come, and we know where he got that from, don't we?"

There was a snort. Sawtooth had been a good friend of Fletcher's, after all. But he also admitted, "I'm beginning to not like the sound of this."

"Well, too bad," she grumbled. "I wasn't asking for permission. But I wasn't expecting to have to prove myself either, when Daddy already knows I'm capable, so this will require some thought."

"Thank God. Spur-of-the-moment actions from you, missy, scare the bejesus out of me."

Chapter 3

There was a fire up ahead, a campfire—at least, Damian Rutledge hoped it was a campfire, because that meant people, something he hadn't seen for the past two days. He'd settle for even the uncivilized sort at the moment, anything that could point him to the nearest town.

He was utterly lost. He'd been assured the West was civilized. And to him, civilized meant people. Neighbors. Buildings. Not mile after mile after mile of nothing.

He should have suspected that this area of the country wasn't quite what he was used to when the towns he passed through kept getting smaller and smaller in population. But he'd been doing fine, traveling on the railroad all the way from New York City, at least until he reached Kansas. That was where he started running into some unpleasantness.

First it was the railroad. The "Katy," as the Missouri, Kansas & Texas Railway was fondly called, was not running that week because of the small incident of a train robbery that had blown up about fifty yards of tracks and damaged the train's engine. He had been told the stage lines were running, and he discovered he could catch another train in the next town, so he thought he'd just have a short detour on the stage. What hadn't been mentioned was the fact that that particular stage hadn't been used in over five years, what with the railroad having made it obsolete.

Most folks traveling in that direction preferred to wait out the repairs, but Damian was too impatient to wait. And that was his worst mistake. He should have realized, when he saw he was the only passenger, that there had to be a good reason for most people to shun the dilapidated vehicle.

There were other stage lines that still ran in Kansas between towns that the railroad didn't pass through, and they had been having a rash of robberies lately. But Damian didn't find this out until a watering stop where the stage driver got a bit talkative. And then he also found out the hard way not long after that . . .

At least when he heard the shots fired, he knew what was going on. The driver hadn't stopped, though. He'd tried to outrace the robbers, a foolish endeavor in such an old, cumbersome vehicle. And then the driver veered off the road, for reasons Damian would likely never know. Mile after mile sped by in a blur, more shots were fired, then the coach came to a crashing halt, so suddenly that Damian was tossed across the interior, slamming against the door, his head connecting with the metal door handle, and that was the last he knew for several hours.

It was the rain pounding against the coach that probably woke him. Night had fallen. And by the time he managed to exit the coach, which was turned half on its side, he found himself completely alone, in the middle of—nowhere.

The horses were gone, stolen or let loose, he didn't know. The driver was gone, possibly shot and fallen along the wayside or taken by the robbers, or maybe he had survived and gone for help. But Damian wasn't to find that out either. He had been covered in blood himself from the wound on the side of his head. The rain washed some of it away while he gathered up his belongings, which were strewn about the area, and stuffed them back into his traveling bag.

He spent the rest of that miserable night inside the coach, where it was at least dry. Unfortunately, it was midday by the time he awoke again, so the sun was no help in determining which direction to take, not that he knew which way he wanted to go. Even the track marks of the stage had been washed away during the night.

His watch had been stolen, along with the money he'd had in his pockets and his bag. The money he'd tucked inside the lining of his jacket was still there, though, small compensation for the predicament he now found himself in. He discovered a canteen of water strapped to the side of the coach which he took with him, and an old, musty lap robe under one of the seats that was much appreciated when he still hadn't come upon anyone or anything by nightfall.

He had traveled south, in the direction of the next town he'd been headed to, but that was only a general direction, since the road they had been on had been a winding one. He could be too far east or west, could pass the town by without even knowing it. He had hoped to run into the road again, but no such luck.

By the end of that first day he was seriously worried about ever eating again. He had no weapon to catch his own food if he came upon anything to catch. Having lived in a city his entire life, he had never imagined he would need one. He stumbled across a small watering hole where he was able to wash off the rest of the blood matted in his hair and change into some clean, if still rain-dampened, clothes. And he went to sleep that night with a belly full of water at least, small consolation, as hungry as he was.

The throbbing headache from the lump on his head that had been with him all that first day began to lessen the second day. But the blisters he'd developed on his hands from carrying his bag, and on his feet from so much walking in his town shoes, were so painful his headache was barely noticeable. And he'd run out of water. So he was more than just a little miserable by the end of that second day.

It was sheer luck that he happened to notice the campfire just before he was about to roll up into his musty lap robe for the night. It was a long ways off, though, so far that he was beginning to think it was an illusion, since he was taking so long to reach it. But then it did start to enlarge from the wavering dot it had been, to define itself, a definite campfire, and finally he could smell the coffee, smell the meat roasting, and his stomach rumbled in anticipation.

He'd almost reached the fire, was only twenty feet away, when he felt cold metal against his neck and heard the click of a trigger being primed for firing. He hadn't seen or heard any other movement, but the sound from that weapon kept him from taking another step.

"Don't you know better than to enter someone's camp without warning first?"

"I've been lost for two days," Damian replied tiredly. "And no, I wasn't aware that it was customary to give a warning before seeking help."

Silence, of the nerve-racking sort. Damian finally thought to add, "I'm unarmed."

Another click sounded the release of the trigger, then metal sliding into leather. "Sorry, mister, but you can't be too careful out here."

Damian swung around to face his savior—at least he hoped he'd found a guide back to civilization. But he was amazed to find a mere boy staring back at him. The kid wasn't very tall and was on the skinny side, with baby-smooth cheeks above a bright red bandana tied loosely around his neck. A boy, probably no older than fifteen or sixteen, wearing denim jeans with knee-high moccasins, and a brown-and-black woven wool poncho over a dark blue shirt.

There was a gun holster there somewhere, hidden by the poncho at the moment. A wide-brimmed hat, which Damian had noted plenty of since he'd crossed the Missouri line, sat atop scraggly black, shoulder-length hair. Light brown eyes were taking his measure, catlike eyes that could have been called pretty if they belonged to a girl. On this boy, they were merely very—unusual.

It was the poncho and the moccasins that led Damian to ask, somewhat hesitantly, "I haven't wandered onto an Indian reservation, have I?"

"Not this far north of the Territory—what makes you think so?"

"I was just wondering if you were an Indian."

A sort of grin; Damian couldn't be quite sure. "Do I look like an Indian?"

"I wouldn't know. I've never seen one before," Damian was forced to admit.

"No, I don't reckon you would have, tenderfoot."

"Are my blisters that obvious?"

The boy stared at him blankly for a moment, then laughed, a throaty, sensual laugh that was a bit disconcerting, coming from a boy. Damian was sure the joke, whatever it was, was at his expense. But then, he must seem laughable in his present condition.

Damian was hatless himself, which made him feel almost naked, his derby having been unsalvageable after the stage crash, and the only one he'd brought with him on this journey. Though he'd changed to a clean suit yesterday, today he was covered in dust and burrs. He probably looked as lost as he felt. But he hadn't lost his manners. Ignoring whatever had amused his young host, he held out his hand to introduce himself properly.

"Damian Rutledge the Third here, and truly delighted to make your acquaintance."

The boy stared at his hand, but he didn't take it, merely nodded before saying, "There's three of you?" Then he waved a dismissive hand, obviously deciding the question had been a foolish one. "Never mind. The grub's hot and you're welcome to share it and my camp for the night." With a slight smirk, he added, "Sounds like you could use a meal."

Damian flushed because his stomach had been making noise ever since he'd gotten close enough to smell the food. But he wasn't about to take umbrage, not when food was being offered. And although he had quite a few more questions he'd like to ask, food was uppermost on his mind, and he headed straight for the fire without further ado.

There were two fires, actually, a large one that was still flaring and lighting the area nicely, and a small one doing the cooking. A pit had been scraped out in the ground, with four rocks set around it to support an iron grill. Beneath it had been placed the smaller branches from the fire that had already turned to embers, used so the meat wouldn't overly burn before it was done cooking. A black tin coffeepot was set on one corner of the grill, a tin box was on another corner, which he was to find held a half-dozen freshly made biscuits, and there was a can of beans heating up. As far as Damian was concerned, it was a feast.

"What kind of meat is that?" Damian asked as he was handed a plate.

"Wild prairie hens."

They weren't a very big bird, but there were two of them, and one was plopped down on his plate, along with three of the biscuits and half the beans. He dug in so quickly, it was a while before he noticed there was only one plate, that the lad was eating right off the grill.

"I'm sorry," he began, but he was cut off.

"Don't be silly. Plates are a luxury out here. Besides, we got a river down yonder for washing up after."

Washing? That sounded heavenly. "I don't suppose you'd have any soap on you?"

"Not any that you'd appreciate" was the cryptic reply. "Just use the silt on the bottom of the river like most folks do if you want a bath. It will scrape any dirt you're wearing right off."

How primitive, he thought, but this whole situation was—camping outdoors with only the barest of essentials. The food was excellent, though, and much appreciated. Damian said so.

"Thank you for sharing half of your meal with me. I don't think I could have gone on much longer without sustenance."

There was another one of those small grins, so subtle Damian wasn't quite sure it was an actual grin. "You really think I could have eaten all that on my own? That's my breakfast you've been guzzling—and don't go apologizing again. Just saves time in the morning to eat leftovers, rather than cook fresh. But I'm not in such a hurry that I can't whip up some jacks in the morning."

Damian was already looking forward to it, whatever jacks were. But now that they had dined together, so to speak, and his belly was satisfied, if not quite full, his curiosity was fast returning.

Damian began by reminding the lad, "I didn't catch your name."

Those remarkable light brown eyes glanced up at him before returning to the coffee he was pouring. "Maybe because I didn't toss it your way."

"If you'd rather not—"

"Don't have one," the boy cut in curtly. "Least I never knew it."

That wasn't exactly what Damian had expected to hear. "But you must go by something?"

A shrug. "Folks tend to call me Kid."

"Ahhh." Damian smiled. That was a name that had come up frequently in the file on the West he'd been given, though each of those names had had another name attached to it. "As in Billy the Kid?"

There was a snort. "As in I'm a mite young to do what I do."

"Which is?"

The coffee cup was handed to Damian. He almost spilled it when he heard: "I hunt outlaws."

"I—ah—wouldn't have taken you for a policeman. I mean, you don't exactly look—"

"A what?"

"An officer of the law."

"Oh, you mean like a sheriff? No; who'd elect me at my age?"

Damian had been thinking the same thing, which was why he'd been so surprised. "Then why do you hunt outlaws?" he asked politely.

"For the rewards, of course."

"Lucrative?"

Damian expected to have to explain that word, but again he was surprised. "Very."

At least the lad was very intelligent, Damian thought.

"How many have you apprehended since you began this career?"

"Five to date."

"I've seen a few Wanted posters," Damian mentioned. Actually, the file he'd been given was full of them. "Don't most posters offer the reward dead or alive?"

"If you're asking how many of them lowlifes I've killed, the answer is none—at least not yet. I've caused a few wounds, though. And one of those five has an appointment with the hangman, so he'll likely be meeting his maker before the new year."

"They take you seriously, these hardened criminals?" Damian ventured to inquire.

The subtle grin appeared again, the one that wasn't quite a grin. "Rarely," the kid admitted. "But they do take this seriously."

The gun seemed to materialize in his hand, there in the blink of an eye. Obviously, he'd already had it palmed under that poncho, and Damian just hadn't noticed him bring it out in the open.

"Yes, well, guns have a way of getting one's attention," Damian allowed.

That was the most he would concede, though. The boy was just too young to have done the deeds he was laying claim to. Even if he were a few years older, Damian would have had doubts. But then, children did tend to boast of grand deeds to impress their peers, easy enough to do when proof wasn't available or required.

However, Damian wisely kept his eye on that gun until it was put away again. Handing the coffee cup back got the weapon back into its holster so the kid could pour a cup for himself.

"Do you live around here?" Damian asked next.

"No."

"Does *anyone* live around here?"

The emphasis Damian used produced a chuckle from Kid, and like his previous laughter, it had a strangely sensual note to it that was quite jarring, coming from a young boy. If Damian didn't know better, and wasn't staring directly at the lad, he would be thinking right about then that a woman had snuck into the camp when he wasn't looking. But then the kid had what was commonly termed "pretty-boy" looks more suited to a female, so it was no wonder Damian was having these weird notions.

Damian pushed those musings aside when his host pointed out, "Well, you're kind of off the beaten track out here, Mr. Rutledge."

"No kidding," Damian said dryly; then, after a moment's thought: "But you know where we are, I hope?"

A curt nod. "About a day or two south of Coffeyville, I reckon."

The name of the town didn't ring a bell. All Damian knew was that wasn't where he'd been headed, so perhaps the stage had taken him farther south than he'd realized before it crashed, and he'd traveled even farther on foot than intended, passing his destination altogether.

"Is that the closest town?"

"Don't know if it is or isn't. This isn't my neck of the woods."

"What are you doing out here, then?"

"I've got business up in Coffeyville, least I hope to have."

The kid didn't volunteer any more. Damian was beginning to suspect he didn't like all these questions, his answers were so brief. Damian, on the other hand, enjoyed conversation, even if it was more of the interrogative sort, so until he was told to mind his own business . . .

"I'd like to think I haven't been running around in circles. Are we at least near a road?"

A slow shake of the head. "I tend to avoid roads as much as I can. You run into less folks that way, and I happen to like traveling alone."

That was blunt enough to bring some color to Damian's cheeks. "I'm sorry to have intruded, but I really am lost out here."

"How'd that happen?" Kid asked. "Your horse take off on you?"

It was there in his tone if not in the question that the boy figured Damian was too incompetent to ride or keep a horse. Understandably, Damian's voice was a bit tight as he replied, "No, I was traveling by stagecoach. And before you ask if I fell off of it and got left behind—"

"Now, hold on, mister," Kid interrupted. "You got no call to take offense at a simple question, specially when you've been asking so many of your own. You walked into my camp, you didn't ride in. It was a logical assumption that either your horse came up lame or you got thrown and he took off. Folks who take the stage don't usually end up on foot."

Damian sighed. Kid was right, it was a logical deduction. And his headache was returning. He wasn't going to apologize yet again, though, not when his own assumption was likely dead on the mark as well.

"The stagecoach I was on was fired upon," Damian said. "The driver tried to make a run for it, but ended up crashing the coach. I was knocked out in the crash. When I woke up that night, the driver was gone, the horses were gone, and my pockets and my bag had been emptied."

The lad perked up considerably. "Stage robbers in this area? When did this happen?"

"The day before yesterday."

A huge sigh of disappointment. "They're likely long gone by now."

Damian frowned. "I would imagine so. You would prefer they weren't?"

"Wells Fargo pays real well for the apprehension of stage robbers. And running into faces that tend to get plastered on Wanted posters beats the hell out of hunting them down when they don't want to be found."

Damian humored his companion. "Yes, I suppose that would make your job easier."

"Easier, no, just quicker. Actually, I consider run-ins something like a bonus, unexpected but welcome. Now it's your turn, Mr. Rutledge. What brings you West?"

"What makes you assume I'm from the East?"

A very definite grin as those light brown eyes—almost amber in the firelight—moved over Damian again from top to bottom. "A wild guess."

Damian scowled. Kid chuckled, then said casually, "You on one of them tour-the-country-type trips you Easterners seem to enjoy?"

Damian was annoyed enough to say, "No, I'm on my way to Texas to kill a man."

Chapter 4

I'm on my way to Texas to kill a man.

Having said it brought it all back vividly, that night nearly six months ago in the spring, the night Damian's world had fallen apart. Everything had gone right that day: the hothouse flowers delivered to Winnifred shortly before Damian arrived to pick her up, the engagement ring he'd had designed finished that morning. They had even reached the restaurant on time, for once the heavy New York City traffic not interfering with his time schedule. And the dinner had been superb. Perfect. As soon as he took Winnifred home, he was going to ask the big question.

Her father had already approved the match. His father had been delighted. They made a perfect couple, he the heir to Rutledge Imports, she the heir to C. W. & L. Company. It wouldn't be just a marriage, but a joining of the two largest import companies in the city.

Then Sergeant Johnson of the Twenty-first Precinct had shown up at their table as they were having dessert. The somber policeman had requested a few private words with Damian. They had walked out to the lobby. By the time they finished talking, Damian was in shock.

He wasn't sure if he'd asked the sergeant to see that Winnifred got home safely. He had raced to the offices of Rutledge Imports. The lights were all ablaze.

The office was usually closed by five o'clock in the afternoon, but occasionally one or another of the employees stayed late to catch up on paperwork, including Damian's father . . . though rarely that late. Even the cleaning crew was usually finished by that time of night. But the only people working there when Damian arrived were members of the New York City Police Department.

The body was still hanging from the flagpole in the large, high-ceilinged office. There were two ornate flagpoles, one on each side of the door. Every July, for the entire month, an American flag was hung from each of them. Throughout the rest of the year, the poles supported an assortment of hanging plants. The plants on one pole had been tossed aside, leaving dirt and broken leaves on the cream-colored carpet, and, that night, had supported the body instead.

If the walls weren't made of brick, a body that size couldn't have hung there, dangling some six inches above the floor. But no, those poles were made of steel and reinforced in the brick, so they would never sag. Two hundred pounds hanging from one of them, and it hadn't bent at all.

So close to the floor, yet so far away. Shoes

might have made a difference, might have allowed the body to get support on tiptoe, at least for a little while, but the feet were bare. Yet the arms weren't restrained either. Those powerful arms could have easily reached the flagpole to keep the pressure of that single rope off the neck. The chair, too, that had been placed just under the flagpole, was still standing there; it hadn't been kicked over, was still within reach.

"Cut him down."

No one had heard Damian. Three men had tried to stop him from entering the office, until they heard who he was. The men in the office were too busy sifting through what they deemed evidence to pay attention to a choked voice. Damian had to shout to be heard.

"Cut him down!"

That got their attention, and one uniformed officer blustered indignantly, "Who the hell are you?"

Damian still hadn't taken his eyes off the body. "I'm his son."

He had heard several mutterings of sympathy as they cut Damian Rutledge II down, pointless, meaningless words that had barely penetrated his shock. His father was dead, the only person on the face of the earth whom he really and truly cared about. He had no other relatives.

His mother had divorced his father when Damian was still a child, and had gone off to marry her lover. Damian had never seen her again and had no desire to. She had been, and would remain, dead in his heart. But his father . . .

Winnifred didn't count either. He'd planned

to marry her, but he didn't love her. He had hoped that they would get along splendidly. After all, he could find no fault with her. She was beautiful, refined, and she would make a fine mother for the children they would have. But in truth, she was little more than a stranger. But his father . . .

". . . obvious suicide," he had heard next, then: "There's even a note." And the "note" had been shoved in front of Damian's face.

When he was able to focus on the words, he read, "I tried to get over it, Damian, but I can't. Forgive me."

He had snatched the note out of the policeman's hand and read it again . . . and again. It looked like his father's writing, if a bit shaky. The note also looked like it had been stuffed into something—a pocket, or a fist.

"Where did you get this?" he'd asked.

"On the desk—in the center of it, actually. Hard to miss."

"There is fresh stationery in that desk," Damian had pointed out. "Why would this note be crumpled if it was written just before . . . ?"

He'd been unable to finish the sentence. The policeman merely shrugged.

But another suggested, "He could have been carrying that note around for days while he made up his mind."

"And brought his own rope, too? That rope didn't come from this office."

"Then obviously he *did* bring it along" was the easy reply. "Look, Mr. Rutledge, I know it ain't easy to accept when someone you know takes his own life like this, but it happens. Do you know what it was that he couldn't get over, as the note says?"

"No. My father didn't have *any* reason to kill himself," Damian had insisted.

"Well . . . looks like he felt differently."

Damian's eyes had turned a wintery gray, pale as shadowed snow. "You're just going to accept that as fact?" he demanded. "You're not even going to look into the possibility that he was murdered?"

"Murdered?" The policeman had been condescending. "There's easier and much quicker ways to kill yourself than dangling from a rope. Know how long it takes to actually die from hanging? It ain't quick unless the neck snaps, and his didn't. And there's easier and much quicker ways for murder to be done than by hanging."

"Unless you want it to look like suicide."

"A bullet in the head would have done the trick if that were the case. Look, do you see any signs of struggle here? And there is nothing to indicate that your father's hands had been tied so he couldn't prevent the hanging. How many men do you think it would take to hang a man his size if he didn't want to be hung? One or two wouldn't have managed it. Three or more? Why? What motive? Did your father keep money here? Anything of value missing that you can see? Did he have any enemies who hated him enough to kill him?"

The answers were No and No and No, but Damian hadn't bothered to say so. The policemen had drawn their conclusions based on the evidence at hand. He couldn't blame them for settling for the obvious explanation. Why should they dig any deeper just on his say-so when they could finish their paperwork on this crime and go on to the next one? Trying to convince them that *this* was a crime that needed further investigation would be a waste of his time and theirs.

Still, he had tried. He'd spent two more hours trying, until the coroner had shown up and each one of the policemen had come up with an excuse to leave. Sure, they'd look into it, they had assured him, but he hadn't believed it for a minute. A sop for the grieving relative. At that point they would have said anything just to get out of there.

It had been midnight before Damian had entered the town house he shared with his father. It was a huge, old mansion, too big for just the two of them, which was why Damian had never moved out when he had come of age. He and his father had lived there companionably, neither getting in the other's way, yet both accessible when one of them felt like having conversation.

He had looked at his home that night and found it . . . empty. Never again would he share breakfast with his father before they left for the office. Never again would he find his father in his study, or in the library late of an evening, where they read and discussed the classics. Never again would they talk business over dinner. Never again . . .

The wealth of tears he had been holding back came then and wouldn't stop. Damian hadn't made it up to his room first, but there weren't any servants about at that late hour to witness his lapse from his usual stern rigidity. He had poured a glass of the brandy that was kept on his bureau for when he had trouble sleeping, although he'd been too choked up to actually drink it.

The only thought in his mind had been that he would find out what had really happened, because he would never accept that his father had ended his own life. There was no evidence to the contrary, no sign of struggle, yet Damian knew his father had been murdered. He knew his father too well; they had been too close.

Damian Senior wasn't a man who prevaricated or attempted pretense. He never lied, because he gave himself away anytime he tried. So if something had been so terribly wrong, if something had made him despair, Damian would have known about it.

Yet they had been planning a wedding. There had even been talk of remodeling the west wing of the house for more privacy if Damian wanted to bring his wife here to live. And Damian's father had been looking forward to having grandchildren to spoil.

Besides all that, Damian Senior had been genuinely happy with his life. He had no desire to ever marry again. He was perfectly content with the mistress he kept. He was wealthy in his own right, but had also inherited a large fortune. And he loved the business that he ran, which had been founded by his own father, Damian I, and which he had since expanded very successfully. He'd had everything to live for.

But someone had felt otherwise. "Forgive

me"? No, those weren't his father's words. There was nothing to forgive his father for. But there was much to avenge . . .

Damian now pushed the memories aside. The detective he'd hired had found him the answers he wanted. Yes, he'd come West to kill a man, the man who'd killed his father. But having said so didn't seem to surprise the boy sitting near him.

Kid simply asked, "Just for the hell of it, or you got a reason to kill this man?"

"A very good reason."

"You a bounty hunter, too?"

"Hardly. This is a personal matter."

Damian would have explained if asked, but he wasn't. His companion merely nodded. If he was at all curious, he certainly didn't give any indication. An unusual lad, to be sure. Most boys that age were brimming with questions, but he'd asked only a few, and those with not much interest. Not that it mattered.

"I think I'll take that bath, then turn in," Damian said, standing up.

Kid pointed his thumb over his shoulder. "It's down the bank there. I'll be turning in myself, so try not to make too much noise when you come back up."

Damian nodded, grabbed his bag, and headed down the hill. Behind him, he heard, "And watch out for snakes," then a chuckle that had him gritting his teeth. Damned kid. And he was going to be stuck with him for another day or so?

Chapter 5

*T*he smell of coffee woke Damian, but he didn't stir from his uncomfortable bed on the hard ground. He felt like he hadn't slept more than an hour or two. That was quite possible. Cracking his eyes a bit showed a sky still filled with stars, though there was a lighter blue cast to the east, where the sun would be making its appearance. But then, he hadn't managed to get right to sleep last night either, despite his exhaustion. So it was little wonder that he didn't feel rested this morning.

It wasn't the first time that the events of his father's death and what followed had kept Damian from sleeping. His rage was always close to the surface, a constant companion these past six months. He relived those powerful emotions so often, the frustration, the disbelief, and finally his resolve to see justice done.

After his experience with the police, he had hired his own detectives, and they had been quick and thorough. The small cafe across the street from Rutledge Imports had been open that night, but business had been slow. The one waiter who had been working had noticed two burly men leaving the Rutledge offices, noticed them because they looked so out of place. And he happened to be an amateur artist. For a small fee, he'd drawn sketches of both men from memory.

Obviously the waiter was quite talented artistically, because the sketches he'd made, passed around in the seedier areas of the city, finally led to one of the culprits, who had been persuaded to volunteer a full confession. But even before that had happened, Henry Curruthers had already come under suspicion.

Damian hadn't wanted to believe Curruthers was involved. He had been his father's accountant for more than ten years. He was an unassuming little man in his mid-forties who'd never married. He lived with and supported an elderly aunt on the east side of town. He never missed a day of work. He was always either in the office or at one of the Rutledge warehouses taking inventories. And like all the other employees, he'd been at the funeral, had seemed to be genuinely grieving over Damian Senior's passing.

But one of the detectives had requested permission to examine the company books, and the books had shown serious discrepancies. When Henry was questioned, the detective wasn't satisfied with the little man's answers.

It still wasn't conclusive evidence, even when Henry disappeared from the city with no trace. But then the sketches paid off.

The two men Henry had hired hadn't known his name, but they described him perfectly, from his thick-lensed glasses to his receding brown hair to the single mole on his left cheek and his owlish blue eyes. It was Henry Curruthers, without a doubt. And he'd hired those two men, for a mere fifty dollars, to kill his employer before it was discovered that he'd embezzled money from the company.

For fifty dollars. Damian still couldn't believe that anyone could hold life so cheaply. It had taken one of the detectives to point out that what was a pittance to one man could be a fortune to another.

It was Henry who had insisted on having the murder look like a suicide. He'd even supplied the forged suicide note. He must have counted on Damian's grief keeping him from going over the books until enough time had passed that the discrepancies in them would be so well hidden that they would never come to light.

Henry Curruthers was the murderer, those two men merely his puppets. And he would have gotten away with it if Damian hadn't been so dogged in his search for answers. Yet so far, he *had* gotten away with it. He had disappeared, gone into hiding. It had taken three months to finally track him down in Fort Worth, only to have him disappear again before he could be apprehended.

Damian had become fed up with the waiting, feeling useless while others did the work. He couldn't stand it that Curruthers was out there somewhere, still enjoying his freedom. He had been spotted in Fort Worth, Texas. Like many other men wanted by the law, he'd gone West, to take advantage of the vastness out there to lose himself. But Damian would find him. He didn't know the first thing about tracking a man down, yet he *would* find him. And he had a badge to make it legal when he killed him.

It paid to have powerful friends, and his father had known quite a few. Damian had been able to pull strings to get an appointment as a U.S. deputy, for the sole purpose of dealing with Curruthers. The file he had been given along with the badge was extensive, listing known criminals in Texas and other Western states and territories, as well as their aliases. Curruthers's name had been added to the list.

"You fellas going to come on in and have some of this coffee, or you just going to lay out there on your bellies till the sun rises?"

Damian's eyes flew open. Kid wasn't talking to him, he was sure; in fact, he then heard a chuckle from a distance. He sat up slowly and could vaguely make out the shadows of two men just now standing up, dusting off their clothes, at least twenty feet away.

Damian glanced next at his host to see his reaction to these visitors. Kid was fully dressed, wearing the same clothes as the night before, with a few extra wrinkles from having slept in them. His hat was dangling halfway down his back from a string around his neck, showing that his black hair wasn't just straggly, it was matted, filthy, actually looked like it hadn't seen a comb in months—if ever.

He was hunkered down by the fire he'd restarted, seemingly relaxed, though his expression was inscrutable. It was impossible to tell if he was wary of these new visitors, glad to have

more company, or indifferent. It gave Damian
pause.

And how the devil he'd known that they were
out there, Damian couldn't imagine. The light
from the fire barely reached ten feet away, the
outer perimeters of the camp in full shadow, the
sun still a good thirty minutes from rising. Damian had had to squint just to see the strangers'
shadows, and that with them standing, yet the
boy had somehow spotted them with those
golden, catlike eyes.

He had to wonder, too, why the two men had
been more or less hiding as they watched the
camp, particularly after Kid had made such a to-
do last night about it being customary to give a
camp warning before approaching it. Apparently Damian wasn't the only ignorant one.

The two men were approaching the fire now.
As they became more visible, he noticed the
taller man was smiling in a friendly way. The
other one was still whacking his crumpled-up
hat against his legs and scattering dust. How
anyone could treat a hat like that . . .

The hatless one stopped in his tracks when he
noticed Damian. His eyes widened as if he'd
seen a ghost, and in fact, he said to his friend,
"I thought you said he was dead. He sure don't
look dead to me."

There was a loud groan from the friend. "You
gotta be the biggest-mouthed jackass I ever had
the misfortune to ride with, Billybob."

He'd drawn his weapon as he spoke, pointing
it at Damian. Billybob fumbled a bit for his own
weapon, but finally got it out and aimed it at
Kid, who was slowly standing up, his arms

stretched out to his sides to show they'd have no trouble from him. And still without expression. No fear. That alone was beginning to annoy Damian. He was obviously meeting up with the men who'd apparently robbed the stage, yet Kid seemed totally unconcerned.

Billybob merely complained, "You got no call to cuss at me, Vince, when it were your fault he surprised me like he just did. Next time you say a fella's dead, make sure they's dead."

"Shuddup, Billybob. You're just putting your foot in deeper."

Billybob actually looked down at the ground to see what he'd put his foot in. His friend, noting where he was looking, rolled his eyes, then nudged the smaller man to remind him where he should be looking, which was at the camp, or rather, at its two occupants. And his smile returned as his eyes lit on Damian.

"Well, now," he said agreeably. "We might as well get down to business, seeing as how Billybob's let the cat out of the bag. We already know you ain't got nothing left of interest, mister, but what about you, kid?"

For a moment, Damian thought they were already acquainted with the boy, calling him kid like that. But then he realized that the word just referred to the boy's youth. Like he'd said, he was so young, people naturally called him kid for lack of a known name.

"Of interest?" Kid said, appearing thoughtful over the question. "I got hot coffee and a bowl of flapjack dough ready for the skillet, if that's what you mean."

That reply produced a chuckle from Vince.

"Matter of fact, that *does* interest me, but you must have something in them pockets as well—"

"Well, there's this—"

There was no question this time: Kid had drawn that gun with lightning speed, when not a second earlier, his hands had been out at his sides. And he didn't just draw it, he fired it, whether accurately or not was a matter of intention. If his intention had been to kill Vince, then he was far off the mark. But if he'd meant to disarm him, then he had a damn good aim, because his bullet pinged against Vince's weapon, causing him to yelp and drop it. Aside from a stinging hand, he appeared unhurt.

But that stinging hand was causing him to cuss and howl a blue streak. His friend was staring at Vince openmouthed and boggle-eyed, which made it quite simple for Kid to saunter over to him and stick the nozzle of his gun in his side.

A dense fellow, Billybob was—fortunately. If he'd been watching Kid as he should have been, there would likely have been an exchange of gunfire, and Damian could easily have been shot in the barrage, sitting there between them as he was.

He quickly corrected the sitting part, getting to his feet as soon as his amazement subsided a bit. He still couldn't quite credit it as he watched Kid take Billybob's weapon out of his lax hand and pick up the one on the ground. He'd disarmed them both, easily and without bloodshed—and still his face was inscrutable. He looked so indifferent about the whole affair, he could have just come back from relieving himself in the bushes, rather than relieving two stage robbers of their weapons.

He tossed one of the guns back toward Damian; the other he stuck in his belt. He was motioning with the one still in his hand as he said, "Sit down and put your hands behind your head. And don't give me no trouble. Taking you in dead would be easier, not to mention quicker, than taking you in alive. Now I don't mind harder, but not when I already got excess baggage, so don't tempt me on the easy route."

Damian didn't hear all of that, at least not about the excess baggage, since Kid had politely lowered his voice before mentioning him. Besides, he was debating whether or not to pick up the weapon that had slid across the ground to end up against his bare foot.

He was not familiar with handguns. In fact, he'd never had occasion to ever hold one before. In New York, they just weren't useful or necessary. Rifles, on the other hand, he was quite familiar with, from marksmanship competitions in his college days as well as hunting expeditions in the country with his father.

He supposed he couldn't just leave the gun on the ground, though, not with the two men still relatively free to make an effort to retrieve it, but the lad was addressing that point next, saying over his shoulder, "Find something in that bag of yours, Mr. Rutledge, to tie them up with. An old shirt ought to do nicely, after you rip it up some."

Damian almost snorted. He didn't *own* any old shirts. The very idea—but then he heard Kid add, "You won't be taking that bag along with you anyways. No room for it with just one horse."

He was glad, then, that he hadn't snorted. Damian hadn't considered how they would be getting to a town from here, but obviously the kid had already figured out the inconvenience of two riding on a single horse, and how little room that would leave for extras.

After rummaging in his bag, Damian came forward with a shirt in one hand, the gun in the other. Kid gave him a long-suffering look, until it finally dawned on Damian that he was to do the ripping and tying himself. Logical, he supposed, since they'd already seen what the boy could do with a weapon and so would be less likely to try anything with him guarding them, whereas Damian would no doubt be as clumsy with his gun as Billybob had been.

Vince got vocal again when the restraints were being put on his friend, demanding belligerently, "And just where do you think you're taking us, kid?"

"To the Coffeyville sheriff."

"Now that'd be a pure waste of your time and ours, since we ain't done nothing wrong."

"I got an eyewitness here who'll likely disagree with that."

"You got nothing, kid. He was out cold."

"I got your confession, too."

"What confession?" Vince said, then turned to his friend with a warning look. "Did you confess to something?"

Billybob blushed, but played along. "Now what would I do a fool thing like that for?"

Kid merely shrugged at that point, but then said, "Don't make no nevermind. A sheriff won't have too much trouble sorting it out and deciding for himself what you did—or didn't do. Stage robbery or plain robbery, I'll warrant he's got posters on you two stashed somewhere in his office for me to collect on, and if not . . . well, I'll just consider this my good deed for the month."

If Damian had been paying attention, he might have noticed that the robber named Vince panicked at the mention of Wanted posters. He also should have realized that Vince was the more dangerous of the two, and started the binding on him first, rather than on Billybob. But in all fairness, he hadn't been expecting any more trouble from either of them. So he was taken by surprise again when Vince made a springing dive for Kid's legs and caught them. They both went down, Kid flat on his back, Vince crawling up his legs to get to the gun. But before they started grappling over the weapon, Damian hauled Vince up and was about to plant a fist in his face when they both heard the trigger hammer click. Both froze.

Vince found his voice first as he glared at Kid, who was already back on his feet and aiming his gun straight at Vince's head. "You ain't gonna kill me."

"I'm not?"

That was all Kid said. It was his expression, or total lack of one, that had Vince backing down with a low grumble. You simply couldn't tell what the kid was thinking or feeling, couldn't tell if he was a cold-blooded killer or just a scared young boy who hid his fear remarkably well.

Damian, on the other hand, couldn't manage to conceal his anger. There had been just one too many surprises for him that morning, not to mention the threat of harm to him and his young savior. He was very strong, and his fist connected with Vince's nose. Vince didn't even see it coming, and was out cold before he hit the ground again.

Damian was immediately contrite. He hadn't resorted to physical violence since he'd been fifteen. That had been when his broken-nose count, on other boys, had reached seven, and he'd received one of the worst blistering lectures his father had ever delivered—about his large size and the unfair advantage he had over other boys his age, who all tended to be much smaller than he was. And his size hadn't evened out with others when he reached manhood. At six foot three inches, he was still taller and bigger than most men.

Kid eased his guilt by saying, "Nicely done, Mr. Rutledge. Now if you'll finish up there, I'll have these flapjacks ready in a few minutes so we can eat and be on our way."

Just like that, said so calmly, as if nothing out of the ordinary had disturbed the morning. The boy must have nerves of steel, or none at all. But Damian nodded and did as had been suggested.

Chapter 6

Kid had hunkered down by the fire again and was concentrating on dropping some very thin dough into a skillet, flipping it, then sliding it onto the single plate before he repeated the process again. At least Damian assumed he was concentrating on his cooking.

He'd reholstered his gun, but then, it had already been established how fast that could be brought into action if necessary. And those cat-like eyes, more golden than brown, which Damian had first thought, seemed to see things that normal eyes didn't. There was no doubt that this kid was an impressive fellow. Damian was starting to believe Kid had caught five outlaws.

Damian took advantage of Vince's unconscious state to bind his wrists behind him extra tight. He then left him on his side. The man's nose was still bleeding and that position at least let it drain. Billybob remained silent, watching Damian warily.

With the robbers immobilized, Damian took a moment to retrieve the coat he'd removed and folded so neatly last night, as well as his shoes. It was when he was about to stick his feet into them that he realized Kid had been unobtrusively keeping his eye on more than his cooking.

He called out, "You really ought to shake those a bit before you put them on. You never know what might consider them a real fine bed for the night."

Damian, quite naturally, dropped the shoes as if they had snakes coming out of them. Billybob started snickering and got Damian's first glare. The boy managed to hide his grin before Damian's eyes swung to him, so all he saw was his usual bland expression. And he simply couldn't help being hesitant about picking his shoes up again, did so by their very tips, and shook them violently before he brought them to the fire to try and peer inside them as well.

Kid said, "I'd say they're safe to wear now."

Damian glanced down at the boy suspiciously. "You weren't pulling my leg, were you?"

" 'Fraid not. Don't know if they've got scorpions in these parts or not, but in some areas—"

"You needn't elaborate."

Damian scowled and stomped off to fetch his bag and a fresh pair of stockings. He hadn't planned to be walking around the camp this morning in his stocking feet. But then, getting robbed again, or having it attempted, hadn't been planned for either.

And he soon found that he should have left the dirty socks on. Removing them disturbed several of his blisters to the bleeding point. And getting his shoes back on after that was pure hell.

As he limped back to the fire, he seriously hoped that Kid's one- or two-day estimate to Coffeyville was closer to the one-day mark. If he never saw another campfire, it would be too soon.

Reaching the fire, he was handed the plate stacked full of flapjacks and a jar of honey with the remark, "My butter went rancid yesterday, so that honey will have to do you. And it kind of spoiled my appetite, having to dish out violence so early in the morn, so you go ahead and finish that, Mr. Rutledge. I'll gnaw on some jerky later if I need to."

Damian spared a glance toward Vince and Billybob. "We're not feeding the other guests?"

"Hell, no. If they had wanted breakfast, they should have kept their guns holstered."

The disgust in his tone and expression was the first emotion Kid had shown that day. At least he felt *something*. Just damned sparing of sharing any of his feelings, apparently.

He stood up then, wiping his hands on the seat of his pants, and approached Billybob. "You got horses hidden hereabouts?"

"A ways up the river."

With a curt nod, Kid headed off in that direction.

Damian turned to keep an eye on the robbers while he ate his breakfast. He didn't think Billybob would try anything with Vince still unconscious, but he wasn't going to be surprised again either.

He was thinking about the extra horses and

the possibility of being able to keep his traveling
bag because of them, rather than leaving it behind, when Kid returned with the two mounts.
Both were about the sorriest-looking horses
Damian had ever seen: One was limping, the
other nearly so. But still, it was a surprise to see
the boy head straight for Vince and give a hard
kick to his backside. Not that it would hurt all
that much, coming from moccasined feet, but . . .

"I *really* hate people who treat animals like
this," he said, glaring at Billybob, who was
scooting back in case any more kicks were coming. "Which one is yours?"

"Neither," Billybob denied, an obvious lie.
"They both belong to Vince."

"Well, one can't be ridden, and the other
won't be doing any hard riding any time soon.
Took a rock out of his foot that was beginning
to fester. And look at them! They're both ripped
up bloody from your damn spurs."

Billybob scooted back even farther, but Kid
was done with his tirade and continued on to
the fire. "Time to move out," he told Damian.
"We'll be lucky if we make any more distance
today than if those two were on foot. They'll
have to share the one horse. The other is going
to go crippled if she takes any more weight before she mends. Damn, but stupid people annoy
the hell out of me."

That was pretty obvious. Under the circumstances, Damian decided not to mention his
traveling bag again. He supposed he would be
able to replace it as soon as he reached civilization again. Finding new clothes of good quality was another matter . . .

He helped break up the camp as best as common sense would allow, which for him was washing the dishes in the river. When he came back up the hill, the fire was completely buried and Kid's horse saddled and packed up with the large saddlebags that carried his trail gear.

This was the first time he'd noticed the chestnut gelding, which had been staked off on the edge of the camp. It was a fine-looking animal, well-groomed and spirited, or at least it seemed eager to be on the move. It was comparable to the Thoroughbreds that Damian had seen when he'd occasionally gone to the races, and he was a bit surprised that the skinny kid would own such an animal.

The boy was in the process of trying to get Billybob mounted, and from the sound of it, not having much luck. "I tell you, I can't do it, not with my hands tied behind me," Billybob was saying. "And even if I get up there, I'll be falling off without something to hold on to."

"Good. Then you'll spend all day thinking about staying in the saddle, rather than thinking up ways to cause me trouble. Now either you get up there or you walk, and it sure don't make me no nevermind which you choose."

It did look like an impossible task, which was why Damian came up behind Billybob and more or less tossed him up into the saddle. The man let out a "What the . . . ?" before he concentrated on not falling off the other side.

Kid gave Damian a genuine grin. His look said, *Guess you're not totally useless*, and then he glanced at the still unconscious Vince. "If he's still alive, you want to see if you can manage that again?"

The allusion to how hard Damian had hit the man had him blushing slightly. He nodded, and did manage to help Vince up into the saddle behind his friend after pouring half a canteen of water on him to get him awake enough to stay in it. But now that it was his own turn to mount, he was wishing someone was there to give him a hoist up as well—not that he could imagine anyone big enough to.

Living all his life in a large city, Damian had never had to deal with horses before, always having footmen or drivers to see to the carriage horses. Today would actually be the first time he'd ever been on the back of a horse, and he'd never realized what big animals they really were, particularly the spirited chestnut.

The boy, mounted and waiting, finally said, "You put your foot in the stirrup, Mr. Rutledge. Haven't you ever ridden before?"

"Only in vehicles, not on the animals that pull them," Damian was forced to admit.

He heard a sigh, then, "I shoulda known . . . Here, use my arm for balance, but push with your leg once you get your foot in the stirrup, then release it once you're seated."

It was easier said than done, of course, but Damian made it after the second attempt, and without landing them in the dust. His perch on top the saddle, though, was precarious at best, and he suddenly felt quite sorry for Vince, sitting behind Billybob with his hands tied behind him and no way to prevent a fall if he lost his balance.

At least Damian had Kid's reassuring "Hold on to me if you have to. We're not going to do any hard riding, so you shouldn't have any problems staying put."

They set out immediately, but it wasn't long before Vince started his complaints, and not just about being forced to ride with his hands tied. He was quite loud and extremely insulting with his choice of swear words in telling Damian what he thought of his broken nose.

But Kid finally put a stop to it with a yelled "If you want to eat tonight, shut up," and Vince shut up.

Damian smiled to himself. He had to admit, Kid had a no-nonsense style to be admired—at least under some situations. Actually, he was forced to revise his original opinion of the boy. Despite his less than perfect grammar, Kid was obviously intelligent. He was also extremely competent for his age, and had strong, if somewhat bossy, leadership qualities. He added up to a very intriguing, if disturbing, young fellow. Damian wished he could figure out what exactly *did* disturb him about the lad, but he couldn't quite put his finger on it.

Considering the ease with which he had taken care of the two stage robbers, and his intent to bring them in to the law, he obviously hadn't been bragging or lying about his profession, or the number of men he'd personally brought to justice. He was damned young to be a bounty hunter, but Damian had to suppose that his skill with a weapon made the job rather ideal for him—dangerous, but ideal.

His personal habits, on the other hand, could

definitely use some improvements. He had just camped by a river that had offered usable, if barbaric, bathing opportunities, but he hadn't taken advantage of them. Or if he had before Damian showed up, it certainly wasn't noticeable. Under such close proximity, Damian soon became aware of the odor that permeated the kid, and it was far from pleasant.

When they stopped for a short period around noon to rest the horses and stretch their legs, Damian was quick to fetch a handkerchief from his bag—he'd been so pleased when he looked back and noticed it strapped to the saddle of the horse that was being led. But the handkerchief, pressed unobtrusively to his nose so as not to give offense if the kid happened to glance back at him, helped only minimally.

Normally, Damian would never have broached such a personal subject, but toward late afternoon, after smelling that odor all day, he couldn't keep back the question any longer. "Do you live in those clothes?" he asked bluntly.

"Pretty much," came the easy reply. "Keeps the critters away at least."

Damian couldn't tell if the boy was joking, so he didn't bother to ask what critters he was referring to. He sighed, figuring he'd have to live with it until they reached town, which was another question . . .

"Will we see this Coffeyville by tonight, do you think?" he asked hopefully.

The kid didn't bother to look back to answer. "We might have, without those two owlhoots slowing us down, but now? I seriously doubt it, Mr. Rutledge."

Another sigh; then, merely to continue the conversation, Damian said, "Considering our close, if temporary, association, why don't you call me Damian? 'Mr. Rutledge' sounds rather— out of place out here, don't you think? And you *must* have something else that you've been called during your short lifetime other than Kid?"

"Well, I use 'K.C.' when I have to sign things legallike, if that's what you mean."

"What do the initials stand for?"

"Stand for?" There was a shrug. "Nothing. I was just making my mark the first time I had to sign for a reward, when the sheriff who saw me make it figured he was reading a 'K.C.,' and it kind of stuck after that—leastways, that particular sheriff doesn't call me anything else."

"K.C., eh? That's actually a nice name, if you take it in that context, rather than as initials. Mind if I call you Casey?"

The kid noticeably stiffened for a moment, then just as noticeably relaxed. "Don't make me no nevermind," was all he said.

That wasn't quite true, but Casey obviously wasn't going to make an issue over it. Damian smiled, imagining the boy objected to a name that was known to be used by either boys or girls. And boys his age did tend to get sensitive about such trivialities.

They fell silent again after that. For the most part, it had been a long and boring day on the trail, which Damian supposed he could be grateful for. Boring meant nothing else unfamiliar and dangerous catching him off guard and making him feel so totally out of his element.

About an hour before sunset, Casey headed back toward the river to make camp. He had a fire going in just a few minutes and quickly prepared some dough and set it aside to rise. But then he mounted up again as Damian was still seeing to getting their guests settled.

Damian was alarmed for a moment, thinking he was being abandoned, until Casey said, "Try not to break any more noses while I'm fetching dinner."

Damian blushed furiously. Casey didn't see it. He'd already ridden off.

Chapter 7

Casey was probably as glad to see Coffeyville the next morning as Damian was. She preferred traveling alone. She couldn't relax and be herself when she had to be constantly on guard. She couldn't manage a quick bath if water was at hand. She couldn't even see to nature's needs without slinking off to hide, while her companions just found any old spot with no thought to who else was around. But she couldn't get annoyed about the embarrassment it caused her, since they all thought she was one of them.

And that was her fault. Not that she went to any concerted effort to appear other than she was. It had never occurred to her when she left home that pretending to be a boy would make things easier on her.

She hadn't exactly been looking for "easy" at the time, just the opposite actually, if she wanted to get her point proved soon. The only thing she had done was hack off her hair to shoulder-length, and only because, with the clothes she needed to wear for the trail, that long braid dangling down her back would have drawn more notice, and she'd never liked being the center of attention.

The male attire that she wore was necessary, suitable as it was for riding, which was how she did most of her traveling. But it was the thick woolen poncho that fooled folks, hiding all her bumps and curves. And she wore that by preference. The poncho, wide in front, was easier to lift out of the way to draw her weapon than a jacket would be. A jacket, typically shoved behind the gun before it was drawn, would sometimes fall forward again or get in the way, and that could be detrimental to one's health.

So folks looked at her and, as tall as she was, just naturally assumed she was a boy. She saw no reason to change that misconception. It kept her from being bothered when in towns. It kept her prisoners from thinking they could take advantage of her because she was of the fairer sex. Funny; how they would have less problems accepting apprehension from a young boy than from a woman. But it was true. Some men just didn't take women seriously at all.

If asked, she'd be honest. After all, she wasn't masquerading, she was merely letting folks keep their first impressions. And if no one wanted to get too close to her, which might help that person notice things he otherwise wouldn't, that wasn't intentional either. That she stank a bit, well, there was a good reason for it.

She had to hunt her own food, and critters could sniff out humans too easily. Masking her scent she'd learned from her father. She could occasionally get right on top of a critter that way, before it sensed danger.

Which was why Casey didn't bother to wash her clothes unless she was staying in a town for more than a day, though she did bathe herself as often as possible. Right now, though, she knew she reeked, because her woolen poncho stank to high heaven every time after getting wet, and it had been drenched in the downpour the area had had a few days ago.

None of which would cause her any grief if she didn't have company, but she did, and she'd been extremely embarrassed a number of times since Damian Rutledge III had walked into her camp.

She'd never met anyone who'd held her attention as much as that Easterner did. He was unusual, to be sure, a big man like that in such a fancy city suit, but he was too damn handsome, too. Brown hair so dark that it looked black in most lighting, broad cheekbones, a very arrogant slant to his jaw, and thick brows made his face very masculine, along with a sharply chiseled nose and a firm mouth. And he had piercing gray eyes that had given her pause more than once, in thinking he could see through to the real Casey.

He distracted her, plain and simple. She'd caught herself staring at him for no good reason, just because he was so nice to look at. He made her feel strange, too, which she didn't like. And a couple times she'd even had this fool notion that maybe she ought to get prettied up, to let him see what she could be like, which was plain stupid. He'd be going on his way as soon as they reached Coffeyville, and she was glad of it. Distractions like him she didn't need.

Casey was doing fairly well for herself, all things considered. For a while, she'd felt really bad about the way she'd left home after that argument with her father, her anger keeping her from leaving her parents any explanation. She'd simply taken off without any good-byes, sneaked off in the night, to be exact.

But she telegraphed notes to her mother every few weeks, to let her know she was fine. She didn't want them to worry about her, though she knew they would. Still, she wasn't going home until she had accomplished her goal.

Chandos had made his way on his own. Now Casey was merely doing the same. She was proving that she could support herself without a man's help, and do it by doing a man's job.

Yet sometimes she felt like the outlaws whom she tracked. Knowing her father, she assumed that he was out there searching for her, and it wasn't easy eluding him. But all he had to go on was her description, and her present description didn't exactly match the one he knew by heart. The irony of the initials she used he hadn't discovered yet, at least not to her knowledge, but only a few sheriffs knew her as K.C. Most folks really did just call her Kid.

Soon she might be able to go home. At least she'd come north on this trip with that hope.

It had been a prime piece of luck, being in the right place at the right time and overhearing Bill Doolin bragging about a double bank robbery planned in Coffeyville this week. Doolin was a known member of the Dalton gang, and Casey

probably could have captured him with ease—
he'd been quite drunk at the time—but had decided to wait and get the entire gang at once.

Casey had done her homework about this
bunch of outlaws, talking to people, reading up
on past newspaper articles, just as she always
did before she set out to apprehend someone.
The three Dalton brothers, Robert, Emmett, and
Grattan, used to be U.S. marshals out of Arkan-
sas. It was purely a shame when lawmen went
bad, but the Dalton brothers surely had.

They'd started their illegal activities only a
few years ago in Oklahoma, horse stealing
mostly, then had moved up to bigger crimes
when Robert, the leader of the gang, moved
them to California. Their attempt to rob the San
Francisco-Los Angeles express of the Southern
Pacific Railroad early last year, a failed undertaking since they couldn't get the safe open, got
them plastered all over Wanted posters in that
area, so they hightailed it back to Oklahoma.
Grattan did get arrested and tried—one man
had been killed in that botched California job—
ending up with a twenty-year jail term, but he
managed to escape and rejoin his brothers.

Apparently they added to their numbers after
that, for there were four newcomers with them—
Charlie "Blackface" Bryant, Charley Pierce,
"Bitter Creek" George Newcomb, and Bill
Doolin—when they robbed the Santa Fe Limited
at Wharton in the Cherokee Strip in May last
year. No one was killed that time, and they escaped with over ten thousand dollars. Blackface
Bryant didn't live long enough to spend his

share, though, dying shortly afterward in a shoot-out with U.S. Deputy Marshal Ed Short.

Later that same month, the gang got away with a reported nineteen thousand after flagging down the Missouri, Kansas & Texas train at Lelietta. But they'd likely been holed up, living off their ill-gotten gains after that, because the Dalton gang didn't appear in newsprint again until this past June, when they robbed another train at Redrock. And their last train robbery, in July at Adair, got bloody again, with three men wounded and one dead.

But apparently they were stepping up their operations to include banks now, and not just one, but two at once. Quite an ambitious undertaking for this gang of owlhoots, if it was true. Casey intended to be there to prevent it and collect the rewards.

The combined amounts offered for the gang members would be well over what she'd been hoping to have in the bank when she finished her "point-proving." She'd be able to go home, which was what she'd been yearning to do only two weeks after she left. Instead, she'd been gone for six months. Six long months and plenty of tears in between.

Chapter 8

$\mathcal{J}$ust one hour further last night on the trail, and they could have slept in relative comfort. But Casey hadn't known that, this being her first time traveling as far north as Kansas. She hadn't figured she would run out of food, either, before she reached the next town, but having three extra mouths to feed had seen to that.

They were late hitting the trail that morning because she'd had to go hunting again for breakfast, having gone through the last of her dough and canned goods with the previous night's dinner. She always bought just enough food staples in each town she passed through to last her to the next town, but that didn't take into account running into lost Easterners and bungling stage robbers along the way. So even though it had been only another hour along the trail, it was still midmorning when they rode into Coffeyville.

It was a decent-sized mercantile town. Casey had figured it would be, if it had two banks. And as they rode down the main street on the way to the sheriff's office, she eyed both the First National Bank and the Condon Bank just across the street from it, then glanced around to find a good place nearby from which she could keep an eye on them.

Workmen were busy on the street and had temporarily removed the hitching rails in front of both banks. As she wound the horses around the men, Casey wasn't sure she was glad to see that.

Bank robbers tended to count on being able to tether their horses within easy access for their getaways, which meant directly in front of or at the sides of their targets. If the Daltons rode in and saw no rails, they might decide not to hit the banks after all and ride right back out.

That would be good for the town, but it wouldn't put these particular outlaws out of commission. In that case, Casey would have to depend on the descriptions she had of them in order to recognize them, if she was going to hold any hope of still bringing them to justice.

But presently everything was quiet, so it looked like she would have enough time to dispose of her current prisoners and get prepared to take on the next bunch.

She still hadn't decided whether to tell the sheriff here what was planned. There was always the chance that he might thank her for the information and advise her to stay out of it from here on, wanting all the glory for himself. As well as the money. There was also the chance that he might scoff, not believing her. After all, the Dalton gang was well known in these parts for train robbing, not bank robbing.

Then there was the fact that she knew what she was capable of, but she couldn't say the same of others. On the other hand, she'd never attempted to apprehend so many at once before, either. She'd just have to decide after she met the sheriff, she supposed, and she was about to do that, having reached his office.

The group of them had drawn attention, coming in doubled up on their mounts as they were, with Billybob and Vince obviously tied as well, so there was a lot of help from the town's most curious, getting the two men off their horse and into the sheriff's office. As it turned out, there was a small reward offered for both men, this not being their first stage robbery, so Damian's account of what had happened wasn't needed, other than to report the crashed stagecoach and the missing driver.

There was a bit of confusion, since, for some infernal reason that annoyed Casey no end, it had been assumed by one and all that Damian had done the capturing. Just because he was so damned big, she thought, while she, on the other hand, was so young-looking—stupid first impressions.

But Damian was out the door as soon as the sheriff dismissed him. Casey followed to bid him farewell before she finished her business.

"Good luck on the rest of your journey," she said, offering her hand in parting.

"I'll settle for uneventful—at least until I reach Texas," he replied.

"Ah, that's right, you're on a manhunt yourself. Well, good luck with that, too."

Damian took her hand, giving it a hard

squeeze. "Thanks for all your help, Casey. I would probably still be wandering around lost out there if I hadn't noticed your campfire that night."

That was debatable, but Casey didn't say so. She yanked her hand back, then blushed because it was so obvious that his touch had unsettled her. But he didn't seem to notice. He was already distracted and impatient to be on his way, looking up and down the street at what the town had to offer in the way of amenities.

"Good-bye, then," she said, and abruptly turned back into the sheriff's office.

It would more than likely be the last she would see of the tenderfoot. He'd probably check into the best hotel the town offered, while conserving money was one of her main priorities, so she'd search out cheaper accommodations. She'd spend time in the saloons at night, a good place to gather information. He'd go to the theater, if there was one.

In her opinion, he ought to go home. The Western regions could be very unkind to folks who weren't raised there. Hadn't he already found that out firsthand? But had he learned from it? Hell, no. Easterners were like a whole different breed of people. They looked at things differently, knew next to nothing about surviving without the things they took for granted . . . Casey was doing it again, thinking about that man when she shouldn't be.

She got back to the business at hand and deciding whether to confide in the sheriff or not. She couldn't say much for his deputies, having to listen to the usual wisecracks about her tender age, that she must have come across the outlaws asleep or drunk, that there was no way she could have captured them otherwise. She didn't try to correct their mistaken assumptions. She never did. The fewer folks who knew what she was capable of, the better.

It was a good twenty minutes more before the sheriff had finished with her and told her to come back the next day to collect her two hundred dollars. It wasn't much for a couple of stage robbers, but then, Vince and Billybob had only just started down the path of crime.

And then the decision to share or not share her information or not was taken out of her hands. Gunfire was heard, unmistakable, and not just one shot. Ignoring her, the sheriff and his deputies dashed out of the office.

Casey hoped, she really did, that the Dalton gang hadn't come to town yet. But with an inward groan, she was afraid her hope was a vain one. And from the sound of it, their plans had definitely gone sour.

Chapter 9

~~~~~~~~~~~~~~~~~~~~~~

Damian stood there with his hands raised, incredulous that he was being robbed again, and of the exact same money. Casey's warning as they sat by the fire last night came back to him clearly now, word for word.

"Chances are, the money that Vince and Billybob stole from you is in their saddlebags or on them. Better to get it now, Damian, because whether the sheriff will turn it over to you any time soon is debatable. I've waited upwards of a week to collect a reward. I swear, lawmen and paperwork just don't get along."

"I'm not worried about that," Damian had told him. "I can have funds transferred. In fact, I should go to the bank as soon—"

"I wouldn't."

"Excuse me?"

"Just take my word for it, Damian, and stay out of the banks when you get to town."

The kid had changed the subject after that. And Damian had retrieved his money in Vince's saddlebag—only to hand it over now to a bank robber.

The three men who had entered the Condon Bank were heavily armed with Winchesters and handguns. If that wasn't enough of a clue to what they intended, they had immediately put the few customers and employees in the bank under the nozzles of those guns.

Two of the robbers were wearing obvious false whiskers. They all appeared young, though, in their early twenties. And they were deadly serious. There would be no bungling here, Damian was sure. It was in their eyes, that each one of them would kill without a moment's hesitation if they didn't get full cooperation.

Damian—again—didn't have a weapon to be uncooperative with, even if he wanted to be. He'd turned the extra handgun that he'd been carrying in to the sheriff.

Robbed again. It was beyond belief. And in broad daylight, in the heart of town, with the streets teeming with people and workers. And the kid had known it was going to happen. He'd tried to warn Damian away. But Damian had decided he was just being overprotective—or being ornery, by trying to make Damian more nervous than the kid already figured he was. What could happen bright and early in the morning, after all, with people everywhere?

There were a few minutes of tense waiting around for the vault's time lock to open at nine forty-five, during which time the customers had been ordered to empty their pockets. No one else entered the Condon Bank during that short period, but Damian did notice someone outside peering in the window. The fellow must have seen the drawn weapons and figured out what was happening, because in the next moment, the alarm was being shouted out in the street.

That put an abrupt end to the robbery. One of the robbers swore. Another paled. They didn't look too confident now, and in fact, they forgot about the vault and ran out the door with their guns firing. But the town was quick to defend its money. Guns had been grabbed all along the street. Pandemonium reigned out there.

Most of the people in the bank had hit the floor with the first shot. Damian didn't notice, or think to do the same. He walked slowly to the door, where he witnessed the first casualty. Across the street, two more gunmen fled from the First National Bank with their stolen loot, and one man stepped out to intercept them. He was gunned down with a Winchester. Seconds later, two more bystanders died as they got in the way of the outlaws' attempt to escape down the street.

And then a bullet flew past Damian's ear, so close he could feel the sting of it, the one bullet out of all those flying around that broke his temper. But he had nowhere to direct his sudden burning anger—until he saw Casey run right by him in the direction the outlaws had gone.

It was a total bloodbath. Casey reached the alley where the Daltons had stashed their horses about a block down the street from the banks before the last shot was fired, but only in time to see it fired and Emmett Dalton go tumbling off his horse.

The gunfire had actually lasted only about five minutes. But in that time, four citizens had been killed, including a marshal who had been in town and had traded gunfire with Grat Dalton there in the alley, neither of them surviving it. That alley had become a death trap. The outlaws had all reached their horses, but there were just too many bullets coming their way by then for it to do them any good.

Robert and Grat Dalton were dead, as were Dick Broadwell and Bill Powers. Doolin, whom Casey had overheard talking about the robberies, wasn't even there.

In fact, his horse going lame that morning had kept him behind, though he obviously didn't learn from the mistake of his dead friends, because he went on to start up his own gang after that to continue his lawless ways. Emmett Dalton was the only one to survive that day, and he was to face a life sentence in the Kansas State Prison when he recovered from his wounds.

Staring at the aftermath, Casey was spitting mad. She could have taken them all alive, at the very least, got them all down and disabled with some very painful leg wounds that would have had them surrendering in short order.

That way they would have survived. Not that she felt sorry for their demise. But they'd taken innocent bystanders with them, and that always turned her stomach.

All those deaths she might have been able to prevent if she had just gotten to Coffeyville a little sooner. And she should have. In fact, she would have arrived yesterday or even the day before, in plenty of time, if not for the excess baggage . . .

Damian and his damn stage robbers.

Vince and Billybob alone wouldn't even have

detained her. They would have slowed her down just as they did, but she wouldn't have felt obliged to go out and hunt for them this morning, knowing she was close to turning them in. It wouldn't have bothered her at all if those two had gone a little hungry for a few extra hours. She still could have arrived in town in time.

But Damian was another matter. It hadn't even occurred to her to tell him that the next meal would have to wait until they reached town, not when it was a known fact that most big men like him had voracious appetites. And he was an Easterner, which equated in her mind with helplessness on the trail. She had accepted responsibility for him when she had let him share her camp, which meant she had to feed him.

But he shouldn't have been here. A big-city man like him never should have come West in the first place. That he *was* here was solely his doing, a decision *he'd* made, and because of that, she could place the blame for this whole fiasco on his shoulders. But he wasn't right there in front of her, which was fortunate—the way she was feeling, she'd probably shoot him.

And then he was . . .

Casey became aware of that fact when she was slammed up against the nearest wall, her feet dangling far above the sidewalk, her poncho, shirt, and even the camisole under it all grasped in Damian's large fist that was holding her up. His other fist was drawn back, aimed right for her face, just seconds from doing some serious bone breakage.

Casey should have been screaming for help by then, but she didn't even flinch. She didn't think he had it in him to hit a boy the age he thought her to be, and to her everlasting relief, she was right. With a low growl of disgust, he let go of her, then pierced her with his eyes, a turbulent, stormy gray at the moment.

She didn't know what *his* problem was, but her anger was unabated. And Casey's scruples were a mite different from his, as least when her temper was running high. Without hesitation, her fist landed right between his eyes, not exactly what she'd been aiming for, but with him being so tall, it was hard for her to gauge. That, of course, had him reaching for her again, whether to throttle her or restrain her, she didn't wait to find out.

She drew her gun. He halted immediately, clenching those large fists at his sides. His face was turning red with what was now impotent fury.

Oddly enough, Casey's temper was gone, now that she had the upper hand. Hitting him had helped some as well, not that she'd hurt him any, using her left hand as she did. But she knew better than to use her gun hand for hitting things. And she ignored the present throbbing in her left hand.

"Real fair about this, aren't you?" he gritted out in a sneering tone.

"Considering your size, you betcha."

The calmness of her tone served to enrage him even more. "You knew those banks were going to be robbed, didn't you? Didn't you!"

Casey didn't answer that, said instead, "Let's take this off the street, tenderfoot."

Not that they were drawing any notice or being overheard, with half the town crowded in front of that alley trying to get a look-see. In fact, the nearby store that she pushed Damian into was quite empty, the owner just as curious as the rest of the citizens in town about what all the shooting had been about so early in the morning.

But as soon as she closed the door behind her, he repeated his question. She saw no reason to deny it now.

Her curt nod didn't satisfy him, because he demanded, "*How* did you know?"

She saw no reason to keep that to herself any longer either. "I was in this hellhole a few weeks ago down south, and recognized one of the gang members. I was going to take him, was moving in for it, when I heard what he was talking about, or I should say bragging about, to his friend."

"About robbing the banks here?"

"Yes."

"The man was actually discussing it where he could be overheard?"

"He didn't know he was overheard. I can be good at going unnoticed when I want to be. Besides, he was swimming in rotgut that night. He wouldn't have noticed a fly on his nose, much less me."

"So you knew exactly what was planned here and said nothing. Dammit, Casey, I could have been killed in that bank. Couldn't you have

mentioned this last night when we spoke of it?"
he asked, disgruntled.

"I only share that kind of information with
lawmen. You should have trusted me and taken
the warning as it was intended—to keep you
safe and out of the line of fire. Why the hell
didn't you?"

To give him credit, Damian did flush slightly,
having been so obviously caught ignoring her
advice. "I was only going to be in that bank for
a minute or two. I just wanted to make sure that
I could get funds transferred out here if I needed
them. And now they *are* needed, since those
bank robbers relieved me of my cash again."

"The least you deserve for not listening to
me," Casey said unsympathetically. "And let
me tell you something else. There's folks laying
dead all over the street out there, if you hadn't
noticed, when they shouldn't be. I could have
prevented that if I had gotten here yesterday as
I should have, and why didn't I? Because *you*
showed up. It's also cost me a *lot* of money, your
slowing me up, more'n ten thousand dollars in
rewards for that bunch."

He stiffened at that point. "Just a damn minute, kid. You can't put the blame for those
deaths on me, or any lost rewards. Or are you
under the impression that you could have captured them all single-handedly, without a shot
fired?" Damian scoffed. "I hardly think so."

Casey sighed. "It's what I do, Damian, remember? I track, hunt, and capture outlaws,
while they do their best to avoid it. If I find a
bunch of them gathered together, all the better.
Most men aren't foolish enough to draw a

weapon when they've already got one aimed at them. That's just asking for a visit from the undertaker."

"Desperate men will. You're deluding yourself if you think otherwise. In fact, you probably would have gotten yourself killed for trying. If you ask me, it sounds more like I saved your life by keeping you from trying."

Casey came just short of rolling her eyes. "We'll never know for sure, will we? All I know is, I would have had enough money to retire after this, but now I don't. I'm going to give you one last piece of advice, Damian. Go home. You don't belong out here. Actually, here's another piece. Stay the hell away from me."

Chapter 10

*D*amian spent the next few days quite literally cooling his heels. He pampered his feet to give his blisters a chance to heal, which meant staying in his hotel room, even taking his meals there so he could avoid shoes. He'd also arranged for the town doctor to visit and have a look at his head wound, and after much tsking was told that the wound *should* have been stitched, but there was no point in doing so now, since it was already mending.

It was no hardship, remaining in the hotel. The room certainly wasn't what he was used to, but it was nicer than some he'd stayed in since heading West. And there was nothing he cared to view or visit in this Western town anyway. He'd buy a new derby, hopefully, before he left—and a rifle. He wasn't going to be caught again without a weapon. But that could wait until he was ready to catch the train to continue his journey south.

Keeping to his room, though, left him little to occupy himself with, other than rereading the file he had on the men wanted by the law west of the Missouri line. The Dalton gang and all of their known members had been in that file. There were more members than had actually shown up to rob the Coffeyville banks, but at least the three Dalton brothers wouldn't be appearing in any more files.

Damian also did a lot of thinking while he was recuperating from his "trail" ordeal. He was sorry, after he thought about it, that he and Casey had parted on such bad terms. He had liked the kid. Casey had given him his final advice that day of the robberies, then simply walked away. Damian hadn't seen him since. Not that he was taking the advice to heart and trying to avoid the boy. He just hadn't been out of his hotel to notice whether Casey was still in town or not.

However, Damian was feeling guilty, all things considered. Casey had helped him when he'd desperately needed it. He'd thanked him, yes, but then he'd also come damn close to beating him to a pulp. Hardly the way to treat a person who'd probably saved his life.

And one remark kept repeating itself in Damian's mind. *I track, hunt, and capture outlaws, while they do their best to avoid it.*

Damian had already owned up to the fact that he personally knew next to nothing about hunting down Henry Curruthers. All he had was the name of the town Curruthers had last been seen in. But someone like Casey would know how to proceed from there to find the man. That was what the kid did for a living.

The idea to hire the boy came to him soon

after that, but he didn't act on it immediately. And the reason he procrastinated was that he was used to getting what he wanted from people, yet he fully expected a flat refusal from Casey. He simply didn't feel like facing rejection right now, after everything else he'd gone through.

Yet his common sense won out. Casey could save him weeks, months even, of wasted time. And it wouldn't hurt to ask. If he got turned down, he could always find another bounty hunter. But he would prefer the kid, already being familiar with him and having witnessed firsthand his capabilities. He also trusted Casey, though he couldn't exactly say why, whereas someone he didn't know ... .

Having made the decision, he was then afraid that he'd lost his chance, that the kid would have moved on by now. But he made an effort to find him anyway. And he got lucky.

It was a rundown boardinghouse on the edge of town, the cheapest accommodations to be found. The slovenly owner steered Damian to the first door upstairs. He was worried that his weight was going to cave a few of the steps in, they creaked so loudly on his way up. And there was no answer to his knock. Surprisingly, the door was open, so he stepped inside to wait.

Damian wasn't expecting the kid to be there at that point, yet he was. He came out of a tiny, closetlike bathroom rubbing a towel to the side of his head, having just washed his hair—which was undoubtedly why he hadn't heard the knock. The poncho had been removed. It was the first time Damian had seen him without it.

For a boy of around fifteen or sixteen years, the kid was skinnier than Damian had thought, with very narrow shoulders. The too-big-for-him, white cotton shirt was tucked into his jeans, showing a waist small enough to be envied by most females. Even his feet were small and delicate-looking, noticeable without his moccasins on.

Actually, cleaned up as he was now, Casey looked damn near like a girl, and a pretty one at that. Perhaps Damian would have been doing him a favor to have landed that punch the other day. A permanently disfigured nose would have detracted a bit from that prettiness.

The boy went perfectly still, except for the narrowing of those golden brown eyes, when he noticed Damian by the bed. "How the hell did you get in here?"

"The door wasn't locked."

"Did it have a sign on it that said 'Walk Right In'?" Casey replied sarcastically as he draped the towel around his neck to hang down his chest, keeping a grasp on each end. "Or have you taken to breaking into other people's rooms now, Damian?"

Damian flushed. "The woman downstairs said you were in. When you didn't answer my knock—I was just making sure you were all right."

"I'm fine. But I'll be even better—just as soon as you leave."

"That isn't very hospitable, Casey."

"Sure it is. At least I'm not shooting you."

Damian smiled. He couldn't help it. Casey, disgruntled, was worse than a pouting female.

"I'd like to apologize for my behavior the other morning. I'll admit, my anger got out of hand."

"I noticed."

"It won't happen again," Damian assured him.

Casey shrugged. "It don't make me no nevermind if you fly off the handle. I won't be around to see it. Now you've apologized. I'll restrain myself from doing the same. The door is behind you."

Damian sighed. The kid was *not* making this easy. And he'd switched to his inscrutable expression, the one that hid his emotions so effectively, and had caused Damian more than a little nervousness on several occasions. This wasn't one of those times, though, since the kid was presently unarmed, his gun and holster hanging over the back of the only chair, which was on Damian's side of the room.

"Before I leave, I have a proposal to make to you," Damian said.

"I'm not interested."

"It will be worth your while to at least hear me out before you decline the offer."

"Now just how do you figure that, when I *said* I'm not interested?"

Damian ignored that comment. "I'd like to hire you to help me find a murderer."

Casey sighed at that point. "Do I look like I'm for hire, Damian? I'm not. I do the picking and choosing of the men I want to go after. Clean and simple, with no one trying to give me orders, or pushing me to get the job done, or complaining that I'm not doing things the way they think I should."

"I'll pay you ten thousand dollars."

That took care of the inscrutable expression. Casey was clearly incredulous. And the amount Damian had settled on wasn't arbitrary, it was the figure Casey had claimed to have just lost out on.

"Are you crazy?" was the first response.

"No, just very rich."

"That's throwing away good money."

"That depends on how you look at it. This man murdered my father, Casey, and it drives me crazy each day that he continues to elude justice. And I've already spent thousands of dollars on private detectives, who at least traced him as far as Fort Worth, Texas. But they lost him from there, which is why I'm on my way to Texas, trying to look for him myself. If your help can find him sooner than I could on my own, then what I pay you will be worth every penny to me."

Casey moved to sit down on the edge of the bed. He stared at the floor for several long minutes. Damian didn't say another word, letting him mull it over, hoping his own sense of justice would influence his final decision.

When he looked up, he said, "I have to be honest with you. I can think of a dozen men off the top of my head who would take on this job for a fraction of what you're willing to pay. All good trackers, too. And then there are dozens of others if you know where to inquire, guns for hire that do this sort of thing for a living."

"Your pointing that out, Casey, is the very

reason I want you for the job. I trust you not to steer me wrong or take advantage of my lack of knowledge about this part of the country. Anyone else I wouldn't know or trust, so the offer is being made to you and you alone."

Several more minutes of silence passed, more excruciating than before, since Casey wasn't giving any indication at all of what he was thinking. Damian knew the boy would prefer not to deal with him anymore. But he also knew the money was important to him, or he wouldn't have gotten so upset over missing out on the Dalton gang's rewards.

Casey finally said, "All right, tell me everything you know about the man."

Damian gave an inward sigh of relief. "I'll tell you on the way."

"You'll what?"

"I'll be going with you."

"Like hell you will."

"That's part of the deal, Casey. I have to be there, to make a positive identification—"

"And then kill him?" Casey cut in, eyes narrowing. "I do recall you saying that was your intention. But if you think I'll just stand there and let you shoot this man in cold blood, think again."

"Isn't that an unwritten rule in your own profession?" Damian pointed out. " 'Dead or alive,' all those Wanted posters read, but without any fine print that tells you how to go about seeing to the 'dead' part."

"I go by my own rules, Damian, and death doesn't show up in them."

"Yes, I'd already gathered that about the way

you do business. So don't worry about it. I'm not going to kill him without provocation. I might be hoping for provocation, but I'll settle for his spending the rest of his life in prison. Some men might consider that a worse punishment than death."

"I have your word on that?"

"If you must."

"Very well, we'll ride out in the morning. Get you a horse—"

Damian cut in. "We'll take the train to save time, at least until it's no longer going in the same direction we are. I'll pick up the tickets, since I will also be covering all travel expenses."

The kid was now giving him a look that clearly said *Orders already?* but all he replied was, "It's been my experience that trains *aren't* always faster, but suit yourself."

Chapter 11

Casey spent the rest of that day castigating herself for succumbing to temptation. She never should have agreed to "stick" herself with Damian Rutledge again. Finding this killer for him was one thing, but taking him along to do it . . . she knew better. She'd already dealt with the difficulties of having him around.

Half the time, he made her feel like a mother with a young child, needing to do everything for him because he couldn't do for himself. But then she'd look at him and not feel that way at all. He jumbled her emotions too much. He made her feel things she wasn't used to. Hell, even after she'd thought she'd seen the last of him, she had still been thinking about him way too much.

But ten thousand dollars for one job—there was just no way she could turn that down, when she could then go home as soon as the job was done. The money offered for a wanted man usually correlated to his dangerousness, but in this case she didn't think so. The killer was an Easterner, after all, so how dangerous could he be?

It would be an easy job, too easy for the kind of money being offered. But it didn't make her no nevermind if Damian wanted to throw away good money. She would just have to deal with the negative aspects of it, though . . . which began the very next day.

Casey showed up at the train depot at the time Damian's message to her that morning had stated. He was easy to find. Dressed in his fine suit, wearing a silly-looking hat that wouldn't do a bit of good to keep the sun off his face, he stood out like a sore thumb.

He was carrying a rifle case along with his travel bag. She really hoped there wasn't a weapon in it, because if he intended to do any shooting, she imagined she'd have to tend to shot-off toes.

"You're late," he said by way of greeting as soon as she came up beside him.

"I'm right on time," she disagreed.

He didn't argue the point. Instead, he walked off toward the train that was already boarding, expecting her to follow. She didn't.

Casey took one look at it and called out, "I don't see a stock car on this train."

He stopped, turning around to raise a brow at her. "A stock car?"

She gave him a pointed look. "You think I'm leaving my horse behind, tenderfoot?"

His flush of embarrassment was immediate. Obviously he hadn't considered her horse in his travel arrangements, but then, a man who'd never been on one until a few days ago wouldn't. And now they'd have to wait for another train, one that transported animals as well as passengers, which could be later that day—or even next week.

Damian said, "I'll be right back," and he was back after only a few minutes to tell her, "They're going to add a stock car."

Casey almost chuckled, but settled for a grin. "That must have cost you a pretty penny."

His nod was curt. He was still embarrassed. And the train was delayed in leaving while the extra car was hooked up to it. It had probably cost Damian even more than she figured. Train engineers prided themselves on keeping to their time schedules, after all.

But they finally did get settled, in one of the plushiest cars Casey had ever ridden in. Damian had lucked out there; this particular train had one of those fancy Eastern Pullman luxury cars attached to it, or so she thought. When no other passengers entered it, though, she found out that he'd arranged to have it delivered from one of the northern stations for his exclusive use.

He'd agreed to pay an exorbitant fifty dollars a day to rent it. But having already experienced the emigrant train cars with their hard, uncomfortable seats, he told her that he counted that a small price to pay for his comfort, especially since they still had Oklahoma Territory to pass through, as well as northern Texas.

Casey couldn't complain. She was in complete agreement with Damian about the fact that the few trains she had ridden on in the past six months hadn't been at all pleasant. Having been raised on a ranch, she actually preferred the outdoors and a good seat on a horse, but if she had to ride the rails, one of George Pullman's deluxe parlor cars was definitely the next best way to travel.

"I should have thought of this when I left New York," Damian told her. "My father owned one of these cars, which we used to travel in when business took us out of the city. It had nearly all the comforts of home, even including a large bedroom. I'm sorry to say it never occurred to me to use it to travel West in."

"What, no beds in this one?" Casey asked him, tongue in cheek.

He missed the sarcasm. "No, but the seats look comfortable enough to sleep in if the train doesn't stop over in a town for the night. Not all of them do, and those hard benches at the out-of-town depot stops allow about as much sleep as the cold ground does."

"Would depend on whether you like sleeping on the ground or not, wouldn't it?"

That remark had him slanting his eyes at her. "I suppose you do?"

Casey sank down in the thick, overstuffed, velvet-upholstered chair, her hands hooked over her belly, and just smiled. That seemed to annoy Damian no end, to go by the look of disgust he gave her. So she added a shrug.

"I was raised on a ranch, Damian. I've spent many a night out on a roundup, sleeping next to a campfire."

Also, some of her fondest memories were from those times she had spent in the wilds with her father and brothers, when he was teaching them all the things he felt they should know. But she wasn't going to mention that, since she'd told Damian she was an orphan.

Being nameless, as she'd claimed to be, sort of took it for granted that you weren't raised by loving parents. But her real name was *not* something she was going to pass around, even after all this time, not when her father was likely still out there looking for her.

"So you know ranching as well as bounty hunting?" Damian asked her casually.

"I know ranching inside and out."

"You say that like it's something you enjoyed doing. So why did you switch to bounty hunting, which is so much more dangerous?"

"More dangerous?" Casey couldn't help grinning. "Now that's debatable."

"I hardly think—"

She cut in, "Have you ever been around cattle to know, Damian? With a gunman, it's your skill against theirs, but with cattle, it's you against brute force. If a bull's charging you or a stampede's started, there's no skill to it, you just get the hell out of the way as best you can."

"But if you prefer that . . . ?"

Casey shrugged. "I'll be ranching again, just as soon as I finish doing what I have to do."

"Which is?"

"You ask too many questions, Damian."

Damian grinned this time. "Not nearly as many as I could, but no matter. I just figured, since we were going to be spending a lot more time together, that we might as well get to know each other better."

"The only thing you need to know about me is I can get the job done. Now, why don't you tell me about this man you want tracked down?"

It didn't take long. The bare facts weren't many. But Damian also recounted all the evidence that his detectives had uncovered. Everyone who knew Henry Curruthers had been shocked to learn what he'd done—his elderly aunt, his co-workers, his neighbors. No one could believe that he would embezzle money from the company he worked for, much less resort to murder to hide his crime.

But circumstances could change people drastically. Casey knew that. She was an example of it herself. And having two confessions, as well as Curruthers's fleeing West without telling anyone that he was leaving the city, not to mention the clear indication in the accounts, which only *he* kept, that the money had been stolen, were damning pieces of evidence.

"He'll be easy enough to find with a description like his," Casey remarked after Damian had finished speaking, though she added, "But I'd like to hear his side of it before I turn him over to the law."

Damian frowned. "After everything I've told you, you can't think that he might be innocent."

"No, it doesn't sound like he is. But he's not the typical sort that I hunt either. The outlaws I hunt all have one thing in common—witnesses to their crimes. If I have to kill one of them, I won't feel too bad about it, being assured of their guilt beforehand."

"You've said that was never the case, that you haven't had to kill any of them."

"True, but it could happen, and actual witnesses pretty much make it a closed case, a trial after capture just a matter for the court records. I've only come across one exception to that, with only one witness claiming this fella by the name of Horace Johnson had shot the man's brother in cold blood. The witness was a known member of the town. Johnson wasn't, having only just moved there, so a Dead or Alive poster went out on Johnson. But after I talked to his mother and one of his friends I tracked down, it started sounding like the witness was the culprit. And sure enough, after I confronted him, his guilt had eaten at him long enough that he broke down and confessed to being the one who'd killed his brother."

"Amazing," Damian said. "You actually saved an innocent man from getting gunned down and likely killed by a less scrupulous bounty hunter. I didn't realize you were so thorough in what you do."

Casey blushed, which annoyed her no end. She hadn't been trying to impress him, she'd merely been trying to make her point.

She said so. "I was only explaining why I'd like to hear Curruthers's side of it first."

"But there are witnesses, the two men he hired—"

"Paid killers aren't witnesses in my book, Damian, they are accomplices. And killers aren't known for being scrupulously honest. For all you know, those two men could have held a grudge against Curruthers for some unknown reason and, being caught themselves, figured they'd get some payback out of it by naming him as the one behind the killing. He could have run for that very reason."

"There is still the embezzled money."

"Yes, there is that. But what will it hurt to question the man when we find him?"

"Suit yourself—as long as we find him."

Chapter 12

*I*t should have been an uneventful trip to Fort Worth, but Casey and Damian were both of the opinion, for different reasons, that luck had plain and simply deserted them. As it happened, they were still a few hours away from the Texas border when their train nearly derailed. But the engineer managed to stop just short of the missing tracks. The suddenness of the stop, however, threw a lot of passengers in the forward cars out of their seats.

Casey, ensconced in one of the big, thickly padded chairs in the parlor car, was merely jarred. She glanced at Damian to make sure he was all right, then moved to stick her head out of one of the windows. She couldn't see the missing tracks, but the masked riders coming out of a clump of trees and heading for the train with weapons drawn were definitely noticeable.

She sat back down, adjusted her poncho, and told Damian, "Relax, it's just a train robbery."

His eyes flared. "*Another* robbery? You're joking, right? Tell me you're joking. The odds on being robbed again this soon—"

"Were pretty high," Casey interrupted, "considering the territory we're passing through."

"And what, pray tell, has that to do with it?" he asked huffily.

"This area has always been tempting to outlaws, Damian. Half of it became a Territory just a few years ago, when the Cherokee Strip was bought from the Indians for white settlement. This half we've been traveling through still belongs to the Indians."

"Indian Territory? You couldn't have mentioned that previously?"

"Why? They're tame Indians. But before '90, the entire area was beyond white jurisdiction, and the Indians that the government had moved here years ago pretty much minded their own business, as long as the outlaws left them alone. Hell, the panhandle isn't too far from here, and it wasn't known as No Man's Land for nothing."

"No Man's Land?"

"It was an outlaws' haven, since neither the whites nor the Indians had any jurisdiction, it being completely unclaimed land. And they've still got their hideouts in that area as well as in the rest of the area. Just because the three land rushes that the government sponsored here in the last couple years moved in a slew of new settlers didn't mean the outlaws were going to move out."

"And you couldn't have mentioned *that* previously?" he demanded.

Casey shrugged, then grinned. "Was hoping I wouldn't have to. After all, despite what you're probably thinking right now, train robberies do *not* occur daily."

"The statistics that seem to be following me on this journey dispute that claim," Damian said as he moved toward his rifle case stored in the corner of the car.

Casey frowned at him. "And just what do you think you're going to do with that?"

He gave her a determined glance. "See to it that I keep my money this time."

"Get yourself killed is more like it," Casey grumbled in answer.

"I'm inclined to agree with that," the man stepping in through the door muttered beneath his bandana, having overheard Casey's prediction. "So sit yourself down, mister, and you might live through this."

Damian halted his movement, but he didn't back off or sit down. He looked angry. Of course he was, but to show it was plain foolish, considering that the stage robber who had joined them looked damn nervous—and young. He didn't appear much older than Casey. A good guess was this was probably the young man's first holdup.

"The big fella there isn't going to attack you, so don't do anything stupid," Casey said.

She was looking at the robber, but the words had been more for Damian's benefit. And the remark didn't ease the robber's nervousness any. His gun was visibly shaking, his eyes darting warily back and forth between her and Damian.

But he gathered up enough bravado to order, "Just toss your money over here and I'll be on my way."

"You might want to consider leaving without

the money," Casey suggested calmly.

"Why?"

"It will be less bloody that way."

Casey wasn't a bit surprised that his eyes flew back to Damian. The big Easterner appeared to be the greater threat. But being dismissed as harmless didn't annoy her this time, since it allowed her to draw her weapon without the robber even noticing.

And because this was the second time someone had tried to rob her in a matter of days, she didn't shoot just to disarm. She hit the man's gun hand squarely to damage it enough that he wouldn't be using it again for robberies, at least not with any proficiency.

The weapon fell with a soft thud on the carpeted floor; blood splattered all around it. His scream was plaintive though brief, but the groaning that followed continued unabated. And his eyes above the bandana were boggled with pain and terror. However, he didn't move, not with Casey's gun still trained on him, other than to grasp the wrist of his mutilated hand, holding both hard to his chest.

Casey sighed inwardly. Stupid people always ignored good advice.

Aloud, she snapped, "Get!" He did, immediately. But she yelled after him as he ran out the door, "And find yourself another line of work, cowboy. This one's going to get you killed in a big hurry."

He probably didn't hear her, he was running so fast. Casey moved back to the window, but only to make sure he headed for his horse and took off, rather than gather his cohorts for a little retaliation. She was glad to see he was already hightailing it back toward that clump of trees. And after a few more minutes, the other robbers were spilling out of the train to do likewise. Whether they'd heard the shot and panicked, or been quick to collect their loot, only the other passengers would know at this point.

And then Casey nearly jumped out of her skin when the rifle went off next to her. She glared at Damian, but only because of the scare he'd just given her.

"Let them go."

He glared right back at her. "Like hell—"

She cut in. "They're just a bunch of young, out-of-work cowboys."

"They're train robbers, plain and simple," he said, firing off another shot. "And let me add, while I'm at it, I am twenty-seven years old, if you hadn't noticed. Having a child protect me is ludicrous, so don't do it again."

"Excuse me?" Casey said stiffly.

"You heard me. I can damn well take care of myself. So from now on, let me make my own decisions, if you don't mind, about how to deal with these unpleasant situations."

Casey shrugged and sat down in her seat. Protect himself indeed. Now *that* she would like to see. As for him firing off that new rifle of his, he wasn't going to hit anything he was shooting at anyway, so it didn't make her no nevermind if he wanted to waste good ammunition. She was surprised to see he was even holding the weapon correctly to fire it. At least she wouldn't be tending any dislocated shoulders from wrong handling.

After four more successive shots, he turned to her, apparently finished, but not quite done with his complaints. "You had one of them captured. Since when do you advocate letting outlaws go on their merry way?"

"Since I got hired to find one particular killer. Or didn't it occur to you how much time would be wasted taking them fellas in?"

"Killing them wouldn't have taken any time at all, and is no more than they deserve."

Casey wasn't surprised to hear an Easterner say that, which was why she snorted before remarking, "Then be glad you can't hit the side of a barn, tenderfoot, because you're angry enough to say that now, but your conscience would be giving you hell for it later on."

He glanced back out the window for a moment. Then he smirked in satisfaction.

Casey shot to her feet to see for herself if he'd actually hit something. But by then the train robbers were mere dots on the horizon, and no dead bodies were littering the ground out there.

She gritted her teeth, figuring he'd just had a go at pulling her leg. Still, she wasn't going to add to his satisfaction by remarking on it.

So instead she told him, "I'm going to go see if it's rail damage that stopped us and how bad it is," then headed for the door.

But his next question halted her momentarily. "What made you think they were just cowboys?"

"The chaps they were wearing. Wranglers get used to wearing them after working the range long enough. And that fella's nervousness. It was pretty obvious he'd never done anything like this before, was either desperate or, more likely, got talked into it when he was drunk."

"That's a lot of presuming, Casey," Damian scoffed.

She shrugged. "I'm not always right." Then she grinned. "But it's rare when I'm not."

She left the car. He followed and kept up, despite Casey's long strides that had him walking much faster than he was used to.

"Are you *always* in such a hurry?" he asked her along the way.

She glanced sideways at him before saying thoughtfully, "Never thought of it, but I guess I am. Suppose it comes from being in a hurry to grow up."

"If you ever reach that point, let me know."

"My, aren't you chock-full of sarcasm today. Remind me to keep you out of any more hold-ups. They purely don't agree with your disposition."

It was his turn to snort, but she didn't give him an opportunity to say anything else that might annoy her. She just strode on a little faster. And then they reached the front of the train, where most of the passengers were gathered. They were in time to hear the conductor announce that they would be returning to the last town they'd passed through, there to wait until a crew could be sent out to repair the tracks. Damian looked like he was about to explode over this new delay.

Casey tried defusing his anger by asking him, "You want to stay with the train or ride on to the next town on the train route and catch another? Would mean doubling up again."

She almost kicked him when he leaned forward to sniff her before answering, "Let's ride on."

Chapter 13

*T*he next town along the route wasn't really a town, though someday it might reach that distinction. Right now it was just several extra businesses that had moved in around the train depot: a saloon that also housed a restaurant, a general store, a bakery, a telegraph office, and what passed for a hotel, despite its having only two rooms.

Considering the late hour when they arrived, Casey sent Damian to the hotel to get them rooms for the night; she went to the train depot to report the robbery and the missing tracks. When she joined him in front of the hotel, it was with bad news.

"The next train isn't due for about a week," she told him without preamble, "which is about how long the fella at the depot reckons it will take to fix those missing tracks for the southbound train to get through."

Damian sighed. "I don't suppose there are any stages that run through here?"

"None, and it gets worse," she warned him.

"There isn't a stable in this settlement, either, to buy you a horse from, and the nearest ranch that might have extra mounts for sale is a good day's ride from here. But it's not guaranteed to have any extra stock available, so could be a pure waste of time riding out there."

Damian gave the buildings around them a sad glance. "So we're stuck here for the next week?"

"Unless you want to continue doubled up on Old Sam. I might not mind, but he's sure to start complaining pretty soon about the extra load."

Damian almost smiled, but not quite. "I have bad news as well. There was only one room to be had in the hotel, so we'll have to share it."

Casey stiffened. Share a *bedroom* with him for an entire week? One night she might manage, but a whole week, not damn likely.

"We'll find you a horse," she said in a tone that brooked no opposition, and in fact, she was eyeing several horses across the street in front of the saloon as she said it.

He followed her gaze. "Stealing is out of the question," he thought it prudent to mention.

Casey snorted, but said no more, already heading across the street. Damian followed the kid with not much enthusiasm. There was no bank in this little settlement either, or he would have no difficulty in meeting the price, whatever it was, to acquire a horse. He still might be able to meet it with the cash he had on hand, but the lack of mounts available in the area made it doubtful someone would be willing to part with his for any price.

Not that Damian wanted to continue on this journey on horseback. Riding doubled up behind Casey was one thing, since he wasn't actually controlling Old Sam. Riding his own mount would be something entirely different, and he'd just as soon not add that to his learning experiences on this hellish trip.

The saloon was the first Western tavern Damian had entered, and if it was typical of its kind, it would be the last. It wasn't large and certainly wasn't crowded, but the smell of sour ale and whiskey, as well as smoke and vomit, permeated the air.

Sawdust constituted the floor. Three round tables, scarred and filthy, allowed for sitting. Only one was occupied. There was a separate room with a sign over the open door that read, "Not the best chow, but all you'll find hereabouts." Only two tables were inside, obviously, because they didn't expect many customers.

Casey was standing at the long bar and looking right at home, as if he were in the habit of frequenting such places. Damian shook his head. There ought to be a law out here about serving children hard spirits.

The kid had already ordered a drink and had it in hand when he turned to survey the one occupied table. Three men were sitting there enjoying a game of cards; money near their elbows suggested they were gambling. They had eyed the kid, but quickly dismissed him. Damian they stared at a bit longer when he entered and moved over to join Casey.

Staring at the three men, Casey asked, "Who owns the pinto out front?"

A young man with a thick untrimmed beard

answered, "Reckon that would be me, 'less there's more'n one."

"You a gambling man?"

"When the mood strikes me," he said and looked down at the cards in his hand with a chuckle. "And I guess it's done struck me."

"I'm in need of an extra mount," Casey told him. "How about a little wager that bets yours against mine?"

Hearing that, Damian hissed at Casey, "What the hell are you doing?"

"Getting you a horse, so just go along with this, will you?" Casey whispered back.

The man was asking, "And where's yers?"

"Across the street in front of the hotel. Take a look. You'll never see finer."

The fellow got up to do just that and, standing in front of the swinging entrance doors, gave a soft whistle. "Now *that's* some horse." He turned back to Casey, definitely interested. "What's the bet?"

"The tenderfoot here is going to drop a coin in front of himself. I'm betting I can shoot it out from between his legs before it hits the floor—making sure I don't hit nothing of his, of course."

There were some chuckles, but only because Damian was beet red—whether in embarrassment or anger, it was hard to say. But the bearded fellow scoffed, "I've seen that trick before. It ain't so hard."

"Did I mention I'd be drawing to make the shot?" Casey added.

The fellow raised a bushy brow. "Drawing, huh? But still, them are long legs he's got, with a lotta leeway. If you miss, you just lose a horse."

"You think that isn't enough consequence?"

Obviously not, because he said, "How 'bout shooting it out of his hand instead—from the draw?"

Damian stiffened. Casey whispered aside to him, "Well, I guess some sore fingers is a small price to pay for getting us on our way."

"As long as it's sore fingers and not bloody fingers," he grouched.

The kid grinned at him. "I'd say make sure it's not your gun hand that you use, just to be safe, but you don't have a gun hand, so it don't rightly matter, does it?"

He did *not* appreciate Casey's humor, but he wasn't really all that worried. He'd seen what the kid could do with a gun. However, he did start to worry when a dime was tossed to Casey with the order, "Use that un," and Casey eyed the thing as if he couldn't see it very clearly, which brought on more laughter from the saloon patrons.

But Casey did relieve his mind immensely when he handed over the coin with the whisper "Relax, tenderfoot. I've done this more times than I can count."

He turned to move down to the end of the bar before he said to the others in the room, "Ten feet distant okay with you fellas—seeing as how there isn't that much more room in here to spread out?"

"Ten feet's fine—just get to it," the gambler said with a grin. "I'm eager for a ride on my new horse."

Casey nodded and lifted his poncho out of the way, waiting for Damian to hold the coin out. Damian couldn't believe he was actually going to let this demonstration of marksmanship continue when it was *his* hand that was going to suffer for it if anything went wrong. But Casey's confidence was reassuring. The kid knew he wouldn't miss.

And then he fired and missed. The coin was still held between Damian's thumb and forefinger. And Casey . . . Damian had never seen such a look of complete devastation on anyone before.

He'd gambled and lost his horse, and he hadn't expected that to be the end result here. While the bearded fellow was being congratulated by his friends, Casey actually ran from the saloon in embarrassment. Damian wasn't sure, but it had looked like there were tears in those golden eyes.

"Here, now, he's not going to take off on my new horse, is he?" the winner demanded.

"I seriously doubt that," Damian replied, staring at the swinging doors. "He's honorable—if not quite the marksman he thought he was."

Chapter 14

*D*amian didn't follow immediately after his young friend. If the kid *had* been crying like he suspected, he'd probably prefer that no one was around to witness it. So Damian had a few drinks of the appalling spirits the saloon sold, then headed to the hotel.

Casey's upset could have been avoided entirely, but as usual, he had dismissed Damian as a means of assistance, wanting to handle the matter all on his own—just like he'd done on the train.

On the train, Casey had assumed that Damian hadn't done any damage shooting out of the window, when he had in fact wounded each one of the train robbers as they rode away. If they didn't have a doctor as a member of their gang, they'd draw quite a bit of attention if they went to one in a town. If nothing else, they'd be slowed down, giving the law a chance to quickly apprehend them.

At the hotel, he found Casey standing in front of the window in the tiny room they would be sharing, no doubt staring down at Old Sam in the street and still brooding over his loss. Damian could say something about overconfidence leading to ruin, but he decided not to. The kid probably felt bad enough as it was.

Casey hadn't heard him enter. Damian had to clear his throat to draw the boy's attention so he could tell him, "You can stop moping. I managed to—"

He didn't get to finish, since the kid swung around and blasted him. "Why did you let me do it?! *Why*? Old Sam has been with me since I was twelve. I raised him from a colt. He's like family!"

Damian was struck completely speechless for a moment. That much emotion from a boy who usually kept all emotion firmly under control was a bit overwhelming. Damian's defenses were quick to rise because of it.

"Now just a damn minute," he said. "You can hardly blame me—"

"Can't I?"

"No, you can't. I wasn't the one who suggested gambling your horse away, Casey. In fact, if you'll recall, I wasn't too pleased about what you started in that saloon and said so at the time."

Damian tried to keep a curb on his own anger, not easy with so much undeserved heated emotion coming his way. He'd had a feeling that Old Sam meant more to the kid than just a means of transportation. He'd been right, obviously, or Casey wouldn't still be this upset.

But keeping his own anger under control only seemed to intensify Casey's, because he ignored

Damian's reasonable reply and shouted, "It wouldn't have happened if I wasn't here, and I wouldn't be here if—"

Damian cut in with the reminder "You didn't have to take the job."

"Good, because I quit!"

Damian wasn't expecting that. He'd figured the kid would have a bit more honor than to renege on a deal because of a setback or two.

He shook his head, saying in disgust, "I've seen some temper tantrums in my day, brat, but you're about to win a prize for the worst."

"How dare—!"

"Oh, shut up, Casey. If you hadn't jumped down my throat the minute I walked in, I would have told you that I managed to get your horse back for you."

Casey's expression of surprise was almost comical. "You did?"

But then he blanched as it dawned on him what he'd just said. He took a step back, dangerously close to the open window, as if he'd been punched backward. And the wail he made was pathetic.

"Oh, God, I'm sorry," he groaned.

"Too late—"

"No, I am *really* sorry, Damian. If you'll let me explain . . . I wasn't really angry at you, I was furious with myself. I don't tolerate stupidity much, and what I did in that saloon was really stupid."

Damian couldn't have agreed more. "I agree, you never should have made that bet—"

"I don't mean that," Casey interrupted. "The bet was a good one."

Damian frowned. "Then what the hell are you talking about?"

"I'm talking about aiming for the edge of the coin, because it was so small. And when it came down to it, I didn't want to take the chance of singeing your fingers."

Damian blinked. "Are you saying you missed the coin on purpose?"

"No." Casey shook his head. "I just didn't center my aim on it as I should have. Allowing a quarter inch of room was a mite too little."

Damian almost laughed at that point. The kid figured trying to keep Damian from getting hurt was stupid, and he considered *that* an apology? Then again, if he hadn't tried, he wouldn't have lost his horse, and chances were, Damian wouldn't have been hurt anyway. So he supposed he was ultimately to blame, after all.

"And I didn't mean that about quitting either," Casey added sheepishly with another blush. "I would have told you so, soon as I'd— well, soon as I'd started thinking clearly again, which I surely wasn't doing a few minutes ago. I'll see the job done, whatever it takes—that is, if you still want me to."

Damian deliberately let several long moments pass before he nodded. "I think we would both do well to just forget we had this little—discussion."

Casey grinned, obviously relieved. "Not a bad idea, except, well, you forgot to mention how you managed to get Old Sam back."

"With money, of course. It does have its uses on occasion, and this occasion includes the pinto."

"You actually got his horse, too?" Casey said in surprise. "Well, hot damn, Damian, you're quite the horse-trader, aren't you?"

"Hardly," Damian admitted. "In this case, it seems the fellow isn't planning on going anywhere any time soon. He's apparently courting the baker's daughter. But he likes to gamble, and a run of bad luck had put him quite short of funds. Not that he was reasonable on an agreeable price for the two animals. He actually wouldn't settle for anything less than all the cash I had on me."

"Which was?"

"Not everything." Damian grinned. "Just what I had in my pockets, which was about three hundred, but at least *he* thought that was all I had."

Casey chuckled. "Damned cheap, actually."

"You're kidding? You mean horses actually cost more than that around here?"

"No, just high-steppers like my Old Sam. Besides, when there is demand but not enough supply, you'd be amazed at how steep some things can sell for. That's been proven time and again out here in the West, especially in the old days, when Indian raids would keep supply trains from coming in, or a new mining town would open practically overnight. It still happens in small towns that the railroads have avoided for one reason or another, and in settlements like this that aren't full townships yet."

For someone in Damian's line of business, that was like music to his ears. Imports and exports, supply and demand. He wondered if his father had ever considered this part of the country for further expansion. It might be something to look into—as long as it didn't require on-hand supervision. Coming West again after this trip would be at the very bottom of his to-do list, after all.

"Well, now that we're all set to continue this journey tomorrow, how about some dinner before we turn in for the night?" Damian suggested.

"I'll skip dinner if you don't mind. The hotel doesn't serve any, and I'm not used to making such a complete ass of myself, so I'd just as soon avoid that saloon again. Besides, we'll need some supplies before the store closes if we're going to set out at a decent hour in the morning. I'll take care of that, then turn in."

Damian wasn't going to argue with him, since the kid was looking quite embarrassed again. "Suit yourself. I'll come with you to the store, though, to settle the bill."

"I've got enough money, Damian—"

"I *did* say I'd pay all travel expenses, didn't I? Besides, it won't hurt me to find out firsthand what you consider necessities for trail riding."

Casey threw his words back at him. "Suit yourself—which reminds me, did a saddle come with that pinto?"

Damian did some blushing now. A saddle was something he wouldn't have thought of, and if not attended to today, it would have delayed their departure in the morning until the general store opened again.

"Actually, he kept the saddle."

"Kind of figured he might. Takes longer to break in a new saddle than it does a new horse.

Well, let's hope the store has some in stock. It might not carry them, though, with no horses for sale here. Then again, it might stock a little of everything, as most general stores do."

Casey didn't appear too concerned about it, but Damian still asked, "And if it doesn't?"

Casey grinned. "Don't go worrying about things ahead of time, Damian. Let's find out first; then you can worry about it after."

Chapter 15

❧

*D*amian had seen nothing wrong with their sharing a bed. Casey had insisted she preferred the floor. It still hadn't helped.

There was just something about being behind a closed door with him, in a bedroom too small for one person, let alone two, that she couldn't handle. She had finally forced herself to remain still long enough for him to fall asleep, then had left the room to bed down in the lean-to that the hotel supplied for the guests' horses. There, crammed in a corner next to Old Sam, she'd gone right to sleep.

Which was very annoying when she thought about it the next morning. It wasn't as if she hadn't already slept near the man. But being on the trail, with a campfire between them and other things to be concerned about, including keeping her senses primed for the unexpected, just wasn't the same. The safety of that hotel room had given her nothing to think about but him. And some of the things she had thought about were quite embarrassing to recall in the bright light of day.

114

She had actually wondered what it would be like to be kissed by Damian. She had wondered if his hair would be as soft to the touch as it looked, what it would feel like to run her hands over such wide shoulders. She had even imagined him holding her in those strong arms of his and had broken out in a sweat from the picture it conjured up in her mind.

The embarrassment came when she saw him in the morning and got the impression that she usually did—that those piercing eyes of his could read her mind. For him to be aware of the things she had been thinking about him would have been far too mortifying.

But he barely gave her a glance when he joined her behind the hotel. She'd been all ready with the excuse of wanting to guard the horses because they weren't bedded down in a proper stable, but it proved unnecessary. He apparently hadn't even noticed that she hadn't slept in the room last night. He just assumed that she'd gotten up and come down sooner than he.

They did not get an early start as she'd hoped they would. She had expected there would be some teaching to do to get Damian mounted on the pinto, but she hadn't realized it would be so difficult.

He couldn't relax. He was too hesitant in taking control of the animal. The pinto sensed that and took complete advantage. Here was a creature, after all, that he could intimidate into staying off his back, and the pinto gave it his best shot.

It was too bad there was such a huge weight difference between her and Damian, or they might have been able to fool the pinto into settling down. She'd had to test him first with her saddle, since there hadn't been one available here to purchase. And the idea of putting Damian on a saddleless mount was purely ludicrous, so until they found one to buy, he was going to have to use hers.

But Casey would have had to test the pinto either way, simply because some animals balked at anything they weren't accustomed to, and new saddles fell into that group. And he'd ridden fine under her control. It was just Damian's weight that had him sidestepping and bucking as if he'd never been ridden before.

She had to give Damian credit, though. He didn't stop trying, despite landing in the dirt four times. He did waste an inordinate amount of time dusting himself off, thoroughly, each time, but Casey gritted her teeth over that, refraining from mentioning that he would likely be eating more dust before they were done.

The man surely wasn't suited for trail riding. He seemed to despise the slightest bit of dirt on him, but he'd have to get used to it. She'd tried to talk him into buying more suitable clothes yesterday, at the very least a decent riding hat, but he had insisted his fancy New York duds would do him just fine. And they would, as long as he didn't mind sunburn, burrs, and snags in his fine woolens from every little bush they passed too close to. Of course, she had a feeling he would mind, tremendously. She'd hate to see what would happen if he ever broke out in a sweat. Actually, that might be quite entertaining.

After the pinto finally figured out that he wasn't going to win the battle, they set out. But it was a long day on the trail, or seemed much longer than it really was, since Casey had gotten little sleep in the night. She was forced to keep the pace slow, just to keep Damian in the saddle. She had little difficulty riding without one herself, had done it many times in her youth. But that had been for rides of a short duration. For long rides like this, it became a strain on her muscles.

They stopped in the early afternoon for Damian's sake. Having purchased bakery goods before leaving the depot settlement, they could have continued on, eating in the saddle, but Casey figured he could use the break. In fact, he groaned when she said it was time to move on again.

That evening, however, he surprised her by offering to do the hunting for their dinner, if shots being fired wouldn't matter. She was damned tempted to say shots would matter. She felt like eating meat, after all, and knew darned well he wouldn't be bringing any back if he went to do the hunting. But he'd had such a lousy day that she didn't have the heart to point out that he didn't know the first thing about hunting and should leave it to someone who did.

She resigned herself to eating beans and biscuits and got them started. The real surprise came when Damian returned a half hour later with a wild turkey large enough to feed them for several days. After the mental scoffing Casey had done, she thought he'd just gotten lucky, especially since she'd heard only one shot.

She said as much as she took the bird and started preparing it. "That was quite a lucky shot."

"Actually, there wasn't much luck involved," he replied nonchalantly.

Casey raised a black brow. "It walked right up to you so you couldn't possibly miss?"

"No, it was far enough away that I wasn't quite sure what it was."

Casey was reminded of the tall tales told in the bunkhouse at home and said, "Sure it was."

It wasn't at all hard to mistake her skepticism, which was probably why Damian suggested, "Perhaps a demonstration is in order."

She wasn't a bit concerned with his being embarrassed now. "By all means," she said, and pointed at a likely target some forty feet away.

Damian aimed, fired, and hit it. Casey blinked, then pointed out another target. He hit that one squarely, too. After the third, she gave up.

"Okay, I'm impressed."

Damian raised a brow this time. "Just impressed?"

"Damn impressed," Casey mumbled.

He chuckled and joined her by the fire. "Your expression was priceless, Casey, but perhaps I should mention that I was class champion of rifle marksmanship in college. I also used to hunt with my father."

"Where? In your backyard? You don't ride, or didn't, prior to today."

"We'd take the train up north to the hunting lodge, and yes, we did our hunting on foot."

Casey said no more, disgruntled. Her opinion of him had altered so suddenly and so drastically. But now she had to allow that he could probably take care of himself in most dangerous situations. He'd helped her well enough with those bungling stage robbers, after all. And she had to wonder just how many wounds those young train robbers had ridden away with. He could have killed them, with as accurate an aim as he had, no doubt of that, yet no bodies had been left behind. His "they deserve to die" had obviously been said only in anger, not because he meant it.

He was still too citified to belong out here. Nothing had changed about that. He still stood out like a sore thumb. But she supposed she could stop worrying about his chances for survival. With a horse and that rifle, he could manage on his own.

She continued preparing their meal, doing her best to ignore him. Yet she wasn't unaware of his close scrutiny. If he was waiting for more praise for his newly revealed shooting skill, he'd have a very long wait. But that wasn't what was on his mind, apparently.

"I hate to say it, Casey, but do you know you look like a girl? Have you tried growing a beard or mustache?"

After a moment of mental groaning, she said, "That'd be kind of hard to do."

"Why?"

"Because I am a girl."

She ducked her head, embarrassed no end by his horrified look. She hadn't had to admit it. She couldn't imagine why she did. And the shocked silence that followed had her squirming until she couldn't stand it anymore and glanced back at him—to find him staring at her chest, so hard, it was obvious he was trying to see through her poncho.

"There ain't much to them, but they're there," Casey managed to say without blushing, then felt it prudent to add, "And don't even think about asking to see proof. You'll just have to take my word for it."

His eyes moved slowly back up to her face, scanning each part of it as if he'd never seen her before, and in fact, that was the case. His expression was intense, and then it changed abruptly as his emotions took precedence over his shock. What remained gave Casey pause.

He was angry, no doubt about it.

Chapter 16

"*H*ow dare you be a girl?"

The idiocy of that question showed exactly how furious Damian was. Casey had expected some surprise, but not this serious anger now visible in every line of his body.

"I don't think I had much choice in the matter." She was pointing out the obvious.

"You know what I meant! You deliberately deceived me," he growled accusingly.

"No. Now *that* I didn't do. I just didn't correct any conclusions you drew on your own. And you never asked. But don't feel bad. It's the same conclusion most folks come to about me."

"I'm not most folks, I'm the man who is traveling with you, and I can't believe how inappropriate this is. We even slept in the same bedroom!"

"Actually—I slept out back with the horses last night," Casey admitted.

But she wished that she had mentioned it that morning when he replied sarcastically, "Sure you did."

She frowned then, trying to figure out exactly why he was so livid. She settled on his word "inappropriate." Was that his problem? Did he think she had relatives who were going to arrive with shotguns in hand and force him to the altar because they'd spent a little time in a bedroom together? Not that that *couldn't* happen, but it wouldn't, and maybe she ought to mention that.

"I hope you're not under the mistaken opinion that my not being chaperoned means we'd have to do something ridiculous like get married. We're nearing the turn of the century, Damian. Consequences like that—"

"Still apply and you know it!"

She cringed at the level of his shouting. "Well, not in this part of the country—at least not when no one but the two folks involved know about it. If you'll just set your anger aside for a moment and think about it, you'll realize that *no one* knows you've been traveling with a woman."

"Woman? I would hardly call you that, kid," he said derisively.

That stung, since Casey had considered herself a woman for the past three years. And this was beginning to remind her of the argument with her father, which was about to set her off. She made one more attempt at reasoning with him before that happened.

"The point I was trying to make to you, Damian, is no harm has been done, so you have no call getting upset like this. Just because I'm a—female—doesn't alter our working relationship in any way."

"The hell it doesn't."

She raised a questioning brow. "Oh? And how is that, when it doesn't change what I'm capable of or why you hired me? I'm still one of the best trackers around, thanks to my father's teaching."

"Father? Oh, so now you miraculously have known parents as well? And I suppose a real name, rather than one you *claim* is unknown to you?"

He *would* have to bring that up, she grumbled to herself, but to him she explained, "Lying about my name had nothing to do with deceiving you."

"Excuse me? Since that's exactly what it did, I fail to see—"

"I don't give *anyone* my real name, Damian, because my father is likely searching for me, and I don't want to be found yet. And don't bother asking why. It's personal. But the easiest way to keep my whereabouts unknown is for the folks I meet not to know who I really am, and rather than use a false name, I simply claim I don't know it."

"And pretend to be a boy."

"No, that I don't do. If my short hair, height, and skinniness give that impression, it's not my fault folks jump to that conclusion."

"Let's not forget your clothes."

"The clothes I wear are necessary for trail riding," she told him. "But I have never once claimed to be a boy. If that were the case, I wouldn't have admitted to being a girl just now, would I?"

"Why the hell did you?"

"Because I *don't* lie about it."

"You should have, Casey."

"Why? It's not going to change the way I deal with you. And it shouldn't change the way you treat me. So why are you making such a fuss about it?"

"You are a *girl*."

"So what?"

He ran a frustrated hand through his hair before he said, "If you think that doesn't make a huge difference, then you haven't much sense for a female."

She stiffened. "I hope that doesn't mean what it sounds like, but just in case it does, maybe I should warn you that men have been known to get hurt if they trifle with me."

"That doesn't exactly solve the problem."

"*What* problem? You can't actually be interested in me in that way."

"Can't I?"

She leaped to her feet, drew her gun, and aimed it straight at his chest. "So get uninterested, Damian."

"You aren't going to shoot me."

"You don't really want to count on that, do you?"

He stared at her, hard. She stared right back without blinking or wavering in her aim.

He finally looked at the gun and said, "Put it away. I'll keep to my side of the fire—for now."

That didn't exactly reassure her, but since she didn't *want* to shoot him, she did as he suggested and sat back down. However, she didn't change her inscrutable expression, nor did she take her eyes off him.

After a painfully long minute passed in silence, with them both still staring, he said, "The bird is burning."

"So do something about it. Where is it written that I have to do all the cooking?"

"Probably in the book that mentions that I don't know how to cook."

She blinked. And then she relaxed. If he could say something like that, then they were most likely done with the fight, such as it was—for now.

But just to make sure, she said, "I'm getting some sleep right after we eat. You should do the same. If we're going to reach the next town before nightfall tomorrow, we'll need an early start as well as a little hard riding. Think you'll be able to handle a faster pace?"

"I'll do what I have to do. I always have."

The words were agreeable enough, but the tone was still a tad disgruntled. However, Casey wasn't going to press her luck by instigating any more conversation. Hopefully, a night's sleep would give Damian a better perspective on the situation. She doubted it would help her, though, to forget that the man had indicated an interest in her.

She wasn't going to get any sleep at all, again, for thinking about that.

Chapter 17

❦ ᴄ᷽ᷓᷓᷓᷓᷓᷓᷓ ❦

𝒟amian gave up trying to get any sleep that night. He found some sticks to feed to the dying fire, then sat there waiting for the sun to rise—and watched Casey. It wasn't an unpleasant task. There was a softness about her that wasn't there when she was awake, a softness that made her sex more obvious.

He hadn't seen her sleeping before, which was perhaps fortunate. Thinking she was too pretty for a boy was one thing when he thought she was a boy. But had he seen this softness, which made her look downright sensual, he would have been appalled to find himself attracted to her . . . him . . . he groaned inwardly.

He still couldn't get over it. He *should* have realized for himself, without being told. He had always been intrigued by something about her. But he had let her skills and accomplishments count for too much. No female could do what Casey did, after all—and yet Casey had blown that reasoning all to hell last night.

A woman—no, a girl. He tried to keep that in

mind, but he couldn't quite manage to. Most likely because she didn't look like a girl lying there; she looked like a mature young woman, one who was certainly old enough to be approached in an intimate manner.

He hadn't realized just how flawlessly smooth her skin was, how lush that bottom lip was that he had the strongest urge to suck on. He'd seen her hair clean, knew that it could float softly about her shoulders, rather than be the scraggly mess she cultivated. But tossed back as it was now, it didn't detract from the delicate lines of her face that made her so lovely—and desirable.

As a boy, Casey had been interesting. As a girl, she was fascinating. Damian had a hundred questions he'd like to put to her, but knew she wouldn't answer a single one. She was adept at keeping her secrets, *and* her emotions, to herself, and just because she had revealed the biggest secret didn't mean any more would be forthcoming.

Even after she'd shocked the hell out of him, she'd still used that damn inscrutable expression of hers on him that gave away nothing. It was recalling how often that particular habit of hers had made him nervous that had caused most of his anger. A *woman* had made him nervous.

He had calmed down enough to get over that, since it was probably something she didn't actually do on purpose, or at least didn't do to deliberately make anyone nervous. But he couldn't get over the fact that he was so strongly attracted to her.

Plain and simply, he didn't know how he was going to continue to travel with her and keep his hands off her. For that matter, he wasn't sure why he should even try, when she certainly didn't adhere to the traditional proprieties that kept men from behaving like utter barbarians in the presence of women. By being here alone with him, she broke all the known rules that he had been raised by, so which rules was he supposed to conform to?

But there was his reason for being here in the first place. And by the time Casey began to stir with the nearby greetings of all the birds in the area as dawn approached, the justice that he owed to his father won out over his newfound lust. So he decided it wouldn't be wise to complicate matters with Casey, that the best way to proceed was to keep his distance from her. She would just do the job he'd hired her for.

It was a decision he *hoped* he could stick to. And to that end, he needed to put Casey's mind at ease with a lie or two of his own so she could go back to ignoring him—for the most part—and make it easier for him to ignore her. He began as soon as she sat up.

"I'd like to apologize."

It was a moment or two before she glanced his way, and even then she yawned and blinked several times before saying in a sleep-husky voice, "My eyes are barely open, Damian. Before you go saying something I'd probably like to remember, let me have my coffee first."

He smiled at her. She didn't notice, poking at the fire, fetching what she needed for the coffee, stretching—damn, he wished she wouldn't do that—and then heading off into the bushes. That was something else he hadn't noticed previously that she had the habit of doing. And since he didn't have a similar habit . . . his blush was almost gone by the time she returned. Fortunately, it was still dark enough for her not to notice his embarrassment.

She didn't look at him directly again until she had finished her morning routine and squatted down across the fire from him with her steaming cup of coffee in hand. And then he got her typical composed look. Now why didn't that surprise him?

"Now, then, you were saying something about apologizing, weren't you?"

Damian couldn't help noticing the way her knees spread wide when she squatted like that. Even though her poncho fell between them, he found it difficult to tear his eyes away from her long legs so he could answer her.

He cleared his throat to begin. "I said a few things last night in anger that weren't really true."

"Such as?"

"Such as implying that I was interested in you in a—well, in a personal sort of way."

She seemed to stiffen, but he wasn't sure. "So you really aren't?"

"No, of course not," he lied with a perfectly straight face. "I was just so—disturbed at the time, I was saying anything that might give you the same sort of shock you'd dealt me. Very despicable on my part, for which I find myself extremely sorry this morning."

She nodded slowly and looked away, staring off at the sunrise that was now in full color. The golden glow from the sky made her face mesmerizing, and it was very difficult for Damian to concentrate on her reply.

"I've been known to say things I don't mean either when my temper acts up," she admitted with a frown, as if she were remembering a time in particular. "Guess I should do some apologizing as well."

"That isn't necessary—"

"But needful anyway, as long as we're clearing the air, so let me say it. I did some conclusion-jumping myself last night by suggesting you might be worried about forced weddings. Pretty foolish on my part, when, for all I know, you could be married already."

Married already? Damian frowned, because he couldn't help remembering his last meeting with Winnifred's father, who had approached him at the funeral. "I know this is a bad time to mention it," he'd said, "but this isn't going to hold up the wedding, is it?"

A bad time? Damian had been incredulous at the man's insensitivity, and he knew that what grew from the stem usually bore the same fruit. Which was why he hadn't seen father or daughter since, and had no further desire to.

"There's no wife," he said flatly.

"I wasn't asking, I was just apologizing for assuming when I shouldn't have. Don't make me no nevermind if you're married or not."

Damian found it amusing, the way she stressed that, as if she were worried that he might think *she* was interested in him in a marriage sort of way. Obviously not. She even appeared a bit embarrassed over it.

So he was quick to assure her, "No, I didn't think it would."

She gave him a curt nod, apparently wanting to be done with the subject, and as a dismissal, she remarked, "Amazing how a good night's sleep always puts a different perspective on things."

Damian wouldn't know. He didn't yet feel the effects of getting no sleep last night, but he didn't doubt he would before the day was over. In fact, by the time they rode into the next town toward evening, he was so tired and grouchy he told Casey that if she didn't see him the next day, she shouldn't come looking for him, that he was going to sleep the clock around. And he did just that.

Chapter 18

Casey had thought Damian was joking about sleeping all day. She was annoyed to find out he wasn't. She went by his room about six times that day, but the Do Not Disturb card was still hanging on the outside of his door, and no sounds of movement could be detected within.

Late that afternoon, she finally did some door-pounding. If they were going to continue on their journey in the morning, he had a saddle to buy before the town closed up for the night. She would have bought it for him, except this town was large enough to offer a selection, and a saddle was a matter of personal preference. Not that Damian likely had any, new to riding as he was, but the choice ought to be his.

He left his bed with much grumbling, which was when it finally occurred to Casey that he must not have gotten much sleep, if any, the night of her confession. And she wasn't sure if she ought to worry that he had apparently had much more trouble than she'd first thought, accepting her true identity.

When he had implied he was interested in her, it had affected her, discomfited her. She hadn't been expecting that. Contrarily, she'd felt much worse when he'd fessed up to that being a lie. What should have been reassuring at that point was damned deflating instead.

But he was making every effort to continue as they had been, ignoring her gender. So the least she could do was the same.

Having finally gotten Damian out of the hotel and into one of the two saddle shops the town offered after a quick trip to the bank, Casey wasn't surprised when he bought the most fancy and expensive saddle to be had, along with some shining silver tack to go with it. That ornery pinto was going to be seen a mile away, all aglitter in the sunlight.

She refrained from making any disparaging comments about the saddle. It was a waste of good money, but still serviceable. However, she did mention, once again, that he ought to get some decent riding clothes.

She wasn't sure if he was being contrary by then, because he *knew* she was right, but he still maintained that his own clothes would do him just fine. And he also pointed out that they should be joining up with the train again by the next town, so he wouldn't need them after that. Whether they joined up with the train or not, it didn't keep him from appearing an obvious tenderfoot everywhere they went, and she was beginning to wish she'd left his carpetbag behind after all.

She also wished her point wasn't proved quite so soon, and so dramatically, but such was the case. On their way to drop off the saddle at the stable where the horses had been lodged, they had to pass a saloon that, from the sounds of it, was quite busy.

Damian was lagging behind, hoisting the heavy saddle on his shoulder, while Casey's long strides had her paced far ahead of him. So although it wasn't intentional on her part, they didn't appear to be together. In fact, Damian was the only one noticed when the four drunk locals stumbled out of the saloon and right into him.

Casey wasn't even aware that he'd been detained until she heard the shots being fired and turned around to see four guns aimed at Damian's feet. She'd seen this sort of thing happen in other towns. There was just something about a new tenderfoot in town that could turn otherwise model citizens into downright bullies.

It was an attempt at power, she supposed, the assumption being that a tenderfoot who didn't carry a weapon could be easily intimidated by men who otherwise couldn't intimidate anyone. And if those involved had been drinking, adding false courage and recklessness to the situation, that only made it worse. She'd seen one Easterner actually shot in the foot when he refused to dance to his tormentor's gunplay. Damian didn't strike her as a man who would play along just to defuse the situation.

He wouldn't. He had dropped the saddle and was simply standing there, letting those bullets get closer and closer to his feet, while his antagonists grew more and more annoyed. He wasn't entertaining them. He might be exceptionally good with a rifle, but it wasn't something you carried around with you at all times, and going shopping was one of those times you'd figure it wouldn't be needed. And without a weapon, there wasn't much he could do.

He must not have figured it that way, though, because after asking them to desist got him no positive response, he stepped toward one of the men to put an end to the shooting in a more physical way—and got the man's gun aimed at his chest instead of his feet. That was when Casey drew and fired a warning shot, because she was afraid Damian was going to ignore what was a real threat now and throttle the man anyway—and get himself killed for the effort.

She shattered a bootheel from one of them, shot the hat off another. It was enough to draw their attention away from Damian. She would have done more, but didn't need to. Damian, in the midst of them, went right to work, slamming two of the men together. Their heads butting knocked both out. The third man he hit so hard, he went sailing out into the street. The fourth was doubled over from a gut punch, probably wondering if he'd ever breathe again.

Then, as if nothing out of the ordinary had just occurred, Damian dusted his hands, straightened his jacket, picked up the saddle, and continued on his way. Casey kept her eyes on the last conscious one of the four, just to make sure he wasn't stupid enough to try anything else. He wasn't. Still gasping for breath, he stumbled back into the saloon.

Casey put her gun away and gave her attention to Damian as he reached her. "You okay?"

"Nice, friendly town this is" was his mumbled response.

"It probably is," Casey said, contradicting his obvious sarcasm. "And I hate to mention this, I really do," she added with a grin. "But that wouldn't have happened if you didn't look like you just stepped off the train from back East. You look like a tourist, Damian, and folks will pull pranks on, try to shock, and otherwise amuse themselves with tourists, who they know don't know any better."

"Then teach me."

She blinked. "What?"

"Teach me how to survive out here."

She tried to digest the implications of that, but couldn't without giving it more thought, so she said, "Well, for starters, let's head back to the general store before it closes. It's time you looked like you belonged here rather than like you're just passing through."

His jaw clenched. She sighed inwardly, expecting his refusal—once again. And she had to wonder what it was about his fancy duds that made him so reluctant to give them up. Did he simply not want to appear common? Was it only that?

But then he surprised her with a nod and an abrupt "Lead the way."

She did, although afterward wished she'd never brought it up. Damian in a fancy suit was handsome enough, but in tight jeans, a blue cambric shirt with a black bandana and vest, and a wide-brimmed hat, he looked too rugged by half—he looked like he belonged. And that gave her a whole different perspective on him. It made him . . . available.

Chapter 19

❦

*H*aving found a watering hole, Casey set up camp a bit early the next day to take advantage of it. And with Damian offering to do the hunting again, she managed a quick bath while he was gone, including washing her hair, which didn't need washing. She tried not to think about why she felt a bath was necessary, other than to use the excuse that she no longer needed to cultivate her grimy look.

She was still drying her hair when Luella Miller showed up. Casey's jaw nearly dropped at the sight of her. And not just because it was a shock to see someone else out here. She did some rude staring without even being aware of it. But then, she'd never seen a woman quite this stunningly beautiful before.

Pale blond hair under a fashionable bonnet. Big blue eyes thickly lashed. Skin so ivory it was almost translucent. Big breasts. A tiny waist. A petite height. Big breasts. All lacy from her parasol down to inserts in her dainty boots. Big breasts. Was she repeating herself? She couldn't help it; those were *really* big breasts for such a small woman. It was a wonder she wasn't stoop-backed from being so top-heavy, but her posture was straight as a board, if not a little thrusting.

"Thank God," was the first thing the Vision said, quite breathlessly, though she hadn't rushed forward. "You can't imagine how glad I am to see you. I don't know what I would have done if I had to sleep out here alone tonight."

Casey wasn't sure what that remark had to do with anything, but to be polite, she said, "You're welcome to share the fire and some grub."

"That is *so* kind of you," the woman said as she came forward with her hand extended. "I'm Luella Miller, from Chicago. And you are?"

Casey stared at those delicate fingers, with impossibly manicured nails, then quickly looked away, afraid Luella was expecting more than a simple handshake, and hand-kissing she wasn't about to do. "Casey," was all she said. The outstretched hand she deliberately ignored.

"Is it all right if I sit on this?" Luella asked with a smile, indicating Old Sam's saddle, which had been placed beside the fire. But she sat down on it before Casey said anything, taking a positive response for granted. There was a long sigh as she added, "This has been *such* a ghastly journey. And here I was assured that it would be a simple matter to get to Fort Worth, Texas."

Since she was staring at Casey expectantly, Casey politely asked, "That's where you're headed?"

"Yes, for my great-uncle's funeral. But my maid ran off on me in St. Louis. Can you imagine? And then the train was delayed, something about tracks needing to be replaced before it could continue south. I was hoping to make it to Fort Worth before the funeral, but I really have to be there before the reading of the will, since I'm likely to be mentioned in it. Otherwise I could have waited for the train."

"So you—er—decided to walk to Fort Worth?"

Luella blinked, then laughed. "How delightfully funny. No, of course not. I met this nice minister and his wife who were journeying south by wagon, and they were kind enough to let me travel with them—at least I thought it was a kind gesture until they abandoned me."

Casey raised a brow. "Abandoned you how?"

"They just left me. I honestly could *not* believe it. We had stopped for lunch today and I went off to—well, to have a few minutes to myself, and when I came back, the wagon was racing down the road and soon gone from sight. I waited for several hours, thinking, well, hoping, they would return for me, but not they or anyone else came along. So I continued south, but the road seemed to just disappear. I suppose it isn't well traveled enough to remain obvious, now that the railroad is so much more convenient—at least when it's running. So I'm afraid I got quite lost quite quickly."

For someone who had been wandering around lost all day, she looked mighty neat and clean. But then, some folks just refused to let dirt get anywhere near them. Which was why she'd confiscated Old Sam's saddle for a seat, rather than attempt to sit on the ground.

"I suppose they took your belongings with them?" Casey remarked.

"Well, now that you mention it . . . and I had quite a few expensive jewels in my portmanteau, as well as all my money in my purse." Another sigh. "You think they meant to rob me all along, that that's the only reason they offered to take me south with them?"

"Appears so."

"But people don't *do* that to me."

Casey managed to keep from snorting. The lady obviously thought that because of her beauty, all offers of assistance were sincere.

"Most thieves aren't particular about who they rob, Miss Miller."

"Well, that minister, if he even is one, must be blind," Luella insisted.

"Perhaps he was posing as a minister merely to gain your trust. But there isn't much you can do about it until you report it to the authorities."

Another sigh. "Yes, I know. And I still have to reach Fort Worth within the week. You wouldn't happen to be going south, would you?"

Casey really wished she could say no, but couldn't see any way around the truth, except to avoid mentioning that she was headed for Fort Worth as well. "We'll be stopping in the next town south of here."

"We? Then you'll take me with you?"

"I meant my friend and I. He's hunting up some dinner for us right now. But yes, of course we'll take you as far as the next town."

They continued talking, at least Luella did, mostly about her life in Chicago. From what

Casey gathered, she was a twenty-two-year-old rich society debutante who lived with her indulgent brother. She was supposed to have married, *eight* times, but each time she had canceled the wedding at the last moment, sighing that she was just never sure if her fiancés wanted to marry her because she was so beautiful or because they really loved her. Eight times to figure that out seemed a bit much to Casey, but she didn't say so.

And then Damian returned, and Casey had to witness him making a complete jackass of himself as he stared incredulously at their beautiful guest. He probably didn't hear a word Casey said as she explained who Luella was and what she was doing in their camp. He didn't even think to dismount, just sat there ogling the lady.

And Luella had definitely noticed how handsome Damian was. Casey had never seen so much eye-batting and simpering from one female before. It was purely disgusting, but Damian didn't seem to think so.

"I told Luella that we'd take her as far as the next town," Casey said, finishing her explanation.

"Yes, of course we will. She can ride with me."

How quickly he said that. And he might even be able to manage it. After all, he and the pinto had been getting along much better. But the idea annoyed the heck out of Casey.

Which was why she pointed out, "The extra weight could set that pinto of yours to bucking again. Better if she rides with me."

He nodded. At least he wasn't going to argue.

But Luella sure looked disappointed.

He finally dismounted and dropped his kills pretty much in Casey's lap—without looking. His eyes he couldn't seem to take off Luella. And he was quite formal about introducing himself. Casey rolled her eyes when he did the hand-kissing bit that she had avoided.

For the rest of the evening, those two talked, finding just about everything in common, both coming from the same social background. Casey was ignored for the most part. Though at one point Luella tried to politely include her in the conversation, if an "I hope we're not boring you, Mister Casey" could be considered polite.

But Damian's thoughtless, "She's not a mister" was the piece of tinder that exploded Casey's temper.

She couldn't believe he had pointed that out. And it didn't help that Luella was sitting there giggling, saying, "Don't be silly, I know a man when I see one." But when no one joined in with her laughter, she looked shocked, giving Casey a closer scrutiny, and then was embarrassed about her remark, all of which had been unnecessary.

But Casey wasn't noticing Luella just then, she was pinning Damian with a you're-real-close-to-being-shot look, and, standing up, told him, "I'd like a word with you—in private." She marched off into the darkness.

He did follow her—thankfully, since that part hadn't been guaranteed—and after a few moments was heard to say, "Hold up. I don't have eyes that see in the dark like you do."

She stopped, but only because they were far

enough away from the camp not to be seen, much less heard. "I can't see in the dark any better than you. I just make sure I note the lay-out of the land before it gets dark, something you should be doing already."

"Fine, if you say so."

She ignored the testiness of that reply. He'd reached her, and she was too busy poking him in the chest—hard. "Why the *hell* did you tell her about me? Do you think that's something I share with just anyone? It's none of her damned business who I am. If I had wanted her to know, I would have done the telling myself, now wouldn't I?"

"Are you annoyed with me, Casey?"

She detected the humor in his tone, as if he were convinced she had nothing, really, to be upset about. It was the last straw. She growled low and swung at him. How he saw it coming and avoided her fist, she didn't know. But in the next moment she found his arms locked around her to keep any more fists from flying.

That was probably all he'd meant to do, just restrain her. But Casey went perfectly still, shocked at having his body pressed so close to hers. And her stillness must have set his mind to thinking of other things, because suddenly he was titling her head back and kissing her.

Chapter 20

*A*n accident. That was what Damian had called the kiss that had shocked Casey to her core. He had tasted her, started her insides churning strangely, her pulse racing something fierce; then, with a soft caress against her cheek, he'd set her away from him.

"This was an—accident. It won't happen again," he told her before he walked away.

He had left her dazed and . . . she couldn't even figure out everything else she was feeling. And he had returned to the campfire, sat down, and resumed his conversation with Luella as if nothing—certainly nothing earth-shattering—had occurred. Casey had gone off to find a boulder to sit on and pulled out a few hairs in her frustration.

She had to face some facts. This attraction she felt for Damian had escalated into something much stronger than she could handle. She wanted his kisses. She probably wanted more than that, but she balked at delving too deeply into what kisses could lead to.

But none of it mattered because she couldn't picture him in her future. He was a tourist eager to get back to his way of life. She knew he'd never fit in her world, nor would she fit in his. But unfortunately, knowing that didn't put an end to the "wants" he stirred in her.

She was going to have to decide whether to further explore these newfound feelings, knowing full well that there would be no permanence involved. Or whether to renew her efforts at keeping her distance from this man, and hope they'd be going their separate ways sooner rather than later. He had no real interest in her, but more *accidents* could happen—that was if they could part company with Luella Miller, whom Damian *was* obviously interested in.

On the one hand, she ought to be glad Luella had shown up, because she kept Damian so occupied that it seemed he wasn't even aware that Casey was part of their little group. But on the other hand, it bothered her too much, the way he all but drooled over the lady.

And it didn't look like they would be getting rid of Luella as soon as Casey might have hoped. The southbound train showed up the next day, rolled past them in the distance, and was waiting there in the town they rode into about an hour later. And it was the same train, with Damian's fancy parlor car still attached to it.

Of course, he just *had* to invite Luella to share it with them, since they were all going to the same destination. And what objections could Casey give without flat out admitting she was jealous?

By the time the train arrived in Fort Worth a few days later, it really looked like the lovely lady from Chicago was about to corral her ninth fiancé.

In the several days that they had traveled together, there had been only one instance when Damian seemed to actually get annoyed with Luella. It was when she mentioned knowing his mother, who apparently lived in Chicago as well and was part of Luella's social circle.

Obviously, or at least obviously to Casey, Damian didn't want to talk about his mother, not even casually. Yet Luella didn't notice that and went on and on about the woman, mentioning how she knew about her first husband, how she'd been widowed several years ago from her second husband, how she seemed quite lonely now, living alone in her big house, and that Damian ought to come visit her.

He finally just up and walked out of the car to the open platform at the back. Casey, ensconced in her plush chair across the aisle, mumbled that some folks just didn't know when to shut up.

Luella, not listening as usual, did glance her way to say, "Now what got into him?"

Casey shrugged, smiled, and replied, "It probably got too stuffy in here for him."

Luella pouted and fanned herself. "I suppose. It *is* rather warm in here, isn't it? But then, he makes me warm, too, if you know what I mean."

Casey didn't, and didn't want to. Luella densely ignored her frown and added, "But I imagine I have that effect on him as well, which is a good thing. We *do* make a splendid couple, don't we?"

Did the woman really want her to answer that? She really was something! Casey allowed that Luella was quite something to look at, a bit too beautiful, in fact, but she couldn't understand how any man could tolerate for very long someone as vainly full of herself as Luella was. Damian ought to have more sense, but then, there was no accounting for some people's tastes.

And there was still another side to Luella—a side Luella had quite carefully kept from Damian. Yet the woman had no qualms about revealing her underlying nastiness to Casey, whether intentionally or not.

It was at the last depot, when the train had stopped for lunch, that she had pulled Casey aside to tell her, "I thought you might be jealous of me, but Damian has assured me that you aren't interested in him. Not that it would matter. You would hardly make a suitable wife for him, you'll have to agree. And besides, when I want something, I don't let anything stand in my way, so do try to remember that, dear."

Casey couldn't imagine why Luella had been prompted to say all that, unless she wasn't feeling quite secure in her position. Casey had been too shocked to reply immediately, then lost her chance when Luella sashayed off to rejoin Damian for the quick meal, and Casey wasn't about to make a scene.

That had been yesterday. But now that they'd reached the large town of Fort Worth, still named after the military post that had started it, Casey was going to make sure that she'd seen the last of Luella Miller.

The lady had talked Damian into escorting her to her uncle's house, but Casey said her good-byes there at the station and went off to see to the horses. She then checked into a cheap hotel, since she didn't know how long it was going to take her to ferret out some information on Henry Curruthers in a town this size.

By the time Damian found her that evening in the small hotel restaurant where she was dining alone, she already had good news, which she had planned to tell him in the morning. She hadn't expected to see him tonight, having figured he'd be dining with his ladylove.

"Why are you staying here?" was the first thing he asked when he came up to her table.

"Because it's cheap."

He shook his head. "Must I remind you again that I'm paying all expenses?"

"One bed's as good as another, Damian," she pointed out. "I'll do fine here."

"There is an excellent hotel just down the street, where I've already paid for a room for you."

"So get a refund," she promptly replied, continuing to eat her meal. "And what are you doing here anyway? Didn't Luella offer you dinner?"

He sighed and sat down next to her. "She did, but I declined. Quite frankly, I couldn't bear to sit through another night of her incessant chatter."

Casey almost choked on the piece of steak she

was chewing. Damian pounded on her back to help with the coughing. Red-faced, she snarled, "You're breaking my bones."

"Sorry," he said. He looked disgruntled, probably because she hadn't been very appreciative of his help. Then he asked, "Is the food any good here?"

"No, but it's cheap."

He stared at her for a moment before he burst out laughing. "What is it with you and everything needing to be cheap? I know you make good money in your line of business. You have to, as dangerous as it is."

"Sure I do, but I won't have much to show for it when I retire if I go splurging what I make all over the place, now will I?"

He gave her a curious look. "That sounds like you plan to retire soon."

"I do."

"To do what?"

"To go home."

"I suppose to get married and raise little cowboys?" he asked.

She ignored his sarcastic tone. "No, to run the ranch I inherited."

He was clearly surprised.

"Where is this ranch?"

"That's hardly important, Damian."

"So tell me anyway."

"No."

His frown was telling. He didn't like that flat refusal one little bit and didn't want to drop the subject.

"Your man Curruthers headed south from here," Casey remarked nonchalantly. "San Antonio was mentioned, but not as a final destination."

Incredulous, he asked her, "*How* did you find that out already?"

"I paid a visit to all the stables in town."

"Why?"

"Because if he didn't leave town by train, and your detectives say he didn't, then he had to have bought himself a horse. And his description is distinctive enough to be remembered, which he was."

"You'd think those detectives would have found that out," Damian grumbled.

"That was a matter of rotten luck. The fellow who sold him the horse took off the next day to visit his mother in New Mexico. He was gone for over a month, which is why your detectives came up dry."

Damian shook his head, smiling. "And here I thought we would be here a week at least."

Casey shrugged. "So did I. Too bad. Now you'll have to cut your courting short—or reconsider letting me finish this job alone."

"Not a chance," Damian said, seemingly little concerned about leaving his ladylove behind. "I told you, I have to be there to be sure you find him. I want to confront him face-to-face. Now, did you learn anything else?"

"Well, he bought a piebald, which is about as easy to spot as he is," she said pointedly.

He chose to ignore that comment. "You're talking about a horse?"

"Yes. He was also asking about any new towns in the area just starting up. When Mr. Melton, the horse trader, asked him why, Curruthers laughed and told him he felt like owning his own town. Melton figured that idea was pretty grandiose for such a little runt—his words—but he steered him south, where the Southern Pacific Railroad is causing towns to sprout along its long route and offshoots.''

"So what is your plan?"

"We'll head down to San Antonio and continue the search from there. It's pretty settled to the east of there, so my guess is he would have headed west if he really is looking for a new town. But we should be able to find someone to confirm that in San Antonio.''

"Does the train connect to San Antonio?"

"Yes—unfortunately.''

He smiled at her sour tone. "Admit it, Casey. The parlor car is comfortable.''

She wasn't going to admit any such thing. "The train isn't wasting any time catching up with its schedule. It leaves bright and early in the morning, so if you've got some good-byes to make, you don't have much time left to make them.''

"Actually, I'm pretty hungry," Damian said and called the waitress over. "Bring me what sh—'' He stopped his order to cough before correcting himself. "What he's having.''

Casey still glared at him for the near blunder and warned, "This isn't going to give you much time to let Luella know you're leaving town.''

He leaned over to pat her arm condescendingly. "Playing matchmaker doesn't suit you, Casey, so why don't you let *me* worry about my love life?''

Matchmaker? She would have spluttered if she'd tried to say anything just then, so she didn't try. But the look she gave him should have fried him on the spot.

Chapter 21

On the way to the train station the next morning, Casey had an unpleasant shock. Riding down the middle of the street, dust-covered, with a scraggly beard, was her father. He looked like he had just ridden in off the plains. Casey wasn't about to ask to make sure.

Without a word of explanation to Damian, who was walking his horse beside hers, she headed quickly into the nearest alley and plastered herself against the wall there, praying Chandos hadn't seen her or, worse, Old Sam, whom he would easily recognize. Damian followed her, of course.

But he merely asked, albeit with raised brow, "What are you doing?"

"What's it look like?" she grumbled.

"Hiding, though I can't imagine why."

She peered around him, but Chandos was taking his sweet time riding down the street. He hadn't passed the alley yet. She pulled Old Sam's head down to hide him as best she could. Damian, still waiting for her to answer, sighed.

"Don't we have a train to catch?"

"We'll get there in time."

Damian glanced out into the street himself now, but found nothing out of the ordinary—no familiar faces from Wanted posters—and gave Casey an impatient look. "Explain yourself."

"My father just rode into town—and don't look again, you'll draw his attention."

Nothing could have stopped Damian from glancing out again. There were several men riding down the street. One appeared to be a businessman. One looked like a desperado who'd rather not run into any lawmen. Another was wearing chaps and leading two steers along. Only two appeared old enough to be Casey's father, so Damian looked at the businessman a bit closer.

"He doesn't look very intimidating to me, certainly not enough to send you running," Damian remarked and got a snort in reply, which prompted a question. "Why don't you want him to find you, Casey?"

"Because he'll drag me home before I'm ready, that's why. And believe me, Damian, my father is about as formidable as they come. You don't want to cross paths with him."

Damian looked at the businessman again and frowned; then his eyes went back to the desperado, noting now the black hair, the high cheekbones, and other things that could be said to resemble Casey. Damian's eyes widened.

"Hell, *that's* your father? The one who looks like an outlaw?"

"He looks like no such thing," she grumbled.

"But yes, that's him. And stop staring! He can sense someone staring at him."

"How?"

"Hell if I know, but he can."

"Do you think he knows you're here in town?"

"There's no way he could, unless he guessed I was on the train and followed it here. But that's not likely, since you've been buying the tickets. You've also been taking care of the hotels we've stayed in, so he had no trail to follow."

"Perhaps I shouldn't mention this, but your rooms have been in your name, Casey."

"What?!"

He flinched. "Well, not exactly your name, but your initials."

"You couldn't make up a name?"

"Why? You told me you've been using those initials yourself."

"Only when I have to, and only when I turn over wanted men to the authorities. My father isn't likely to go sifting through every sheriff's office he comes across, but he *is* likely to be checking with every hotel and boardinghouse."

"So those are your real initials?"

"No, but they're initials he'd notice right off," Casey explained.

"They're his?"

"No."

"Then whose?"

"You ask too many questions, Damian. And my father has passed us by. I'm getting on that train pronto. Think you can get the horses boarded without drawing too much attention to Old Sam?''

"He'd recognize your horse, too?"

"Of course he would. He gave him to me."

Casey headed to the train station, at a much quicker pace than before. She didn't hold much hope that she'd get out of Fort Worth without having to face her father, but she did. The train left on time, and without Chandos barging into the parlor car for a major confrontation.

That had been a close call, but only a coincidence after all. Nothing more than that—at least she kept trying to convince herself of it all the way to San Antonio.

But just to see if she could prevent it from happening again, she sent off a telegraph to her mother that read: "If you can, call off the hunt. I'll be home soon now."

As for her job and getting it finished, there were no easy clues to find in San Antonio. In fact, the trail, such as it was, ended. If Curruthers had taken the train from there, the depot clerks sure had no memory of it. But Casey was betting he *had* headed west on the Southern Pacific—if he really was looking for a new town to settle in. They wouldn't find that out, though, without following the same route.

Damian, of course, arranged to have his fancy parlor car transferred to the new train. Actually, Casey was getting used to the comfort of it and just complained now on general principles. And with half the stops being made at depots that did no more than feed you, they started doing a lot of sleeping in that car—at least Casey did, until the night she woke up and found Damian leaning over her.

Chapter 22

Casey had been sleeping on one of the thickly upholstered benches in the parlor car. It was narrow, but much softer than some beds she'd been in lately. She had also been dreaming about Damian, which was probably why she was in no hurry to wake up.

It was a pleasant dream. There was a party at the K.C., and they were dancing together. She hadn't wondered what Damian was doing in her home—it had seemed perfectly natural for him to be there. Even her parents had treated him like they were used to seeing him around. And then suddenly he was kissing her right there in the middle of a dozen dancing couples, but no one seemed to notice. And it was like that other time, only this kiss didn't end.

All those feelings he had stirred in her before rose up again, but in her relaxed state they were even more intense. And this kiss wasn't only longer but deeper. He was using his tongue quite extensively to explore the recesses of her mouth. He would suck on her lower lip as well, as if he meant to keep it. And she could feel his hands caressing her, but not on her back where they should be. Strange.

She wasn't sure why she finally woke up to the fact that the kissing part, at least, wasn't a dream. Perhaps it was the shock of Damian's hand gently kneading her breast. There was something too intensely pleasurable about that for Casey to remain relaxed or asleep.

Then her whole body stiffened with the full realization that Damian was actually kneeling there beside her bench with his hands and lips on her. She tried to think of an explanation for it, but her mind wouldn't work properly.

All she could think to say was, "Damian, what are you doing?"

She had to repeat the question three times before he finally leaned back to look at her. From the dim light of the single wall lamp that had been left on, she could see that he appeared somewhat confused.

But that was nothing compared to her confusion when he replied, "What are you doing in my bed?"

"What bed? There're no beds around here, just these benches big enough to fit only *one* person," she said emphatically. "And you're on *my* side of the car, Damian."

He glanced around him then, couldn't help but see that she had stated the case correctly, and said, "Well, damn, that was quite a dream."

Casey blinked. She'd just been having a dream about *him* that had been too nice by half, so she had to allow that he might have been experiencing something similar. Not necessarily about her. In fact, more likely his dream had been about Luella.

Yet her eyes still narrowed. "Do you always get physically involved in your dreams?"

"Not that I was ever aware of—until now. Did I—that is, do I owe you an apology?"

Apologize for giving her some serious pleasure? But then, he didn't know what he'd made her feel, did he? How could he? She hadn't made any sounds or movements to indicate how much she'd liked what he was doing—had she?

Actually, she had no idea how much she had participated in what he'd been doing, for she'd been too involved with . . . feeling to take notice. He hadn't been awake, though, so even if she had given herself away as to how much she'd liked his kissing, he wouldn't have realized it.

"It don't make me no nevermind if you walk about and do things in your dreams, Damian. Just try to keep any active involvement to your side of the room."

"Certainly," he replied. A long pause followed. "Although I sense that this was nice."

She blushed clear to her booted toes. But with the dim lighting, he probably didn't notice her embarrassment. And he still must have had "nice" on his mind, considering what he remarked next.

"Would you perhaps like to see what I mean?"

She already knew what he meant. What he was suggesting was that they continue kissing, and he was leaving the decision of whether to do so up to her. Damn, the temptation was incredible. And this time it wouldn't be Luella he was dreaming of kissing. He knew exactly whose lips would be surrendering to his.

She didn't dare say yes. If he had just kissed her again, without asking, she probably wouldn't have objected. But by asking, he was making her admit she wanted him to kiss her, and she couldn't do that and still maintain that she wasn't interested in him. She still wanted to maintain that impression. She had to.

Damn him, what'd he have to ask for? But it was just as well. They were getting closer to the time of parting, heading their separate ways. It was going to be hard enough saying good-bye to him this second time. A shared intimacy would make it even worse.

So before she changed her mind, she said, "What I'd like is to get back to sleep, Damian. I'd suggest you do the same—and keep your dreams to yourself."

Was that a sigh she heard? Probably not.

He nodded and stood up. However, he seemed to hesitate before he turned his back on her, a long enough pause to make her tense in anticipation. But then he went back to the chair he usually slept in—the benches were a mite short for his long frame—and made a big production of getting comfortable. There was some definite sighing now.

Casey turned over to face the wall, wondering how she'd ever get back to sleep.

Chapter 23

Casey was in the habit of asking around, in each stop the train made, to see if folks remembered someone of Curruthers's description passing through. But it was starting to seem pretty pointless, and in fact, just when Damian was beginning to think they were wasting their time following the Southern Pacific west across the lower half of Texas, she came up with a positive response.

Since Damian had two hours to kill while waiting for the train to move on, he had followed Casey around that day while she did her questioning. When she approached the town barber, though, he figured she was really pulling at straws. Yet the barber remembered Henry.

After Damian had given it some thought, he recalled how meticulously neat Henry had always been about his appearance. Just because the man was on the run didn't mean he'd suddenly get sloppy, so a barber *was* a likely candidate to have dealt with him.

This particular barber was the sort that kept

up a running conversation while he worked on his customers, and he'd managed to get Henry to talking. One of the things he remembered Henry asking about was when this town was due for its next elections, and whether the people were happy with their current mayor or not.

Taken at face value, it could have been just idle curiosity on Henry's part, or a simple attempt to keep up the conversation. But when they added this piece to the previous knowledge that Henry was looking for a town to "own," it gave the information a different slant.

After all, someone with the authority of a mayor could be said to control a town, which in many cases could carry more power than "owning" a town. Had Henry changed his mind about how he meant to obtain the power he was looking for, or was politics the way he meant to go all along?

But a town that had a mayor was usually well-established. So now they seemed to have more places to search.

Casey was disgruntled over their conclusions. "We know he came this far, but it means we'll have to start checking out the offshoots of the rail line as well from here on," she pointed out.

That was true, and likely meant even more time before they finally found Curruthers. But more time also meant that Damian would be in Casey's company even longer, and he wasn't as disappointed about that as he should have been.

On the one hand, he would like to find his father's killer and return home, to return to the life he was accustomed to. But on the other hand, he had to admit, the thought of running

Rutledge Imports without his father was rather depressing. He'd always known that someday he would have to—he'd been groomed for it—but he'd never thought he would step into his father's shoes this soon.

And then there was Casey.

He'd known it was going to be difficult keeping his hands off her, but he hadn't counted on wanting her every minute of the day. Luella Miller had helped to distract him for a while, but not long enough. The Chicago debutante might be exceptionally beautiful, but her incessant, vain chatter had very quickly become extremely annoying, to the point where all he wanted to say to her was, "Please shut up."

As to his quiet Casey with her closely kept secrets, he found it hard getting her to talk at all, especially about herself. Yet he constantly wondered about her, about her motives for doing what she did, about her background, about why she was hiding from her family, if she had even more family than just that ominous-looking father of hers.

But most of all was his desire to make love to her. And the other night on the train he'd succumbed, he couldn't keep his distance any longer.

He'd been unable to sleep, and unable to stop watching her sleep. And seeing her face all soft and yielding again as she slept was just too tempting to resist this time. And then she'd woken. He wasn't used to pretending, but he'd done so to keep the peace when she came awake and had sounded so accusing.

Acting out his dreams. He all but snorted

every time he thought of that lame excuse. But in the throes of passion, he hadn't exactly been thinking clearly, and at least Casey had believed him. He couldn't stop wishing she had remained asleep, though, because her response to him had been all that he could have hoped for—at least until she woke up.

The next evening brought them to the small town of Langtry, where the train was laying over for the night so the passengers could get a decent night's sleep in the local hotel. Damian found rooms and retired early. Casey said she'd do her investigating that night, since they were leaving early in the morning.

Damian fell right to sleep.

But the next morning when he went to look for her, Casey wasn't in her room. She wasn't at the depot or with the horses. In fact, Damian had no luck finding her anywhere—until someone suggested that he check the jail. And there she sat behind some sturdy-looking iron bars, her face composed—as usual. Yet on closer inspection, her golden eyes banked a furious fire.

"Is this serious?" he asked when he was allowed to approach her cell.

"Ridiculous, is what it is," Casey growled.

"You didn't shoot someone you shouldn't have, did you?" was his first conclusion.

"My gun didn't clear leather."

"Then what are you doing here?"

"Hell if I know" was her unsatisfying reply. "I was having a whiskey in the Jersey Lilly saloon last night, standing at the bar minding my own business, when a fight broke out. I was still standing there minding my own business when it was over, and half the folks in the room were down on the floor, dabbing at their bloody noses."

"So if you didn't do anything—"

"I was getting to that," she cut in. "Old Judge Bean, drunk as a loon, was there and started ranting that his court had been destroyed."

"Are you trying to tell me the saloon here doubles as a courthouse?"

"That's not so unusual, Damian. Lots of small towns that don't have their own courthouse, let alone their own resident judge, make use of a saloon when the circuit judge comes to town, because it's usually one of the bigger open rooms in a town. But most judges don't spend all day and night in their courts whether court is in session or not."

"Why do I get the impression you know this Judge Bean personally?"

"I don't, but I sure got an earful about Roy Bean from the other jail guest I had to share this cell with for a few hours last night, until his wife came to drag him home. Seems the judge uses his Revised Statutes of Texas to suit his own purpose, which is passing out fines whenever he gets short of drinking funds. He does his fair share of hanging horse thieves and murderers without batting an eye, though—as long as they aren't one of his drinking pals."

"What's that mean?"

"Means he twists the law to suit himself, and gets away with it. If one of his pals shoots someone, he figures out a way to acquit them. In one of his more infamous decisions, he ruled that the victim shouldn't have gotten in front of the gun his friend had been firing."

Damian shook his head. "I'd say your cellmate was pulling your leg, Casey."

"I'd like to think so, but I doubt it."

"Why?"

"Because I vaguely recall hearing about Judge Bean before, from a young cowboy who'd passed through Langtry several years ago. He was here when a man just dropped dead in the street in front of the saloon where the judge was lounging on the porch. The judge immediately waddled down—"

"Waddled?"

"He's got such a large drinking gut that he can't quite walk a straight line," she explained. "But as I was saying, he waddled down to act as coroner first. Then, after searching the dead man's pockets and finding some money and a revolver, he assumed his judicial authority again to hand down a posthumous fine for carrying a concealed weapon. The fine, of course, equaled the amount of money he'd found."

"And he gets away with this?"

"Why wouldn't he, when he's the only law around here? But as I was saying, he was having himself a fit last night because his court got all smashed up, and he arrested everyone on the spot. Then someone pointed out to him that his jail wasn't big enough to hold the whole room, so he amended his 'official' arrest to just me."

Damian frowned. "Why?"

"Believe me, I asked that myself, and was told that seeing as how he knew everyone else involved, he knew where to find them to collect his fines. Hell, half of them were his damn drinking cronies, so he probably won't fine them at all. But me he didn't know, so I'd be spending the night in jail to make sure I didn't take off before he convened his court in the morning."

Damian sighed. "So this is just a matter of you paying a portion of the damages before you get released—even though you had no part in creating those damages?"

"That's about it."

"Knowing how you like to keep things to yourself, did you even point out that you hadn't been involved in that barroom brawl?"

Casey glared at him for that. "Do you think I like spending the night in jail? 'Course I mentioned it. But he made an 'official' ruling that everyone there was going to chip in for the repairs, with no exception."

"Himself included?"

Casey snorted. "With all the fines going to him, and him then paying for the repairs, he probably figures that's doing his part."

"I suppose we're going to miss the train because of this?" he remarked.

"Maybe not. Someone has already gone to rouse the judge. I was told it won't be much longer."

"Well, whatever you do, Casey, don't rile the man, or you're liable to end up back in here."

"I've already figured that out," she mumbled sourly. "It still goes against the grain, being fined for something I didn't do."

"Don't worry about it. I'll pay the fine."

"That's not the point."

He smiled. "No, but it will get us out of here and on our way."

As it happened, Damian should have stayed away from that courthouse-saloon altogether. But then, they couldn't have known that Judge Roy Bean would be in one of his more ornery moods that morning.

Chapter 24

*T*he Jersey Lilly, where Judge Roy Bean held court whether court was in session or not, was a typical-looking saloon with one exception, the built-in jury box. Bean wasn't a typical-looking judge, however. He could barely get the top button of his waistcoat closed, he was so fat, and the other buttons were a lost cause.

The judge was approaching seventy, and his bloodshot eyes attested to his passion for rum. Rope burns around his neck spoke of his having met up with a lynch mob at some point in his past. Likely true, since there were rumors that he'd been in a few less-than-honorable gunfights that had ended with him still standing and the other fellow needing a pine box. All this before he got appointed justice of the peace.

Casey had been so upset over getting arrested the night before that she hadn't actually noticed that there wasn't all that much damage done to the saloon, certainly not enough to account for Bean's ranting and raving. But then, she wouldn't be at all surprised if his fury had been contrived just to support a new opportunity for levying fines.

In the large room, one table was missing a leg. One chair had been busted over someone's back. But that was all, other than broken bottles. And she couldn't recall having seen anything worse than that last night, such as something that might have been removed in an effort to clean up. Actually, it didn't look like any effort had been made at cleaning up the place yet.

Even that early in the day, some of the judge's cronies were bellied up to the bar having their morning eye-openers, waiting for him to finish "business" and join them. From what Casey had heard, even if there was a trial and the jury box filled, drinking was encouraged.

Bean himself had a tall glass of rum placed next to his gavel on the table he sat at to pass out his verdicts. No special podium for him. Guess he had figured the jury box was enough to give his saloon the distinction of a court-house, that anything more would have been a waste of his good money. His court was so in-formal that even his bailiff shared a corner of his table, sipping a cup of coffee rather than standing alert to protect the court as he should have been doing.

Casey was escorted into this travesty of a courtroom by one of the court deputies. Damian had followed right behind her and, in fact, moved to stand beside her in front of Bean's ta-ble, which drew the judge's immediate atten-tion.

"Just find yourself a seat, young man. I'll get

to you as soon as I finish with the little lady here."

Casey stiffened, wondering how the hell the old coot had discerned that she was a female when everyone else looked at her and saw differently. He actually made a cackling sound, having noticed her reaction, and apparently was pleased as punch that he'd managed to surprise her.

"I've got good eyes, missy," he bragged. "Always could and always will take notice of a pretty lady, don't matter what silly duds they cover themselves in. I'll admit I don't get many before my court, though," he added with a disapproving frown that almost made her blush.

The judge then raised a bushy gray brow in Damian's direction. "Why're you still standing there, son? You hard of hearing?"

"I'm with—her," Damian explained. "Here to pay her fine so we can be on our way."

"Well, now, you shoulda said so," the judge replied with an avaricious gleam in his eye. "For participating in the destruction of private property, as well as disturbing the peace—one hundred dollars. Pay the bailiff."

"One hundred dollars!" Casey practically screeched.

"You got a problem with that, missy?" Roy Bean asked with a warning look.

She sure as hell did, but Damian's nudge reminded her that she better keep it to herself. And it was probably fortunate that the wad of bills that Damian pulled out and counted off added up to only a hundred and sixty dollars, or Bean was sure to have come up with some other excuse to fine them some more. As it was, Damian handed the money to the bailiff, who immediately handed it to the judge, who showed no shame when he stuffed it into his own pocket.

"So she's free to go?" Damian wanted everything clarified.

"Yes, yes," Bean said impatiently, eager to get out of his judiciary role now that he had a pocket full of money again. "But why'd you pay her fine? You her husband?"

"No."

"Her lawyer?"

"No."

"But you're traveling together?"

From Damian's look, he was starting to get worried about these personal questions, so Casey spoke up. "We're searching for a man who committed a murder back East, to bring him to justice."

"Commendable." Bean nodded. "And you're welcome to bring this killer before my court if you find him. I'll be glad to hang him quick and proper. But you're still traveling together, which speaks for itself, missy, now don't it?" the judge said with a frown.

Casey frowned right back at him. "Speaks for itself how? Just what are you implying, Your Honor?"

"It's pretty obvious you two have been cavorting in sin, traveling alone together, and I really can't tolerate that. No, sir. Never could, never will. But I'm glad to say that's easily rectified. So by the powers invested in me, I pronounce you man and wife, and may God have mercy on your souls." He banged a gavel before adding, "That'll be an extra five dollars for the marriage. Pay the bailiff."

Casey was rendered speechless.

Damian got out, "Now wait a minute—" before Roy Bean narrowed one of his bloodshot eyes on him.

"You aren't *really* thinking about arguing with me about due process and moral duty, are you, young fella?" the judge demanded ominously.

At that point Casey dug in her own pocket to toss the five dollars at the bailiff, grabbed Damian's arm, and dragged, yanked, and otherwise got him out of there before they both ended up back in that lousy jail cell.

Out on the porch, though, she ran out of steam, since Damian wasn't cooperating in being rushed. And she was still too dazed herself over what had just happened to point out that they really ought to get on the train pronto.

"That wasn't what it sounded like, was it?" Damian asked her.

"If you mean that it sounded like he hitched us together then, 'fraid so, that's what he did."

"Very well, at least tell me it wasn't legal."

"Sorry, wish I could. But he's a bona fide judge, legally appointed."

"Casey, things like that just don't *happen*," he said in a frustrated tone. "Usually the bride and groom have to say a few words—like they agree."

He was being sarcastic, and she couldn't blame him one bit. "Not in all cases," she was forced to remind him. "And not when faced with the kind of arbitrary power that Bean wields. That ornery old coot was determined to be ornery, and there isn't a thing we can do about it—here.''

''Why'd you pause?''

''Because it's occurred to me that we're getting upset over nothing.''

''I'd hardly call suddenly being married *nothing*.''

''Well, no, 'course not, but the thing is, we can get unmarried just as easily. In fact, all it will take is to come across another judge and explain what this one did. And for sure it's easier to find a judge than it will be to find Curruthers, so let's just get the hell out of Langtry before something else goes wrong, okay?''

He had no trouble agreeing with that, and they did manage to collect the horses and make the train just as it was whistling its departure. But Judge Bean's bailiff had no trouble catching up to them either and held the train up even more. He had Casey's gun to return to her—she was amazed that she'd been walking around half naked without it and hadn't even realized it. He also had a couple signatures to collect for the court records, concerning their marriage.

Casey turned stubborn at that point. ''And if we don't sign?''

''Then I'm instructed to escort you back to the court,'' the man told her.

She had her weapon back, barely sheathed. The decision was really hers, whether to comply or just kick the bailiff out of the train car.

She was leaning toward the latter when Damian said, ''We've already decided to remedy this, so just sign the damn book, Casey.''

She supposed he was right. And since he'd already said her name aloud, she signed the book "Casey Smith." Seeing what she'd done, he signed "Damian Jones."

At least they had *something* to smile about as the train pulled out of that hellhole.

Chapter 25

*E*ven though she realized that it was only temporary, being married to Damian preyed on Casey's mind something fierce. There was something nice about it—in her mind. He was probably hating it, and in fact, the first thing he asked in each town they came to was if there was a judge, or where the nearest one could be found.

Casey hated that an event that was supposed to be really special had been accomplished in only a few seconds, without the courting, without the asking—without the bedding afterward. And for some fool reason, her thoughts kept coming back to the bedding part.

But the fact was there, staring her in the face: She could make love with Damian now and not suffer a bit of guilt over it. She hadn't asked to have it so. A rum-soaked judge had made it so. But it *was* so. And that knowledge was very hard to live with day after day, because having "permission," so to speak, made her want to experience Damian's lovemaking even more than she had previously.

In the town of Sanderson, Casey had another scare, which at least got her mind off her "marriage" for a while. She could have sworn she saw her father again, entering one of the local boardinghouses. She hadn't seen his face, though. And really, anyone could wear the type of clothes that Chandos favored. Besides, it would be quite impossible for him to have traveled this far from Fort Worth by horse so soon— unless he'd been on the same train as she. And he hadn't been on the train. There *had* been other horses riding the stock car with theirs several times, but none had been Chandos's horse. She would have recognized him immediately.

Later that day, they came up with new information. A new town, barely a year old, had sprung up along an old trading route about a two-day ride north of the Southern Pacific tracks. The railroad didn't have a spur line to it yet, though one was planned in the near future, since Culthers was growing so fast. It had its own schoolhouse already, three churches, its own town council and mayor.

The mention of a mayor had Casey and Damian heading that way, though it meant taking to the trail again. Also, the name alone, sounding so much like Curruthers, might have drawn their quarry in that direction. But, still worried that her father might be in town, Casey didn't want to take any chances. So when she woke before daybreak, she sneaked into Damian's room and roused him out of bed, and they more or less fled town then and there.

Damian, unexpectedly, complained. "You know, though I haven't benefited too much from this 'marriage' of ours, *you* certainly have."

Casey ignored him. Keeping to a slow, careful pace on the road, at least until sunrise, she had no trouble hearing Damian grumble again, "No, this temporary 'marriage' of ours hasn't given *me* any benefits."

He sounded so sour Casey was primed to argue, "What benefit do *I* have?"

"Haven't you realized that, as a married woman, your father can't drag you home or anywhere else, for that matter—at least not without my permission? Husband's rights do take precedence over parental rights."

Casey was grinning by then. "You know, that's an excellent point. Not that I would dream of standing up to my father like that, especially since this isn't a real marriage—but *he* wouldn't know that, would he?"

"Not unless you mention it."

"Yes, well, I'd just as soon not put it to the test, if you don't mind. So why not stop complaining about missing a few hours' sleep? We can make camp early today if you like."

He didn't stop complaining. She hadn't really thought he would. He was just in a complaining kind of mood today, she supposed. But they did make camp early, and luckily, near a freshwater stream.

Casey had planned on suggesting forgoing a fire that night, just to be on the safe side. She'd stocked up on supplies that didn't require heating, and the weather was quite warm. But Damian was so disagreeable she didn't mention it. Then she spotted fish in the stream. Fried fish sounded too good to pass up.

She left Damian to see to the horses while she went off to whittle herself a fishing spear. She was standing knee deep in the stream, having caught only one fish so far, when Damian showed up.

"There's an easier, more relaxed way of doing that," he remarked from the riverbank.

She didn't bother to look up, too intent on the fish that kept darting away from her. "I don't see any string lying around handy—unless you're of a mind to unravel one of them fancy shirts of yours."

"I'm of a mind to wash the dust off. You won't look, will you?"

Casey blinked. "Look?" Her eyes swung up to him, to see him in the process of removing his vest. "Now hold on. You can just wait on doing any washing until after I've finished catching dinner."

"I'm too dusty to wait."

"You're going to scare all the fish away!" she shouted up at him.

"I'll barely make a ripple," he replied as he started unbuttoning his shirt.

"You're crazy."

"I'm dusty."

She'd never heard anything so ornery-stubborn, but she could be just as stubborn. "Suit yourself then," she growled, "but you're the one who won't be eating fish tonight if I don't catch any more, not me."

She refused to budge from the stream merely because the fool man was going to get naked. It didn't make her no nevermind. She'd just keep her back to him and go about her business. But that was easier decided than done.

A few seconds later, he was in the stream. It was slowly driving her crazy, knowing that he was just a few feet away from her and buck naked. She could hear him splashing water on himself. No ripples indeed. Not that it mattered, because if she saw a fish just then, she wouldn't have really seen it. Her mind, her whole body, was centered on Damian and what he was doing.

She tried moving inconspicuously farther upstream so she at least wouldn't hear him. The water was colder there because it was deeper due to a debris blockage, but not freezing cold. She barely noticed the cold, though, her body had grown so hot.

And then she heard, right behind her: "Are you running away from me, Casey?"

She swung around in startlement. Damn, what a mistake that was, and too late to correct.

Damian had come up silently behind her. He was sunk down in the water, but he slowly rose up, the water slewing over his chest and arms as he did, glistening in what little sunlight remained, until his whole upper torso was revealed. And Casey was purely mesmerized by the masculine shape and contour of him. He was more muscular than she had imagined, his arms so thick, his hair-covered chest so very wide in comparison to a taut, narrow waist.

She hadn't answered him, couldn't even recall there had been a question, but he asked another. "Or perhaps you just decided on a bath yourself, up here where it's deeper?"

She still wasn't really hearing him, but she sure had no trouble seeing him, or feeling him when his finger came to caress her cheek and dribbled cold water down her neck. It was the shiver that followed that brought her out of her daze, if she could be said to be thinking clearly yet, which wasn't exactly the case.

But she did hear "It looks like you need some assistance, though."

Her poncho was lifted off her, and from the corner of her eye, she saw it sail through the air to land in a heap on the riverbank. Her gun followed and managed to land right on the poncho. It was seeing her gun thrown out of her reach that brought her out of her mesmerized state quite quickly.

"What are you—?" was as far as she got.

In truth, she did get the rest of that question out, but it was lost to anyone hearing it underwater. He had dunked her. He had actually pushed her under the water.

Casey came up sputtering in disbelief. She glared at Damian through a face full of wet hair, saw the grin he didn't have sense enough to hide at the moment, and shot a palm stream of water in his direction. He gasped at the new coldness hitting him square in the chest, raised a brow, then dived at her.

Casey shrieked and leaped to the side, but the splash of Damian hitting the water full blast with his body completely drenched her again. By the time she got the water out of her eyes enough to see, she couldn't find him. And then her legs were yanked out from under her.

It had been a long time since Casey had cavorted in a pool of water with her brothers, but she hadn't forgotten how to "get even." About twenty minutes later, Damian was calling for a truce. Casey was completely out of breath, mostly from laughing. Who'd have thought she could have "fun" with an Easterner? She certainly would never have imagined it.

She crawled to the bank, leaving Damian sitting back in the water, watching her. She was still smiling to herself. So was he, for that matter. And then she finally noticed why. Her clothes had been plastered to her skin. She might as well have been as naked as he was.

Her blush was immediate, but it didn't last, not once she noticed Damian's eyes. They were usually a very soft gray, pale almost, but right now they were a darker, more turbulent color, indicating strong emotion. And he'd started to wade toward her. He wasn't really going to walk out of the water with her staring at him, was he? He wasn't . . . He did, and before she had sense enough to look away.

She'd probably carry that image to her grave, so strongly did it imprint itself on her mind. He was like a statue carved to perfection, the artist too proud to add the slightest flaw to such a splendid creation. And just that brief sight of him made her feel all tingly inside.

She sensed more than heard him kneeling there beside her on the bank. She wasn't going to look again to be sure, but her breath caught in anticipation. She ought to get up and leave, yet she couldn't get her legs to cooperate for some reason. And then his hands were cupping her cheeks, forcing her to meet his gaze.

A fire raging out of control; that was what his eyes brought to mind. The sun was beginning to set, casting them both in a golden glow, but there was still enough light to recognize such immense intensity.

"It's not working anymore, Casey," he remarked in a husky rasp.

Did he expect her to say something when she could barely think? "What . . . isn't?"

"Telling myself our marriage isn't real."

"But it isn't real."

"Right now, at this exact moment in time, it's very, *very* real."

He must not have wanted another reply from her, because his mouth was now preventing any further comments. Raging fire? *Volcanic eruption* was more like what his kiss was all about. And within mere seconds, Casey's own passion was ignited to a similar degree of intensity.

This *was* what she had been thinking about ever since that ornery judge had hitched her to Damian, so she was inclined to agree wholeheartedly with him. Right now, right this minute, their marriage was real—and Casey was tired of fighting to ignore the things her *husband* could make her feel.

There was no ignoring what she felt right now, even if she still wanted to, which she didn't. The wild turmoil simply took over as she rose to her knees to get closer to Damian, wrapped her arms around his neck, and kissed him back for all she was worth. Having his own arms gather her even closer to each shape and nuance of him was thrilling beyond belief, while his lips continued to ravish her mouth, pulling her even deeper into his passionate kiss.

She was so consumed with his kiss that a while later, she wasn't even aware that he had to pry her arms away from him to get her shirt off. The silky camisole he ran into next gave him pause, as did her lacy drawers, but only because they were so feminine compared to the rest of her attire. And she barely noticed him spreading her poncho out on the ground, or picking her up to place her on it. But she noticed when he lay beside her and began to introduce her body to the feel of his hands.

There was no hesitancy in his touch. His hand moved over her arms, her neck, spent a great deal of time learning the shape and sensitivity of her breasts before continuing down her belly, all with a possessive boldness she wouldn't have expected but which she reveled in.

And then he set about inflaming her passion beyond what her limited experience could handle. He bent to lick at the hard nub of one nipple, drawing an uncontrolled whimper from her. She tried to pull him closer, but he wouldn't budge. He was going to torment her breasts for as long as he liked, never mind that they were so sensitive already that it was driving her crazy. When he finally did bring the full heat of his mouth over her breast, she thought she was going to go up in flames.

And that was when the hand on her belly moved again, lower, until his fingers slipped into the moistness between her legs. Casey's response was immediate, a burst of such incredible pleasure, she could never have imagined the like. It spiraled outward, that pulsing ecstasy, spreading languor, draining all tension.

Damian's weight settled on top of her as a reminder that she wasn't alone. She opened her eyes to see his gentle smile and couldn't help returning it. She felt a closeness to him now that had nothing to do with the proximity of their bodies. It was a nice feeling, too nice, actually, but she wasn't going to worry about that now.

He kissed her again as another part of him pushed for entry between her legs. Much thicker was this new intrusion, much hotter, too, and then she felt a brief popping sensation inside her that startled her eyes open again. That intensity was back in his. And immediately the tension returned, pulsing around that part of him that had gained entry and was steadily filling her.

Casey forgot to breathe, so wondrous were these new sensations that his deep penetration caused, and then she was breathing too hard, because he had started to move inside her, started a tempo that she couldn't help but join. It was happening again, but she expected it this time and held on tight, gasping, letting the pleasure surround her and take her swiftly to repletion.

Afterward, as he held her to his chest, his lips on her forehead, one hand tenderly caressing her back, she felt the most incredible contentment. She could have stayed there indefinitely if she hadn't heard Damian's belly rumble. She smiled—and ended up sharing that single fish for dinner after all.

Chapter 26

At first, Damian found it quite amusing; Casey's legendary composure was gone. Every time she looked at him the next day, her cheeks would noticeably pinken. It wasn't until he began to wonder why that it started to worry him.

Of course, she was probably having mixed feelings over what they'd done. He knew he certainly was. But he hoped she wasn't regretting it. He *should* be, but he wasn't.

Previously, his sexual habits where women were concerned had been quite simple. Spend a few hours with a woman and then go home to his bachelor bed. See them again or not; it never really mattered much. Casey was the first woman he'd ever spent the entire night with, then shared coffee with in the morning. It was a new experience for him, and one he wasn't quite sure how to handle without making her embarrassment even worse.

He should have made love to her again this morning to ease the sexual tension they both seemed to be having. It was what he wanted to do. But she was being her efficient, let's-hit-the-trail self again, so he didn't attempt it. And besides, she *had* been a virgin. What little knowledge he had of them included a certain soreness they were reputed to experience for several days following their first sexual encounter. The very last thing he wanted to do was give Casey any pain now, when she had fortunately seemed to experience very little of it last night.

He did have a great deal of self-castigating to do, however, for yielding to temptation in the first place. He had been hoping against hope that they would find a judge quickly, because their temporary "marriage" had pretty much been driving him crazy, having the right to make love to Casey more or less handed to him, but trying to do the noble thing and not take advantage of it.

Yesterday, however, he sure hadn't been thinking of anything noble—just the opposite. He had come up with one excuse after another to rationalize why he was being so foolish, suffering so much, when he didn't have to. But that was all they had been—excuses. He *knew* he should have continued to keep his hands off her.

He still couldn't regret it, though. She had proved to be too much of a delight in every way imaginable. And so very passionate. Now *that* had been surprising indeed, especially when she was so adept at keeping her emotions such a mystery.

They were still barely talking to each other by the time they reached Culthers late that afternoon. The town was, as reported, a small but quickly growing community. Comprised of two main blocks, with evidence of another under way, it offered a variety of businesses to tempt settlement in the area. It also seemed much more peaceful than many towns they'd been through, with both children and their pets romping in the streets, an indication that not much gunplay disturbed the peace. There was more than one saloon, but they'd also seen more than one church on the ride in.

As soon as they arrived, Casey asked for directions to a boardinghouse. It was almost a slap in the face, her doing that, knowing how Damian was accustomed to staying in the best a town had to offer, and there *was* a hotel, albeit a small one. He knew she was in effect telling him to stay on his side of town, she'd stay on hers. In other words, she wanted no more intimacy with him.

She couldn't have been more clear about it if she'd spoken the words aloud. How Damian felt about it was another matter. He didn't like it at all, would have checked them into the same room if she'd asked his preferences. But he would respect her wishes. She obviously *was* having regrets, and wanted to make sure she'd have no more to add to them.

They parted after stabling the horses, agreeing to meet for dinner in a restaurant they'd noted in passing, where they would discuss how to proceed if Henry did happen to be here in Culthers.

As Damian walked into his hotel he saw the newspaper on the check-in desk—and Henry's face was plastered on the front. He stopped dead in his tracks. Curruthers *was* running for mayor here, in an election to take place in several weeks.

Reading quickly through the article, Damian noted it was pretty much a case of one candidate slandering the other, the one slinging all the accusations being Henry. Strictly political in nature, the article didn't say anything personal about Curruthers, such as how long he'd been a resident of Culthers or where he hailed from previously. It didn't even mention his first name, but in a small town like this, everyone likely knew everyone, so maybe it was understood.

Damian had two choices. Find Henry immediately and deal with him. Or find Casey first, so she could be there for this long-awaited confrontation. As eager as he was to get the whole thing over with, he owed Casey a front-row seat, so to speak, for all the time and effort she had devoted to leading him to Henry. She's earned her bounty money.

It was a simple matter to locate the boarding-house that she'd been directed to. This one was at least clean and somewhat homey in appearance, owned by the local schoolmarm, as it happened. That very proper young lady probably wouldn't have let Damian up her stairs for any reason—if she'd known Casey was a female. But since she didn't know, she directed him to the second door on the left at the top of the stairs—which was open, the room being empty.

Hearing water running led Damian to the only other door up there that was closed. He knocked impatiently. "Are you in there, Casey?"

"What are you doing here?" she called out immediately.

He didn't like talking through doors, so rather than answer that, he asked, "Are you decent?"

"Barely. I'm about to have a bath."

Not surprisingly, the thought of Casey in a steaming-hot bath sort of changed the direction of Damian's thoughts. He wondered if the door was locked. He was about to find out when he heard from her again.

"You still there?"

"Yes." He sighed, recalling why he was.

"You didn't say what brought you."

"Henry is here."

"I know."

Damian frowned at that reply. "What do you mean, you know?"

"I probably saw the same newspaper you did, with his picture on the front page."

His frown got a little deeper. "And you come up here to bathe instead of coming to tell me?"

"He's not going anywhere, Damian. He'll still be here when I'm done with my bath."

"I'm not waiting."

He heard a low growl of annoyance before the door jerked open. In disappointment, he noted Casey *was* completely dressed, just lacking her poncho and her gun belt.

"What's your big hurry?" she demanded.

"Considering how long I've been searching for Henry, do you really have to ask?"

Her belligerence fled. She even sighed. "No, I guess not." She turned to reach for her gun belt and glanced down to buckle it on, adding, "Did you take the time to ask someone where Curruthers can be found at this time of day?"

"At Barnet's Saloon. It would appear that he runs his political campaign from there."

"Don't sound so disgusted." Casey grinned at him. "Saloons happen to make excellent places to conduct business other than the usual business of drinking, gambling, and—" She paused to cough. "Well, you get the drift."

He did, but denied it, "And?"

She turned stubborn, refusing to spell out anything of a sexual nature. "And having a generally good time," she improvised with a frown.

Damian leaned forward and stole a quick kiss from her, then said while she was still too surprised to speak, "That kind of good time?"

Casey snorted and grabbed her poncho, but she was blushing again, and she refused to meet his amused glance. She did give one last, wistful look at the hot water she was leaving behind, before heading out the door with a curt "Well, come on, let's get this over with."

Chapter 27

❦

*T*he very first thing she noticed about Barnet's Saloon was how clean it was. The second thing was, it didn't look like any saloon Casey had ever been in before. The tables were covered with red leather. The chairs were upholstered. The bar was a work of art, thickly carved and highly polished and inset with a marble top. The walls were actually wallpapered. There was a thin carpet on the floor, and, for crying out loud, not a spittoon in sight. If not for the bar, it looked like the lobby of a fancy hotel, or an exclusive men's club.

Casey was impressed. She even stepped back outside to look at the placard again, just to make sure they were in the right place. They were, but Barnet's was just too foreign-looking, as if designed by someone from Europe—or back East, and that brought Henry Curruthers back to mind.

He was sitting there, so easily recognizable with those thick glasses and that mole on his cheek, exactly as Damian had described. He sat at a table with three other men. Two others stood around, listening to the conversation. All wore business suits, though all but Henry looked seriously awkward in them. The group appeared as if they ought to be in some hideout, discussing their next robbery, rather than sitting in this fancy saloon discussing political strategies.

Casey shook that thought away. She was being too suspicious. Just because the five men with Henry had that peculiar look of menace typically associated with gunfighters didn't mean they were gunfighters. They weren't even wearing guns.

Damian didn't seem to notice the decor or think that it was unusual, but as soon as he spotted Henry, his focus remained on him and him alone. He was waiting for Henry to notice him. Casey was waiting for that, too, as a confirmation of identity. Not that one was really needed, but Henry *would* recognize Damian, and in that moment of surprise, his reaction could give away his guilt.

But that wasn't the case, unfortunately. When he finally glanced over toward the door and saw them standing there, he did show a speck of surprise, but that was all. And, heck, maybe the place had rules of dressing that allowed only suited-up folks to enter, and she and Damian certainly weren't that, having just come off the trail. If that were the case, everyone there would be surprised at their presence, not only Henry.

That did happen to be the case. Everyone else was now looking at them in something less than curiosity, a few in actual outrage.

One fellow spoke up querulously. "Here, now, this is a private saloon, members only. If you're looking for a drink, head over to The Eagle's Nest across the street."

They weren't budging, of course. And Casey was figuring she might have to back up their stance with her Colt, at least until they got their business finished here, but that wasn't necessary.

"I'm placing you under arrest, Henry," Damian said. "Will you come along peaceably, or will you give me the pleasure of dragging you out of here?"

Casey had to admire Damian's bluntness, even if he didn't have the authority to do any legal arresting. The others in the room, though, found his statement hilarious; almost all of them were laughing, Henry included.

"What'd you do, Jack, kick Mrs. Arwick's dog again?" someone snickered.

"No, wait," another said with a chuckle. "Old Henning must be having Jack arrested for ridiculin' him in the newspaper—as if every word weren't true."

Henning was the other candidate currently running for mayor, whom Henry had slandered in the local two-page newspaper, but who was this Jack they were referring to? Someone else was a mite confused as well, though in the reverse.

"I've heard you called many a thing, Mr. Curruthers, but a Henry?"

Curruthers was smiling as he answered, "Actually, I *have* been called Henry before, but, dear me, it's been more than twenty years since anyone's made that mistake, getting me and my twin brother mixed up." Then he looked at Damian and asked pointedly, "Is that what you've done, mister? Mistaken me for my brother, Henry? And just who are you, anyway?"

Damian was frowning something fierce, obviously not liking the implications of those questions. "Damian Rutledge—and let me get this straight. You're saying you and Henry are identical twins?"

"Yes, unfortunately."

"Unfortunately?"

Curruthers shrugged. "I've really got nothing against my brother, although I've always considered him a bit of a Milquetoast, if you know what I mean. But I've just never liked having someone around who could pretend to be me, and get away with it, simply because he's got the exact same face that I do. It's why I left New York and my family ties behind as soon as I was old enough to get out on my own. And I've never gone back or regretted leaving. I've kept in touch, and I hear from Henry every so often, but if I never saw my brother again, it wouldn't bother me much."

"When was the last time you heard from him?"

"Actually, a couple times this year. It surprised the hell out of me when he wrote last spring that he was thinking about coming to pay me a visit. Never figured Henry would want to leave New York and his comfortable job there. He's an accountant, you know."

"Yes, I'm aware of that."

"But he's such a timid sort, if you know what I mean, and this country out here, well, it's not for the timid." There were a few chuckles from his friends over that remark, before Curruthers added, "He must have changed his mind, though, since he wrote again a few months ago from San Antonio—he'd made it that far—but he never showed up here."

"Then you don't expect him to show up?"

"After all this time? It doesn't take three months to get here from San Antonio. My guess is, Henry probably got scared off. For someone who's lived their whole life in a big city like New York, Texas can seem quite primitive. Takes a certain kind of man to settle out here, and Henry just isn't that kind, if you know what I mean."

"But you are?"

"Well, I've lived in Texas for the last fifteen years, so I guess that speaks for itself."

"This town isn't that old," Damian pointed out.

"I said I've lived in Texas, not this town," Jack said, his tone turning condescending now. "No, I've only lived here in Culthers for the last eight months or so—isn't that right, boys?"

"Yep, was about eight months ago that you showed up here, Jack," the man to Curruthers's right said.

"Was a couple months into the new year, as I recall," another confirmed.

Jack nodded, wearing a bit of a smirk now as he glanced back at Damian. "By the way, what's Henry done, anyway, to warrant arrest?"

"He committed murder."

"Henry?" Curruthers started laughing. It took him a while to compose himself. "You've got to be mistaken—again. The only way Henry might kill someone is to pay to have it done. He wouldn't have the guts himself."

"But you would, wouldn't you—Jack?"

The little man stiffened, possibly because the pause Damian had inserted before his name indicated that Damian wasn't believing everything he was hearing. Not surprising, since Casey wasn't either. But it was only the question that Jack addressed right now.

"I'd kill someone in self-defense, without a doubt. But then, I didn't say I was like my brother. Matter of fact, we're as different as night and day. I don't tolerate weakness, though that's about the only category my brother has ever fit in—if you know what I mean."

Casey had gotten that impression with the first words Jack had uttered. There was an unmistakable arrogance about this little fellow that didn't match up at all with what Damian had said about Henry. She didn't need it spelled out that one brother was a bit of a coward, while this one was more or less a braggart. Now, whether it was all for show or if he really did have the gumption to back it up, that was what she was interested in.

But she was keeping out of this interrogation, since Damian was doing just fine. She was amazed, actually, sensing how furious he was over this unexpected turn of events, how well he was keeping his temper contained. This was *supposed* to have been the end of his search. It had to be utterly infuriating for him that on the surface, it looked like they might have come up against a complete dead end instead.

Damian's silence, or perhaps it was the skeptical expression he was still wearing, must have caused Jack to change his "offended" stance, because he sighed now and said, "Look, Mr. Rutledge, if you're having any trouble believing me, and I suppose you are since you've never heard of me before, then I would suggest you send a telegram to my aunt in New York. Last I heard, she was still living. And she can verify that Henry and I are twins."

"Where is the telegraph office?"

At that point Jack was grinning again. "We don't have one here in Culthers. We expect to before the end of the year, but right now the closest you'll find one is in Sanderson, one or two days' ride south of here. Of course, I will expect you to return and offer a full apology. Can't have any slurs against my good name during an election, if you know what I mean."

The little man was nothing if not confident, but it was a confidence that grated.

Chapter 28

*"T*wo brothers, both wanting to be mayors? Do you believe that, Casey?"

Damian had deliberately refrained from talking about the meeting they'd had with Jack Curruthers until now. He and Casey were halfway through with a couple of nearly raw steaks—which at least *she* was enjoying. His disappointment that it hadn't been Henry in that saloon had made him furious at first. One bottle of red wine and working their way into the second had helped get him calm enough to talk.

Casey chewed thoughtfully on some fried potatoes before she remarked, "Maybe Henry decided to follow in his brother's footsteps. You know, like sons do with fathers," she added pointedly, since Damian fell into that group. "Then again, Henry could have just been asking questions everywhere he went that would lead him to his brother. Perhaps he forgot the name of this town but remembered it was new. In that case, he'd be asking about new towns, wouldn't he?"

"That's a bit far-fetched, Casey."

"Maybe, but possible. Try picturing it. Henry needs a place to disappear to and decides his brother can help. He gets halfway here, but he misplaces the letter he had from Jack that mentions the name of the new town where he's recently settled, and he can't remember the name of it to save his soul, so he starts asking about new towns. Or maybe two towns in Texas have the same name and he gets to the wrong one. Anyway, he also knows that Jack plans to run for mayor, so he narrows down his search to small towns with mayors. But finally he realizes that Texas is just way too big, that he won't be able to find his brother this way, so he gives up and heads back East."

"Well, I *hope* you're wrong, because with a cold trail like that to go by . . ."

"I wouldn't count this a dead end just yet, Damian," she said cryptically.

"You think Henry might be here, and Jack's doing his part to hide him?"

"I suppose that could be a possibility. But in that case, why would Jack even admit that Henry was planning to visit him?"

"Because we tracked him this far."

Casey nodded slowly. "Yes, there is that. Still, let's consider brother Jack for a minute. He seemed tough as nails, but any coward can get delusions of bravery with five big, menacing hired hands backing up his every word, which is what they did. He could be paying for his arrogance—if you know what I mean."

Damian grinned at her use of what appeared to be Jack's favorite phrase, but as to the point she was making, he said, "Yes, I thought of that. Except it's Henry I know, not this bold brother. It *is* more likely that they'd be cut from the same cloth, rather than being so dissimilar, as Jack would have us believe."

"Oh, I don't know. I've got two brothers myself who happen to be complete opposites. One would rather have his nose in a book all the time, hates ranching, and in fact he should be a practicing lawyer pretty soon, while the other's about as ornery as they come, hard to drag him in off the range, and—"

"You've got *brothers*?"

The question brought an instant blush. Apparently, she hadn't meant that reference to slip out, but she'd been drinking her fair share of the wine—and while drink could be stimulating, it could also loosen a tongue enough to forget that some things were meant to be kept secret.

"Well, yes," she replied tepidly.

"What else have you got?"

She took another drink of her wine before saying testily, "How about a mother, just like you've got?"

She'd mentioned his mother deliberately because she knew he didn't want to talk about that lady—her way of saying, Keep the personal questions out of the conversation. That would be fine if he weren't craving to know every single thing there was to know about her.

"Sisters? Uncles and aunts?"

Golden eyes narrowed on him and she retaliated with a direct hit. "How come you don't like your mother, Damian?"

He wished she didn't play so dirty. The mere

thought of his mother made him angry.

"If I answer that, will I get some answers from you in return?"

That he wasn't ignoring her question as she had his surprised her somewhat, but she gave him a noncommittal shrug. "Maybe."

Not a very satisfying answer, but the best he'd get, he supposed. "Very well. To begin with, I should mention that I loved both of my parents in the natural way that a child does. But my mother didn't return that love—or at least, her love for another man was much more important to her. She divorced my father many years ago, causing him untold personal as well as public distress. She might as well have divorced me also, because when she left New York to marry her lover, I never saw her again."

"Never? Her choice or yours?"

"Excuse me?"

"I guess what I'm asking is, did she ever return to New York to visit you? And if she didn't, did you ever make an attempt to find her to discover why not?"

"No, to both counts. But why would I expend the effort when I already knew why? She simply didn't care enough about me to bother. She went off to make a new life for herself, and to hell with what she left behind."

He couldn't manage to keep the bitterness out of his tone. Why the hell did it still hurt after all these years?

"I don't know," Casey said, her look more sympathetic than he was comfortable with. "If it had been me, I would have tracked her down and demanded some answers from her. And if

I didn't like those answers, then I would have at least made her feel miserable for abandoning me so callously. 'Course, callous folks don't usually feel guilty about anything. That's why they're callous. But I would have given it my best shot.''

Was she trying to make him laugh? ''Verbally—or with that gun you tote?''

She gave him a sour look. Apparently, she had been quite serious.

''You've lived all these years under an assumption, Damian. Doesn't that bother you? I'd want confirmation one way or the other, if it were me.''

''She wasn't there when I might have needed her. I don't need her now. So what would be the point?''

''Maybe for your own peace of mind. Maybe because she's the only family you have left. Maybe because you've recently found out that she's a widow again—and lonely. But that's just how I'd feel about it, if it were me. 'Course, both my parents have always been around, so what do I know?''

Scolding and contrite in the same breath. Amazing how she could do that. But perhaps she was right. Maybe he *should* have confronted his mother long ago to find out what she had to say for herself. It couldn't have made him feel any worse. He already believed the worst.

''I'll think about it,'' he conceded in a low-voiced grumble.

Her answer was a smile and a change of subject. ''Now, about Jack Curruthers—''

''Not so fast,'' he interrupted. ''Are you forgetting your 'maybe'? Fair is fair, Casey. Let's hear a bit more about your family now."

Casey gave him a long-suffering sigh and swiped up the wine bottle to refill her glass. "Well, you already know that both my parents are still living."

"Together?"

"Oh, yes, it's quite a deep and abiding love they share. Gets downright embarrassing sometimes, when they can't keep their hands off each other."

She managed not to blush when she said it. He shouldn't have asked, though. Most married people with children *did* stay together, especially when divorce, in high society at least, could be so scandalous.

"I have two brothers, no sisters," she continued. "Tyler's not quite a year my elder. He's the one who's going to be the lawyer in the family. Dillon's the hell-raiser, though he's only fourteen. I lost one grandpa recently, a cantankerous old cuss I dearly loved. But I still have another who's been a doctor all his life, and still practicing at it, though only with his regular patients. No other relatives, though, since neither my mother nor my father had any other siblings."

"And the reason why you left home?"

She frowned. And nearly a minute of silence stretched out before she finally said, "It was just a small disagreement with my father."

"It couldn't have been all that small, Casey, to have sent you out on your own."

"Well, it was important to me, is all. He didn't think I'd be capable of handling certain things because I'm a woman. And he was being pigheaded-stubborn about it.''

"So you set out to prove him wrong—by being a bounty hunter, something most women would never think about being?"

"Something like that," she mumbled.

"Considering how dangerous the line of work you chose is, who was really being stubborn?"

"I didn't ask for your *approval* of what I did, Damian," she reminded him.

"No, you didn't. And you can stop glaring at me. I know I pushed you into revealing so much. But I won't apologize. You *are* a fascinating woman, Casey. I can't help wanting to know all there is to know about you."

She was blushing now. And she attacked the remaining portion of her steak with a vengeance.

He probably shouldn't have said that. She obviously didn't want the conversation to get any more personal than it already had. But after sitting across from her all this time and being able to stare at her to his heart's content because staring was acceptable during conversation, he was having a problem with another "wanting" as well.

And he *really* shouldn't act on it, knew what answer he'd likely get, but he asked anyway. "Come to my room tonight, Mrs. Rutledge?"

Her scowl was immediate as she glanced at him. "You mean you haven't found out yet whether they have a judge in this town or not?"

"They don't."

Her lips twisted a bit sourly. "Now how did I know that you'd know that already?" She stood up, still scowling. "I have a room, thank you very much. And if we're to leave early in the morning, I think I'll go make use of it."

"Casey . . ."

She didn't let him finish. "Get your mind back on what's important, and stop acting like I'm the only female around. I'm not, and you might want to take advantage of that before we hit the trail again."

She walked off in a huff. Well, he'd been expecting that kind of response from her, after the way she'd been acting all day. But that she'd more or less suggested he find himself a willing prostitute was ludicrous. He didn't want just any woman, he wanted the one he was married to.

Chapter 29

❦

Casey wasn't in top form the next morning. She'd stopped in a saloon after leaving the restaurant the night before, to pick up another bottle of wine to take to bed with her. Not very bright on her part, but her emotions had been in a wild turmoil all day yesterday. She'd never have gotten to sleep otherwise.

Yesterday, she'd been certain that Henry would be in Culthers, so she'd been sure that she and Damian would be parting for good before the end of the day. She still felt in her bones that Henry was there, either hiding or doing a good job of pretending to be his own brother Jack. But the hunt hadn't ended. And Casey's turmoil continued.

She never should have made love with Damian the other night. She never should have let her body dictate the matter when her mind knew better. Appeasing her curiosity had accomplished only one thing. She now knew what else she'd be missing when he was gone. It was bad enough that she was going to miss him at

207

all. Yet she knew she would. She'd somehow gotten attached to him in a way that had nothing to do with their temporary marriage. A real fool thing to let happen—not that she'd had any choice.

And she was already experiencing the loss. That was the unusual part. He wasn't even gone yet, but she knew he would be, and soon—and she hated the way it made her feel, which was downright rotten.

She shouldn't be taking it out on him, though, which was pretty much what she'd done yesterday. It wasn't his fault that they weren't, nor ever could be, compatible. They both were raised too differently, in two completely different cultures. She'd be miserable in his, and he'd be miserable in hers, and there was no getting around that.

She hadn't done her job thoroughly yesterday either, but she corrected that this morning, stopping for a chat with Miss Larissa, the town's schoolteacher and boardinghouse owner. She also spoke to a few folks whom she came across on the way to the stable. They all had about the same thing to say about Curruthers, which was what she reported to Damian when she joined him at the stable.

"Jack Curruthers hasn't been here as long as he claims. That was an outright lie, backed up by more lies from those cronies of his."

"Is that just your opinion, or have you confirmed it?" Damian asked.

"I only suspected it, but I figured he couldn't have everyone in town on his payroll, so it was easy enough to find out the truth. The schoolmarm says he arrived here about the same time she did, less than five months ago. Two others said the same thing."

"What about Henry showing up?"

"None recall a twin brother, were surprised to even hear Curruthers had one. But one fellow did mention that he was *advised* by Jack's election committee that he better be voting for Jack."

Damian raised a brow. "Does that infer a threat of violence?"

"Coming from those particular hired hands? I'd say it was more of a promise."

"So he actually intends to strong-arm his way into the mayor's office?"

"Wouldn't be the first time."

"In a big city, I quite agree. I would have thought it would be different out here, though, where people are starting new lives for themselves."

"Ah, but Curruthers doesn't hail from out here; he hails from the big city. Besides, you can find corruption anywhere, Damian, if you look hard enough. It's just not as prevalent when everyone knows everyone else, which is the case in most Western towns. But as for Jack, the question is, why would he lie at all if he's really Henry's twin—and not Henry pretending to be Jack?"

"You think he's sending us off on a fool's errand just to give himself time to escape again?"

"No, I don't think he wants to leave what he's got going here. If anything, we've created a problem for him that he'll try to eliminate."

"You're expecting trouble, then?"

"You betcha." And in her present mood, Casey was looking forward to it.

"Then why are we even bothering to go back to Sanderson to send off that telegram?"

"Because you'll need all the facts you can get before you confront him again. Which reminds me—I assume you already know the name of this aunt in New York, since you didn't ask for it yesterday."

"Yes. After Henry disappeared, she was questioned. She swore he was innocent, incapable of doing anything so dastardly—her words. Remember, he had supported her for most of his life. I would have been surprised if she hadn't staunchly defended him in this."

"She never mentioned him having a twin?"

"No, but then, she wasn't very cooperative, as I'm sure you can imagine. She answered the questions asked of her without volunteering anything extra that might help to find him."

Casey nodded. "Well, let's get going. The sooner you send that telegram off, the sooner we can get back here and finish this thing."

"Then you *do* think Jack is Henry, don't you?"

"Actually, no. What I do think, though, is that he knows where Henry is. Here or elsewhere, he knows. Getting him to say where ought to be interesting."

Damian frowned. "You aren't suggesting I beat it out of him, are you?"

Casey grinned. "Only as a last resort."

Chapter 30

❧

*E*xpecting trouble, Casey didn't get much sleep that first night on the way back to Sanderson. Damian didn't either, so they took turns keeping watch throughout the night. But no one showed up to insist they leave the area and soon-to-be Mayor Curruthers alone.

Damian sent off his telegram and checked into the hotel to await his reply and catch up on lost sleep. Casey was still too keyed up to retire. She sauntered into the noisier of the two saloons on the main street, had at least one drink at the bar first, then asked to join one of the three poker games in progress.

She picked the table that looked like it was having more fun than conducting any serious gambling, with three easygoing fellows who were doing a lot of joking and talking while they played, which was what she wanted to do, at least the talking part. And they took right to her, as if they'd known her for years, even to teasing her about her age and if she really knew how to play.

She let a good thirty minutes pass, during which time she lost consistently, before she introduced her first casual question. "Any of you fellas hear of Jack Curruthers, the man who's running for mayor over in Culthers?"

"Not much. Why?" John Wescot asked.

John had introduced himself as the only dentist in town and guaranteed that he'd make it a painless experience if Casey should happen to require his services. She had managed to keep from snorting while she declined.

"I've heard he's a bandy rooster trying to fill shoes too big for him." Bucky Alcott said.

Bucky was an old range cook for one of the local ranches. Until he'd mentioned that, it hadn't occurred to Casey that it was a Saturday night—which was why the saloons were so full, what with ranch hands coming into town for a bit of typical weekend hell-raising

"I was just there," Casey replied, again in a casual way, as she studied her cards from the current hand. "Heard it said more'n once that his men are *leaning* on folks to get them to vote for him."

"Now why don't that surprise me none?" Pete Drummond remarked, shaking his head.

Pete was somewhat of a tenderfoot, having come West only two years ago, though he had adapted fairly well, even to speaking the lingo, which was a case of butchering the language he undoubtedly could speak with perfect diction if he chose to, but he didn't choose to. He sold firearms for a living and had opened a store here in Sanderson.

"Then you know Jack?" Casey asked Pete.

"No, but I seen him when he passed through here on his way to Culthers. Little fella acted like he owned the town—the whole dern state, for that matter. Never met anyone that blatantly arrogant."

"Do you know who the men are that he has working for him over in Culthers?"

"Might be Jed Paisley and his boys," the dentist said with a thoughtful frown. "They were working on the Hastings spread for a while, 'bout halfway 'tween here and Culthers, but I heard they complained that was too tame for them and they moved on."

"You're probably right, John. My sister was up that way a few weeks ago and mentioned she saw Jed and one of his boys in Culthers—and wearing suits, no less. Imagine that hombre in a suit?" Pete said.

"Who exactly is Jed Paisley?" Casey asked.

"Well, it's all rumor, you understand, nothing ever proven, but they say he used to run with the Ortega gang down Mexico way, terrorizing the peasants and killing just for the fun of it." Pete was warming up to the subject. "That was for a couple o' years, before he tried his hand at lawful employment, working for the ranches around these parts. He did kill a fella last year right here in this saloon. Was a stupid excuse for killing, if you ask me, but he got away with it just the same."

Casey was too curious to ignore that one. "What was the reason?"

"From the way I heard it, the victim was doing Jed a kindness to try and save him embarrassment by whispering to him that he'd forgotten to button up after coming back from the john. Instead Jed took it as an insult that the fella had even noticed and shot him dead."

Casey shook her head. "A mite touchy."

"No, mighty touchy. Jed's not a nice sort by any means. Didn't none of us miss him when he stopped coming here." Pete's emphatic nod punctuated his words.

"I had to pull one of his teeth once," John put in. "Don't think I ever sweated so much. He had his hand on his gun the whole time."

"I suppose his *boys* are cut from the same cloth?" Casey asked.

"Oh, yes," Pete volunteered. "There were five of them in all. Running into one or two of them wasn't so bad, since they didn't exactly go out of their way to make trouble, just never ignored it if'n it came their way. But when all five of them were together, and drinking to boot, well, someone usually always got hurt. And the dern sheriff was too afraid of them to do anything about it."

"So is it a safe guess that they're all fast guns?" Casey needed clarification.

John shrugged. "Can't rightly say. 'Accurate' is more like it."

"Mason is fast." Bucky spoke up now. "I saw him demonstrate his draw once when he was tryin' to impress Miss Annie, back when he was a-courtin' her. But like John said, Jed could definitely hit whatever he had a mind to aim at. Couple of kids stirred up a wasp's nest one Sunday when Jed was passin' near it, and damned if he didn't shoot them poor wasps instead of just gettin' out of the way, even reloaded to finish every single one of them off. Most folks said the kids were lucky he didn't shoot them instead, and most other folks were inclined to agree. Fact is, if they hadn't run like hell, he mighta."

"Do you know anything about the other three?" Casey asked.

"The youngest is Jethro, who's also Jed's younger brother. He came out here to join Jed a few years back. He's a little bully who glories in his brother's reputation and takes advantage of it, but he'd be nothin' on his own."

John chimed in again. "Elroy Bencher, now, likes to push his weight around without resorting to actual gunplay. He considers himself unbeatable when it comes to using his fists. Fact is, he was forever trying to get someone to try to go a round or two with him, but we don't raise stupid folks around here. The one man who did give Elroy a go for it got his spine broke in the fight and hasn't walked since."

Casey grimaced. "And the last one?"

Pete shook his head. "No one knows much of anything about Candiman, which makes him the more dangerous, if you ask me. He's quiet, too quiet, and always watching."

"Funny name," Casey remarked.

"It's what he calls himself. His friends just call him Candy, and when they're all together, you're sure to see at least one of them toss him a piece of candy. Don't think I've ever seen him not sucking on something sweet."

"I'd love to get him in my chair." John chuckled. "That's if he'd leave his guns outside the office."

They all were chuckling over that; then Pete finally thought to ask, "Why all the questions, Kid?"

Casey gave the simplest explanation that didn't require details. "I had a little run-in with Curruthers and his bunch when I was there, but since business is going to take me back, just wanted to know if I had anything in particular to worry about."

"I'd stay away from the lot of them if I were you," John suggested.

"Wouldn't even go back to Culthers if it were me," Bucky added.

"Be glad you escaped in one piece the first time, Kid. Don't tempt your luck a second time," was Pete's comment.

Good, well-meaning advice from nice, friendly folks, for which Casey thanked them before parting company. It was too bad she couldn't take their advice, though. But then, she wasn't *that* worried about Jack's hired guns, only a little worried. After all, they didn't even wear their guns, probably because it was bad for Jack's political image. But without them, how dangerous could they really be?

Chapter 31

*T*he ambush occurred about an hour out of Sanderson the next morning. The first shot came
from a clump of trees on their left that skirted a
very steep ravine. The second came from the
bottleneck up ahead that was caused by a pile
of boulders the narrow trail passed through. It
wasn't the only way to get to Culthers, just the
quickest route—and, at the moment, blocked.

But then, they weren't being asked simply to
turn around and find another route. Those were
some serious bullets, serious enough to cause
Casey to quickly seek cover and shout for Damian to do the same. Unfortunately, they chose
opposites sides of the path, Casey diving behind
one of the larger boulders on the right, while
Damian headed into the trees on the left.

That prevented any discussion of strategy, but
Damian didn't appear to need any advice. He
was already returning fire. Casey retrieved her
rifle and did the same. She was expecting shots
to be coming from five different locations, but
could spot only two—which didn't mean much,

since she didn't have a clear view of the entire area.

She hadn't been expecting an ambush in broad daylight, though. A night raid, yes, but during the day, when there would be a good chance of spotting who was doing the shooting? Of course, if the shooters didn't plan on leaving any witnesses behind, then night or day wouldn't matter.

But she supposed, after everything she had learned about Jed Paisley and his cronies last night, she should have expected this. And since this could have occurred before they'd even reached Sanderson—there'd been plenty of time and opportunity—Jed had obviously waited before doing anything, just in case Casey and Damian had decided to move on instead of returning to Culthers. Jack must have given orders to stop them *only* if they were on their way back.

She sent off a couple of rounds into the trees, about twenty feet from where Damian had taken cover. That spot held the closest shooter to Damian, and therefore was the one she was most worried about. Of course, if she hadn't been worried about someone sneaking up on him, she might have been more cautious of the same thing happening to her . . .

"Hello there, Kid. Shoulda took our advice and headed back to wherever ya hails from."

She recognized that voice behind her instantly. John Wescot, the Sanderson dentist. It just didn't make any sense to her that he would be here and aiming a rifle at her back—she'd recognized the sound of one being readied for firing, too, a minute before he spoke.

But when she started to turn around, to confirm his identity with her own eyes, since her mind was not accepting it, she got a "Don't move—'cept to set that rifle down real slow-like."

She did. The rifle was too cumbersome for any quick moves, anyway, and he hadn't mentioned disposing of her six-shooter, possibly because her poncho had kept him from noticing it. Yet. Not everyone wore a gun strapped to his thigh—leastways, not "boys" as young as he thought her to be.

"You're lucky it's us and not ol' Jed," he went on to tell her in his nonchalant tone. "Fact is, he's much worse'n we let on. He likes to torture his victims before he kills 'em. Finds something amusing 'bout it. Me, I get paid to kill, I just do it quick and clean. No need for extra suffering. It's just a job, after all. So where would ya like it, in the head or the heart? Both are pretty quick in my experience, so shouldn't hurt all that much."

Casey couldn't believe what she was hearing. He spoke of death as if it were merely a small inconvenience. And how the hell would *he* know if it hurt or not?

"Answer me one question, if you will," she said, managing the same casual tone he was using. "Did you get hired for this job before or after I joined you last night?"

"It was after you left us. Fact is, we enjoyed yer company, Kid. Ain't often we get to brag about our friends like that," he said with a chuckle. "It was purely fun. And if it's any consolation to you, Bucky didn't feel too good about takin' the job, seein' as how we got to know you and you're such a young un. But a job's a job. It's nothing personal, you understand.''

Oh, she understood perfectly. Hired killers usually did take that attitude, to absolve themselves of any guilt that *might* trouble them. Of course, most of them didn't have a conscience to begin with, so guilt never entered their small minds one way or another.

She asked another question, more to stall for time than out of any real curiosity. ''You aren't really a dentist, are you?''

''Hell, no,'' he practically snorted. ''What would I want a fool job like that for when this kinda work pays so much better? Now you answer my question, 'cause time's a-wastin'. Where ya want the bullet?''

''Between the eyes will suit me—if you've got the guts to look in them first.''

''Sassy-mouthed for such a young un, ain'tcha? All righty, turn around, but do it *real* slow, Kid. Don't want this to get messy.''

Messy for whom? For her, of course. Either he had nerves of steel, or he really didn't think he'd have any trouble from her, and her guess would be the latter. And it was John Wescot standing there. What she still found so incredible was her own gullibility, that these men had managed to fool her so easily into thinking they were just harmless townsfolk out having a good time on a Saturday night.

''Satisfied?'' he said as he took more careful aim with his rifle. ''Now it's time—''

Casey dropped to the ground as she drew her weapon. But even as fast as she was couldn't compensate for a rifle ready to be fired. All she did was mess up John's aim some. She got a bullet off, but the explosion in her head at the same time kept her from seeing if she was at least going to take him to the grave along with her.

Chapter 32

*D*amian couldn't see behind the boulder that Casey had claimed as hers, but he could see over it. And when he heard two shots fired almost simultaneously and saw two puffs of smoke float up above that same boulder, his heart seemed to drop into his belly.

There was about forty feet of open, flat area between him and that boulder, but that didn't stop him from racing toward it. Bullets hit the ground at his feet, flew past his head; he didn't notice or care that he made such a big target, nor did the shots have anything to do with the fact that he'd never run so fast in his life.

What he found when he got to the boulder was one body sprawled on the ground and another leaning back against another boulder, standing there at a slight angle—dead. Blood was splattered everywhere.

Casey was the one on the ground and Damian couldn't stand it. She looked just as dead as the other body, lying on her back, her arms spread out, her gun still gripped in her right hand. He couldn't tell if she was breathing. And she was covered in blood, making it impossible for him to pinpoint immediately where her wound was.

It would have helped his peace of mind to realize that most of the blood wasn't hers, but came from the man she'd shot in the chest at such close range. However, Damian couldn't determine that as he dropped to his knees beside her to gather her gently into his arms.

At that moment the ambushers could have moved in to finish him off, for he was focused only on Casey as he rocked her in his arms and dealt with his anguish. But since the remaining gunmen couldn't see what had happened behind the boulder, they continued to send their bullets in that direction, chipping away at the hard rock, once even sending dangerous slivers of it down on the ground around him. But they didn't approach.

This was all his fault, Damian thought. He had brought her here. He had tempted her with more money than she'd ever earned on a single job before. If he had been reasonable in his offer, she would have had no problem turning him down and going her own way, but he hadn't wanted to take that chance, so he hadn't been reasonable. And now . . .

Her heat should have told him she wasn't dead yet, but he was too upset to even think of that. Guilt and recriminations were too easy to wallow in, and he could barely breathe himself for the knot in his throat as he did his wallowing, not noticing that she was still breathing.

It took a pretty loud moan to finally break through his grief, a moan caused not from her wound but because he was squeezing her too tight. He let out a shout of joy as he carefully laid her back down on the ground. Her eyes fluttered for the briefest moment, though didn't quite open. Yet she was alive—alive and possibly bleeding to death.

The thought sent Damian into a new panic, to find her wound and get it stanched immediately. Poking around her didn't stir her, but as soon as he touched her head, she moaned again and her eyes flew open—just in time to shoot the man sneaking up behind him.

Damian swung around to see the fellow fall forward, face-first. Casey was unconscious again by the time he glanced back at her, her still smoking gun dropping from her lax hand this time. He quickly stuffed it in his own belt before he examined her head again.

There was about a three-inch bloody path where the bullet had slid by just above her right temple. Her hair was missing from the line, scraped off as if she'd been scalped in that narrow area. The tip of her ear had been singed black from the heat also.

The wound was still bleeding, but only lightly. It was her continued unconsciousness that had him most worried now. Blows to the head could affect people in many different ways. He had been fortunate that his own recent head wound had caused him only headaches.

He needed to get her to a doctor. And he needed to make sure that she wouldn't get shot again along the way. That meant seeing to the remaining ambushers first—or the last one, since he heard fire from only one weapon. Of course, that didn't mean much; there could be others. Finding where they'd left their horses would help to clarify the count, which was what he set out to do after tying his bandana around Casey's head.

He crawled over and around the big rocks, sometimes on his belly, working his way toward the bottleneck up north. He figured the horses would be behind it, but when he reached the summit, no horses or sign that any had been hobbled there, so he worked his way back.

The gunfire had continued being directed to where he'd last been seen. But by the time he'd reached the bottleneck, it had stopped completely. Again, that didn't mean much, since it could mean so many different things, but he nevertheless hurried to get back to Casey—only to find her gone.

The two bodies were still there, Casey and their weapons were not, and neither was her horse. Yet he *knew* she wouldn't just leave him there. She'd have no reason to, unless she thought he was dead. But she'd verify if he was dead or not first—unless she had no recollection of him at all. And that was one of those peculiar effects he'd been worried about.

He had heard of head wounds that had caused someone to forget friends, even family, even a full lifetime of living. If she had regained consciousness and left the area, then what else was Damian to think? At the moment, she might not remember him at all.

Chapter 33

❦

*C*asey awoke to find herself belly-down over a saddle on a horse that was pounding away at the ground and causing a piercing pain to streak through her temples. Her first thought was that Damian could at least have held her upright on his lap rather than in this ignoble position. She started to tell him so when she noticed the leg next to her wasn't his—at least the boot wasn't.

She had shot John Wescot. She wasn't positive, but she thought she'd shot Pete Drummond as well. Did that mean it was Bucky, the last of that threesome, who was carting her off? But why? If he'd found her, why hadn't he just finished the job they'd been hired for?

And if it's any consolation to you, Bucky didn't feel too good about takin' the job, seein' as how we got to know you and you're such a young un.

She recalled those words now and took comfort in them. Bucky didn't want to kill her. He was taking her away so he wouldn't have to— *if* it was Bucky and not Jed Paisley or one of his boys.

But what would be Bucky's alternative? Just let her go? She doubted it. He'd accepted the job, even if he hadn't liked it. She couldn't imagine what he intended to do instead. For that matter, how should she deal with him? Be outraged? Blister his ears for trying to kill her? Appeal to his guilty conscience? That might backfire on her.

The pain stabbed at her head again, reminding her how serious the situation still was. She refrained from trying to feel the wound to determine how bad it was. She didn't want Bucky to know she was awake yet. But it couldn't be that bad, since she had all her thoughts about her . . .

That was it! She could play dumb, pretend the wound had damaged her memory. He'd have no reason not to let her go, then, if she had no memory of him, Culthers, or anything else. She'd be solving his dilemma for him. That is, if he was smart enough to figure that out for himself, which she certainly hoped would be the case, since she couldn't help him do that if she didn't know why she'd been shot.

Now, if he'd just get to wherever he was taking her before she lost the contents of her belly all over his boot . . .

From her upside-down position, it looked as though they were headed to a farm, though not one that was currently being worked, but had probably been bought cheaply from a farmer who'd given up and moved on. A nice place for someone like Bucky to call home—that is, if he wasn't wanted by the law. He might even have shared it with his two deceased buddies. The house itself was certainly big enough for three to live comfortably.

He didn't even check to see if she was awake before he dismounted and hefted her over his shoulder to carry her inside the house. It was all she could do to keep from grunting as her belly met his bony shoulder. And then she was dumped, quite literally, on the floor. Maybe she'd been harboring false hope. He'd carried his lack of concern for her condition a bit too far, but it did give her an excuse to wake up—groaning.

Her eyes fluttered open to see it was indeed Bucky Alcott hunkered down next to her, peering at the blood seeping through the bandana still tied around her head. "Who are you?"

"Don't be pullin' my leg, Kid. You know me well enough from the other night."

"You are mistaken, mister. I've never set eyes on you before."

"Now look here, boy, I'm not stu—"

"Boy?" She mustered an offended tone for her interruption. "What do you mean, *boy*? Are you blind? I'm a woman, as if you didn't know."

He squinted his eyes at her, then shot to his feet and yelled, "Hell's fire and damnation, a woman! Then what in tarnation are you doing in them clothes, lookin' like a fresh-off-the-farm fifteener?"

She glanced down at herself, but all she noticed was the blood, and her surprise was natural and made her forget for a moment the role she was playing. "I'm dying, aren't I? With this much blood—"

His snort cut her off. "Don't think that blood is all yours."

She recalled herself in time to play dumb again. "Whose, then?"

"Beats me," he lied. "It's what you were wearing when I found you."

Was he making a joke? She chose to think not, and got back to what she *was* actually wearing, saying with a frown, "As for these manly-looking clothes, I don't rightly know why I would be wearing them, to tell you the truth. I suppose because I've been doing a lot of riding. I wear jeans on the range, I'm sure of that."

"You say that like you *ain't* sure."

Her frown got deeper. "Well, I'm not exactly. I seem to be having a little trouble recalling some things. Have I been given some kind of medication? Is that why my memories are suddenly so fuzzy? And why the devil does my head feel like it's on fire?"

He coughed. "I—ah—think you got yourself shot in the head, missy."

"I did what?! Who would dare!"

"Now, don't be flyin' off the handle. Fact is, you oughta be dead. 'Nuther fact is, I shoulda done the killin'. But with both John and Pete—"

She was immensely disappointed that he'd admitted that. Obviously, he hadn't yet figured out the benefits of her memory loss. But she continued to play dumb. "*You* shot me?"

"No, I didn't," he said in a low grumble. "But like I said, I shoulda."

"Why? What could I possibly have done to you to warrant something so outrageous as—"

"You didn't do nothin' to me. It were just a job I got paid for. Nothin' personal, you understand."

My, how friends did tend to have the exact same philosophies to ease their consciences. "Then you still intend to kill me? Is that what you're saying?"

"You'd be dead already if that were my intent. I brought you here to talk you into stayin' away from Culthers so I won't have to kill you."

"Who is Culthers?"

"Who? It's a—never mind. If you don't know, all the better."

Finally he was figuring it out. She was beginning to wonder . . .

"Do *you* know who I am?" she asked him. "I can't even manage to recall where I come from. Damn, but this is so frustrating!"

He didn't look very sympathetic, in fact looked downright glad to hear it. "I noticed the K.C. brand on your horse. That's a ranch over in East Texas. Might be, you could ask around if anyone knows you there."

She was amazed that he knew of the K.C. Ranch this far west. Thinking of the brand was actually nice detective work on his part. And for him to even mention it meant he *was* letting her go.

"That's an excellent idea. I never would have thought of it. But—just where is this ranch?"

"Over Waco way, I think. Never been that way myself, just heard tell of it 'cause it's a big un. Easiest just to take the train east."

"There's a train near here?"

"Oh, yes, and I'll be glad to put you on it," he assured her.

"How kind of you," she replied. "But shouldn't I see a doctor first?"

"Well, I dunno. Let me have a look-see at that head of yours."

He had pulled off the bandana before he had her permission and was lifting her hair out of the way—hair that had gotten stuck already. The new pain brought tears to her eyes, but she gritted her teeth and let him poke around for a minute.

"It could use a stitch or two, I suppose," he said. "Want me to fetch a needle?"

"It's actually that deep?"

"Well, no, but stitchin' never hurts."

Like hell it didn't. "I'll pass, thanks. But maybe some water to clean it up? And my saddlebags—I ought to have a change of clothes in them, don't you think?"

He was very cooperative, all things considered. And he did take her into Sanderson, straight to the train depot, where he bought her a ticket himself. She was hoping they'd have to wait for the train so she'd have time to figure out what she should do next, but no such luck; they were just in time for him to escort her right onto it. Why did she get the feeling she was being run out of town?

He left her with this parting advice: "If, that is, *when* your memory comes back, missy, do us both a favor and forget why you came to this part of the state. Be a shame if I still had to kill you."

It would also be a shame if *she* had to kill *him*.

In a roundabout way he'd saved her life—by deciding to spare it. But she *would* be back. Her job wasn't nearly done here. She'd just try to avoid Bucky, was all.

Chapter 34

*I*t had been days since he'd seen Casey. Damian had very quickly reached the point where if someone even looked at him wrong, he'd probably take the man's head off. He was completely frustrated in his inability to discover what had happened to Casey. It had taken him a day and a thorough search of Sanderson to finally realize that she might not have gotten up and left under her own steam. That last ambusher could have found her and carried her off.

Why, though? was the agonizing question that had run through his mind that entire sleepless first night. Had she walked off? Had she seen the gunman leaving and tried to follow him? Or had he followed her? Clearly both had left, since he'd found only his own horse around the area.

He'd quickly gone back to Sanderson and fetched the sheriff later that day. But the horse tracks had been impossible to follow: They crossed too many other tracks, ending that avenue of pursuit.

The sheriff claimed not to know either of the

dead men, and he flat out denied having any idea who the third man might be. Damian didn't know whether to believe him or not, though the man hedged enough for Damian to lean toward the "not." Yet there wasn't much he could do about that without any proof.

But that left him with only one alternative, to confront whoever had hired the ambushers. And he didn't doubt that the gunmen had been bought. Curruthers.

Within a day and a half he returned to Culthers, not bothering to stop for sleep. His pinto wasn't very appreciative, nor was his body, but he was too worried about Casey to be concerned with comfort.

He arrived in the middle of the night and went straight to the boardinghouse that Casey had stayed in, not because he thought she might be there, but because he figured the schoolteacher probably wouldn't be on Jack's payroll. A hotel clerk, in his opinion, was far less trustworthy.

Unfortunately, the landlady was difficult to rouse, nor was she very anxious to let him in at that hour. He had to give her a quick explanation of the events of the past few days before she would agree to offer him a room. Luckily, she detested Jack Curruthers.

Much as Damian wanted to immediately search out Curruthers or one of his buddies, he was about dead to the world and simply had to get a little sleep first. But he asked to be wakened at dawn, and the landlady obliged him. She also gave him the names of all the men who she knew worked for Jack, and the address of at least one, which was where Damian headed first.

He found Elroy Bencher still in bed at that early hour, and fast asleep, which had made getting into his house simple. The man actually left his doors unlocked and most of his windows open. And he was alone, fortunately. Damian didn't want to be scaring any women with what he was about to do—which was to beat the man senseless if he didn't get the answers he needed.

The landlady had failed to mention, though, how big Elroy was, and Damian hadn't really noticed when he'd last seen him, his full concentration having been on Jack at the time. But he noticed now, when he put the cold barrel of his rifle against Elroy's cheek before nudging him awake and the man sat up bare-chested and growling.

"Don't move too much, Elroy," Damian warned. "Or you might find your head traveling to the other side of the room without you."

Elroy squinted up at him. The sun was just barely rising, and the bedroom, located on the west side of the house, wasn't receiving much of its light yet, so his question was understandable.

"Who the hell are you?"

"Does the name Damian Rutledge sound familiar? I tried to arrest your boss, remember?"

"Oh, you," Elroy grunted. "Didn't expect you to be stupid enough to come back here."

"And I didn't expect you and your friends to be stupid enough to try and prevent me from returning. Sort of admits to guilt, doesn't it?"

"I don't know what you're talking about," Elroy said belligerently.

"Sure you do," Damian disagreed. "But if I have to spell it out, I will. I'm talking about the three men you sent to attack me and the kid on our way back here. Two of them are dead, by the way."

He noticed the tensing of those thick muscles at his added remark. And as far as he was concerned, that was all the confirmation of guilt he needed. But Elroy was determined to play dumb.

"You're crazy. Some no-account saddle-bums attack you and you blame it on Mr. Curruthers? Like he cares where you go or what you do? He's got nothing to fear from you, Rutledge. He's not the man you were looking for."

"No? Well, that's a moot point at the moment, because oddly enough, Elroy, all I want from you are the names of those men and where they lived. It's the one who's still alive that I want."

Elroy snorted. "Can't help you there, and wouldn't if I could. And you got your nerve, breaking into my house. We got laws in this town, you know."

"Do you? The sheriff in Jack's pocket, too?"

"Just get the hell outta here before I get annoyed," Elroy growled at him. "I ain't got no answers for you one way or the other."

"I disagree," Damian replied calmly. "And you *will* tell me what I want to know—one way or the other."

"Yeah?" Elroy smirked now. "And just how are you going to make me? You shoot off that rifle, you'll have the sheriff here arresting you,

U.S. marshal or not. So how do you plan to make me tell you, little man?"

Damian knew he was being deliberately goaded. Elroy was just itching to take him on; he could see it in his eyes. And although it had been many a year since he had enjoyed a good fistfight, one in which he didn't have to worry about breaking someone's nose, there was the possibility he might not win this one. But what the hell. *He'd* been itching to pound out his frustrations on someone, and at least Elroy Bencher promised a good fight, not one that would be over after just one good punch.

Damian stood his rifle against the table next to the bed and said, "Well, let's start with this, shall we?"

Amazing how his fist always managed to connect, but Elroy's nose was as susceptible as most were—breaking with one single punch. The big man howled, blood dripping onto his bare chest. In the next instant, he tried to bring Damian down by launching himself toward him. Not very wise, starting from a sitting position. Damian merely stepped back and Elroy's large frame ended up sprawled on the floor at his feet.

He should have kicked him while he was down, he really should have, but Damian's sense of fairness wouldn't let him. However, allowing Elroy to get to his feet was one of the bigger mistakes of his life. The man's fists were like solid steel hammers, and he had an incredible amount of strength backing each punch he landed. And he immediately started landing them far too frequently.

Damian managed to stay upright by dint of

will, despite the pounding he was taking. And he was still getting the occasional punch in, though they didn't seem to be doing much damage. A long fight? He was beginning to think it would never end. But then he got lucky . . .

A single punch managed to crack not one but two of Elroy's ribs on his right side, causing him to gasp with pain. From that point on, the man protected that side with his right arm. And either the pain was also affecting his left-handed blows, or he simply had a weak left-hand punch to begin with.

In a few more minutes, Elroy was back on the floor, and this time Damian wouldn't have hesitated to do some kicking, principles or no principles.

"Unless you want my foot coming down on those broken ribs, you'll give me the names I want."

Elroy did.

Chapter 35

❦

*I*t was the middle of the following afternoon by the time Damian reached Bucky Alcott's farmhouse outside Sanderson. To reach that town so quickly, he'd gone with very little sleep. The house was located about a mile out of town, just where Bencher had said it was.

There was the possibility that Alcott would recognize him right off, despite the bruises he was wearing on his face and his having one eye nearly swollen shut. But Damian didn't care.

Smoke coming out of the chimney indicated Alcott was home, so he simply rode up to the narrow front porch, dismounted, and knocked sharply on the door. If Bucky had seen him coming and fetched a gun, well, he guessed they'd be having a shoot-out. Damian would just have to make sure he didn't kill the man until he had his answers.

The door opened. The man standing there wasn't holding a gun. He was middle-aged, not very tall, but exceptionally thin. Brown hair that was fading and brown eyes went with a weathered face. And he had the peculiar bowed legs that some people developed from spending too much of their lives on the back of a horse.

He didn't recognize Damian either, at least not right off. Damian must have caught him cooking, because he was wearing a full-length chef's apron, seriously stained, and had smudges of flour on one cheek. He was also wiping flour from his hands on the lower half of the apron.

What Bucky did recognize, however, was an aggressively held rifle. He was frowning as he said, "It's bad manners to go knockin' on someone's door with a weapon in hand, mister. Gives the wrong impression in most cases."

"Not in this case," Damian replied, then asked, just to be sure, "Bucky Alcott?"

Bucky nodded, but his frown got much deeper as he inquired in turn, "Do I know you?"

"Since you tried to kill me a few days ago, I guess that qualifies as a yes, you do. Now, you tell me what happened to the kid before I—"

"Whoa, there!" Bucky exclaimed. "Someone's led you up the wrong creek. I got no idea—"

Damian backhanded the man, sending him sideways to trip over a crate of rubbish parked by the door. He moved into the room to stand over him, in no mood to deal with denials again before he got at the truth.

"My knuckles are sore from beating your name and address out of Elroy Bencher," he said, rubbing the scabs on those knuckles. "I really don't want to have to do the same with you—but I will if you insist."

"Now hold on there, mister," Bucky said, raising his hands defensively. "I don't know no El-roy Bencher. Whoever he is, sounds like he lied to you about me, just to tell you what you wanted to hear so you'd leave him alone. If you think about it, why would he tell you anythin', let alone the truth? Just 'cause you beat him up a bit?"

It sounded logical, too logical, and, dammit, too sincere as well. Damian was beginning to have some real doubts now. A harmless-looking middle-aged man like this, a hired killer? A man who was apparently very serious about his cooking, a hired killer?

The man was a farmer, for crying out loud. Damian had seen the barn as he rode up, the chicken coop next to it, the pigpens, though no nearby crops, but this *was* a farm. And Bencher, that belligerent bear, he *could* have lied there at the end, said anything just to get Damian to leave his house—and his broken ribs—alone.

Damian took a step back. If he'd been led wrong, and it looked like he had been, then he was seriously out of line here, having just accosted someone who appeared to be an innocent man.

He was about to apologize, and profusely at that, when he happened to glance down at that old crate of rubbish next to Bucky—and noticed a blue denim pant leg, splattered with blood, hanging out over the edge of the crate.

Casey's denim jeans . . .

His rifle came up immediately and aimed at Bucky's head. It was all he could do to keep from pulling the trigger right then and there, he was that furious over how easily he'd been gulled.

"Those are *her* clothes in that pile of rubbish you just fell over," he told the now cowering man. "You've got five seconds to tell me what the hell you were doing taking off her clothes. And then you'll tell me exactly where she is. If you even think about lying again, you'll be left here to rot—quite dead. One . . ."

"Wait! Wait! Okay, mister, I give up. It won't be the first time I didn't finish a job I got paid for. And considerin' I lost two good friends on this one, I don't feel a bit obliged to return the blood money."

"Two . . ."

"I didn't take her clothes off! Hell's fire, what kinda fella do you think I am?"

"Three . . ."

"Will you stop with the countin'? I'll tell you everything I know. I *helped* her, for cryin' out loud. I didn't want to kill no young un, even when I thought she was a he. I certainly don't kill no women."

Damian didn't lower his rifle yet. "And just how did you find out he was a she?" he asked doubtfully. "It's not something she goes around mentioning."

"The heck she didn't. She told me, and she was plumb indignant about it, too, for me callin' her a boy. That purely ticked her off."

"You're lying again . . ."

"I'm not, I tell you! It was like this. She got shot in the head. The wound wasn't all that bad, but because of it, her memory went fishin'. She couldn't rightly recall nothin' 'bout herself, and

I guess that included why she was pretendin' to be a boy."

Damian sighed at that point, his own suspicions confirmed. He lowered the rifle, then said, "She's really lost her memory?"

Bucky nodded, adding, "She was a mite upset about it, too. Understandable, though. Think I'd go crazy myself if I couldn't remember my own name."

"You said you helped her. How?"

"I was gonna try and talk her into leaving the area; that's why I brought her here. But when I figured out she didn't know why she'd been shot, well, I fetched her some clean clothes, helped her get all the blood off her head, and put her on the train headin' back east."

"What?!" Damian exclaimed incredulously. "What the hell did you do that for?"

" 'Cause it ain't safe for her around here. And 'cause she wanted to find out who she is."

Damian was about ready to shoot the man again, this time for his idiocy. "And how is she supposed to find out who she is on a damn train, not knowing where to go or who to talk to to ask?"

"Sheese, mister, I didn't send her off blind," Bucky said indignantly. "She's headin' over Waco way, to the K.C. Ranch. Her horse comes from there, leastways that's where it got its brand from. Figured someone there might remember her, or at least remember the horse, fine-lookin' as it is, and they'd be able to tell her who she is."

Very well, so the man wasn't a complete idiot, but still . . .

"It didn't occur to you that I could do that? After all, we *were* traveling together."

"Mister, with the kind of men that are after your head, I didn't figure you'd be alive long enough to help anyone. And I didn't want that little lady involved in the hornet's nest you stirred up. So I sent her lookin' for answers where she might find them and not get shot at in the process. And hopefully, if she gets her memory back, she'll be smart enough not to come back here."

Damian sighed. There was no point in berating the man further, when all he'd done was try to help her in the end. He couldn't have known that Casey's father had given her that horse, nor would she have had the memory to point that out. And there was no telling whom her father had bought the animal from, or how many owners it had passed through before that. Casey was off chasing needles in a haystack.

And all Damian could do was follow . . .

Chapter 36

~~~~~~~~~~~~~~~~~~~~~~~~~~

*I*t was a frustrating dilemma, whether to chase
down Casey immediately or finish with Curruthers first. Curruthers was only a day away,
just needed a final confrontation. But Casey,
there was no telling how long it would take
Damian to catch up with her.

And where would she go after she reached
Waco and found no help there? Would she even
think to come back to Sanderson to find her answers? Or had she lost her amazing deductive
reasoning along with her memory?

The train schedule decided the matter for him.
The next eastbound train due to depart Sanderson wouldn't be leaving for another four days.
Damian could finish his business here in that
amount of time. He could even catch up on
some much-needed sleep before heading north
to Culthers in the morning, which was what he
did.

He should have skipped the sleep, however.
Timing turned out to be more important than
he'd figured. If he had only gotten back to

Culthers a few hours sooner, he might have been able to prevent the gunfight he arrived to witness—and the all-out battle that followed . . .

Entering Barnet's Saloon in Culthers dressed as she was wasn't a good idea. So Casey waited, and sure enough, Jack and his *campaign crew* filed out of the saloon around lunchtime to head to the restaurant across the street.

A few minutes later, Casey entered the same establishment and took the table next to theirs. Only two of them even glanced her way when she came in, one dismissing her, the other showing some male interest. But they were too busy joking around and teasing the biggest member of their group about his busted nose and general sorry condition to pay her too much mind.

That had to be Elroy Bencher, the one who liked to throw his weight around. The teasing was understandable. He looked like he'd been stomped on by a horse and then stomped on some more. She couldn't imagine another man doing such damage to him, big as Bencher was, but one of his disgruntled remarks led her to change her mind.

"Least I gave as good as I got. He ain't lookin' too pretty now either. If I hadn't tripped and broke my ribs, he wouldn't be a problem no more."

Which led Casey to wonder if they might be talking about Damian . . .

After stopping the train that Bucky had put her on, much to the engineer's chagrin, she'd come straight back here, hoping this was where Damian would have headed. And he *had* been here, according to Larissa the schoolmarm. Thank goodness. Her largest fear had been put to rest—he hadn't died that day. But he'd already left Culthers again, looking for her. It sounded like they had missed each other by only a few hours.

But she was sure he'd return, and in the meantime, she had decided to see what else she could discover about Jack Curruthers. The plan, hasty and not well considered, she had to admit, was to see if she could get to know the want-to-be mayor on a personal level, and the quickest way to do that was as a woman.

She had Larissa to thank for the clothes she was wearing. She'd bought the schoolteacher's last unaltered outfit from back East, one the woman claimed was too fancy for these parts anyway. An abundance of lace and bows wasn't Casey's style, but was suitable for her purpose, which was to look as different from the *kid* as possible.

After a few more minutes, she managed to catch Jack's eye and smiled at him. That was all it took to gain his full attention. He wasn't exactly a ladies' man, after all, being too short, too nondescript in his looks, and he was twice her age as well, so it wasn't surprising that it took only a coy smile from a young woman to lure him over to introduce himself.

"You're new to our fair town," he said after tossing out his name and pulling up the chair next to her without waiting for an invite. "Just visiting?"

She nodded, aware that his men were also paying her much more attention now, which wasn't what she had intended. Too many eyes on her, and at least one pair was bound to see a resemblance to Damian's sidekick.

"You look somewhat familiar," Jack remarked thoughtfully, making her groan inwardly. His eyes hadn't been the ones she had figured would be that discerning. "Have we met somewhere else, perhaps?"

"Well, I am widely traveled, at least here in Texas. You?"

"Very."

"I've stayed in San Antonio recently, as well as Fort Worth," she told him.

Those two names had him frowning. She knew she was pushing it, mentioning towns that Henry—or Jack himself—had passed through, so she quickly added, "And Waco. Now *there* is a lovely town."

"Well, it doesn't matter if I've seen you before, because I'm sure we haven't actually met. That I would remember. And your name, ma'am?"

"Jane" was the easiest name that came to mind, and she grabbed a last name from the condiments before her on the table. "Peppers."

"And who is it that has the pleasure of your company while you're here?"

"I beg your pardon?"

"Who exactly are you visiting here?" he clarified.

"Oh, Larissa Amery. You must know her, since she's Culthers's only schoolteacher right now. We went to school together, and haven't seen each other for the longest time, so I figured we were due for a visit."

"You're from the East as she is, then?" He was frowning again. "Strange, but your accent is distinctly Western—Texas, to be exact."

"Well, I should hope so. I *was* born and raised here. I merely finished my schooling in the East. But since you mention it, you sound like an Easterner yourself. So you're fairly new to Texas?"

"Let's not talk about me, Miss Peppers. I'm much more interested in you."

That had been said to flatter her, but all it did was have her mumbling mentally. This was turning out to be a bad idea, after all. He wasn't stupid enough to let something slip, especially to a new acquaintance. And two of his men at the next table were watching her like hawks. She was wondering what excuse to use to get up and leave when Jed did the getting up and came over to whisper in Jack's ear.

The little man shot to his feet immediately, bellowing obscenities. Casey didn't have to wonder why as she caught the look of outrage that he turned on her. She stood up. It was automatic to reach for her gun—which wasn't there.

She did have a gun, though, in her large reticule, one she had bought as soon as she got to town, since her holster had been empty the day Bucky had carted her off. Her holster was in there, too. The problem was, how could she get to it now.

But none of the six men were wearing guns either. And this was a public place they were in. There were other customers present, employees—witnesses. Running for public office, Jack wasn't going to do anything stupid like have her killed on the spot. His style was to send out lackeys to do his killing, and in less than honorable ways—just as Henry had done with Damian's father.

So Casey tried extricating herself from the confrontation. After all, Jack hadn't revealed anything to her. No harm had been done. Just because six men were all looking as if they'd like to get their hands around her neck didn't mean she really had anything to worry about.

"I believe I've lost my appetite," she said as she reached down for her reticule.

A hand clamped to her arm, preventing her from getting it. "You've got some nerve, lady," Jed said. It was his hand, and he wasn't letting go.

"Really?" Casey replied. "And here I thought I was just hungry, and this was a likely place to find some vittles. Or is there a law against having lunch in this town that I wasn't aware of?"

"Lippy-mouthed—"

"That's funny—"

Jack cut off the comments of his men with a whispered hiss. "I know exactly what you tried to do, girlie, and that *is* a crime in my book."

He then glanced at Jed, and Casey didn't need much intelligence to interpret that look. It plainly said, Take care of her and see to it personally this time. When she felt the pressure on her arm change, as if she were about to be dragged out of there, Casey figured she'd better start worrying—and change her tactics.

So she blurted out, "Okay, which one of you is going to take me on?"

"Take you on?" It was Jed who asked, giving her a blank look.

"In a fair fight," Casey clarified.

Elroy smirked. "I will."

"In a fair *gun*fight," Casey clarified further. "Or are you all too cowardly for that?"

There was a chuckle before someone said, "Don't think she knows who she's dealing with."

"Oh, I do indeed," Casey replied contemptuously. "Ambushing is more your style."

That remark produced a few red faces. Then the one sucking on a candy jawbreaker said quietly, "I'll take her on."

"No, I want to," the youngest among them put in eagerly. "Let me, Jed. I don't mind killin' no woman—if she is a woman," he said with a derisive sweep of his eyes down her body. But then he continued with a chuckle. "Guess the undertaker will find out for sure afterwards, won't he?"

"Just take it out into the street," Jack said fastidiously. "Gunsmoke lingers, and I'd just as soon not smell it while I'm eating."

Chapter 37

They'd marched her back over to the saloon, where with a single word the bartender had reached down and started piling weapons on top of his bar. Their weapons. So they'd never really been without them, just didn't wear them handy, probably for political reasons.

It had been decided that Mason would face her. Jed's younger brother was pouting over being passed over, and had nearly gotten backhanded for complaining. But Jed wasn't taking chances here. He wanted his fastest gun.

They all strapped on their guns, though, making Casey wonder just how fair a fight it was going to be. They even offered her a weapon. She wouldn't have been surprised if it didn't have a single bullet in it. She declined, of course, and retrieved her own.

She would have liked to have time to change her clothes, but didn't think she'd get any approval if she asked. It just felt . . . odd, strapping on her gun belt over such a fancy dress. The snickers she was receiving weren't at all surprising. Not one of these men expected her to know much about guns. They were expecting an outright slaughter—hers.

Back outside, Casey moved down into the middle of the street. Mason was the last to leave the saloon. He was a tall, slim man, with black hair floating about his narrow shoulders and a very neat, trimmed beard. He'd removed his coat, despite the chill of that October day. Underneath was an embroidered silk vest that went with his business suit. He looked about as unusual with his double-holstered gun belt as she did. Nothing like looking civilized and uncivilized at one and the same time.

The street had been cleared immediately, as if the townsfolk knew what to expect. Just having Jack's bunch step out wearing their guns had seen to that. Made Casey wonder how much blood had been spilled outside Barnet's since Jack had arrived in Culthers.

Her father would blister her hide if he ever heard about this. Capturing outlaws was one thing. Chandos had taught her long ago about the element of surprise, and she had made good use of that knowledge in her bounty-hunting career. She didn't give outlaws a chance to draw on her, and even if they did, her weapon would already be out, already be in command of the situation.

This was entirely different, standing there facing someone, giving him the opportunity to draw on her. She was fast with her draw. She was also very accurate with her aim. But still, timing would be everything here, and it was downright disconcerting, knowing that. And

Bucky and his friends had said Mason was fast . . .

Her palms were actually beginning to sweat. To have suggested this had been real stupid on her part. She could have thought of some other way to get out of that restaurant in one piece—if she'd had more time to think on it. She could even have started screaming, playing the threatened female. Someone might have come to her defense—and gotten himself killed as well. No . . . but damn, she had the feeling she was going to die.

And Mason, he looked as calm as it was possible to be. *He* was used to this sort of thing. Casey didn't look nervous either, but then, she was drawing on inner resources so she wouldn't show what she was feeling. She was, in fact, as nervous as she'd ever been in her life.

She watched Mason's eyes, cold, impartial. He didn't mind killing folks, didn't mind killing her either. It took a certain kind of man to be that way, the kind she didn't care to get to know. Then suddenly it was happening and she didn't have time to think about it anymore, just reacted naturally as she'd been taught to do.

And she had to allow that she'd been taught well. She was still standing. Mason was falling. She was so surprised over that, she didn't notice Jethro drawing his gun on her. A rifle cracked to her left. Jethro's gun hand was hit. He started screaming. Other weapons were quickly drawn to retaliate.

Casey hit the dirt and rolled before she fired off another shot. And now other bullets besides those coming from the rifle were peppering the street and the front of the saloon, forcing everyone to run for cover, though the shots weren't hitting anywhere near where Casey was lying. She couldn't see where they were coming from either, but obviously, someone else in this town didn't take kindly to Jed and his boys ganging up on a woman.

She wasn't going to lie in the open with her frilly dress all bunched up, just asking for a bullet. Fortunately, the rifle was giving her plenty of opportunity to get up and get moving, which she did, dashing toward the restaurant. Once stationed next to the door inside, she returned the favor, and in another moment, Damian was there glowering at her.

"Not now," she said, knowing he was just dying to lay into her, he looked so furious.

The window shattering next to them must have encouraged him to agree, because he moved over to it and started firing off his rifle again. Now that she had a chance to actually look at the scene outside, she saw that Elroy Bencher hadn't made it to cover in time, probably because of his broken ribs. He'd taken a bullet in one knee and was curled up in a ball on the porch of the saloon, moaning something terrible.

Candiman was lying across the steps. He looked a mite dead. Mason was still in the street, unmoving, dead or not, Casey didn't particularly care at the moment. The other three had managed to get inside the saloon, and at least one was firing from behind the door.

"I take it you've recovered your memory?" Damian asked between shots.

"Never lost it."

He snorted. "Just what did you think you were doing out there?"

So he wasn't going to wait? "I didn't go issuing challenges, if that's what you're thinking. I just figured since I had time to kill, waiting for you to show up, I'd try to get Jack to open up a little. Men are known to do a certain amount of bragging when women are around, and I don't exactly look the same in this outfit."

"You really thought they wouldn't recognize you?" He shot her an incredulous look.

She managed to keep from squirming. "Well, they weren't exactly paying attention to me that day you first confronted Jack. You announce that you're arresting their money supply, and every eye in that saloon went to you and stayed on you. I was simply a no-account kid who happened to be at your side. So yes, I didn't think they'd recognize me, and they didn't—least not at first. And the rest you can imagine. Jack realized I was trying to trick secrets out of him and took exception."

He said no more on the subject—for the moment. But after firing a couple more shots out the window, he did glance her way again. "You—uh—you look very pretty in that dress, by the way," he remarked.

Casey snorted this time. "Bows! It figures you'd like silly bows."

"Excuse me? I give you a compliment and you snap my head off?"

"No, I'm feeling like ten kinds of a fool, that's why I'm snapping your head off. And you wouldn't happen to have any extra bullets, would you?" she asked after loading the last from her gun belt.

A box of bullets came sliding toward her from the back of the restaurant, compliments of a very frightened cook. Her own weapon came sliding toward her from Damian's direction. Well, hell, with this extra firepower, she started thinking about ending this thing for good.

"Maybe one of us should try to get in the back of the saloon," she suggested to Damian as she stuck the extra gun and bullets in her reticule, which was slung over her shoulder to keep it handy but out of the way. "Before they think about leaving from it."

"One of us, as in you? Forget it. And I'm not letting you out of my sight, so forget that, too. Where the hell's the sheriff when you need him?"

"Conveniently gone fishing, probably. But they felt no qualms about pulling an unfair gun-fight, so I'd say if he was here, he'd be shooting from their side. It's just as well if he doesn't show up."

"A moot point."

"Why?"

"Because I just saw one of them dash across the back of that alley next to the saloon. Looks like they're leaving after all."

Casey peered across the street again. She fired off another shot, waited, but there was no return fire this time.

"Only one?" She frowned.

"I barely noticed that one. The other two could have crossed already."

Casey nodded. "I'm not going to step out

there to make sure. How about we head out the back ourselves and see if we can cut them off at the stable?"

"Now *that* I'll agree to. Come on."

The stable was about a block and a half away. Taking the back-street approach when there wasn't a back street required hopping a few fences. At least Damian did some hopping. Casey got lifted over any obstacles that got in their way, and, after the first such unasked-for help, didn't bother complaining again. If she was going to wear a dress, then she would damn well be treated like someone wearing a dress, he told her.

Particulars—from a man still furious about coming into town and finding her in the middle of a gunfight. She wasn't dumb enough to argue, though—at least not now. But later, she'd be sure to mention to him that wearing a dress did *not* define a person or her capabilities. Hadn't she left home to prove that very point?

The stable was, fortunately, on their side of the street. The back of it was fenced off for an exercising corral, but was still the easier path to enter without getting shot right off. That is, if Jack and the two Paisley brothers had arrived there yet—and if that *was* their destination. Which didn't seem to be the case. The stable owner was slowly pitching hay into a nearby stall.

But at second glance, the man looked a mite nervous, too nervous considering he didn't know why they were there. They might have their weapons out and ready, but neither was pointed at him . . .

Casey tried to grab Damian's arm to stop him from proceeding further, but he'd stepped too far in front of her. And quicker than giving him a warning, she threw herself at him, knocking them both to the ground—just as the shot was fired.

The stable owner ran, yelling, out the wide-open front entrance. Damian rolled to his left before firing off a shot, at nothing in particular, since he didn't have a visible target yet. Unfortunately, Casey rolled in the opposite direction at exactly the same time, and right within Jack Curruthers's reach.

A gun nozzle pressed into her neck, while "Drop it" was hissed in her ear.

Dropping her gun went against every instinct she had, but she couldn't think of any way to keep it and stay alive. She dropped it, and was assisted to her feet none too carefully, Jack having more strength than one would imagine for such a little man.

"Back off, Rutledge, or the little lady gets it right now," Damian was warned. "We'll be taking her with us for insurance. You follow, she dies—simple as that."

Damian just stared at them, probably trying to figure out a way to shoot Jack without hitting her instead. But it wasn't going to happen, not when she was a bit taller than the target and he was doing a good job of hiding behind her. She was about to try dropping to the ground again to give Damian his shot, but the Paisley brothers came out in the open just then, and with Jed's weapon aimed directly at Damian, *she* wasn't taking any chances.

Damian was pretty much rendered harmless if he wanted to preserve her life, and they knew it. They didn't even ask him to disarm, they were that confident he wouldn't interfere now. And he didn't.

She rode out of there doubled up on Jack's horse, sitting in front of him with his gun still pressed hard against her. Things didn't look very promising at the moment—for her anyway. In fact, she wondered how long it would be before Jack decided he didn't need her for insurance purposes any longer and pulled the trigger.

Chapter 38

*T*he little cabin must have been a regular hideout, because they rode directly to it. At least that was Casey's first thought when she was taken inside and thrown into a corner. The place didn't look lived in; in fact, it contained a serious coat of dust over everything. Yet she soon saw that the room was also well stocked with canned goods that had been stashed under a loose board in the floor. There were blankets in that rather large storage hole as well, and a small crate of extra guns and ammunition.

A place prepared in advance to hole up for a last stand? It looked like something Jed would have a use for, considering his line of work, but Jack?

Casey, sitting in the corner and keeping her mouth shut for the time being, wasn't feeling as dejected as she'd felt earlier. It had taken about four hours to reach the cabin, and once she'd finally remembered that she still had that borrowed reticule hanging from her shoulder, her whole perspective had changed.

The men weren't the least bit worried about the bag she was carrying, weren't going to bother taking it away from her, because they'd already searched through it back in the saloon and had found only the one weapon in it—which had been left behind in the stable on Jack's orders. They had no way of knowing that between the saloon and the stable, she'd gotten another weapon and still had it.

She just needed to bide her time until they stopped paying such close attention to her. And that ought to be soon, with the dinner hour approaching.

So she was not pleased to hear Jed order his brother, "Don't take your eyes off of her."

Jethro had been busy rewrapping his still bleeding hand with the same bloody cloth, so the sour look he gave Jed was understandable. "I still don't know why you didn't just kill that marshal while you had the chance. Then you wouldn't need to worry 'bout him following, or keeping her around in case he does."

"Idiot, you don't kill a U.S. deputy marshal, at least not when there's a town full of witnesses, unless you want thirty more to come knocking on your door" was Jed's sharp reply. "They seem to take it personal when you kill one of theirs. Might as well call yourself dead."

"I'm not sure he really is a marshal," Jack put in in a tired voice. The little man wasn't used to the hard riding they'd just done. "He comes from upper-crust New York society, and is rich to boot. It's ludicrous for someone like that to become a lawman."

"We've already been over this, Jack. He could

have got the badge *just* to hunt you down. So whether it was a convenient lie or the truth, I'm not taking any chances. You want him dead, you do it when there are no witnesses. Hopefully, he'll show up here and we can end it."

Casey just loved the way she was being put in the "no witness" category. Of course, that simply meant that once they were done using her as a shield against Damian, she'd be as dead as they planned to make him. Not that she was going to let things progress that far. Funny, though, how Damian's little lie about being a U.S. deputy was all that had kept him from being killed in the stable today. And she wasn't about to point out that it was a lie.

She hadn't missed the significance of Jack's words. For him to know that Damian was a rich society Easterner, when Damian had never mentioned any such thing to him, pretty much confirmed that either Jack was Henry and knew Damian personally, or Henry had very recently confessed everything to his brother. She would have bet it was the former, except for one little glitch. Jack really didn't add up to everything she'd been told about Henry. People *could* change, she supposed, but this much?

She decided to find out the truth. After all, Jack had no reason to stick to his original story at this point. He was on the run again. It would take some rather far-fetched excuses to explain away what had happened in the street today, which meant he could pretty much forget about becoming mayor of Culthers. And since he fully expected to kill her before this was over, he had no reason to maintain his secrets.

So she asked him right out, without wasting breath leading into the subject, "Which is it, Curruthers? Are you Jack—or Henry?"

He turned his owlish eyes on her and said derisively, "I would think you'd be scared enough to keep your mouth shut, little lady. What is someone like you doing with that Easterner anyway?"

"I'll be glad to answer your questions just as soon as you answer mine."

He snorted, but then he shrugged. "You want your morbid curiosity appeased? Very well, Henry's dead. He's been dead about a year now."

That wasn't exactly what Casey was expecting to hear, but did he mean that figuratively or literally? Before she asked for clarification, though, something else occurred to her that was even more pertinent.

"You killed him, didn't you?"

Another shrug. "In a manner of speaking. I'd gone home for a visit, figured it was time after all these years. We got into a fight, he tripped and hit his head. It was an accident, but one that didn't bother me much."

"And you didn't tell anyone, did you?"

"What for? So I'd get blamed for it? I don't think so. Besides, old Henry wasn't missed at all," Jack added with a smirk.

It was his smug, self-congratulatory look that made it all click together in her mind. "You pretended to be Henry, even at his job."

Jack chuckled. "And why not? I don't know much about numbers, except to make them work in my favor. I was already there. It was an easy way to make the trip profitable. And it wasn't as if that company couldn't afford a few losses. Old Man Rutledge had already made his fortune. The fool should have kept his nose out of the books, though. I was getting ready to quit the city when he started nosing around and demanding explanations."

"Then why didn't you just leave if you were already planning to? Why kill him first?"

"Because some of those questions he was asking were too personal. It's easy to pretend to be a weakling like my brother was, harder to try the reverse. But I guess I wasn't that good at it," he concluded with a chuckle.

"Meaning?"

"Meaning Rutledge was suspicious of my behavior, probably because I just didn't bow down enough to him like my brother would have," Jack replied derisively. "Because he had his doubts about me, it wouldn't have been hard for him to question my aunt and find out that Henry's twin had recently come to town for a visit."

"That wouldn't have been hard for anyone to do," she pointed out.

"Yes, but only the old man suspected something wasn't quite right with Henry. Why would anyone else ask about a twin? They wouldn't have a reason to, now would they? No, the plan was, Henry would get blamed and be the one hunted down, not me. So the old man had to die, to keep it that way. And it would have stayed that way if Rutledge's son wasn't so hellbent on revenge."

"Revenge?" she questioned. "How about simple justice? You killed the man's father. Maybe some folks would just shrug that off and figure they can't do anything about it, but then again, some won't."

"It was set up to look like he took his own life!" Jack complained heatedly. "That should have damn well been the end of it."

"Unless someone knows the victim well enough to know they wouldn't kill themselves. But I guess you didn't take that into account, did you? And by the way, why didn't you do the actual killing yourself instead of paying to have it done? Simply because Henry wouldn't have?"

"Well, there was that," Jack said with still another shrug. "But there was also the fact that Old Man Rutledge was a huge son of a bitch, just like his son. To have it look like a suicide required some brute strength, not something I could have handled alone. Now it's your turn. What are you doing tagging along with Rutledge, aside from keeping his bed warm?"

It was beyond annoying, how so many men jumped to assumptions like that, refusing to admit that some women might have capabilities other than cook, breeder, and bed warmer. That perhaps some women might be able to do what men could do, possibly just as well or even better. They couldn't accept it, much less allow women to prove it.

Casey's resentment had her pointing out, "I outdrew your fast gun, that maybe give you a clue? I'm the one who tracked you down, Jack. Got offered a nice ten thousand to do it, too. And someone with *half* my tracking know-how

could have done the same. You don't cover your
trail very well, Jack."

Her effort to belittle him resulted in the expected glower. "Maybe I won't kill you after all,
little lady. I might keep you around for a while,
for what you're really good for."

"Come anywhere near me and I'll show you
how the Comanches deal with scum," she shot
back. " 'Course, you don't have much hair to
work with, so it might be a bit painful."

Heat suffused his face as his scowl grew
darker. Jed's busting out laughing might have
been responsible for some of Jack's present anger, though.

"What the hell did she mean by that?" he demanded of his lackey.

"The way she talks, Jack, I get the impression
she's learned stuff from an Indian along the
way. They always were the best trackers around.
So she's probably not kidding about the scalping
part." Jed let out another chuckle. "Wouldn't be
surprised if she knows how to skin in less time
than it takes to spit."

"I need a doctor, Jed," Jethro interrupted at
that point in a whining tone. "This hand won't
stop bleeding, and I'm getting dizzy."

"Lay down, Jeth, and get some rest," his
brother told him with very little actual concern.
"I'll wake you later for the third watch."

"Get a fire started and I'll get that blood
stopped," Casey offered.

Jethro paled, but Jed laughed again. "Yep, definitely some Indian training there."

She shrugged indifferently. She'd made the
offer only because it *would* be painful, cauteriz-

ing the wound, and the boy didn't look like he had much tolerance for pain. He might faint, and one less pair of eyes to watch her every little move was what she needed if she was going to manage to get herself out of this cabin in at least a breathing condition.

Chapter 39

*I*t was becoming dark real fast, too fast. Jethro had lain down as suggested on one of the bare mattresses in the room—there were several pushed up against the walls. It was doubtful, however, that the pain in his hand was allowing him to sleep, though he was trying.

Jack was sitting at the only table in the one-room cabin and had taken over the task of keeping an eye on Casey, while Jed piddled around getting a fire started and opening up several of the canned goods. These he was apparently offering still cold, since he did no more than shove an open can at Jack, who ignored it for the moment.

No food was offered to Casey, but then, she was too tense to eat anything anyway, so she hardly noticed the significant slight. Why waste food on someone you had every intention of killing, after all?

She was still biding her time, though she didn't have all that much left. She had considered removing her empty gun belt to put it away, using that as an excuse to open her reticule and get at the gun inside. But the problem with that meant the action would have to be immediate. In other words, she'd have to bring the gun right out and start using it.

They knew, or rather thought, that she had nothing else in her bag, so there was no reason for her to rummage around in it. Yet she needed at least a few moments to check how many bullets were actually in the gun, which she foolishly hadn't done before putting it away, and she couldn't remember how many were left after the last time she'd used it.

If the gun was empty, she'd be getting herself killed real quick no matter what she attempted. If only one or two bullets were left, she'd have to do some serious threatening and make sure these men believed her, to keep from having to use the ammunition. But if she had at least three bullets left, which was what she was hoping was the case, then she'd have no problem if they insisted on shooting it out with her instead of surrendering. She'd be prepared for either of those possibilities.

But she needed to do something pretty fast, because she was afraid Damian was going to show up, just as they were hoping he would. And if they even suspected that he was within hearing distance, they could and would use her to bring him out in the open so they could kill him. And he could be out there already.

Even if he hadn't seen in which direction they'd headed upon leaving town, with the little she'd shown him about tracking, he should have been able to find the cabin before dark. If he was out there, then he was wisely waiting for full dark, which was just a matter of minutes away.

What worried her the most, however, was *what* he would do when he made his move. He didn't have very many options, after all, and trying to parley with these fellows would be the worst of them.

The cabin had windows, but those had been boarded up at some point. And the door had one of those old wooden-plank locks, which had been lowered firmly into place and would take more than a few attempts to break through. There was no easy way to get into the cabin or to see inside it beforehand. All of which put the safest and easiest way out of this on Casey's shoulders.

Jed was the only one she really had to worry about. Jack had a gun, but whether he was any good with it was questionable. And young Jethro wouldn't be using his right hand for quite some time. The odds were far against his being able to use his left hand with any accuracy, so he was the last she needed to be concerned with.

Actually, now that she considered it, one bullet was all she would really need. If she got Jed out of the picture, the other two men would be manageable, at least long enough for her to retrieve Jed's gun, which she'd already seen him reload. Besides, she didn't want to kill Jack. If at all possible, she wanted Damian to have the satisfaction of bringing him to justice.

And she had to have at least one bullet in the gun. Damian wouldn't have slid her a completely empty gun when she'd asked for bullets, now would he? So there was no reason, really, to wait any longer.

Jack was even being cooperative—in a sense. He was staring right at her, but actually, he didn't appear to be *seeing* her. His mind seemed to be elsewhere, no doubt worrying over his present predicament just as she was, so it was possible that he wouldn't notice what she was doing until it was too late.

Casey made her move. And she didn't bother with the removal-of-the-gun-belt plan that she had worried over. The long-strapped reticule was resting on the floor by her right hip. She simply lifted her knees so her skirt partially hid it from view and her hand inched toward it, also concealed by her skirt. In another moment she had the gun in her hand and was leaping to her feet.

Unfortunately, even with her weapon aimed right at Jed, who had immediately glanced her way with a "What the hell?" he still reached for his own weapon. She didn't have time to waste on scrupulous morals this once. He was drawing to kill. She aimed for his heart and pulled the trigger—and felt as if her own heart had just stopped when she heard the soft click of an empty chamber.

Death. She was looking it in the face once again. And when she heard the resounding blast of Jed's gun . . . but it wasn't his gun that had made the sound that had drained all the blood from her face. It was the door crashing open, and not after several attempts as Casey had thought it would take, but in one solid heave. God love him, again she had forgotten to give extra credit to Damian's huge size and strength. He came in with his rifle in one hand and his finger already on the trigger.

Jed had barely turned in Damian's direction when the rifle shot, at such close range, lifted him completely off his feet and slammed him into the wall behind him. Jethro sat up, terrified and enraged at the same time, when he saw his brother's dead body slumped against the wall. He didn't have a weapon handy though— hadn't been smart enough to take one to bed with him—but Casey, being nearest to him, did—an empty gun still had some uses. She slammed it against the back of his head.

Jack, however, was digging in his pocket for his gun as well. He didn't have much choice, life in prison or taking Damian down first.

Which choice Damian would prefer Jack make, Casey wasn't sure, but he did attempt to get Jack to halt all movement by aiming the rifle directly at his head. "It's not pretty, what a bullet from a weapon like this can do to someone's face," he explained. "Of course, that someone won't care much afterward . . ."

Jack decided prison might be a better option, after all. He froze completely. Casey moved over and retrieved the gun in his coat pocket, a small derringer.

They had done it, or at least Damian had done it, gotten them both out of this dilemma and without bloodshed—theirs anyway. Her first instinct was to throw herself at Damian and kiss the hell out of him, but, of course, that was out of the question. First of all, he still needed to keep his attention on both Jack and Jethro. So she resorted to her second instinct.

"What took you so long?" she demanded in a tone about as grumpy as it could get.

He gave her only a brief, surprised glance before he answered in a sarcastic tone, nearly as surly as hers. "Nice to see you, too, Kid. Is there any rope around here to tie these two up with?"

"Probably not, but I've got lots of useless petticoats under this skirt that will make do."

That was said just as caustically, yet it had the opposite effect on Damian. It made him smile. Probably because he knew she'd rather be in her jeans than in a confining dress, which she was stuck with for the time being.

She didn't resent his humor—well, yes, she did—but she didn't remark on it. She got busy looking for some rope instead. She didn't find any even after locating a small shed out back that contained odds and ends, but a knife made quick work of her petticoats, and the tough cotton did serve just as well as a rope.

It was a few hours after dark by then, and Casey had no desire to spend the rest of the night in that cabin, nor was she the least bit tired. Her adrenaline was still flowing, in fact, though she couldn't imagine why, now that they were safe. So she suggested they head back to Culthers immediately, and Damian agreed.

Jed was rolled up in a blanket and tied to the back of his horse. The other two men were left outside, fully trussed up and gagged—they weren't going to be making any plans they could discuss together if they got left alone. They did get left alone when Damian went into the cabin one final time to put out the fire.

Casey wasn't sure why she followed him, but she did. And then she kind of figured out why her blood was still pumping so strongly.

"I thought you were going to die today," Damian said when he turned and found her behind him.

"So did I," Casey replied in a small voice.

And then he yanked her to him and was kissing her in the way she'd wanted to kiss him earlier. So he felt it, too? A need to reaffirm life after thinking more than once today that they were each not going to see another sunrise? And damn, it was a powerful need. It didn't matter that there was blood on the floor, or that there was no sheet on the bare mattress that he lowered her to, or that Jed and Jethro had been dumped on the ground outside. For her, all that mattered was the contact with someone she cared about—and the blazing desire that sprang immediately to life and blocked out every other thought.

He didn't undress her, there was too much urgency for that; just raised her skirt and ripped off her drawers, probably not intentionally—the thin material simply didn't withstand his strong tug. But she didn't even notice until later. All she noticed at the moment was the welcoming taste of him as he continued to devour her mouth with his, and the incredible pleasure as he entered her.

Such a feeling of rightness, as if she had been missing something intangible but was now whole again. And the passion flared brighter. Yet it was over too quickly. It was almost immediate, the swift climb and then the soaring burst of ecstasy. Yet it was more intense than before, more wildly satisfying in a different way as well. And such peace settled over her afterward.

It *was* something she had needed, apparently, and needed very badly. It was just a singular, blaring misfortune that she was afraid Damian was the only one she'd ever experience it with. Had she admitted she cared about him? Dammit all, she cared too much.

Chapter 40

A bright, nearly full moon allowed them a quick ride back to Culthers. It was still deep in the middle of the night when they arrived, the town silent, only a few dogs barking to note their passing. Casey was definitely feeling exhausted by then and suggested they head for the boardinghouse, where the prisoners could be tucked behind a locked door until morning, when she and Damian could decide what to do with them.

Damian nodded in agreement, but said, "There's only one decision to make—what to do with young Paisley. Jack will be returning with me to New York to stand trial."

She had expected as much, but then, they hadn't spoken since leaving the cabin, had merely concentrated on getting the horses back to town without any coming up lame. They hadn't spoken of what had happened in the cabin either, but what was there to say, really, about that? That it shouldn't have happened, sure. That it had been beneficial, sure. That it wasn't going to happen again, sure. None of which could be said without embarrassing them both.

But it was safe to speak of anything else. Casey waited until they had put Jack and Paisley in Larissa's lockable storeroom at the boardinghouse. They'd had to promise the schoolteacher a full accounting in the morning before she'd taken herself back to bed.

On the way up the stairs to their respective beds, Casey finally told him, "I didn't get around to mentioning it, but Jack definitely isn't Henry."

That, of course, stopped Damian cold. "You're saying this isn't over yet?"

"Sorry, I didn't mean to imply that. You've got the right man; it just wasn't Henry to begin with. The way Jack told it, Henry died in a fight they had, *accidentally*, though Jack didn't have much remorse over it. Jack had gone back to New York to visit his family, and with Henry dying, he decided to make it a profitable trip by assuming Henry's identity and his job—just long enough to steal that money from your company."

"But why kill my father if all he is is a thief?" Damian demanded.

"I guess your father knew Henry better than most. Jack said he was starting to notice that Henry was acting—well, strange, you could call it. Jack didn't do such a good job of pretending, I guess. Your father was starting to ask questions. His suspicions were becoming obvious to Jack. You can figure out the rest."

"So if my father hadn't noticed anything

wrong with Jack's performance, he'd still be alive?"

"That's the gist of it. Jack wanted Henry to take the full blame for the theft, and, of course, Henry would never be found because he was already dead and disposed of. And Jack, unknown to anyone except his aunt, wouldn't be the one anyone looked for. It was a foul, though logical, plan, if you think about it. But Jack got worried there at the end that your father, already suspicious, might question his aunt and find out that Henry had a twin, one who had recently been in the city. That would have been all it took to point the finger at the true culprit."

Damian sighed. "So now I could wish that my father hadn't been quite so discerning."

"You could, but there's no point, is there? It happened, and now you have the man responsible for it. Justice will at least be served."

"Yes, small consolation, but better than none at all," Damian replied.

Casey nodded and continued up the stairs. But once at her door, she decided to bring up a different subject, and spoke in a somewhat disgruntled tone. "By the way, the next time you toss me an empty gun, how about letting me know that it's empty? I came within seconds of dying because I shot Jed without a bullet to back it up."

"I'm sorry," he said, his face reddening. "You know handguns aren't my area of expertise. I never even thought to check to see if the gun was empty or not. You asked for bullets. Those you got, a whole boxful. I figured you might like to have an extra gun handy, is all."

She blushed, after that explanation, which put the fault back in her corner. She could have taken an extra moment in the restaurant to load the darn thing.

"It doesn't matter now." And then she admitted, "But your timing was excellent, if you didn't notice. You saved my life in that cabin, Damian. Thank you for that."

"Now that's the last thing you have to thank me for," he replied with a half smile.

But then he was suddenly staring at her with that piercing look of his that could make her so flustered inside. She probably ought to mention to him that she had—feelings—for him, if he hadn't already figured that out. She just couldn't see what difference it would make, though. He still wouldn't want to stay married to her. He still wouldn't want someone like her for his wife. And she was going to get choked up if she continued to think about it.

So with a quick "G'night," she entered her room and closed the door, then stumbled in the dark toward the bed and fell on it. Tears had already sprung to her eyes.

There was very little left to do, to finish up the job she'd been hired for. Actually, her part of it was done. As soon as she was paid, she'd have no reason not to tell Damian good-bye. And that thought was tearing her up inside something fierce.

Out in the hall, Damian stared at the closed door for a long moment, debating whether to knock and get Casey back out there. He even raised his hand halfway, then slowly lowered it.

Again, she was acting as if they hadn't made love, hadn't shared that intense intimacy. She avoided meeting his eyes. Was she that ashamed of what they'd done? Or was it more that she was just ashamed that she'd shared intimacy with him in particular?

That idea hadn't occurred to him before, but he was well aware she found him lacking in all the traits she apparently admired in a man. *Tenderfoot* was what she called him in the purest derogatory sense. But Casey lived in a land that still lived in the past. There was very little difference in a Western town today from one that existed fifty years ago. Whereas the cities in the East were growing by leaps and bounds, as they should be with a new century right around the corner. Was he supposed to ignore progress that made life easier, just because she did?

Why did he even wonder about it? They would be parting soon. She was eager to go home and prove herself to her father. She'd shown in every way possible that she felt the intimacy they had shared was a mistake. Not once had she given him any encouragement to press the issue.

Damian sighed and returned to his own room. It was just as well, he supposed. He couldn't imagine Casey presiding over a business dinner with him—which his wife would be expected to do—without laying a six-shooter on the table. He couldn't picture her running his rather large household. He *could* certainly see her in his bed for the rest of his life, but where would she insist on that bed being located? In some obscure Western town? Independent little darling that she was, she'd probably want to support him as well.

No, it was just as well that they'd be parting. He only wished he could stop feeling so damned miserable about it.

Chapter 41

By the time they dropped Jed off at the undertaker the next morning, they had drawn quite a crowd, but that was to be expected, considering that Jack and Jethro were trussed up like game hens. Folks who looked like prisoners always drew notice. It never failed, actually, and was usually beneficial. This time was no different.

The sheriff was out on his porch to meet them, having become aware that a near mob was ascending on him. Whether he had been in Jack's pay or not wasn't relevant at this point. If he wanted to keep his job, he'd be abiding by the law, at least in this situation. And the reason was, there were many in the crowd throwing accusations, now that Jack had been dethroned, so to speak. They had been too afraid to complain previously about the threats over voting but weren't now.

Damian even made it easier for the sheriff to switch sides by letting him know right off that Jack was being taken back to New York to stand trial for murder. Only Jethro was being turned over to him. Elroy would still have to be arrested, but he'd be easy enough to find, since his wounds left him bedridden.

Damian had pulled a piece of paper out of his pocket and unfolded it for the sheriff to read. Casey's jaw had nearly dropped when she glanced over his shoulder and saw what it was—his appointment to U.S. Deputy Marshal. Well, hell, he could at least have told her he *was* really a deputy, rather than let her draw her own conclusions. Of course, he didn't know she hadn't believed him.

It was still a surprise, though a nice one. And she had to allow that, with the way he dressed now, having put his fancy suits away for the time being, he made a fine-looking U.S. deputy, even if it was only for the temporary job of finding and arresting Curruthers.

They rode out of Culthers for the last time later that morning, with Jack in tow. There was time to spare to catch the eastern-bound train in Sanderson, and soon they were traveling in comfort again—Damian's parlor car was still there waiting for them.

He had yet to come across a bank capable of transferring the funds needed to pay Casey with, so she was still traveling with him for the time being. She wished it were otherwise, because the longer she remained in his company, the more she resented that it couldn't be permanent. So she settled for second best and *tried* to ignore him as best she could. And if he happened to catch her staring at him, well, she just pretended she was deep in thought, and where her eyes had settled meant nothing at all.

They had to pass through Langtry again, but it was only a few hours' stop this time, so they both agreed that the wisest course would be to simply remain in the car. Neither of them wanted to risk another unpredictable run-in with Judge Bean, for obvious reasons.

Unfortunately, the parlor car was remembered in that town, and the judge must have been short on his whiskey funds, because his bailiff came knocking on the door about twenty minutes after the train arrived. Casey seriously considered declining the *invite* to appear before the judge's judicial bench again. She could get Old Sam off the train and be gone before the bailiff managed to round up a posse to force the issue. But she'd be abandoning Damian if she did, since he'd already disposed of his horse and Jack's, figuring they wouldn't be needed again. And she certainly couldn't fit all three of them on Old Sam.

So with little choice in the matter, she ended up walking into Roy Bean's courtroom with Damian at her side. Bean's drinking buddies were all there. And Bean himself was giving them an ear-to-ear smile, which made Casey even more wary.

The bailiff who had fetched them took a moment to whisper something in the judge's ear. Bean looked surprised. For whatever reason he'd demanded their presence, he now had something else to sink his teeth into.

He didn't leave them in suspense, saying, "My bailiff tells me you've got a prisoner in that

fancy train car of yours. The fella you were looking for?''

Damian answered, ''Yes.''

''Well, hot damn,'' Bean said and then, with a
grin, glanced toward his cronies, who were
lined up against the bar, almost like permanent
fixtures. ''Looks like we're going to have us a
hanging, boys.''

Damian shook his head and tossed his appointment paper on the table for Bean to look
at. ''I'm afraid not. As a U.S. deputy, I have the
authority to return this man to stand trial in the
state that he committed his crime in.''

Bean was definitely disappointed, even sighed
heavily before he allowed, ''So you do. Well,
that's a shame. I would have been glad to hang
him for you.''

Damian retrieved his paper and said, ''Thank
you, Your Honor. And if that's all—''

''Now, hold on,'' the judge interrupted. ''That
ain't all, actually. You two still hitched up?''

Casey couldn't help recalling how diligently
Damian had searched for a judge to change that
fact, and she replied churlishly, ''Only because
we haven't found a judge between here and Sanderson—Your Honor.''

Bean was back to grinning. ''They don't call
me the only law west of the Pecos for nothing,
missy. Now I have to tell you that after you left
town, I got to thinking I'd been a mite neglectful
in your case. I did my duty as I saw it, since you
were clearly traveling in sin. But I forgot to mention what I usually tell the folks I hitch up, that
at any time thereafter, for another five dollars,
I'd be glad to unmarry 'em if'n it don't take.

And seeing as how you just admitted you're looking to get unhitched, I guess I can't do less than I'd do for other folks. So by the power invested in me, I hereby unmarry you." His gavel banged once on the table. "That'll be five dollars. Pay the bailiff."

Chapter 42

*T*here was an overnight stop in the next town, as well as a larger, more affiliated bank, one that could handle the transfer of such a large amount of money. And they arrived early enough that Damian was able to secure the bank draft for Casey, which he handed to her that night at dinner in the small restaurant they found near the hotel.

That was it, then. She'd been paid, and they were no longer married. They were still traveling in the same direction, but they didn't have to do it together. Casey could just as easily wait for the next train or ride out on her own. She couldn't see prolonging her misery, now that she didn't have to. And misery it was.

She stared at Damian across the table in that little restaurant and felt like her heart was breaking, while he was perusing the menu, unaware of her turmoil. He'd been moody since the "divorce," but she could understand that. He'd wanted it, yet it still went against the grain, having it forced on him in the same manner the marriage had been forced on him.

Ornery judges like Bean who toyed with people's lives just for self-serving, monetary reasons ought to be outlawed, and hopefully, they were a dying breed. But the folks who got toyed with had no recourse in the meantime—except to get on with their lives.

Casey was going to do exactly that. She wasn't going to say good-bye, either. Crying in front of Damian was out of the question, and that was what she was afraid she'd do if she had to actually say the words that would sever their relationship for good. He expected to see her on the train in the morning. She wouldn't see him again after tonight.

They were staying in the same hotel—she hadn't even bothered to look for a boarding-house. The walk back to it was excruciating, though. He spoke of mundane things. She didn't say anything at all, the knot in her throat too tight for words.

But after opening the door to her room, she turned to gaze at him one last time, noting little things for her memory to savor: the slight stubble on his checks, the firm lips that could be extremely soft at times, the fact that he'd let his hair get longer than he preferred, and that his pale gray eyes were as intense as ever.

It was too much to resist, one last contact. It was meant as a kiss good-bye, no more than that. But it turned into something quite different.

When she reached up, he must have read more into it than she'd intended, seeing it as an overture on her part. He gathered her close and wouldn't let go. And that, too, was too much for her to resist. How could it hurt, after all, to say good-bye to him in this way? And how much more special it was, for her knowing it was the last time.

He must have felt the same. Even though he expected to see her again, he must have realized this would be their last shared intimacy. He was all the more careful for it, all the more tender.

He picked her up and carried her to the bed, cradled in his arms. He was very slow in undressing her, too distracted in kissing each area that he bared. Her shoulders, her neck, even her fingers received special attention. There was no urgency, just a poignant tenderness in his kisses as well as the caresses that followed.

Casey wasn't hesitant, either, in her own caresses. The sounds she wrung from him were encouraging, and there was so much of him to explore. His muscles rippled beneath her fingers. She found his soft spots. She marveled at what was so hard. She was emboldened further, leaving no part of him untouched. Even that strong male length of him felt the daring of her fingertips, as well as the strength of a firm grasp.

Contrasts, so obvious and yet so amazing, the different textures, the things that set them apart. Nevertheless, what pleasured him pleasured her. In that there was no difference, just the wonder that it was so.

His body was so fascinating. Even the smell of him was intoxicating to her senses. And the taste—she wasn't sparing in her kisses. By setting the pace of lazy, sensual exploration, he was allowing her the time to do all that she had previously only fantasized about doing.

But pleasure like that had its limits. Their blood slowly heated. Skin that had reveled in a soft caress was soon too sensitive to receive more. Brief fluttering became constant churning. Every nerve was pulsing vibrantly. And when she thought she couldn't bear it anymore, he finally pulled her into the curve of his nakedness and that velvet hardness filled her.

His gaze locked with hers, nearly as erotic as the thickness of him inside her. And then his thrusts began, a slow withdrawal, a swift surge forward, a heated kiss in the interim, only to repeat the cycle. It was so exquisite, his lovemaking, so consuming.

Soon that wave of pure sensation arrived, which lifted her into the realm of ecstasy, exploding on her senses in a pulsating crescendo, draining her to repletion. That he experienced his own climax in that same moment filled her heart with joy.

She held him close to her. She somehow held back her tears. For that short time, he was hers. They would go their separate ways, but she would never forget him—nor would she ever stop loving him. But she would try, she really would, to put the pain aside; and hopefully, she could one day look back on this time without regrets, and simply remember it as a cherished part of her life.

Chapter 43

❦

*C*ourtney was on the west range of the ranch when she sighted Chandos riding toward her. She immediately dug her heels into her mount and raced toward him, praying that this time he was home for good.

The past seven months had been difficult for her, not just because Casey was gone and not just because she had taken over many of the responsibilities of running the K.C. while Chandos had been away, but simply because she hated being parted from her husband like this.

She reached him, and just managed to get out, "Well, hell, it's about damn time," before she threw herself out of her saddle and into his open arms.

She heard him chuckle before his mouth fastened on hers for a searing, it's-been-too-long sort of kiss. By the time she leaned back enough to feast her eyes on him, she was breathless. And he was grinning. That was the thing she noticed most, not the shaggy beard or the hair that had grown so long he was braiding it. That

292

grin—and the lively sparkle in his light blue eyes.

He'd changed; he was more like the old Chandos. She'd seen it the few times he'd come home in the past seven months, and it was even more pronounced now. The anger was gone. Life was back in his eyes. As much as she had hated having both her daughter and her husband away, she could thank Casey for this change in him.

It had been a good, healing time for him, doing something he considered useful, something he was good at, rather than the monotonous running of the ranch, which he found quite boring at times since Fletcher's death. At least when his father was alive, there had been a reason for him to excel at ranching, to show up the old man, to do it better than he. But that motivation died when Fletcher did.

"Can I hope that this isn't going to be just another brief visit?" she asked.

It hadn't taken Chandos very long to find Casey after she'd left that night so long ago. Courtney had expected that would be the end of it, that he'd be bringing her straight home. But that wasn't what he'd done at all. His guilt, over causing her to leave in the first place, had prompted him to let her prove whatever it was she'd gone off to prove. He'd merely "watched over her" while she did it.

"It's over, Cateyes," he replied with a brief sigh. "Casey came in on the noon train today. Now, whether she gets to the ranch before dark is the question. She's been dragging her feet like she's on her way to her execution."

"That's understandable. She's probably dreading facing you."

He shook his head. "I don't think it's that. If anything, she should be looking forward to crowing about what she's accomplished. But the few times I got a good look at her since she started heading home, she seemed—I don't know, like she's in mourning."

"Did something happen recently that you didn't mention in your telegrams and letters?"

"Yes, a lot of things, but nothing that I can figure would have affected her so much. She finished that last job she took on, parted company with the tenderfoot who hired her—unless coming close to death has made her realize she took on more'n she could chew."

"Close to death? Close to death! When the devil did *that* happen? You were supposed to be assuring that she was never in any real danger."

He smiled at his wife wryly. "I wasn't able to be there every single time she had a mind to draw that gun of hers. She did manage to lose me occasionally, leading me a ragged chase to catch up to her again."

"When, exactly, did she come close to death?" Courtney demanded. "And how?"

"The last job she took on was a bit more dangerous than I figured it would be. The Easterner hired her to find someone named Curruthers. I learned that much by questioning the same folks she questioned. Curruthers was an Easterner as well, which is what misled me."

"He was more dangerous than you figured?"

"No, actually, he was harmless enough himself, but had surrounded himself with hired fast guns who weren't. By the time I caught up with Casey after she found the fellow—she pulled a fast one on me in Sanderson, taking off in the middle of the night without leaving a trail—she was involved in a damned showdown."

"What?!"

He grinned. "Settle down, Cateyes. She won it hands down, and it's damned funny, thinking about it now, though it sure wasn't at the time, of course, with all those bullets flying. In fact, that was the end of it for me. I was going to drag her home just as soon as the dust settled."

"And what, pray tell, was funny about our daughter participating in a damned shoot-out?" she asked tightly, not about to settle down as suggested.

"Well, if you can picture what I saw, her standing there in the middle of the street in what looked like a peaceful little town, wearing one of the fancier dresses she's ever worn, with her gun belt strapped to her hips over the lace—"

"You find *that* funny?"

"So will you when you stop glaring at me—and recall that she's safe and sound and just about home."

Courtney sniffed indignantly, but wasn't quite glaring at him anymore. "Very well, I might find it funny—when I'm a hundred and ten. Now tell me why you didn't drag her home at that point."

He frowned, remembering. "Because my fool horse went lame on me."

"But you were there in the same town she was," Courtney reminded him, frowning as well. "So what's your horse got to do with it?"

"Because those bastards she was up against never intended it to be a fair fight. I got into it at that point, giving her enough cover to get off the street, which she did. The tenderfoot showed up at that point, too—they'd apparently gotten separated somehow, after leaving Sanderson. But anyway, the bullets were flying from both sides of the street, only when they stopped, I wasn't quick enough to realize that both sides had taken off out the back of the buildings. They met up again in the town stable, and whatever happened there, they managed to end up riding out of town with Casey in tow."

Courtney sighed. "Okay, I can see where your horse going lame would have made it difficult to put an end to it right then."

"It was worse than that," he said with another frown. "I set out after her immediately. So did Rutledge, and he was ahead of me."

"The Easterner?"

Chandos nodded. "The trail headed south on the road to Sanderson, but that was just to throw off any pursuers. I found where they left the road to head west and even finally spotted them. Rutledge hadn't figured that out yet, so wound up behind me."

"But then your horse went lame?"

He nodded, sighing. "I was going to waylay Rutledge and take his horse. Didn't think the tenderfoot could do Casey much good if he caught up to them. But that damned fellow flew by me, too far away for me to stop him. Don't think he even saw me, he was so hell-bent on catching up to Curruthers. And I was a good five miles from town by then. By the time I got another horse and headed after them, they were already returning to town with prisoners in tow."

"*He* rescued her?"

Chandos snorted. "I doubt it. She probably had everything in hand by the time he found her, though I'd dearly like to know how she managed it. One of those owlhoots was dead, the other two trussed up like turkeys ready for the oven."

"So ask her what happened when she gets home," Courtney suggested. "Or do you still intend to let her think you never found her?"

Chandos shrugged. "Don't know. Let's wait and see what she has to say for herself first. But it's over, Cateyes. At least I'm sure of that. And maybe you can figure out why she's not as happy as we figured she'd be when she got around to coming home."

Chapter 44

❦

*C*asey paused on the hill overlooking the Bar M Ranch and had to wonder, in retrospect, if it all had been worth it. She was afraid she had too many of her father and grandfather's traits, being too stubborn, headstrong, and sure that only she knew what was best. In the end, she wasn't sure what she'd proved.

She'd wanted to keep Fletcher's legacy from falling to ruin, a noble endeavor, or so she'd told herself at the time. But would this ranch have fallen to ruin if she never stepped foot on it again? Would Chandos really have let that happen? Probably not. She'd simply been too full of herself, thinking only she could save the day. She gave herself a mental snort. She'd been gone seven months and the ranch was apparently still running fine.

And now she had to explain her reasoning to her parents, when she no longer felt her reasons had any validity. She'd done a fool thing and needed to own up to that.

Casey swung Old Sam around and dug her

heels in for the last leg home. She arrived at the dinner hour, so chances were she'd find both her parents in the dining room. And she did. But standing there in the doorway of that elegant room, feeling so out of place in her dusty poncho and jeans, she couldn't get the words out that she'd planned to say. It was so good to be home, she'd missed her mother and father, missed them terribly, yet for some reason she just didn't feel like she belonged here anymore, and that realization was cutting deeper than all the other things troubling her.

She hoped it was merely a passing sense of sadness. This was her home, after all. She knew she'd always be welcome here. Yet she also always figured that someday she'd leave here for good, when she found a man . . .

"Did you have to cut your beautiful hair, Casey?" Courtney asked in a disapproving tone.

That certainly wasn't what she had expected to hear after having been gone for seven months, and in fact, Casey stared at her mother incredulously. Was that all the scolding she was going to get? She was afraid to even look in her father's direction, dreading the anger she expected to see from him. He wasn't yelling yet—but he would.

"It will grow back," she replied lamely.

Courtney smiled and stood up to hold out her arms. "So it will. Now come here."

That was what Casey had been waiting for, hoping for, and she didn't hesitate before she flew into her mother's arms—and promptly burst into tears. Her mother's soothing voice reached her through the noise she was making, but the tears wouldn't stop, just got worse.

Casey had so much to be forgiven for. She had so much bothering her that could never be made right. Parents were usually able to "fix" everything that went wrong in a child's life, but she was past the age of having problems easily "fixed."

All she could think to wail was, "I'm sorry! I never should have left, I know that now!"

"Casey, honey, shhh," Courtney continued to murmur. "All that matters is that you're home now, safe and sound. Everything else will fall into place."

It wouldn't, but Casey wasn't going to argue with her mother. She was being given a reprieve. She wasn't even being asked for an explanation . . .

"Perhaps if you told us why you felt the need to leave like you did?"

Casey almost chuckled. She did manage to wipe the tears off her cheeks and lean back to give her mother a half smile. At least *this* was something she'd expected.

"Well, why I left like I did, sneaking off in the middle of the night, is pretty obvious. If I'd told you what I planned to do, you probably would have locked me up and thrown the key down the nearest well."

"Quite possibly." Courtney smiled back. "And why you left?"

Casey finally glanced at her father, who was still sitting there, staring at her—inscrutably. It didn't make her no nevermind that he wasn't yelling yet, but at least he could *look* like he was furious with her.

"It was a fool reason that I wished I'd never thought of. I just wanted to prove that I could handle the Bar M fine on my own. Daddy claimed that only a man could run it proper. I set out to do what only a man would consider doing, and I earned more'n some men earn in a lifetime."

"Did you have to pick a profession that was so dangerous?" Chandos asked quietly.

Casey cringed. "So you got close, did you? Close enough to find out what I was doing?"

"Closer than that, little girl."

Casey went very still, and not because he'd called her "little girl." She hesitated before saying, "What do you mean?"

"Did you really think you could elude me all these months?"

Casey sighed inwardly. She'd never thought any such thing. In fact, she'd expected her father to show up from day one. That he hadn't had caused her some worry.

"When did you find me?" she asked.

"A couple weeks after you left."

She frowned. "I don't understand. Why didn't you just confront me then?"

"Maybe because it was my fault that you left and I didn't want to compound that mistake. I figured that if you reached your goal, that would be the end of it, and I wouldn't feel so damned guilty about it anymore. Just wish it hadn't taken so long—or that the whole thing wasn't so dangerous."

"But it *wasn't* that dangerous—for the most part. When I was just hunting bounties, it was easy enough to catch my targets unawares."

"I know."

Those two words really had her worried. "You know? You're not saying that you didn't just find me, but you also stayed with me?" Then Casey answered her own question. "Of course you did. You would. You were waiting for me to get in trouble, weren't you? You expected it!"

"No, now, you're barking up the wrong tree there, little girl. I knew damned well that you were competent enough for the job you chose. But you're my *daughter*. If you think I could have just left you out there, knowing the kind of people you'd be dealing with, think again. I had to be around—just in case. There was no other way, Casey. Either I stayed near, or you came home."

Casey nodded. She didn't know why she'd been surprised. He had always protected her. Why would she think this would be any different?

And then it dawned on her and she nearly blanched. He'd been following her all along. He'd been there, watching her. When she and Damian had made love on the trail—had her father witnessed that, too?

She had to ask. "Were you always there? Every step of the way?"

He shook his head. "There were quite a few times you managed to lose me. The longest was when you were headed toward Coffeyville. It took me more'n a week to catch up to you that time. When you left Fort Worth just as I got there, I had to ride like hell to make it to the next whistle stop before the train pulled out again. When you sneaked out of Sanderson in the middle of the night, you lost me for several days. Didn't catch up to you then until you were in the midst of that showdown in Culthers.''

Casey sighed mentally and yet cringed at the same time. He hadn't witnessed her and Damian making love. But that damned gunfight . . .

"That was pretty stupid of me," she admitted.

"Yes, it was."

"I don't mind telling you, I was so scared I don't know how I managed to get my gun drawn, much less hit the fella. You were the one who gave Damian and me cover to get off the street, weren't you?"

"Yes."

"Sure wish I'd known you were out there when they had me in that cabin later that night, waiting for Damian to show up so they could kill him."

"I wasn't. My horse came up lame. But I assume you managed to extricate yourself from that mess just fine on your own. At least it looked that way when I finally caught up to you and found you heading back to town with prisoners."

Casey managed to keep from laughing at her own shortcomings. "Me? No, I just managed to come within an inch of dying, after drawing an empty gun on those fellas. It was Damian who got us out of that mess, and not a second too soon, breaking the door down when he did. He saved my life."

"The tenderfoot did?"

"Don't sound so skeptical. He's never used a handgun, but he's an expert marksman when it comes to a rifle. And he was adapting pretty good to our part of the country, before he headed back East."

"Why did you even hook up with him to begin with? That's something I never could figure out."

Casey pulled the bank draft out of her pocket and tossed it on the table for her father to read. "Because he offered me way more'n the job was worth, too much for me to refuse for a couple weeks of easy work. And I was ready to come home. Figured a bit over twenty thousand dollars was enough to prove I don't need a husband—till I'm ready for one."

Courtney lifted her hand to her mouth to cover a grin she couldn't restrain. Chandos put on his inscrutable look again, which gave no clue to what he was going to say next. What he did say surprised Casey.

"Yes, that proves *that* point well enough. And if any one of the Bar M hands could have seen you in action these last months, you'd probably have no trouble there either. But I still think you will have trouble, Casey, getting a bunch of wranglers, young and old, to follow your orders without argument. Trouble with men is, most of them think they know the right of it, and most of them have a hard time keeping their mouths shut if they disagree with their boss—and that's if their boss is a man. If their boss is a woman, then they will *know* they've got the right of it, even if they don't, and won't hesitate to show the little woman up, if you get my drift. Now, when you prove them wrong, what's going to happen?"

Casey sighed, understanding what he was getting at. "Bad feelings, of course. Wanting to get even by showing me up again, then more bad feelings if they're wrong again. Or me being forced to fire them if they're right, because it sets a bad precedent, feuding with the boss."

Chandos nodded. "Now, having pointed all that out, which I really regret I didn't do before, I won't stop you if you still want to try running the Bar M. As long as you know what to expect, and, if you fail, that it won't be a personal failure." He grinned at her before adding, "Then again, little girl, anyone who's accomplished what you have these last months can probably figure out a way to avoid what I'm predicting. Be a proud day for me if you prove *me* wrong."

Chapter 45

Later, in her spacious bedroom, a room still in the pink-and-white tones of her youth, Casey sat in front of the vanity, wearing an old white cotton nightgown. Her mother stood behind her, brushing her hair as she used to do when Casey was much younger. Courtney was tsking every so often over its length, but Casey was enjoying the brushing anyway.

Courtney had knocked on her door not long after Casey had come upstairs. Casey had pretty much expected her. They'd always been close, always been able to talk with ease. And there were some subjects that just weren't for discussing in front of Chandos.

"You've put on weight—but in the right places," Courtney pointed out.

Casey blushed. She hadn't really noticed, but her breasts and hips did have a bit more curve to them—at long last. She should be delighted by the observation, after waiting so long for it to happen. But all she felt was indifference, really, which was telling.

"Guess I finally reached that magic sprouting age you used to assure me would come around."

Courtney nodded, but after a few more brush strokes, she remarked, "Your father seems to think something else is wrong, that you're unhappy for some reason that doesn't have much to do with everything else. Has something unusual happened that you'd like to talk about?"

"If you can call falling in love unusual, then I guess you could say so."

Casey had sighed as she said it. She shouldn't have said it. There was no point in talking about something that couldn't be changed and couldn't be resolved.

But Courtney seemed delighted. "Did you really? I was beginning to think that no one around here would ever hold your interest—but then, he's not from around here, is he? The Easterner, I presume?"

Casey nodded with another sigh, though she assured her mother, "I'll get over it."

"Why should you?"

Casey blinked up at her mother in the mirror. "Maybe because he doesn't return the sentiment. Maybe because he's from the upper crust of New York society, and I'm just a country girl he'd never consider taking for a wife. And maybe because I'd feel so damned out of place in a city that big, I can't imagine living there. And maybe—"

"Maybe you're throwing up too many obstacles," Courtney chided. "Are you sure he doesn't return the sentiment? I find it hard to believe that any man couldn't love you—once they get to know you."

Casey chuckled. "Spoken like—my mother."

"I'm serious," Courtney insisted. "You're beautiful, intelligent, and incredibly versatile in all the different things you've learned. You think nothing of taking on a man's endeavors, yet are quite capable in your own. I think you've proved that there isn't much of anything you can't do, once you set your mind to it."

"I don't think all men would appreciate that," Casey said wryly.

"No, perhaps not," Courtney replied. "But your abilities give you a certain confidence that shines through and adds to your overall appeal. Was this—Damian, was it?"

"Damian Rutledge—the Third."

"The Third, eh? Sounds impressive. But was he not attracted to you at all?"

Casey frowned, remembering the passion they'd shared. Still, had that stemmed from a mutual attraction or simply because, from Damian's point of view, she'd been the only female around for most of the time they were together?

But to answer her mother, she pointed out, "A man can be attracted to a woman without wanting to marry her. There are other things to consider where a wife is concerned, like if she'll fit into his life. He didn't want me for his wife. That I am sure of."

"Why are you so sure?"

"Because we were married and he couldn't wait to get us unmarried."

The brush fell out of Courtney's hand. "You were *what*?"

"It wasn't consensual, Mother, and it's already been set aside."

"What do you mean, it wasn't consensual? Someone *forced* you two to marry?"

Casey nodded. "You may have heard of that ornery judge, Roy Bean, over in Langtry. He took it upon himself to decide that Damian and I were traveling in sin, which we weren't, but he was after the five-dollar charge he'd get for marrying us, so he married us without a by-your-leave, and there wasn't a thing we could do about it."

"That's—that's outrageous!"

Casey agreed. "Yes, it was. Damian was furious, naturally, and looked for another judge to undo the marriage in every town we hit thereafter. We didn't find one, but when we came through Langtry on the way back, that old judge did it again, took it upon himself to unhitch us, again without asking, just for another five-dollar charge."

Courtney sat down next to Casey on the vanity bench and gathered her daughter into her arms. "Oh, honey, I'm so sorry. That must have been especially hard for you, if you already loved him by that point."

Casey tried to shrug it off. "It doesn't matter. I knew all along that he wasn't for me, that our lives were just too different for us to be compatible. He's not comfortable out of a big city, I wouldn't be comfortable in one, and there's no middle ground there. I just wish my heart had kept that in mind instead of getting all soft on me."

Courtney didn't seem to want to accept that.

"Remember what I just said about your being able to do anything you set your mind to? Why have you given up on this man? You captured killers. You're going to take on the running of the Bar M. Why do you shy away from going after your heart's desire in this case?"

"Because failing with him would hurt in a different way that I don't think I can handle."

"You're handling losing him now? Aren't you? Or are you utterly miserable because you *didn't* give it your best shot? The obstacles you imagine in your mind can be dealt with, too, honey. Who says you'd have to live in the city all the time, or that he'd have to live in the country from now on? Who says you couldn't live part of the year in both places and enjoy it—because you'd be together?"

"But he didn't want me for his wife!"

"So change his mind," Courtney said pragmatically. "If you can't figure out how to do that, I'll be glad to advise you."

Courtney was blushing now. Casey smiled at her mother. She meant well. She wanted Casey to be happy. She was just overlooking one little point. How could Casey be happy, even if she managed to snare a proposal of marriage out of Damian, if he didn't really love her?

Chapter 46

$\mathbf{D}$amian was having a real hard time traveling with Jack Curruthers, despising him as much as he did. Being certain that the man was heading for a prison sentence after his trial didn't help much. He'd stolen from a company, but rather than just run with the money, as most thieves would, he had tried to place the blame elsewhere and ordered a man's death because of it, turning theft into murder.

Curruthers deserved whatever the courts dealt him. But Damian didn't deserve to have to suffer his constant company on the long trip back to New York.

Jack didn't show an ounce of remorse. He smirked, goaded, and bragged of his crime every chance he got. And in the parlor car on the train, there was no way for Damian to escape his presence. A gag could be shoved in his mouth, but the goading was still there in his owlish eyes.

Which was why, in St. Louis, Missouri, Damian left the train to find another parlor car, one with a separate compartment that Jack could be locked away in. Out of sight—at least partially out of mind. And he found just what he was looking for, a car with a separate bedchamber. Unfortunately, Damian was gone for several hours, arranging for the rental—the car had an in-city owner—and the delivery. By the time he returned, Jack had escaped.

It was the last thing Damian had expected to happen at this point. He had taken precautions against it. Jack had been chained hand and foot, shackles obtained from the Culthers sheriff, as well as the foot chain being secured to one of the bolted-down benches. And the car had been locked with a key, only the porter who serviced it having a duplicate.

The porter wasn't under suspicion. He had had an obvious aversion to Jack after hearing about his crimes, and besides, he'd taken the opportunity of the train's being in the city for the night to visit relatives he had here. Damian was quick to find several witnesses, one who had heard the noise in the car, which had been the breaking of the bench, and another who had seen Jack tumble out of one of the windows and hobble away. He was gone, and St. Louis was a large city, easy for him to find places to hide.

Damian immediately reported his loss to the local police, who were quite helpful, but not to the extent of finding Curruthers. After three days of dead ends, he telegraphed the detectives he'd used in New York; they put him in touch with contacts of theirs in St. Louis.

It still took another week before a definite trail was found, one leading directly to Chicago, Illinois. Apparently Jack had given up on losing himself in the vast openness of the West. He was going to try a huge city now, and Chicago ranked right up there in size with New York.

This certainly wasn't how Damian had figured he would experience Chicago for the first time. In the back of his mind was the fact that his mother was there somewhere, but he managed to keep that out of his conscious thoughts. Maybe someday he would look for her, but he had too many other things on his mind to even consider it on this trip.

Casey, now, was a lot less easy to keep out of his thoughts—was constantly in them, actually. He was still angry at the way she had taken off without a bit of warning, simply sneaked out of the room they'd been sharing in the middle of the night. No good-bye. No chance to speak of meeting up again in the future . . . or anything else.

He had decided to talk to her about their marriage—or rather, their divorce. He wasn't displeased that Bean had "unhitched" them. He'd just been furious that the judge had again forced a legality on them without asking. And that marriage had been a farce anyway. He'd been planning to take his pride in hand and ask for a real one. But Casey hadn't given him a chance.

Just hours after getting her money for finishing the job he'd hired her for, she'd run off. Which pretty much proved how eager she had been to part company with Damian. She couldn't even wait for morning to roll around. Nor had she been on the train when it had pulled out. He'd checked every car, hoping to find her, before he even went to collect Jack, who'd been stored in the local jail for the night.

Now, several weeks later, he was still stewing over her departure, and with time on his hands—the detectives had been adamant about not wanting an amateur tagging along with them—he had nothing to do *but* stew. At least when Casey had been searching for Jack, Damian had been actively involved, had even felt somewhat useful—occasionally.

When the thought occurred to him, Damian jumped on it like a starving man on a haunch of beef. Casey ought to be here in Chicago with him. He'd paid her ten thousand dollars to bring Jack to justice, but Jack was eluding justice again. Damian had *not* gotten his money's worth.

But how was he going to find her when he didn't know where she lived, didn't even know her full name? Even the name he called her wasn't hers; it came from the K.C. initials she used, which she had probably taken from the brand on her horse for lack of better inspiration the first time she'd been pressed for a signature.

There *was* that brand on Old Sam . . .

Bucky Alcott had sent Casey off to that ranch near Waco to look for her roots. Damian had dismissed that as a wild-goose chase, considering he knew she hadn't bought the horse from the K.C. Ranch but had received it as a gift from her father. Yet that ranch was the only clue Damian had, since she had never once mentioned anything about her home that would point to its location.

It gave him something useful to do, heading

back to Texas. There was another reason he was going, but he was still too angry to admit that, even to himself. Yet because he didn't have much real hope of actually finding Casey, he figured he would probably just be wasting his time.

But wasting his time was preferable to sitting in his hotel room waiting for the detectives' daily progress reports, which were monotonously the same—no leads yet. Jack had lost himself in Chicago, was smart enough not to use his real name this time. And how did you find a needle in a haystack, which was what he was in a city so big?

Surprisingly, Damian had every confidence that Casey would know how.

Chapter 47

*I*t was a mansion by any standards, the K.C. ranch house. Damian had thought he was coming to another town when he saw it and the surrounding buildings from a distance. It was like no ranch he'd seen before in his travels in the West, and he'd passed by many.

He was impressed and yet disappointed by its huge size, since a ranch so obviously successful would probably have no record or recollection of a single horse a young girl had named Old Sam, purchased by her father many years ago. Even if they did keep that type of record, he didn't know her father's name either.

He'd been hoping someone might remember the man from the description Damian could offer, but now he seriously doubted it. They must sell dozens of horses here every month. The many stables he could see as he got closer suggested they bred them as well as cattle.

He still had to try. Whoever had sold the horses here five or six years ago might have an excellent memory *and* still might be working here. And someone as dangerous-looking as Casey's father appeared to be, when Damian had seen him that day in Fort Worth, had a better chance of being remembered than an average buyer.

He'd rented a horse in Waco after getting directions to the K.C. Ranch. Funny how he had done it without much thought, hadn't even looked for a buggy to rent instead. But now he actually felt comfortable on a horse, something he would never have imagined a year ago.

There was a very long, wide porch on the front of the house. Two hitching rails, just as long, spread out on each side of the stairs leading up to the porch. Damian tethered his horse to one before approaching the front door.

While he waited for his knock to be answered, he faced the front of the porch. There wasn't much to see out there but open plains, cactuses, and the occasional tree—then he realized the porch faced westward. And he'd seen some of the incredible sunsets they had in this part of the country. The porch must be extremely relaxing at the end of a hard day's work, with such a magnificent view. The many chairs and tables scattered along its length said a number of the ranch folks here probably took advantage of that serenity.

The door opened. A quite handsome, middle-aged woman stood there; her light brown eyes were vaguely familiar, though in Damian's nervousness he couldn't think why. His hope of finding Casey through this place wasn't high, yet it was the only chance he had. It was because he would find out today, one way or the other, that had him so nervous.

"Can I help you?" the woman asked curiously.

Damian doffed his hat and cleared his throat. "I'm looking for a young woman who rides a horse that came from this ranch—or at least, it was branded here."

"What's her name?"

"I'm afraid I don't know her real name," he admitted. "Her father purchased the horse for her, probably about five years ago. And no, I don't know his name either. But I was hoping someone here might remember him and know who he is, maybe even where he lives."

She seemed to be waiting to hear more, but when no more was forthcoming, she said, "A lot of horses get sold here. Is there anything special about the horse that might distinguish it? Or anything unusual about the man who purchased it? Without a name, it's going to be pretty hard to—"

"I can describe him," Damian interrupted, though he didn't mean to, had just realized he should have said so right off. "He's probably about as tall as I am."

"Well, that helps," the woman said with a grin. "Since you're quite a bit taller than average."

Damian smiled back, feeling slightly more at ease. "He's got black hair that he may or may not wear extremely long. The one time I saw him, it was very long, but that was recently. He's probably in his mid-forties now, so figure around thirty-eight or nine back then."

The woman chuckled. "Sounds like any number of men around here, including my husband. Anything else to set him apart and make him memorable? Scars, maybe?"

Damian shook his head. "I didn't get a very close look at him. But there was a quality about him, a dangerous quality that would probably make some people nervous. To be frank, he had the look of an outlaw."

"Goodness, are you sure you want to find him again?" she asked.

"It's his daughter I need to find."

She nodded thoughtfully. "What about the horse? Was it unusual at all?"

"It's an exceptionally fine-looking animal. It could probably be termed a Thoroughbred, even though Casey calls him Old Sam."

The lady stiffened. "Casey? I thought you said you didn't have their names."

Her reaction was encouraging, but he explained first, "I don't. Casey is just a name I gave her, since she was going by the initials K and C—probably taken from the brand on her horse, though I never got around to asking her about it. Actually, all she called herself was Kid. Do you by chance know who I'm talking about, ma'am?"

"Oh, I might. Why are you looking for her?"

"That's a bit private—"

"Then I guess I can't help you," the woman cut in and actually started closing the door on him.

"Wait!" Damian said. "She was a bounty hunter when I met her. I hired her to find my father's killer, which she did. But before I could get him back to New York for trial, he managed to escape."

"So you're looking for her to hire her again?" she asked sharply.

That was certainly none of her business, which was why he replied, "Something like that."

"And that's the only reason you're here?"

It was Damian's turn to stiffen somewhat at her persistence. "Why else?"

She was frowning as she said, "I think maybe my husband would like to talk to you. Come inside."

He did. She immediately walked away from him with a curt "Wait here," leaving him no choice but to obey.

Her behavior had him utterly baffled. She was definitely angry about something. Her eyes had turned hotly amber. And it had started when he'd said Casey's name. Could that really be her name? The woman did seem to know who she was. That "I might" she'd said about knowing her had clear connotations of "Yes, I do."

Damian went very still. Amber eyes?

Sounds like any number of men around here, including my husband.

Hope surged through Damian. Had he actually found Casey's home? Was that her mother he'd just spoken to who had eyes like Casey's when she was angry? And the woman's husband he'd described . . . ?

The tap on his shoulder turned him around, and sure enough, it was Casey's father standing there with his fist drawn back. Damian had no memory beyond that except for stars exploding in his eyes.

Chapter 48

❦

I'm beginning to think I never should have told you that Casey was in love with him," Courtney said to her husband as they stood over Damian's long body, sprawled there in the entryway, a trickle of blood under his nose.

"Of course you should have," Chandos replied, rubbing his knuckles in a satisfying way, his look reflecting the same feeling.

Courtney huffed, saying doubtfully, "Really? When I had to talk you out of going after him, all the way to New York, no less? And here the fool man shows up on our doorstep. He might as well have just handed you his head."

Chandos raised a brow. "Then why'd you tell me he was here? You could have just sent him on his way, and I'd never have known the difference."

Courtney made a tsking sound. "So for a very brief moment, I *wanted* you to beat some sense into him. But it was only for that brief moment," she insisted.

Chandos almost grinned. "I take it he said something to annoy you?"

321

Courtney's lips tightened. "He's come looking for Casey to hire her again. Can you believe that? Not that she would even consider working for him again, but just seeing him is going to prolong her heartache. But does he consider that? No, the man is a selfish, insensitive son of—"

Chandos placed a gentle finger to her lips to silence her. "I love it when you get riled, Cateyes, but in this case, there's probably no reason for it. Weren't you the one who had to convince me that he didn't know that Casey's in love with him? Didn't she admit that when you asked her? Kind of makes him innocent of any wrongdoing, doesn't it?"

"Well, yes," she said, but then narrowed her eyes on him. "Then why did you come in here and immediately punch him, if you now hold him blameless?"

"For the plain and simple reason that he's made my daughter miserable. Call it a father's prerogative."

She raised a brow now. "Oh, and a mother doesn't have one of those?"

He chuckled at her. "Your prerogative was to come get me because you knew I'd tear into him."

She blushed guiltily. "Maybe we shouldn't be discussing the whys of our respective dislike of this young man, but rather, what we're going to do about his unexpected and unwanted appearance on our doorstep. I would prefer it if Casey didn't know he's been here, but she's been dividing her nights between here and the Bar M, and tonight she'll be sleeping here. Considering how late in the afternoon it is, she could show up any time now."

Chandos nodded. "I'll get a couple of the hands to dump him in a wagon and haul him back to town. Hopefully, the reception he received here showed him that he's not welcome to return."

Courtney frowned thoughtfully. "I don't think that will do it."

"Why not?"

"Because he struck me as being a bit stubborn," Courtney said. "And he's come all this way to hire her. I don't think he'll leave until she tells him herself that she won't work for him again."

"You're sure she won't?"

"Not positive, but why would she? The only reason she did before was for the money, which she wanted so she could prove things to you. She's got nothing to prove now. She's running the Bar M and doing fine so far."

"Excellent reasoning for a man, but what about a woman in love?"

Courtney almost growled, "You're right, of course. That might affect her decision if she has to make one. She could agree because she might like to spend a bit more time with him. Or she could agree because he apparently needs help and she loves him. She might want to help him for that reason alone. So perhaps we should try and assure that she doesn't have to make the decision in the first place."

"You aren't suggesting that I dispose of him permanently, are you?"

"Don't be ridiculous!" Courtney snapped,

then saw that he was teasing. She glared at him. "Perhaps just a talk with him will convince him not to return here, and you can have that by escorting him to town yourself. And if that doesn't convince him, then tell him she's not here, that she's gone—oh, I don't know . . . to Europe. Yes, Europe—quite far enough away for him to realize that if he's going to get the help he needs, he should start looking for it elsewhere."

"I'd just as soon *not* have words with him. Don't know if I'd be able to resist swinging at him again."

"Then I will—"

"No, you won't," Chandos said adamantly, then sighed. "Very well, I'll take him to town." He leaned down to haul Damian over his shoulder, adding with a groan, "Damn, he's as heavy as he looks."

"Chandos . . . ?"

"What?" he grunted on his way out the door.

"Don't let him know how Casey feels about him."

He turned back toward her. "And why not?"

"She didn't choose to tell him, and he was too dense to figure it out for himself—"

"Or he knew and didn't care, which is what I figured was the case, though I let you convince me it was otherwise."

"Ah, so that's why you hit him instead of saying hello first?"

He snorted. She smiled and got on with her point. "Either way, I don't think she'd appreciate him knowing. I know I wouldn't if it were me."

He nodded and continued down the porch steps, where he pushed Damian over the saddle of the horse he'd left there, belly-down. After gathering the reins, Chandos looked up at his wife.

"I should be back before dinner," he told her. "Oh, and make sure he hasn't left any blood on the floor from his broken nose."

"You really think you broke it?"

"I damn well tried to. But why else would a man his size go down so easy?"

"Maybe because you always did swing a nasty punch," she offered with a wave.

Chandos chuckled at her. "And you always give me more credit than I'm due."

"Nonsense. I married an exceptional man. At least *I* know it."

Chandos was smiling as he led Damian's horse around to the stable to collect his own. But the pleasure he found in his wife's words didn't last long, not with the task she'd set before him.

That task didn't take very long, though. About a mile down the road, Damian started making noises indicating he was waking up, so Chandos halted both horses to give him a chance to slide off his without further injury. That he did, though he was disoriented for a moment as he stood there in the middle of the road.

His first question when he finally spotted Chandos was "May I ask where you were taking me?"

"Back to town," Chandos replied. "You're not welcome on the K.C."

"You couldn't have just said so?" Damian grouched, carefully feeling his nose.

"Broken?"

"Doesn't seem to be."

"Just a low tolerance for pain, then, huh?" Chandos said this with a smile that could pass for a smirk.

Damian scowled and pointed out testily, "Just coldcocked with no warning."

Chandos shrugged. "And just what kind of reception did you think you'd get from the parents of the young woman you nearly got killed?"

Damian flinched, surprised that Casey would have mentioned details about what she'd been doing while away from home, but he said in his defense, since her father obviously already knew, "She's a bounty hunter and damned good at it. It's her profession—"

"It's something she dabbled in temporarily, hardly a profession."

"Regardless," Damian said. "She was ideal for the job, so she took the job."

Chandos made a sound of disgust. "And now you think she'd take the job again?"

"The man she helped me find has escaped," Damian pointed out. "I have detectives looking for him, but they're having no better luck this time than they did before. Casey has better luck."

"Casey's just got good sense, is all."

"That really is her name?"

Chandos frowned at the change in subject. "You didn't even know her name?"

"Why does that surprise you? She volunteered very little information about herself. It was quite a while before I knew she was a woman!"

"And just how did you finally find that out?"

The question was asked with so much condemning insinuation that Damian knew exactly what Chandos was thinking, and since he was as guilty as the man was thinking he was, he stuck with the literal truth.

"She told me," he explained. "When I suggested she grow a beard."

A peculiar look appeared on Chandos's face, and if Damian had known him at all, he'd know the man was just short of laughing. But he didn't know him, and all he saw was that brief lapse from the otherwise thunderous looks he was getting. Casey's father no longer looked like the man Damian had seen that day in Fort Worth. He was clean-shaven now, his hair cut to a moderate length, though still long by city standards. Yet one thing was absolutely the same: that quality of danger that was so easy to sense about him.

"You might as well catch the next train back to where you came from, Mr. Rutledge. Casey no longer works as a bounty hunter."

"This is a special case, since she was already involved in it," Damian said. "Besides, I'd like to hear what she has to say—"

"Forget it," Chandos broke in very quietly. "And take some advice. Don't make me repeat this. Stay the hell away from my daughter."

Damian thought to protest again, but considering there wasn't another soul anywhere in sight, and the man's hand was resting too close to his Colt revolver, he thought better of it. Her father wasn't going to be reasonable, didn't care about Damian's motives. And frankly, Damian didn't trust him not to shoot to make his point.

So he nodded curtly and mounted up. "It's been—somewhat—of a pleasure," he said dryly.

Chandos rubbed his knuckles and agreed. "Yes, from my standpoint it was."

Chapter 49

Casey found her father sitting on his horse outside the small, fenced-in graveyard. This was the first time she had come to visit Fletcher's grave herself since she'd been back home. She was surprised to find Chandos there. Nothing else was near that lonely plot of land, shaded by a single large oak tree, that could have given him a reason to be there. The Bar M graveyard was reserved for Bar M folk, and he had known no others in it—just his father.

She stopped her horse next to his but didn't say anything, waiting for him to acknowledge her presence, which he couldn't have missed. He didn't, just continued to frown toward the grave that marked Fletcher's resting place. She finally dismounted with the fistful of scraggly wildflowers she'd gathered on the range, and opened the low gate, rather than stepping over it, which she could easily have done.

She glanced up at her father and said, "You know, it's okay to come in here. I really don't think he's going to sit up and point any accusing fingers."

She had said it lightly, to get a smile out of him. His reply lacked all humor. "He should."

It was such a telling remark, coming from him. It held a wealth of festering guilt. She didn't know how to respond to it. She knew Fletcher had held him blameless, had accepted full responsibility for their rift. But try to get her father to listen to that, when he'd always closed his mind to any mention of Fletcher . . .

So she said nothing and continued toward the grave and knelt there on one knee to spread out her flowers. But after a few moments, she saw her father's shadow pass over the grave as he came to stand behind her.

"I've begun to realize something recently that I'm not proud of."

Casey went very still at those words. A confession? And here, in front of Fletcher—so to speak? Maybe she ought to leave. Her father had come here for a particular reason, obviously, and had decided not to postpone it simply because he was no longer alone.

She got up, but his gentle hand touched her arm to stop her from leaving him there alone, and his voice was filled with regret when he said, "I think I was trying to control you just as much as that old man tried to control me when I was your age. I've done exactly what I hated him for doing. But it has opened my eyes to why he tried to mold me. It's made me understand him better."

Tears came to Casey's eyes. My God, Fletcher couldn't have asked for more than that. If only he were here to hear it himself. But then, he *was* here . . . at least, Casey had always felt his presence at the Bar M, liked to think he was still watching over her. And his presence was strongest at his grave.

Having spent so much time with Fletcher when she was growing up, perhaps she was the only one who could reassure her father now—and point out a few things that Chandos might not know.

But as to his confession, she asked carefully, "And forgive him, maybe?"

"Yes, that, too. It's just killing me now, that I hadn't figured this out before he died, and let him know that I at least understand."

"He never asked for that. He would have been glad that you understood, but it wasn't something he needed to hear. He knew he'd made mistakes aplenty. He mentioned them often," she said, adding with a smile, "Almost with pride. But then, that's the way he was. He believed that a man learned and benefited from his mistakes, that they toughened him, added directly to his strengths."

Chandos nodded. "Yes, I can imagine he would think that way."

She was glad to note there was no bitterness in his remark, as there might have been just months ago. "But in your case, Daddy, he was too proud of you to feel the full sting of his regrets."

"What do you mean?"

"If you had turned out bad, then he would have blamed himself. But you didn't, you see. There wasn't anything about you that he didn't find pride in, and, well, guess what? He took full credit."

Chandos burst out laughing. "Son of a bitch."

Casey grinned. "Exactly. Since you did turn out so well, Grandpa figured that the mistakes he made with you must have had something to do with it. It purely tickled him pink, the success you made of the K.C. He crowed to anyone who would listen that you did it all on your own, that you wouldn't accept his help. You were his son. You did good. You did better than him. You 'showed the old man.' He took such pride in that, Daddy—in you."

"I didn't know," Chandos said softly.

"No, you didn't, but everyone else did."

"Thank you, little girl."

That "little girl" was back to being the endearment it had always been, which Casey could find no objection to. "No need to thank me for speaking the truth. No need to regret, either, that you couldn't tell him of your understanding. You just did. He's here, he knows."

He smiled sadly. "Perhaps, but it's not the same. We never talked, my father and I—"

Casey's snort cut in. "You talked plenty—you just did it in a rather loud way."

Chandos chuckled. "Is that what you call our shouting matches?"

"At least you never denied him access to you or your family, and you settled right next door to him. You think he didn't know how much that counted, that there was forgiveness in that, just unspoken? You let us kids visit him whenever we liked. You think he didn't see understanding in that? He had no regrets there at the end. He left a fine legacy that he was proud of. He left a fine son he was even more proud of.

He was happier than you know, Daddy."

"But I *didn't* know it."

"Mama can verify that everything I've said is true. She's heard his bragging about you. She's probably even mentioned it to you before, hasn't she?"

"Yes, I suppose she has."

Casey nodded, continuing. "You had a need to do better'n him, but deep down, you knew that doing so would make him proud—and you did it anyway. That kinda speaks for itself, doesn't it? He certainly figured it did. I mean, if you had really wanted the message to be that you hadn't forgiven him and never would, you could have been a failure instead and let him fester, blaming himself for it."

He gathered her close for a hug. "Where'd you get so much wisdom at your age?"

She leaned away to give him a gamin grin. "From you, maybe?"

"Hardly," he retorted.

"Okay, from Mama, then." She chuckled.

She imagined she could feel Fetcher's warmth, and pleasure, in what had been said and what had been put to rest. She hoped her father felt it, too.

Chapter 50

*D*amian should have gotten on the next train heading north. He really didn't want to tangle with Casey's father again. Not that he didn't think he could win if they came to blows again. The man had merely gotten in one lucky punch. But he didn't want to fight her father at all. Not to mention that the man might pull his gun next time instead—and use it. He'd certainly insinuated as much.

But considering all that, there was still no way that Damian was going to leave without at least talking to Casey first. So he made use of what little information he had about her and took his sore nose to Casey's grandfather after a short search located which doctor he was.

Dr. Harte refused to see him, of course. Casey had warned Damian that the old man saw only his longtime patients these days. But the doctor changed that policy when it was mentioned that his son-in-law had done the damage. And as Damian had hoped, he learned a bit more about the family from Harte, after he explained how he came to know Casey.

"Casey's staying mostly at the Bar M these days, the ranch she and her brothers inherited from Fletcher Straton," Edward Harte told him. "That ranch was the reason she took off all those months ago. She wanted to run it, but Chandos wouldn't let her, so she set out to prove some things. He took off after her, of course, though he didn't bring her back as soon as we expected. My daughter, Courtney, wasn't too happy with them both gone for so long."

"Then he's letting her run it now?"

"Indeed, and I hear she's doing fine so far. But then, if they both weren't so hot-tempered, they could have figured that out back in the spring-time."

Damian wouldn't have met Casey if that had been the case, but he didn't say so. He hadn't been surprised, either, that Casey was running a ranch now and doing a good job of it. Her capabilities never ceased to amaze him. He was surprised, though, after having met Chandos and talked to him, that the man had never caught up to Casey in all those months. After all, she'd learned most of what she knew from him. But again, if Chandos had found her right off, he would have taken her home and Damian would never have met her.

After speaking a bit more with the good doctor, Damian decided to wait a few days before seeking Casey again. Actually, he hoped she'd come into town. Less likelihood of his running into Chandos that way. So he kept watch on the doctor's house and the general store, the two places she would most likely show up at. But she didn't show, and he was too eager to see her again to continue to wait.

Which meant it wasn't long before he headed out into the countryside, this time to the Bar M. Because the ranch had belonged to Casey's grandfather, and because she was now running it single-handedly, Damian was expecting something on a much smaller scale than the K.C. Ranch. But no, incredibly, two ranches in the same family, both resembling small towns in the amount of buildings spread out around the main houses. And now he understood why Casey's father hadn't wanted to turn the Bar M over to her. A ranch this size would be daunting for most men, much less a young girl.

Unfortunately, Casey wasn't there. He was informed that she was out on the north range. He was warned not to try to find her, that it was easy to get lost out there. He chose to ignore the warning—and got lost.

It was sundown before he spotted buildings again. Just his luck, they turned out to belong to the K.C. rather than to the Bar M. He almost wished that Edward Harte hadn't mentioned that Casey divided her evenings between the two ranches. Being there already, he couldn't leave without finding out if this was one of those evenings.

He'd been right about that porch come sundown. A few lanterns had been lit, but their light wasn't yet necessary with the bright red hues that bathed the porch in a warm glow. He took a moment to sit in one of the rockers and just gaze westward, marveling at how incredibly beautiful this part of the country could be, the vast openness . . . the kind of peace he'd never find in the city.

It was too much to hope that Casey would suddenly appear on the porch and share that profound moment with him. He could imagine taking her hand in his and rocking side by side with that panoramic view before them . . . well, he could if he wasn't still so furious with her over their parting—or lack thereof.

He really had to put that anger aside if he was going to obtain her help. She would hardly be conducive to an agreement if he was glaring at her while he stated the facts . . .

Damian sighed and got up to knock on the door before it got much darker. He sincerely hoped someone other than one of Casey's parents would answer. He hadn't forgotten Chandos's warning; he was just choosing to ignore it. Ideally, he hoped not to see the man again at all.

Apparently a house this size didn't have the large staff of servants one might expect, or at least not the kind who answered doors, because Courtney Straton once again stood there when the door opened. And she made no bones about being displeased to see him. Her frown was immediate. He was surprised she didn't slam the door shut on him.

"I could've sworn you wouldn't be back," she said in a somewhat amazed tone.

"I wish it weren't necessary, ma'am, believe me, but I really *must* talk to Casey before I leave the area. Could you please not summon your husband this time, and simply tell me if she's here or not?"

She opened her mouth to respond, but then

closed it. Her frown grew deeper, though it was more thoughtful now. Damian held his breath. She was the one who sighed.

"All right, since you're not going to be sensible about this, you might as well come inside." She closed the door behind him, then called out, "Casey, honey, come here a minute. You've got a—visitor."

For her to merely say it without shouting meant Casey was going to appear within seconds, and she did, stepping through the open doorway of the dining room, napkin in hand. She moved no farther, though, halting immediately when she saw Damian standing in the entryway next to her mother, her expression mirroring shocked surprise.

He was surprised as well, by her elegant appearance. He was so accustomed to seeing her in jeans and a poncho, except for that one time in Culthers, that it hadn't occurred to him that she might dress differently now that she was home. Her black hair was arranged in an artful coiffure that was dotted with jewel-tipped pins. The tight-waisted gown she wore was emerald-green velvet, the low, rounded neckline bordered with several inches of the same colored lace so soft, it draped like short, capped sleeves over her shoulders.

She was incredibly lovely, incredibly alluring as well with that low neckline framing the soft curve of her breasts. Staring at her, Damian almost forgot why he was there.

He'd interrupted their dinner, obviously, and they apparently dressed for it here, just as high society did in the city. Her father came to stand behind her, also finely tailored in a black evening coat with a black string tie, so utterly different from the man who'd ridden into Fort Worth that day. And if an inscrutable expression could be called deadly, his would be. Chandos was even less pleased to see Damian again than his wife had been.

Casey shook off her shock long enough to ask, "What are you doing here, Damian? And what happened to your nose?"

He flinched, having forgotten how obvious the damage on his face was. The swelling had gone down considerably, but the bruise that had shown up spread beneath one eye and between his brows. There had been a small break after all, according to Dr. Harte, though it could have been worse if the blow had landed more centered on his nose, rather than at the top of it and slightly off center.

Damian spared Chandos only a single look before he replied, "It ran into your father's fist. Seems he felt I was owed some pain for risking your life."

Casey's shock was back. "Daddy punched you? When?" she exclaimed.

"Several days ago."

"You came here and no one bothered to tell me?" The question wasn't for him, and in fact, she turned to Chandos.

"What was the point?" her father said offhandedly. "He left. He was not supposed to return."

"Daddy, didn't we *just* have a talk about making decisions for me that I'm capable of making on my own?"

"Ask him why he came here, little girl, before you go jumping to conclusions. It's still my right to protect you, no matter how old you get."

She frowned at that cryptic remark. Damian did as well. It implied he had come here to harm her in some way, which was ridiculous. He started to say so, when Casey's eyes swung to him and narrowed.

"Why *are* you here, Damian?"

He would have preferred to speak to her privately, but it didn't look like her parents were going to allow that, so he got right to the point. "Jack escaped in St. Louis. He's been traced to Chicago, but his trail was lost there. It's too easy to hole up in a city that size, too many places to hide. My detectives have run out of ideas for finding him. Their suggestion is to send out Wanted posters to every state and hope some lawman who takes notice of them comes across him someday. Which could be never . . ."

She nodded, slowly. "Which still doesn't say why you're here."

"You found him once, Casey."

"Out here in the West, sure, but he's in a city now," she pointed out. "What do I know about cities?"

"But you know Jack."

"You've already got people working on it, Damian."

"Yes, and they're competent enough, but they're already giving up," he said. "And they don't have a vested interest. You do."

"I do?" She raised a brow at him. "And just how do you figure that?"

"Because you impressed me as someone who

will see a job done to the finish," he told her. "Because the job, though finished for you, has basically been extended, so it's not actually done yet."

"It's not *my* fault you lost him."

He sighed. "No, it's not. But after all the effort you put into finding Jack, do you really want to see him go about his merry way now?"

Damian was putting her on the spot and he knew it. Couldn't she see that she was his only hope?

"You came all this way to what? Hire me again?"

"I didn't think money would be an issue, but if that's what it will take—"

"I needed money before, Damian, I don't now. I just want to make sure I have this straight. This is the only reason you came here? Just to get me to find Jack for you again?"

"Just? You know how important it is to me to bring him to trial. Why else would I travel all this way when I wasn't even sure I'd find you here?"

"Why else indeed?" she said, then glanced at her father. "I see what you mean, Daddy."

At that, she walked away, leaving Damian incredulous. He hadn't expected her to flat out refuse to help him. Actually, he'd pretty much taken it for granted that he would only have to let her know of Jack's escape to get her on the train to Chicago with him.

"I believe you've gotten your answer, Mr. Rutledge."

He turned to see Casey's mother holding the

door open for him to leave. Yes, he had his answer. And it felt devastating, as if he'd been
turned down for more than just the help he
needed.

Chapter 51

❧⸻❧

*D*amian was about halfway to Chicago when he decided to head back to Texas. He'd given up too easily. Nor had he used all the options available to him—guilt, moral obligation, or any number of other things he could have tried to sway Casey's answer. He'd let that feeling of rejection send him packing with his tail between his legs. Disgusting. And if he was going to be turned down, he could at least have gotten the other things that were bothering him off his chest. There'd been no need to be diplomatic at that point.

So he left the train to find out how long a wait he'd have for the next train heading south—and came across Casey having lunch inside the depot. He was so amazed to see her there, it took him a few moments to believe it.

That couldn't be Casey in a bright yellow traveling dress with matching bonnet, even matching shoes; it was just someone who resembled her. That was his first reaction, yet he knew it was she. His whole body coming alive with tension told him for sure.

343

But that meant she'd been on the train since Waco, and how could he have missed knowing that—of course he wouldn't know. He'd made arrangements with the new porter who came with the larger parlor car, to bring him his meals in the car. He'd barely left that car since Waco, his less-than-happy frame of mind making him want to avoid people at the frequent train stops.

He approached her table slowly, still afraid it was just wishful thinking that had put her there before him. And when she glanced up at him with that inscrutable expression of hers—he now knew where she got that habit from—it was a bit more than disconcerting. No surprise on her part, no smile, no "Well, imagine running into you here," nothing that he could grasp and deal with.

So he said simply, "You came."

"Yes."

And then, with less neutrality: "When were you going to let me know?"

"I wasn't."

He stiffened. "And why not? I thought we worked rather well together before."

"We did some things well together, but finding Jack wasn't one of them."

That candid reply was so unexpected, Damian was rendered almost speechless. And she wasn't even blushing for having more or less stated they'd been good in bed together. But she'd brought it up, and his anger was there to take quick advantage of that fact.

"Funny you should mention that, Casey. I wouldn't have gathered you thought so, not with the way you went off in the middle of the night without saying good-bye, go to hell, or it's been fun."

"I thought we parted rather nicely. No words could have added to that."

Looked at that way, she was right. It was a very nice way to part company—if both parties were desirous of parting. But when one had had other ideas . . .

"*One* of us might have had a few more things to say," he pointed out.

"*One* of us had ample time to say anything that needed saying," she shot back.

He ground his teeth together. She was right again. He was the one who had procrastinated, trying to get up the nerve to suggest they not part at all. And considering the tone they had both just taken, now wasn't an ideal time to mention it either. And then, seeing Casey's mother, followed by her father, walk into that small lunchroom had a way of changing the direction of his thoughts.

"You brought your *parents* with you?"

She followed his gaze and smiled at the couple approaching them. "Actually, we just seem to be traveling in the same direction," she told Damian. "My mother decided she'd like to do some major shopping in Chicago. My father wasn't about to be separated from her again, when the last separation only just ended, so he had to come along. Of course, they assure me that my deciding to go to Chicago at this time had nothing to do with their making the trip as well."

She rolled her eyes to show how much she believed that. He wasn't amused. He had requested her help, not that of her whole family. But he was forgetting that she'd had no intention of letting him know that she was going to hunt for Jack. That was, if she really was—that hadn't been made clear yet either.

Damian sighed. He simply had too many things to take exception to at the moment, and now that he no longer had the privacy to do so, he might as well keep his mouth shut. Except on one point...

"*Are* you going to look for Jack?"

"That was my intention," Casey replied.

"But you don't want my assistance? Don't even want to see the detectives' reports?"

"You've already pointed out how big the city is that he's gone to ground in. Seems to me, the only way to ferret him out is to start thinking like he does. So no, reports on your detectives' progress won't help me none, so I don't need to see them."

"I seem to recall my assistance being of some help on at least one occasion of dealing with Jack. I didn't ask you to get involved in this again to turn you loose where I couldn't aid you if necessary."

She sighed. Her father, having come up in time to hear Damian's remark, said, "Now, if I had been assured of him backing you up, Casey, I probably could have talked your mother into shopping closer to home."

And Courtney said, almost in the same breath, "Afternoon, Mr. Rutledge. I see you finally found her. Perhaps now you can offer us the comfort of your private car for the rest of the trip."

Damian's jaw almost dropped. He was rendered speechless again. They wanted to travel with him, but Casey didn't? And her father would actually trust him to protect her? What the hell had happened to reverse their attitudes toward him since he'd left Waco?

He finally found his voice to answer, though somewhat hesitantly, since he was still waiting for the rug to be pulled out from under him, proving he'd misunderstood.

"Certainly, ma'am," he said. "It would be my pleasure to share the parlor car with the three of you."

Casey's lips pursed in displeasure. This obviously wasn't her idea, nor did she care for it one little bit. Courtney smiled in acceptance, though, so apparently that settled the matter.

Chandos, of course, was noncommittal either way, his expression utterly neutral as usual. He might have just told Casey that he more or less trusted Damian to protect her, but he sure wasn't going to verify that by word, look, or deed for Damian's benefit.

Perhaps their opinions hadn't changed all that much after all. He was reading more into it than was intended. And had he really offered to enclose himself in the small confines of a parlor car with Casey's parents for several days? He had to be out of his mind.

Chapter 52

⟡

*C*asey and her mother took over the separate bed compartment in the parlor car. Chandos moved Damian's few things out of there without asking, taking it for granted that he'd allow the ladies the privacy of that room. He would have, of course, but he would have liked to be asked.

But that was the tone those remaining few days assumed. The Stratons took a lot for granted; at least Casey's parents did. Casey herself wasn't very communicative—except with her parents. Damian got to see, firsthand, the easy relationship she shared with them.

It was Courtney Straton who made the time he spent with the three of them at least bearable. Her manner of gentility, so different from her daughter's and husband's, spoke of her social upbringing in her early years. She tried, continuously, to bring Damian into any conversations that were started in the main part of the car, which was where they spent most of their time each day. She encouraged him to talk about himself as well, and his father, and the company that had been so long in his family. She even mentioned his mother . . .

Casey had blushed, and rightly so, when Courtney remarked, "Casey tells me your mother lives in Chicago. Perhaps we'll get to meet her while we're in the city."

The look he gave Casey pretty much said, *And what else did you tell your parents that was none of their business?* But to Courtney, he merely replied, "I doubt it, ma'am. This isn't a social visit, after all."

And then there were those excruciatingly uncomfortable nights, after the ladies had retired behind the closed bedroom door, that he was left alone with Chandos Straton. The first night set the tone for the next as well, which was, they were simply going to ignore each other. Except for one remark that was said just after Chandos settled down on the long bench across the room from Damian.

"My wife is giving you the benefit of the doubt, thinks your determination speaks for itself. But I'll be reserving judgment."

Damian wasn't going to let that cryptic statement pass. "What the devil are you talking about?"

"You figure it out, tenderfoot" was all Chandos replied before he turned over to go to sleep.

And so it went for the next three days. By the time the train pulled into Chicago, Damian actually felt as if he'd long been friends with Courtney. Not so with the other two, who both gave the impression they were merely suffering his presence. And he never did get to talk to

Casey alone again. One or the other of her parents was always at her side.

He recommended to them the hotel he had previously stayed at and intended to again, thinking that at least there he might find Casey alone at some point. But Casey would have refused even that. Her expression, when her mother said that was an excellent idea, was telling, but she didn't try to reverse the decision.

There wouldn't have been much point, actually, since it had already been agreed that if Casey did discover Jack's whereabouts, she wasn't to try to apprehend him alone—her father's mandate, which she had grudgingly agreed to. Damian was to be kept apprised of her progress as well, and that would require their meeting frequently—which was when Courtney had suggested they might as well all gather each evening for dinner. Not how Damian would have preferred it, but where Casey's time was concerned, he'd take what he could get.

Casey had also stated her immediate plans when she'd told Damian, "Jack's gotten used to throwing your money around. He's hiding, yes, but chances are he's doing it in style. I'm going to start by questioning the employees of the higher-class rental agencies, as well as of the more expensive hotels. I'll work down from there."

Which meant that any assistance on his part wouldn't be required, at least for the first few days. Even her father couldn't foresee any trouble arising during this questioning phase.

As it turned out, Casey was in such a big

hurry to get Jack found so she could head back home, she didn't show up for dinner the first night at the hotel, or the second. She'd left messages, though, that there were just so many people she needed to talk to, she didn't have time to sit down to a full dinner, and would be continuing her interviews into the evening hours.

Chandos wasn't a bit surprised. "When my daughter starts something, she digs her teeth in good."

Damian was disgruntled, to say the least. He wanted Jack found, and as soon as possible. But he also wanted some time with Casey before she disappeared on him again. And since she refused to let him accompany her on these interrogations, he'd been counting on the agreed-upon dinner hour to spend with her.

She did show up on the third night, and in splendid array. The hotel offered a very elegant restaurant that was frequented not only by the hotel's guests, but by many affluent residents of the city as well, who found this an ideal place to show off their expensive jewelry, expensive mistresses, or whatever else they took pride in.

But Casey put all the other ladies to shame with the simplicity of her lavender silk gown and a single black ribbon locket at her throat. Funny, how she seemed to grow more and more beautiful every time Damian saw her.

Tonight, she actually preceded her parents. When she saw that they hadn't joined Damian yet, she slowed her approach, was probably thinking about making a quick retreat. But the look he gave her must have changed her mind—he'd damn well drag her to his table if he had to, was what she gathered, and she wasn't going to risk the scene such an outlandish act would cause. Good thing, because he didn't care what kind of scenes he caused at that point.

He stood to seat her. Their waiter appeared immediately to offer her a choice of refreshments. Damian didn't wait for him to leave before saying, "You look exceptionally beautiful tonight, Casey."

She hadn't expected a compliment. It produced a rosy blush. And before she could say anything, he added, "But then, I liked you in your jeans and poncho, too."

That seemed to surprise her, but she still said nothing, possibly waiting for the waiter to leave first. The second they were alone, Damian had one more thing to add, however unwisely. "Actually, I liked you best when you were wearing nothing at all."

Her blush turned bright scarlet. Her eyes swiftly dropped to the table and she hissed at him, "Are you *trying* to embarrass me?"

"No, just stating a few truths," he replied huskily.

Her golden eyes came back up and locked with his. And he had the strangest feeling that in her mind's eye she was seeing him naked as well. He was certainly picturing her that way, couldn't stop the memories of their last night of lovemaking from filling his mind.

It was a breathless moment. He wanted to take her straight up to his room. He wanted . . .

"Damian, is that you?" A high-pitched squeal sounded. "Oh, it is! Whatever are you doing in Chicago without letting me know? You must have arrived tonight, and decided to wait until the morning to call on me."

Damian closed his eyes briefly in dread, then stood up to greet Luella Miller.

Chapter 53

Casey couldn't believe her rotten luck. To go from that pulse-racing moment, when she actually thought Damian might be going to say something of an intimate nature, to hearing that jarring voice she had come to despise—yes, despise, just as she despised the owner of it for her petiteness, her glowing beauty, but mostly for her proprietary attitude where Damian was concerned.

Okay, so "despise" was a bit harsh, but Casey certainly didn't like her. Yet the one person she'd hoped to never run across again was standing there gushing her surprise over finding Damian in Chicago. Hell, Casey had put Luella Miller so far from her mind, she'd forgotten the lady even lived in this city.

"I'm here on important business, Luella," Damian was telling her. "I'm afraid I don't have time for social amenities this trip."

"Oh, really?" Luella said, staring daggers at Casey. "And who might this be?"

Now that was funny. Luella was jealous of

her? And she didn't even recognize her. Which showed how superficial the woman was. She might give a man she was interested in her undivided attention, but anyone else didn't merit even minimal scrutiny.

"Now I'm hurt, Luella, I really am, that you don't remember me," Casey said dryly.

"Oh, it's you, Casey," Luella sniffed. "Sorry, I thought you were—well, you know—one of those"—in a whisper now—"ladies of the street."

She'd thought no such thing, was just being catty. But it didn't make Casey no nevermind. She was about to excuse herself, in fact, and let these two get on with their reunion, when her mother and father showed up. She was stuck.

She actually had to sit through an entire dinner with Luella because the lady insinuated her company on them, and politeness precluded telling her to get lost. It reminded Casey too much of the time spent with Luella on the way to Fort Worth. Just as before, she monopolized any conversation, and managed to keep all talk centered on herself.

But Casey was definitely skipping dessert, had developed a headache she had no qualms about mentioning. And then Luella appeared to have found someone else she was acquainted with, and began craning her neck to see around the table next to them. With the slim chance that she might desert them and go off to plague someone else with her incessant chatter, Casey waited another moment before excusing herself.

"Oh, my, if this isn't the most amazing coincidence," Luella gasped. "Damian, I do believe that's your mother dining across the room there—and the dear woman hasn't noticed you yet."

Luella didn't even bother to look to see what that statement did to Damian. She shot right to her feet, obviously intent on rectifying the "hasn't noticed you" part. She screeched instead, as Damian's hand gripped her arm and yanked her back into her seat.

She looked at him now, incredulously. She still wasn't paying attention to the signs he was giving off, so hadn't figured out yet that Damian was furious, and mostly with her.

"Have you gone mad?" she pouted.

"Quite possibly," he gritted out. "And if you even think about approaching my mother again, then most definitely I have. If you had paid attention, Luella, when you thrust yourself into our private dinner, you would have heard me tell you I was here on business, *not* social discourse. If I have to be even plainer than that, it means I have no desire to see my mother at this or any other time."

"Or me, obviously," she said. Obviously she was expecting an immediate denial.

She didn't get one. And that produced a becoming blush. She still wasn't insulted enough to get up and leave, though, more's the pity. Perhaps she was too dense to realize she *had* been insulted.

Courtney tried to ease the tension by mentioning dessert. Chandos was all but laughing. Casey continued to gaze worriedly at Damian. He'd looked toward the table where his mother apparently sat, the moment he finished blasting

Luella. And as tall as he was, he had no trouble seeing over the heads of the other patrons in between.

She knew the moment that his mother must have caught his eye. He went so still, she couldn't detect a twitch, not even a breath out of him. And the pain in his eyes wrenched at her heart.

He got up and marched out of the restaurant. She got up and followed right behind him. She vaguely heard Luella say, "Well, I never. Not even a good-bye?" She figured her parents would explain—or not.

Damian went straight up to his room. He didn't realize that Casey was behind him until he slammed the door shut, or tried to, but it didn't slam, catching her instead as she walked into the room. He swung around as if he were ready for battle. He must have thought it was his mother who followed him, because the tension went out of him when he saw it was Casey.

"I wasn't ready," he said by way of explanation, as if she would know what he was talking about.

She did. "I know."

"That silly woman could drive a saint to lose his patience," he added.

"I know that, too."

"But that's not how I want to face my mother for the first time, already aggravated by someone else. I'll need every bit of control I can muster to sit through whatever explanation she has to offer."

"You're right. If you're going to face her, do it free of emotion."

He nodded, dragging an irritated hand through his hair. And then his intense gray gaze impaled her, the pain back in his eyes.

"She recognized me, Casey," he said in a bewildered tone. "She hasn't seen me since I was a child. How in hell did she recognize me?"

"Maybe the same way you recognized her," Casey offered hesitantly.

"No, she hasn't changed that much. Amazingly, she really hasn't. A little gray on her temples, but hardly any wrinkles to change that lovely face I remember. But I was ten when she left. There is nothing about me now to resemble the child I was then."

"Damian, a mother can have certain instincts, intuitions. And you were staring at her a mite intensely. It's not unreasonable to think she could make a lucky guess and figure out who you could be."

"Yes, of course. That must be it," he said with a sigh, "Not that it matters," he insisted lamely.

She wanted to hug him in that moment, but didn't. "Will you be all right?"

"Certainly. And please extend my apologies to your parents for my abrupt departure."

She smiled gently. "They aren't insensitive. No need for apologies." She turned, reached for the doorknob.

"Casey?"

She stopped, held her breath. But he didn't get to say whatever he had meant to. The door hadn't been closed completely when Casey entered the room. Another person entered now, stepping carefully around it, looking past Casey to fix her eyes on her son.

"It is you, isn't it, Damian?" the woman said hopefully. "Have you come here to see me?"

Casey swung around to catch Damian's reaction. He had none. He wasn't going to give his mother even an inkling of his feelings.

"No," he replied tonelessly. "I'm here to find my father's murderer."

She sighed. "Yes, I had heard of his death. I'm very sorry."

"No need to be, madam. He was nothing to you, only a small part of your youth."

Now that was telling, fraught with resentment, no matter how neutral the tone. The woman merely nodded, perhaps trying to control emotions of her own.

"Forgive me, then, for intruding," she said in a whisper as she turned to leave.

Only Casey saw the tears in her eyes. She glanced swiftly toward Damian, but he'd already turned his back, and it was a stiff back. Fists were clenched at his sides. Now wasn't the time to mention those tears.

Chapter 54

❦

*T*wo days later, Casey arrived halfway through the dinner Damian was again sharing with her parents, to give them the news. She really hadn't thought it would be this quick. When she had decided to come to Chicago, her reason hadn't been just to find Jack Curruthers.

She still remembered her mother questioning her motives when she found her packing. "You're going to help him, aren't you?" she'd asked.

"Yes."

"Why?"

"Because I like to finish something I start. And this isn't finished."

"That's your only reason?"

"No," Casey had admitted with a sigh.

Courtney had tapped her foot impatiently. "Well, don't make me drag it out of you."

Casey had sat down on her bed to explain. "I'm going to take your advice, Mama—to a degree. I'll at least give Damian a chance to suggest marriage. But if he can't do it on his own, then I don't want him. So don't interfere, Mama, and I mean that."

Courtney hadn't been too happy about that, but had agreed. And Casey had thought there would be ample time for Damian to figure out that she could make him a fine wife. It had even seemed promising when she'd caught him staring at her a number of times in that way of his that could set her insides to fluttering. But in the end, he seemed only concerned with finding Jack.

And now she'd found him.

She didn't make excuses for joining them late and not sending a message this time. She simply sat down at their table and announced without preamble, "I've located Jack."

Chandos nodded at her, not the least bit surprised by her swift success. Courtney huffed, "Well, I haven't even begun my shopping," to which Chandos chuckled and said, "What shopping?"

Damian wasn't listening to either of them; he was incredulous, demanding, "Already? Are you positive?"

Casey shook her head. "Positive, no. I haven't seen him yet myself. But he fits the description, as well as the time frame of his arrival in the city."

"But how did you find him so easily, when I've had detectives working—"

"Don't be hard on your detectives," she cut in. "It was luck more'n anything else, and maybe asking things they didn't think to."

"Such as?"

"Well, I discovered that Jack had stayed at a

hotel near the river. But he wasn't there long, only a few days. Yet it was a definite path to follow, so I talked to anyone and everyone who would have had anything to do with him or his room while he was there."

"My detectives had checked *every* hotel in the city," Damian said. "If you had bothered to read the reports, you would have known that."

"If I'd read the reports, I might not have been as thorough, might not even have bothered checking the hotels. But you aren't listening, Damian. I said it was a matter of luck. Turns out Jack was taking all his meals in his hotel room, and the young man named Milton Lewis, whose chore it was to collect the trays afterward, was sick one day while Jack was there. Milton's brother had filled in for him, with only one other hotel employee aware of it. Apparently Milton'd been sick quite a bit this last year and had been threatened that he'd lose his job if he failed to show up again, so he'd tried to keep his supervisor from knowing he wasn't there that day."

"And he's the one who knew something about Jack?" Damian asked.

"He didn't, no. And I only got the information about his not being there from a slip he made when I was questioning him. He certainly hadn't been willing to admit his deception—his brother and him look a lot alike, which is the only reason he'd managed it."

"So you got to talk to Milton's brother, whereas any others questioning Milton never even heard about this brother?" Chandos guessed.

"Exactly," Casey said. "Milton gave me his

brother's name and address, and I went to see
him this afternoon. Seems Jack had gotten suspicious of the fellow's nervousness. Jack would
be, with so many folks searching for him. But
the young man's nervousness had nothing to do
with Jack, of course, and to keep Jack from complaining to the supervisor, he was forced to admit the ruse the brothers were playing. Jack
must have realized the man could help him,
since he wouldn't be there again, wouldn't be
one of the hotel employees who might get questioned about Jack, and so wouldn't lead anyone
to him."

"But help him how?" Courtney asked.

Casey grinned. "Just goes to show how smart
Jack is. He told the young man he'd say nothing
about his taking over his brother's job if he
could find him a nice place to rent that he
wouldn't have to go through an agency to get."

"And the young man did?"

"Oh, yes, he came back with an address that
same day, he was so worried about it. Actually,
it was *his* place. The young man figured it would
be no big inconvenience for him to give it up
and move in with his brother until he could find
another rental himself. He just wanted to get
Jack satisfied so he wouldn't report the brothers.
Jack wasn't all that thrilled with the place and
told him so, probably because it's not in a high-
rent area. But he must have figured it was too
good to pass up, since chances were very low
that anyone would be able to trace him to it,
considering how he found it."

"And he's still there?"

Casey nodded. "According to the landlady.

He's going by the name of Marion Adams, probably hoping the 'Marion' would be misleading, in that it's a name a woman could have as well—just in case anyone on his trail got lucky enough to check out the building he's in."

"Then what are we waiting for?" Damian said as he stood up to leave.

"Morning," Casey replied.

"Why?"

"Because Jack isn't there right now," she answered offhandedly. "I checked."

That brought two immediate frowns from the men at the table. "You checked?" Chandos said first. "If you tell me you knocked on his door, I'm probably going to be locking yours, with you behind it."

"Now, Daddy—"

"Didn't you agree you wouldn't try to apprehend Jack by yourself?" Damian said next. "I swear, Casey, that's it, I'm not letting you out of my sight again."

"Will you two stop?" Casey said in exasperation. "I have no desire to play the heroine here single-handedly. No, I didn't knock. His room is on the third floor, right next to the stairs. The landlady had already told me he wasn't in. She's a nosy sort and keeps track of her tenants. But just to make sure, I threw an object up at his door, then waited out of sight on the second floor to hear if his door would open. It didn't. I then retrieved the object so he wouldn't wonder about it, and got out of there."

"He could have returned while you were there and walked up behind you," Damian pointed out, still not convinced she hadn't been at risk.

Casey merely smiled and pulled down the thick gauze on the upper edge of her bonnet. It covered most of her face, and was thick enough to conceal her features.

"He could have," she said. "But he wouldn't have recognized me."

"All right," Damian conceded. "But I still don't want to wait until morning. He'll return at some point tonight, and I want to be there..." His voice trailed off when Casey started shaking her head. "Why not?"

"It's too dark in that building, with only a single window at the far end of the hall from his room, and that facing another building only a few feet away, so hardly any light gets in there in the day. None would get in after dark. And the hall lamp on his floor is broken. He's probably been coming up to his room with a candle lately. Also, there are only two exits from any of those rooms—the door, and the fire escape behind the building. I checked out the back. Too many places for concealment if he managed to get down that way. The fire escape also goes up another two floors to the roof. That's too many possible ways he can go in the dark, too easy for us to lose him again. At least in the morning, in full daylight, he won't find concealment easy."

Damian sighed, giving up. Chandos grinned and told him, "She doesn't leave much to chance."

"No, she doesn't," Damian mumbled.

Chapter 55

*T*hey all gathered just before sunrise the next morning, while the hotel was still quiet and the city reasonably so. The hope was that Jack would still be abed. Damian was good at breaking doors down, after all. Couldn't manage a better surprise entrance than that.

Chandos decided to go along to cover the fire-escape exit. Casey had figured he would. It was all well and fine to allow that she and Damian could handle most any situation that arose, but as long as her father was already there and had no other plans . . .

Casey had brought her jeans along for the occasion, not wanting to be hampered by skirts. The poncho she'd left at home, though, the weather this far north requiring something a bit warmer than that mild-season garment. One of the thick, fleece-lined jackets she wore on the range in winter was more suitable.

They weren't really expecting any trouble; at least Casey wasn't. Jack didn't have any hired guns here to protect him like he'd had in Texas.

If they did manage to catch him unawares, with no bullets fired, then they could conceivably be back at the hotel in time for breakfast.

The carriage that Casey had rented when she arrived in the city got them to Jack's building just as the sun broke over the horizon. Chandos headed down the alley to position himself where he could still see the street out front as well as the fire escape in the back. Damian and Casey headed immediately upstairs.

Damian had his rifle with him. Casey had felt odd wearing her gun belt in the city, so she'd tucked her six-shooter in the pocket of her jacket, along with a slew of extra bullets just in case, but she drew it out now as they approached Jack's door.

There was no sound inside the room, no light coming from under the door. Damian positioned himself, glanced back at Casey to see if she was ready, then threw his shoulder against the door.

It opened immediately. He was able to catch himself from falling into the room. But the room was empty. Jack's belongings were still there, but he sure wasn't.

Casey started checking around to be sure, while Damian growled, "Where the hell is he?"

She didn't answer. She could feel his frustration; it was twice as bad as her own. And then she heard the bird call, faint but distinct, a bird not known to the cold climate of a northern city.

"That's my father . . ."

"What?"

"He must have seen something. Get downstairs fast!" she said, running toward the door.

Damian didn't argue. And he passed her on

the stairs, his longer legs sending him flying down. He was already climbing into the carriage when she burst out of the building. Chandos was waving at her to hurry. This wasn't the time to ask what had happened.

Casey dived into the carriage just before her father set the single horse into a gallop. The animal wasn't used to racing, but Chandos got some speed out of it. Damian helped Casey up onto the seat next to him, facing forward.

"Okay, what happened?" she asked the moment she caught her breath.

He pointed up the street in front of them. It wasn't hard to notice the other vehicle driving just as recklessly as they were. But that didn't tell her what had gone wrong with their plan—her plan. So she crawled up on the opposite seat from which she could better talk to her father in the driver's perch, and tapped him on the shoulder.

He volunteered what she wanted to hear, shouting back at her, "Don't know if he spotted you two or me, but I chanced to see him leap into a passing carriage before he was beyond my sight. He must have just come home, but got suspicious enough to want to leave in a big hurry. By the time I reached the street, he'd already pushed the driver out of the carriage and was halfway down the block. Left the poor man on the curb, screaming about a broken foot."

"So we're going to be as crazy as he is?" she shouted back. "This is dangerous!"

It was that. The street was teeming with traffic even at that early hour. Delivery wagons, people crossing the street, coaches and carriages of all sizes. But Jack was plowing a path straight through it all, uncaring if he actually hit anything—and they were right behind him, their path already cleared by him. But curses and shouts followed both vehicles from angry folks who just managed to get out of the way in time.

"You're right—and this old horse you rented isn't going to last much longer," Chandos told her. "Get ready to take him down. I'll try to get a little closer."

Hit him with a Colt from a bouncing carriage? Sure she would, Casey mumbled to herself as she dropped back into the seat next to Damian.

"You heard?" she asked him.

He nodded curtly. She stared at the rifle still gripped in his hand, then said, "You're going to have to do it. There's no way I can get off an accurate shot with all this motion, but you can brace that rifle of yours. Fire over his head first. Maybe he'll have enough sense to stop before some innocent people get hurt."

Damian didn't answer, just moved into a better position on the other seat. With the rifle, they didn't need to get any closer. It could span the distance between the two vehicles easily enough, whereas a handgun couldn't.

Damian fired off the first shot. It didn't stop Jack. But it might have been the deciding factor that caused him to turn into the next side street, hoping to get out of the line of fire. Jack's horse was willing to follow his direction, even at that speed, but unfortunately, his carriage couldn't manage such a sharp, abrupt turn. It flipped over onto its side, spilling Jack out of it, and continued a few more yards before screeching to a halt.

A wagon had to veer up onto the sidewalk to avoid running over Jack, who'd been dumped right in front of it. That would have made no difference to Jack. The fall had killed him.

Chapter 56

*C*asey was already packing by the time Damian arrived at the hotel after dealing with the police. The hotel kept an updated train schedule on hand for its guests. The next train heading to Texas departed that afternoon.

She'd already told her parents that she meant to be on it, which hadn't pleased them very much, all things considered. They'd been hoping for a different conclusion to this trip, after all—at least her mother had been.

Chandos was still of an "I'll reserve judgment until after I see results" mind. In other words, he wasn't going to like or accept Damian until he had witnessed him making Casey happy. There wasn't much chance of that happening now.

Perhaps she was departing a bit quickly—again. She wasn't really giving Damian an opportunity to think of other things, like marriage, now that his mind no longer had to dwell on Jack Curruthers's capture. But the truth was, she was afraid to put it to the test, since he'd given her no reason to think that marriage would ever enter his mind where she was concerned. And there had been enough occasions when he could have given her a hint or two, or at least have told her that he'd like to talk when they were finished with Jack.

But he hadn't done that, so what difference would a few more days make? For all she knew, he could be planning on catching the train today as well.

He did show up at her room, though, to tell her the results of his meeting with the police—and that he had officially retired from his deputy marshal appointment. He said this standing outside her door, since she hadn't opened it wide enough to invite him in. And it wasn't until he had finished that he noticed the bed behind her and her clothes spread out on it, next to her traveling bag.

"You're leaving—already?"

"Why not?"

He shoved his hands in his pockets. "Why not indeed?" he fairly growled. "I suppose you weren't going to say good-bye this time either?"

"Did I miss something, or did you only ask for my help with Jack? That you got. But you sure do set a lot of store in good-byes, don't you? Very well, consider it said."

He burst out, "I swear, Casey, you can be the most exasperating—"

"What'd I do now?" she interrupted, frowning.

"Nothing. Not one damn thing," he snarled and turned to leave.

She hated to see him go like that, annoyed

with her for—whatever reason. She would have liked to spend the rest of her life making him happy, but since that wasn't going to be possible . . . there was one other thing she could do for him, or try to do, as a parting gesture.

"Damian . . . ?"

He swung around so swiftly, he startled her into jumping back. She took a few seconds to calm her heartbeat. She didn't notice he was trying to do the same.

"I didn't want to mention it while your mind was so preoccupied with Jack," she said, "and it doesn't look like I'll get another chance, so . . . that night your mother followed you to your room—"

He'd stiffened at the mention of his mother, and now cut in. "What about it?"

"There were tears in her eyes when she turned away from you, Damian." He went deathly still. He paled as well. Casey quickly added, "I thought that was kind of—significant, kind of indicating she's got powerful feelings where you're concerned. You really ought to find out what those feelings are before you leave the city, don't you think? I've got her address. A bit presumptuous of me, but—"

"Would you go with me?"

She wasn't expecting that, had only wanted to get him to speak to his mother again, come what may. "Why?"

"Because I don't want to go alone," he said in a near whisper.

Her heart wrenched. How could she refuse? "All right. Now?"

He nodded curtly. "Now, or I'll probably change my mind."

Chapter 57

Casey had taken the time to find out a few things about Margaret Henslowe when she went after the woman's address after seeing her that night in the hotel. Margaret had been left a very rich widow by her second husband, Robert Henslowe. She lived in a large brownstone mansion that had long been in his family, but now belonged to her.

She was very well thought of, a social matriarch, so to speak. But she didn't have any really close friends, as least none that could be thought of that way by the few people Casey had talked to about her. And there had been no children in her second marriage. Since her second husband's death, she was alone in that big house, and she spent too much time inside it, according to those questioned, like she had given up on living, was just waiting to die herself.

Casey didn't mention any of this to Damian on the way there. She didn't want him feeling sorry for the woman, if it turned out that she didn't deserve his pity. But that wouldn't be

known until he heard what she had to say—
about him.

They arrived just after noontime, might be in-
terrupting the woman's lunch hour, but Casey
wasn't taking any chances about being turned
away. She had brought her Colt along to insist
if it came to that—that is, if the woman was
home. It would be real unfortunate if she
weren't, since Casey doubted Damian would
make another journey here if this one didn't pan
out.

She was home. The butler who answered the
door showed them to the parlor, where they
were asked to wait. A stuffy gent, to be sure.
Damian's name hadn't surprised him, so was
likely unknown to him. And why would it be
otherwise? No reason for the lady to talk of a
previous marriage in the house of her current
one.

Margaret arrived in the parlor a few minutes
later, a tad breathless. She'd rushed, probably
not believing that Damian had actually come to
see her. And she looked so amazed—and delighted—to see him standing there next to her
fireplace. She didn't spare even a glance in
Casey's direction. She had eyes only for her son.

It took a few moments for her to realize that
Damian wasn't as pleased as she was. He was
stiff as a board, his hands locked behind his
back. His expression was guarded, though there
were hints of bitterness and anger in his eyes.
Her expression now showed a measure of sadness. But all they did was stare at each other.
They weren't going to say anything.

Casey sighed and dropped down onto a sofa,

spread her gray velvet skirt wide, then blushed when she felt the weight of her gun in the large reticule she set in her lap. She should have known she wouldn't need it here. Then again, maybe that was what it would take to get these two talking . . .

She tried a little verbal nudge first. "I'm Casey Straton, ma'am, a friend of Damian's. I believe he'd like to ask you some questions . . ."

That was Damian's cue, but he didn't take it. Margaret had to ask, "Questions about what?"

Casey glanced at Damian. He still didn't look like he was going to say a single word. She sighed again. This wasn't progressing as she'd hoped it would.

"Why don't we start with the divorce and why you wanted it?" Casey suggested.

That got a response out of Damian. He said bitterly, "I already know why she wanted it."

Margaret frowned. "No, perhaps you don't know, at least not everything. It wasn't that I didn't love your father—well, I didn't actually, but I was quite fond of him. Our marriage had been one of mutual benefits, prompted by the pressures of marrying one of a like social standing, which didn't leave all that many choices, as you might imagine."

"He loved you," Damian spat out.

"Yes, I know." Margaret sighed. "But I didn't feel that way about him. That would have been all right, I suppose. Many women live unfulfilled lives like that. But then I met someone who made my life worth living. I fell in love with him completely. I couldn't stay with your father after that. It wouldn't have been fair to either of us."

"So to hell with ten years of marriage and a child you produced in that marriage."

"You really think it would have been better if I had stayed and made three people miserable instead of just one?" she asked.

"Just one? I see even now you feel I counted for nothing back then."

She gasped. "That isn't so! I would have taken you with me, Damian. I wanted to. But I knew how much your father loved you. And you were at that age when a father's influence is most important for a young boy. I was hurting your father by leaving him. I knew that. I couldn't hurt him more by taking you away from him as well."

"All right, I can understand that. What I can't understand is why you never visited. You didn't divorce just my father, you divorced yourself from me, too. Did I mean so little to you that you couldn't write occasionally, that you couldn't come even once to see how I was faring?"

"My God, he never told you, did he?"

Damian stiffened. "Told me what?"

"Your father made me promise I would never try to see you or contact—"

"You're lying!"

"I'm not, Damian," she insisted. "It was the only way he would give me the divorce. But don't think harshly of him for it. I don't believe he wanted it that way for any vindictive reasons. He was merely trying to protect you, and I could understand his reasoning. He felt it would be hard enough on you, losing me like that. He wanted you to have time to get over it, without visits from me that would make the pain even worse. He promised, though, that he wouldn't prevent you from visiting me when you were old enough. But you never did," she said sadly. "Yet I still didn't abide fully by that promise, though your father never knew. It really had been too much to ask of me, to never see you again."

"What do you mean?"

"Once every season, I have traveled to New York just to catch a glimpse of you. I never let you see me. In that I did keep the promise. But I wasn't going to be denied at least the sight of you, to see how you were growing, if you seemed happy. Even after you were grown and working at Rutledge Imports, I still made the trip, four times each year. I used to sit at that tiny cafe across the street, to wait and see you leaving work. One time you crossed the street to have a quick dinner—you must have been working late that night. I was sure you would notice me, but you were preoccupied. Another time I had my driver circle round and round the block for hours, just waiting for you to leave the mansion, and when you did, you were apparently in a great hurry to get somewhere, because you tried to get my driver to stop and take you up. I had to screech at him to get us away from . . ."

Casey rose quietly and left them alone. She shouldn't be there, listening to these confessions. It was a private moment between a mother and son who'd been separated far too long.

Damian was hearing what she'd hoped he'd hear. His mother loved him, had always loved him. The moisture in his eyes as he listened to her said he believed it now. Casey's tears were a bit more obvious. Her collar was getting wet, for crying out loud.

Chapter 58

Good comes with the bad and vice versa. Damian tried to remind himself of that as he raced back to the hotel—alone. No one could have everything he wanted. That was too much to expect. But he couldn't help wanting everything.

On the one hand, he felt such peace of spirit now, after talking to his mother, as if a weight that had been crushing him was finally lifted from his shoulders. To learn that he hadn't been unwanted or abandoned, as he'd always thought, made such a difference. And he couldn't have asked for a better parting from her. The hug had been immensely healing. The agreement to become part of each other's lives henceforth had been reassuring.

But then, on the other hand, there was Casey, ripping up his emotions something fierce—and disappearing on him again.

When he'd left his mother's house, he'd expected to find Casey waiting in the carriage. But no. She'd had the driver take her back to the hotel, then return for Damian. No message.

No nothing—again.

And she had left the hotel. That was the last straw. She'd already checked out, already left for the train station. Left him.

Driving to the station reminded him of his mad chase after Jack. But he'd slipped the driver an outrageous tip to have it so. He *wasn't* going to miss seeing Casey one last time just because of the heavy traffic found in all large cities. Fortunately, the train station was close to the hotel. Unfortunately, it was a huge station.

Damian still managed to get there before the southbound train pulled out. But the mass of people waiting for other trains made it difficult for him to locate the Stratons. It was Chandos he spotted first and approached.

The man sounded surprised to see him there, though he didn't look it. "I could've sworn Casey mentioned that she'd said her good-byes to you. Once wasn't enough?"

"Her idea of good-byes and mine aren't exactly the same, but then, what should I expect, when your daughter holds me in utter contempt?"

Chandos actually chuckled at that. "You really think she could love someone she holds in contempt?"

Damian's heart leaped into his throat. "Are you saying she loves me?"

"Now how would I know that? Seems to me that's a question you should be asking her."

Devastating, that letdown. "Where is she?"

Chandos nodded down the track, to where Casey was standing at the end of the train with her mother, the older woman's arm around her shoulders as if she were consoling her. Which, of course, wouldn't have been the case. Would it?

They were both probably glad to be going home, just as Chandos admitted to being when Damian wished him a safe journey in parting. "This is the farthest I've ever come into the heart of this country," Chandos remarked. "There's much to be said for progress, as long as you don't have to live in the midst of it. At least in Texas, you can still ignore it for the most part—and still breathe fresh air not clogged with chimney and factory soot."

If he wasn't under a time constraint—the damn train whistle had already blown—Damian might have replied to that and even admitted that he could agree in some respects. At the moment, though, he just wanted to reach Casey before she got on the train.

"Ma'am." He nodded to Courtney.

"If you'll excuse me, I think Chandos is calling me," she said and left them alone.

Damian didn't look back to see if that was true. He simply grabbed Casey the moment her mother walked off and kissed her, hard. His frustration was in that kiss, as well as his exasperation with her—and himself. He should have done this long ago.

"Now that's a proper good-bye," he said when he set her back on her feet.

"Is it?" she replied a bit breathlessly. "I wouldn't know. I don't say too many good-byes."

"Neither do I, and I don't like this one at all," he grumbled.

"You don't?"

"Casey, I—" Whatever he'd started to say, he got tongue-tied over and said instead, "You know, I liked that town of yours. I've been thinking of opening an extension of Rutledge Imports there."

She blinked. "You are?"

"Yes, and I was wondering if you might allow me to court you when I move to Waco."

"Court me?" she echoed in disbelief. "As in— *court* me?"

"I'm not asking to build an extension on your house, Casey. Yes, court you. One of these days, I'll get up the nerve to ask you to marry me, and a nice, long courtship will—"

"You want to marry me?"

He smiled at her incredulous look and said softly, "I can't think of anything I want more."

He'd rendered her speechless. In fact, she was silent for so long, just staring at him, that he thought he was going to perish of suspense.

And then she said in her abrupt, no-nonsense way, "To hell with courtships. Ask me—now."

He was holding his breath. "Would you?"

"Say it."

"Marry me?"

"Oh, yes. Yes!" She threw her arms around his neck and shouted it once more. "Yes!" And then demanded, "What took you so damn long?"

He laughed. "Uncertainty—the most I've ever felt. I might have figured out long ago that all I need is you, Casey, to give my life meaning. But finding out if you'd marry me turned out to be the most important question of my life, so it was

taking me awhile to get up the nerve to ask it.
Yet I'd planned to ask it on our way back from
Culthers. You just took off before I could."

"We'll have to work on this hesitancy of
yours, Damian. I was miserable when I left you.
You could have saved me, and it looks like
yourself, a lot of heartache if you'd just come
right out with it back then. My answer would
have been the same. I was already hopelessly in
love with you."

He gathered her close. "I'm so sorry—"

"No, don't apologize, you silly man. I'm just
as much a tenderfoot as you when it comes to
matters of the heart. I could have spoken up myself. I mean, if I was going to be miserable anyway, I could have been miserable knowing for
sure that there was no hope for us. I guess I was
just as afraid to find out the truth as you were.
It was just too important. So if there's any blame
to place—"

"I don't think there is any," he cut in with a
grin. "If you'll overlook those few weeks of misery, so will I—and make every effort to see that
it never happens again."

"Ah, now that's a promise I like hearing—and
will hold you to."

There was much more promise in the tender
kiss he gave her in answer, promise of a love
that would never end.

A short distance away, Courtney said to her
husband with considerable pleasure, "Looks
like we're going to have us a wedding."

Chandos followed her smiling gaze to find his

daughter in the middle of one heck of a passionate kiss. "It does, doesn't it?"

She glanced at her husband worriedly now and said reproachfully, "I hope you'll give him a chance to prove himself before you start riding him."

"Me?" He grinned at her. "Sure I will, Cat-eyes. Wouldn't think of doing anything else."

"Sure you wouldn't," she muttered beneath her breath.

Enter the World of Johanna Lindsey

Welcome to the world of Johanna Lindsey, and enter into a fantasy of your choosing. Immerse yourself deep into times when men were warriors, tamed only by very special women, and romance reigned supreme. Whether it is against the backdrop of glamorous Regency England society, the pageantry of a medieval court, the wild wilderness of the American West, or any other you can imagine, Johanna Lindsey knows how to make a love story come alive. Enjoy!

Captive Bride

Johanna Lindsey touched deep into the soul of her readers with her first romance. The world knew a new star was born with this tale of an arrogant Arab prince cut down to size by a strong-minded English miss.

Philip Caxton saw Christina as soon as she entered the room. She turned away with contempt when she saw him. Well, he didn't expect an easy conquest. She had seemed to hate him last night.

He sighed, cursing the lack of time. But perhaps Christina Wakefield was just playing hard to get. After all, young women came to London to look for husbands. And he wasn't such a bad catch. But still, with only one day's acquaintance, the odds were against him. Damn, why hadn't he met her sooner?

Anne Shadwell drew Christina toward Philip. "Miss Wakefield, I would like to introduce—"

She was cut off abruptly.

"We've met," Christina said contemptuously.

Anne Shadwell looked startled, but Philip made an arrogantly graceful bow, took Christina's arm firmly, and walked her out onto the balcony. She resisted, but he was sure she wouldn't cause a scene.

When they reached the railing, she whirled to face him defiantly.

"Really, Mr. Caxton! I thought I made myself quite clear last night, but since you don't seem to understand, let me enlighten you. I don't like you. You are a rude, conceited man, and I find you quite intolerable. Now if you will excuse me, I am going back to join my brother." She turned to leave, but he grabbed her hand and pulled her back to him.

"Christina, wait," he demanded huskily, forcing her to look into his dark eyes.

"I really don't think we have anything to say to each other, Mr. Caxton. And please refrain from using my first name." She turned to leave again, but Philip still grasped her hand in his. She faced him once more, stamping her foot in fury.

"Let go of my hand!" she demanded.

"Not until you've heard what I have to say,

Tina," he answered, pulling her closer to him.

"Tina!" She glared at him. "How dare—"

"I dare anything I damn well please. Now shut up and listen to me." He was amused at the disbelief written on her lovely face. "Tina, I want you. I would be honored if you would consent to be my wife. I would give you anything you want—jewels, beautiful gowns, my estates."

She was looking at him in a most unusual way. She opened her mouth to say something, but the words wouldn't come out. And then he felt the sting of her hand across his cheek.

"I have never been so insulted in my—"

But Philip didn't let her finish. He gathered her in his arms and silenced her words with a deep, penetrating kiss. He held her tightly against him, feeling her breasts pressed against his chest, crushing the breath from her body. She was struggling to free herself, but her efforts only increased his desire.

Then, unexpectedly, Christina went limp in his arms and threw him off guard. Philip thought she had fainted but winced when he felt a sharp pain in his shin. He released her instantly to grab his leg, and when he looked up, Christina was running into the drawing room.

He should have known better, Philip told himself.

He should have gone to her home in Halstead and courted her slowly. But that wasn't his way. Besides, he had never courted a woman before. He was used to getting what he wanted immediately, and he wanted Christina.

A Gentle Feuding

*Sheena Fergusson is the most prized beauty in Scotland.
Every man wants to possess her—except for Jamie
MacKinnion, the avowed enemy of her clan. But when
the proud laird finally lays eyes on Sheena, his warrior's
heart is conquered by the ethereal magnificence of this
woman.*

James MacKinnion moved slowly. An envelop-
ing mist still clung to the dewy ground, and he
was sopping wet from crossing the second of the
two Esk rivers. He was tired from lack of sleep
and the rough ride south. There was something
wrong in all this, but he didn't know what it
could be.

The mist swirled and parted before him in a
gentle breeze, revealing for a moment a wooded
glen not far ahead. Then the mist settled again,
and the vision was gone. Jamie rode for it; the
trees were a pleasant change from the barren
moors and heather-clad hills.

He had never been this far east on Fergusson
land before. He had never raided Lowlanders in
the spring before, either.

Jamie's anger warred with his common sense.
Dead men demanded he ride to avenge them. A
scrap of plaid demanded he ride south. Yet . . .
why? He would have given anything for more
evidence. The act bordered on insanity. Was he
sure of what he was doing?

The mist was rising steadily as Jamie entered
the wooded glen.

Then he heard a sound, and in a flash he slid
off his horse and ran for cover. But when he

listened again, he recognized the sound as a giggle, a feminine giggle.

Leaving his horse behind, he moved stealthily through the bracken and trees toward the sound.

When Jamie saw her, he wasn't quite sure he believed the vision. A young girl was standing waist-deep in a small pool, the mist swirling about her head. She looked like a water sprite, a kelpie, unreal, yet real enough.

The girl laughed again as she splashed water across her naked breasts. The sound enchanted Jamie. He was mesmerized by the girl, rooted where he was, watching her play. She was frolicking and having a joyous time of it.

She was like nothing he had ever seen before, a beauty, and no mistake about it. In a moment she faced him, and he saw nearly all of her loveliness. Pearly white skin contrasted starkly with brilliant, deep red hair. Almost magenta, it was so dark and gleaming and long. Two strands waved around her breasts and floated in the water. And those breasts were tantalizing, round, high and proud in youthful glory, the peaks sharply pointed because of the caress of icy water. Her features were unmistakably delicate. The only thing not clear to Jamie was the color of her eyes. He was not quite close enough to see, and the reflection of the water made them appear a blue so clear and bright as to be glowing quite impossibly. Was his imagination running wild? He wanted to move closer and see.

What he really wanted was to join her in the water. It was an insane idea, born of the strange effect she was having on him. What if she let him come to her, let him touch her as he ached to do? He had to leave before common sense completely fled. As if to point out his folly in tarrying, the first rays of sun broke through the glen, showing him the time he had wasted. His brother and the others would have all returned to the men by the river. They would all be waiting for him.

Jamie was suddenly sickened. Watching the girl, being transported to what seemed a sphere outside reality, he was appalled by the contrast between the lovely scene before him and the bloody one he would see in just a short while. Yet he could no more stop the one that was soon to happen than he could forget the one he was watching. Both seemed inevitable.

Jamie's last look at the girl was a wistful one. Beams of sunlight dotted the pool, and one touched the girl and lit her hair like a burst of flame. With a sigh, he turned away. That last vision of the mystical girl would be etched in his memory for a long time to come.

Love Only Once

With Love Only Once, *Johanna Lindsey introduced her beloved Malory family. The romances of these outrageous and outspoken sensualists, set in the ever-popular Regency era, are pure magic. Nicholas Eden, the rakish fourth Viscount of Montieth, is as enchanted as readers during this first encounter with Regina Ashton. Having just discovered that he has accidentally kidnapped the Malory ingenue, he is now setting her free. But if he is expecting anger from his unintended hostage, he's in for a surprise.*

She stood framed by the window, gazing at him in a startlingly direct way. There was no shyness in her look and no fear either on that exquisite, delicate, heart-shaped face. The eyes were disturbing, with an exotic slant. Such dark blue eyes in that fair face, so blue and clear, like colored crystal. The lips were soft and full and the nose was straight and slender. A thick fringe of sooty lashes framed those extraordinary eyes, while black brows arched gently above them. Her hair was raven black, too, in tight little ringlets surrounding her face, giving her fair skin a glow like polished ivory.

She was breathtaking. The beauty didn't stop with her face, either. She was petite, yes, but there was nothing childlike about her form. Firm young breasts pressed against the thin muslin of her rose gown. He wanted to pull the rose muslin down a few inches and watch those lovely breasts spring free. He received another jolt then, feeling his manhood rise against his will. Lord, he hadn't lost control like that since his youth!

Desperate to bring everything under control, he cast about for something—anything—to say. "Hello."

His tone implied "What have we we here?" and Reggie grinned despite herself. He was gorgeous, simply gorgeous. It wasn't just his face, though that was striking. There was a sexual magnetism about him that was quite unnerving.

"Hello, yourself," Reggie said impishly. "I was beginning to wonder when you would realize your mistake. You certainly took enough time about it."

"I am just now wondering if I have in fact made a mistake at all. You don't look like a mistake. You look very much like something I did right for a change."

He quietly closed the door and leaned back against it, those beautiful amber eyes boldly moving over her from head to foot. It was not at all safe for a young lady to be alone with a man of his stamp, and Reggie recognized that. Yet for some reason she couldn't fathom, she wasn't afraid of this man. Scandalously, she wondered if it would be such a terrible thing to lose her virtue to him. Oh, it was a reckless mood she was suddenly in!

She eyed the closed door and his large frame blocking that only exit. "Fie on you, sir. I hope you don't mean to compromise me more than you already have."

"I will if you will let me. Will you? Think carefully before you answer," he said with a devastating smile. "My heart is in jeopardy."

She giggled, delighted. "Stuff! Rakes like you don't *have* hearts. Everyone knows that."

Nicholas was enchanted.

Hearts Aflame

Kristen Haardrad has been imprisoned by the Saxon warlord Royce when her shipmates dared to attack Royce's lands. The Viking maiden has been searching for a man who could stir her senses and make her blood sing, and now she's finally found him in Royce. So with the full force of her Viking determination she sets out to win the heart and love of her captor.

Kristen had been stretching when she heard the steps crossing the floor, coming from the entrance. She jumped up curiously, her heartbeat quickening when she saw Royce coming out of the shadows, his direction not the stairs, but toward her, straight to her.

She did not move, waiting for him to reach her. His expression was intense, harsh, and her heart beat even faster, not in fear but in expectation. When he stopped, she felt only a moment's surprise when his hand went to the back of her neck, his fingers gripping her hair to yank her head back. She held her breath as his eyes moved angrily over her face.

"Why do you tempt me so?" He asked this not of her but to himself.

"Do I, milord?"

"You do it apurpose," he hissed before his mouth slashed down over hers.

Kristen had waited for this, to know the feel of lips, to be able to touch him. She had wanted this to happen, but she had not guessed how devastating the actuality would be. Nothing could have prepared her for such a violent jolt of desire, when she had never felt desire before.

His mouth moved over hers brutally in his anger. He gripped her hair, holding her still for this ravishment, yet he did not touch her otherwise. Kristen was the one to lean into him, until she could feel the full length of his body and know the extent of his desire. This inflamed her more. She didn't care that this was not what he wanted, that he was kissing her against his own will, and probably hating her more because of it, she wrapped her arms around his back, moving her hands up over the hard muscle there until she gripped his shoulders, holding him tight to her.

She heard him groan at her complete acceptance of him, and his other arm slipped about her waist, crushing her tighter to him. His tongue plunged into her mouth and she drew on it, capturing it like a prize, refusing to let go. God in heaven, this was wonderful, more thrilling than anything she had ever felt before. She would have let him take her there, in the hall, on the table, the floor—she didn't care. She wanted to make love with him now, before he came to his senses and stopped.

He did stop, and Kristen sighed miserably when his lips left hers. He looked down at her, his eyes fierce, filled half with passion, half with fury. She met his look boldly, but this served only to anger him more.

With a snarl, he shoved her away from him. "My God, you have no shame, do you?"

"I feel no shame in wanting you," she told him softly. She smiled then at his snort of disbelief. Deliberately, she added in a teasing tone, "You are my heartmate, Royce. Begin to accept it. You will eventually."

"You will never count me as one of your lovers, wench," he stated emphatically.

She shrugged, the sigh she gave louder than necessary. "Very well, milord, if that is your wish."

"Not my wish, the truth," he insisted. "And you will cease to use your tricks on me."

Kristen could not help but laugh at this order. "What tricks are those, milord? I am only guilty of looking at you, mayhap more than I should, but I cannot seem to help myself. You are, after all, the most splendid man here."

He drew in his breath sharply. "God's mercy, are all Vikings as brazen as you?"

"What you call brazen, I call honesty. Would you rather I lie and say I hate you, that I despise the sight of you?"

"How can you not hate me? I have enslaved you. I keep you shackled and I know you hate the chain. I think you do hate me, that you tempt me apurpose, hoping to have revenge by bewitching me."

Her eyes narrowed at him. "I am through telling you what I hope for, through speaking the truth to you when you will not believe it. Think whatever you like."

She turned her back on him, but was tense, waiting for him to walk away. He did not do so immediately. She imagined he was fighting to control a new fury that she would dare dismiss him like that. She would have been much appeased if she had seen that his eyes had simply moved over her, revealing for one unguarded moment the yearning in his soul.

Once a Princess

What woman hasn't dreamed of being Cinderella, of being rescued by a handsome prince to a better world than the one she lives in? In Once a Princess, *that fantasy comes alive for Tanya, but the lovely orphan isn't quite ready to believe that fairy tales can happen for her.*

Tanya couldn't hold back the incredulous thought any longer. "Do—do you know who my parents are?"

"It is possible—if you carry a certain—birthmark that is—hereditary."

She didn't even notice his hesitation over those pertinent words. She was trying to tamp down her excitement, because what he was suggesting was just too unlikely to be true. And yet—ever since she'd found out that she was unrelated to Dobbs and Iris, she'd wondered about her real parents, where they came from, what they were like, *who* they were.

Other girls had backgrounds, rich in detail and color. Her life was a blank page begun in a tavern. Now here were four strangers hinting at knowledge she craved as much as, if not more than, her independence. To finally have a real identity, a family history, possibly even relatives still living—a birth date! It was just too wonderful to be true, and if she allowed her hopes to be raised, she'd be doomed to disappointment. And to have it all hinge on a birthmark?

"We are certain of your identity, mistress. The mark that will prove it should be found on the underside of your seat, on the left cheek. It will no doubt require a mirror for you to examine it, but go and do so now, and do so carefully, so you may return and describe the mark to us."

"And if I won't?"

"Then you may possibly be offended when we locate the mark ourselves, to end all doubt, you understand."

She was quickly learning that Stefan could be cruel in his remarks. Her cheeks flaming, she hissed, "You bastard," but he merely crooked a brow at her, showing her how little it mattered to him that he'd insulted her—again. "What happens if the mark *is* there?"

"Then you will return with us to Cardinia."

"Where is that?"

"It's a small country in Eastern Europe. It's where you were born, Tatiana Janacek."

A name. Her name? God, this was becoming real again, her hopes soaring again. "Is that why you're here? To take me back?"

"Yes."

"Then I have family there? They sent you to find me?"

"No." His tone softened for the moment. "Regrettably, you are the last of your line."

Up and down, these hopes. Why did she let herself be lured in by possibilities? All right, no family. But a name, a history—if they were telling the truth, and if she had the mark.

"If I don't have any family left, then why did you bother to find me?"

"These questions are pointless, mistress, until you prove to us all, yourself included, that you possess the mark that names you a Janacek."

"I don't care how pointless you find my questions, I'm not moving an inch until I know the real reason you came here."

Stefan took a menacing step closer, but she didn't budge. He growled down at her, "For no other reason than to collect you and return you—"

"*Why?*"

"For your wedding!"

"My *what*?"

"You are to marry the new King of Cardinia."

Angel

Angel never thought of himself as a hero. He was just a man with a gun and a reputation who had always walked a solitary path. But when a debt lands him in a marriage with a refined young woman who interferes in everyone's life, including his own, the inscrutable loner finally learns what it means to need someone.

"Are we divorced yet?"

Cassie woke with a start, that soft drawl echoing in her ears. "What?"

"Are we divorced yet?"

She knew instantly who he was, she just couldn't believe he was there. "Angel?"

His hand slipped into her hair as his body moved to cover hers. "Just answer the question, Cassie."

"We're not. I just haven't had the time—"

His mouth came down to cut off the rest of her explanation. Obviously, he wasn't interested in her excuses just now. But what he was interested in was bundled up in warm flannel.

"How come you don't sleep naked?"

It was a question born of frustration, not one for a lady to take seriously. Cassie answered anyway. "I do in the summertime."

He groaned, knowing full well an image of her naked was going to haunt him now. And his tongue slid in deep, eliciting an answering groan out of Cassie. It was a while before they drew breath.

"You got the sweetest, softest lips I ever did taste," he said against them.

"Your voice makes me tingle, Angel."

"What does my mouth do to you?"

"It makes me weak."

His mouth moved up to suck on her earlobe. "What else?"

"Hot," she whispered.

"Oh, God, Cassie, I'm going to burst if I can't get inside you right now."

"Then what are you waiting for?"

He laughed and kissed her again. Then he rolled to her side to shove the covers off her. She tore the top of her nightgown open, popping off three buttons in her impatience to get it off. He yanked his shirt out of his pants and sent his buttons to join hers on the bed and the floor. In seconds he was back, pressing her into the mattress. Her arms and legs wrapped around him, locking him in place. And then he was inside, deep inside, and that familiar throbbing came so quickly, bursting on her senses, pulsing around him, drawing his own climax to mesh with hers.

Cassie lowered her legs slowly. Her toes slid against leather. Angel was still wearing his boots, and his pants. She wanted to laugh, but she felt like crying.

God, how she hated the reality that surfaced after the passion was spent. She resented that. She resented Angel, too, at the moment. And she particularly resented the fact that he hadn't taken off his boots.

She let him know it with the curt admonishment, "Next time take off your boots."

"I'll take them off now."

"No, you won't. You aren't staying."

"I'm not ready to leave yet, Cassie. And that was too intense. We're going to try it again, slow and easy."

Her stomach fluttered in response to those words. She suppressed the feeling.

"No, we aren't," she told him stiffly. "You're going to get out of here before my mama hears you and comes charging in with her gun blazing."

"Where is she?"

"In the next room."

"Then we'll have to be quiet, won't we?"

"Angel—"

His mouth was back, slanting across hers with tantalizing skill. She couldn't let that work this time. She couldn't.

She did. She'd missed him too much, wanted him too much, to be sensible about it. And there had been the thought, haunting her ever since he'd ridden out of her life, that she'd never know his touch again.

Now his touch was breaking the last of her resistance with a slow sweep of his hand over her breasts and belly. Gooseflesh followed in wake; nipples tingled to hardness. She'd just had the most incredible explosion of pleasure imaginable, but her body was firing up to experience it again. And in no way did Angel hurry her toward that end. He'd said slow and easy, and that was exactly how he proceeded.

It was nearly dawn before Angel finally got his fill of her. Cassie was too sated to feel any more resentment. And he'd been right. The first time had been over with too quickly. The rest ... Lord love him, the man was as good at loving as he was with a gun.

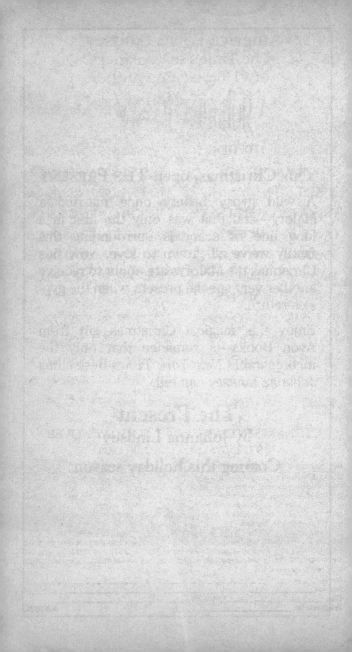

Elizabeth Lowell

THE NEW YORK TIMES *BESTSELLING AUTHOR*

"A law unto herself in the world of romance!"

Amanda Quick